THE PLACE WHERE
DREAMS COME TRUE

Tory Bacher—Young, gay, and gorgeous, he worked his way up from one-night stands to run the city's most sensual nighttime palace. But there's no pleasure without pain.

Brad Rothman—he tried to warn his college chum about the dangers of living in the fast land, but who could tell Tory anything?

George Keller—Tory loves him. He loves Tory. Can two hustlers live happily ever after?

Mona Brett—She introduced Tory to a fast crowd, but forgot to tell him there were no brakes.

Tory's

WILLIAM SNYDER

AVON
PUBLISHERS OF BARD, CAMELOT AND DISCUS BOOKS

TORY'S is an original publication of Avon Books. This work has never before appeared in book form.

AVON BOOKS
A division of
The Hearst Corporation
959 Eighth Avenue
New York, New York 10019

First Avon Printing, January, 1981

For Judy

Chapter One

TORY Bacher danced into his apartment singing "After You've Gone" in an upbeat tempo. He tossed his keys and sunglasses on the foyer table, flipped through the junk mail and bills and then tossed them in the same general direction, took a few steps into the living room and tried to ignore the empty glasses and full ashtrays, threw his suede cardigan over a sofa and kicked off his Bally loafers. He finished the song by holding the last syllable for a challenging eight bars, applauded himself enthusiastically, and bounded up the spiral staircase to the kitchen. Giving a defiant sneer to the clock that read ten-thirty, he poured a glass of wine from the carafe in the refrigerator. He smacked his lips loudly and smiled after the first sip, shrugged his lamb's-wool turtleneck over his head and tossed it on a dining-room chair. Sipping his way slowly down the stairs back to the living room, he studied the shelves of albums and selected Ella Fitzgerald singing Gershwin, Bobby Short singing Cole Porter, and Noel Coward singing himself. Between wine sips he assisted Ella with "Someone to Watch over Me" and ambled into the bedroom, moaning loudly with exaggerated relief as he unzipped his French jeans. They landed forlornly in front of a closet while he searched through a pile of *After Dark, W, Interview, GQ,* and *Specialty Food Trade News* for his address book. He noticed it on the floor next to the bedside telephone, and emitted a loud, contrived laugh of surprise, then a genuine chuckle of pleasure at the sound of his own voice. He

1

threw the book onto the bed along with the telephone,
cigarettes, lighter and ashtray, slipped out of his Boulet
bikini briefs, gave his reflection in the full-length mirror
a lecherous stare, and jumped onto the bed. Opening the
book to the first page, he contentedly began to organize
a party, his favorite pastime.

Organization came naturally to him, an ability that
seemed to have been passed down through his father's
German Mennonite chromosomes. As a child, he'd always arranged the neighborhood bicycle races and the
secret clubs in the garage. In high school, he'd always
managed to stab a pivotal position in running the newspaper and the plays. After he dropped out of college
and got a job in a supermarket, it wasn't long before he
was making up the time schedules and revamping the
gourmet department. It all came so effortlessly to him,
and he'd been labeled an underachiever since kindergarten. But the name never bothered him much unless it in-
terfered with his fun.

Parties were a special pleasure, a gift of his maternal
Italian heritage. His happiest childhood memories were
of parties with his mother's sprawling family; Sunday
afternoons at an aunt's house in South Philadelphia or
Wildwood with the women chattering endlessly over
coffee and cake in the kitchen, the uncles drinking beer
and shouting at a television ball game in the living room,
the cousins running wild through the house and the
streets; holiday dinners at Uncle Joe's farm, Grandmother
deLuca and the aunts in the kitchen making their own
pasta in all shapes and sizes and the secret deLuca
spaghetti sauce, the huge table groaning with heaped,
steaming dishes, chairs reclaimed from the attic to accommodate the loud, laughing mob; the annual summer reunion at the farm with wet kisses and tickled ribs from
great-aunts and uncles, second and third cousins, people
rarely together but invisibly bound by affection, eating
bushels of clams, drinking kegs of beer, dancing to the
five-piece band with the accordion player, planning pea-
nut scrambles and sack races with silver dollars from
Uncle Joe as the prizes. The thought of a party still gave
Tory a warm glow and a shiver of excitement, and he
indulged good feelings whenever he could.

How this unlikely mixture of German Mennonite and

South Philadelphia Italian came about was the subject of one of Tory's favorite bedtime stories. Uncle Joe seemed like a storybook king with his big farm and the rest of the family his loyal subjects. They were surrounded by hostile kingdoms of strange Mennonite people who hated them for intruding into their lands and feared their foreignness, the way they still sometimes spoke Italian and drove in a caravan of Fords and Chevrolets behind Uncle Joe's Buick to the Catholic church in the city, forty miles away. But Uncle Joe was a fearless ruler, able to ignore the enemies and prosper. Tory's mother, Claudia, was the beautiful princess, Uncle Joe's niece from the city spending the summer in fresh air and sunshine. His father, Russell, was the handsome knight who won her heart, an enemy from the neighboring kingdom. The romance almost started a war and the lovers had to flee to far-off Maryland to be married.

As Tory grew older, he realized that they didn't live happily ever after. Now he could look back on the beautiful couple in the wedding picture and realize that they had probably been drawn together by motives less than fairy-tale pure. His father had the hint of a lustful stare in the picture, an expression that Tory had since become more than familiar with on other men. His mother's chin jutted out almost imperceptibly, a subtle gesture of rebellion that Tory only recognized because he used it himself when he was refused what he wanted.

They were never completely forgiven when they returned from Maryland and bought a house in Stoltz Grove, the community nearest the family farms. Tory wondered if the marriage would have worked out better in another location, someplace far away from the mass disapproval. Tory grew up listening to Claudia complain about Stoltz Grove and its residents, how the women in their bonnets and dark dresses gave shocked stares to her slacks and red nail polish and how they almost fainted when she'd spice her grocery-store conversation with a *hell* or a *dammit*. Though she may have yearned for the neon lights of the city, the censure seemed to give Claudia a perverse pleasure. Sometimes she'd sit on the front porch with a gin and tonic and loudly play Sinatra records, or hang wash on Sunday mornings while the neighbors were on their way to church. Tory was sure that she blamed Russell for imprisoning her among the "narrow-minded clodhoppers," and they argued constantly. Soon, even the arguments seemed to bore Russell, and he was seldom home.

Tory grew up feeling he was different. His mother ensured that by naming him Vittorio, after his grandfather, then plunging him into a world of Johns and Roberts. She drilled him to feel her disdain for Stoltz Grove, and by the time he was ten he was making plans to move to the city. His longing soon surpassed hers. Lucy and Ricky lived in the city, and Ricky worked in a nightclub. It looked like much more fun than anyone ever had in Stoltz Grove. He'd rush home from elementary school to watch the Philadelphia teenagers on *American Bandstand*, all wearing the newest clothes and dancing the latest dances. Frankie Avalon and Bobby Rydell and, most important of all, Fabian, were from the city. He thought that it must be an amazing place.

He copied the city ways as best he could, satisfying himself and impressing his peers. With his pudgy body and lack of coordination, he couldn't compete for recognition in the standard athletic ways, so he styled himself the class sophisticate. He constantly pleaded with Claudia to let him take the train to Philadelphia for a shopping trip and a matinee. It became the one withheld treat that could prod him into perfect behavior. He was always delighted when a classmate admired a new shirt or sweater and he could say it came from Wanamaker's or Strawbridge's and not one of the local clothing stores. When a movie finally found its way to the Stoltz Grove Theater, he took great pleasure in telling friends that he'd seen it months before at the Boyd or the Goldman, where they had balconies and uniformed ushers. He couldn't compete with his classmates on their own territory, but a self-promoted worldliness served as an adequate substitute.

He began to understand his manic devotion to Fabian with the onset of puberty. It wasn't easy for him to deal with being a homosexual at twelve, but he'd always been different, and it made its latest manifestation easier to accept.

Puberty had its bright side. Through no effort of his own, the baby fat seemed to melt overnight and he suddenly had broad shoulders and a slim waist and long legs. His tall, well-proportioned frame was a replica of his father's and one of the few things for which he cared to thank the man. His face was his mother's, and that underwent changes, too. The round, rosy cheeks that Uncle Joe used to pinch with one hand while he handed out a quarter with the other disappeared to reveal high cheekbones, a firm jaw, and the beginnings of pleasingly symmetrical adult features. He inherited Claudia's slight pug nose, full sensual lips, luminous brown eyes with thick, dark lashes and a head of lush, dark, loose curls that took on coppery highlights with exposure to the sun. He began to spend hours in front of mirrors, more in awe than in vanity. He'd never been an ugly child, but the transformation was breathtakingly dramatic. He felt a need to check his reflection constantly, in store windows or rearview mirrors, chrome appliances or stainless-steel flatware, half expecting the powers to revoke their gift at any moment.

He reveled in being attractive. God or Fate or the powers had given him so many disadvantages, differences that he'd had to make the best of. It seemed only fair that he should get some rewards to make up for them. He'd always been bright, an attribute that he exploited whenever possible. It got him into an accelerated program in high school, where a cut class or a cigarette in the boys' room was punished with a kindly lecture instead of two weeks in detention hall. He began to notice that an attractive face and body also merited special attention. The signs were subtle in school; invitations to certain parties, a seat with the right group in the cafeteria, more than a passing interest from certain teachers. Tory looked for the signs eagerly, ready to pursue the advantages he considered his due.

The dream of city life became a reality after high school graduation. He left for Philadelphia University with few regrets. The city became even more important to him; not only was it the womb of glamour and sophistication, it was also the center of gay life. The clues had become more and more obvious to him as he'd grown through adolescence, and he accepted the fact without surprise. The city had long been his release from dreary rural life, and it seemed natural that it should also be an

escape from straitlaced moral standards. He was still in
Philadelphia six years later, satisfied that he was achiev-
ing some degree of glamour and sophistication.

Tory finished up the P's in his book, the buttery-soft,
warm-red, brass-cornered address book from Cartier,
with as little success as he had anticipated in finding company for Friday night on the same afternoon. The R's
were no more interesting: Alan Rorer was in Pittsburgh
on business; Ed and Jane Roberts were pleasant but
they'd be uncomfortable with so many gay people; Jeff
Randall could be hysterically funny before he got incoherent but the memory of the cigarette burn in the dining-
room oriental from his last visit was still too fresh in
Tory's mind. He was puzzled by the Richard with no last
name until he noticed the South Philadelphia telephone
exchange. It summoned a happily torrid memory of an
eighteen-year-old picked up on a street corner, a sweet
child but not quite suitable for social presentation. Richard and South Philly had warmth and good looks, but not
much style.

He came to Brad Rothman, cradled the telephone on
his shoulder, and dialed the office number from memory.
The receptionist connected him immediately.

"Hello, toots, do you want to come to my party?"

"When?"

"Tonight."

Brad laughed his usual vaguely vexed laugh. "St.
Patrick's Day isn't until next week."

"This is a retirement party."

"Whose?" Brad asked warily. Tory could never understand why he hated surprises.

"Mine! I got fired!"

"What happened?" Brad finally asked in a doomed
tone.

"The old codger finally caught me with my hand in
the till," he answered brightly. "Talk about your standard
cheap scene—he carried on for hours."

"Is he going to have you arrested?" Brad's voice was
urgent.

"Arrested?" Tory hooted indignantly. "I could tell the
state tax collectors things about him that would make me
look like Snow White. He's letting me collect unemploy-

ment and promised to give me a good reference, should I ever choose to work again. Perhaps I was too kind," he added thoughtfully. "I probably could have held out for a cash settlement."

"Why not? What's a little blackmail after all these years of embezzlement?"

"Let's not be unkind," Tory answered evenly. "I may not be a saint but I'm not evil."

"Just a bit misdirected."

"And let's not analyze my moral standards again today. Come over after work and I'll whip something up for you and you can give me dark looks while I polish off the last bottle of Montrachet."

"Who's coming?"

"Just Art and Kathy from work and Jim and Danny from down the street. And Alice from downstairs with her new boyfriend, who's adorable, a little mustache and shoulders for days. If I get drunk enough I'll put the moves on him and we can watch Alice try to stay neighborly."

"Anything to keep us entertained."

"I take my host duties quite seriously. And Gary and his lover are coming later—you met them at Barbara Woods' party last fall. Gary's opening a shoe store or something—maybe you can suck up to him and get his legal business. And Michael, the bartender from Roscoe's and maybe a few others. I've got to keep it small; it's time to start cutting corners."

"I guess it is. How much are you getting from unemployment?"

"One-forty-three."

"That should take care of cigarettes and dry cleaning. What do you plan to do about the rent and charge accounts?"

"Please, Bradley, not today," Tory sighed dramatically. "These things have a way of working themselves out. I'll think about it tomorrow."

"At Tara?"

"Yes. Tomorrow is another day, you know."

"Tory, be serious. What are you going to do?"

"I'll sell Mama's garnet earbobs. That will pay the taxes and tide us over until the cotton crop comes in."

"Really."

Tory hated to be confronted with unpleasant thoughts, something Brad did to him regularly. His tone turned angry. "Do you really want to know what I'm going to do? For starters, I'm going to relax for several weeks. I'm going to drink and dance and get high a lot and carry on every morning until four and have a string of cheap affairs. I've had it with drudgery, and I'm glad Goldman finally caught me red-handed. I have no idea of what I'm going to do, I only know that I'm finally out of that dreary store and I'm going to enjoy it. And I wish you'd stop worrying about it."

"I can't help it. I always worry about you."

"You Jews, you're always worrying about something. Just try to enjoy yourself tonight. Maybe I'll fix you up with Michael."

"Why are you so hot on fixing me up lately?"

Tory was happy to change the subject. "Because eligible young lawyers are a valuable commodity and they shouldn't go to waste. You'll make some lucky young man very happy someday, and if I'm the one who fixes him up it's only fair that I collect a finder's fee. Perhaps I can make a career out of it."

"Selling lawyers?"

"Matchmaking! In the respected tradition of Dolly Levi. I have a perfect temperament for the work."

"How can you be so flippant about losing your job?"

"The secret is to think of it all as a musical comedy. Everything will work itself out by the finale. See you after work."

Tory felt vaguely annoyed as he hung up the telephone, an emotion that Brad often aroused in him. Sometimes he wondered if he had latent masochistic tendencies that drove him to seek constant criticism. If so, Brad was the perfect answer. He'd been dispensing stern advice practically since the day they'd met at Philadelphia University. When Tory looked back on it, he wondered how they'd ever become friends.

Brad was a sophomore who lived two doors down the hall when Tory moved into the dormitory. He wasn't sure what course his college social life would take, but he didn't expect it to include Brad. Tory had blithely joined his fellow students as a smiling young soldier in the

late-sixties war against the military-industrial complex.
Brad was an enemy sympathizer. His hair was unfashion-
ably short and neat and he seemed content to pursue his
pre-law degree and go on to accept his proper place in
society.

Tory had eagerly anticipated becoming part of the
youthful counterculture. Conservative Stolz Grove looked
upon its emergence with fear and disgust, so Tory threw
himself into it with gleeful abandon. He stopped going to
the barber before high school graduation, and his loose
curls tumbled wildly over his ears and collar. He supported
the antiwar cause and filled his room with peace symbols
and political posters, though he never bothered to delve
deeply into the philosophical fine points of his position.
He eagerly experimented with marijuana and LSD. He
wavered only on the flower-child notions of fashion and
it was with grave misgivings that he traded his Bass
Weejuns and creased wool flannels for tie-dyed T-shirts
and faded jeans.

His educational plans pointed vaguely toward liberal
arts. Though he'd lost interest in studying years before,
General Hershey and his selective service still manning
the Vietnam War made school seem the most sensible
alternative. Most important of all, it gave him the reason
to move to the city.

Tory's roommate flunked out after the first semester,
but before that they'd established their dorm room as a
center for marathon rap sessions, loud acid rock, and
clandestine pot-smoking. Tory cheerfully joined in marches
and demonstrations to protest the war, pollution, nonunion
grapes, police brutality, and any other available cause.
Some days he wasn't sure exactly which wrong he was
righting, but it all seemed so radically chic, and he smiled
brightly for the newspaper photographers.

Brad sometimes dropped into his room, usually to complain about the noise. The constant guests engaged him
in arguments about all the pertinent topics of the times,
occasionally drawing Tory into a political discussion. Brad
supported a moderate position and always won by default
when Tory forgot which examples he was supposed to cite
to demonstrate his points and dismissed the subject with
shouts of "Bourgeois!" and "Fascist pig!" The arguments
sometimes turned personal as Brad took a maddeningly

keen interest in Tory's casual attitude toward class attendance and the legal risks of drugs and membership in radical groups.

They developed a friendship only because of the movies. Tory guiltily felt that he should regard the social relevance of *Easy Rider* with the same awe as his peers and one Saturday afternoon he was mortified to discover Brad three rows behind him at a matinee of *Funny Girl*. It was too late to cover his tear-swollen eyes, but fortunately Brad was almost as affected as he. Tory was pleasantly startled, and they spent the next four Saturdays in the same theater together after Brad promised not to talk about it on campus. He annoyed Tory regularly but he did understand glamour.

Gayness wasn't openly acknowledged in the dormitory, where sexually conservative attitudes still prevailed. Tory found that hypocritical in a supposedly liberal setting but he wasn't about to risk his popularity by making an issue of it. He discovered the cruising area of Spruce Street, far from campus, and made discreet trips there. He was sure that Brad was also homosexual, even if he didn't yet realize it himself. They didn't discuss it until the following year, when Tory came back from summer vacation with an off-campus apartment and David Cunningham.

Tory dialed his parents' number and hoped that his mother would answer. He used to keep his finger poised above the cradle buttons and quickly terminate the call if he heard his father's voice. Time and minimal contact had since resolved many of their differences and they could be cordial to each other at holiday gatherings, weddings, and funerals, though Tory still preferred not to speak to him about anything that might cause an argument.

"Hello." Claudia's melodious greeting covered at least two octaves. It always made Tory smile. He remembered vividly how she could be in the middle of a screaming match with Russell and still answer the ringing telephone in her most refined voice.

"Hi, Claudia."

"Hi, doll!" she said in happy surprise. Her tone immediately changed to wary alertness. "What's wrong?" She always suspected that something was wrong when she didn't initiate a call, and she was usually right.

"I just wanted to tell you not to waste a dime trying to get me at the store. I don't work there anymore."

"What happened?"

"Nothing dramatic. It was just one of those things. You know we've never gotten along, and it finally passed the point of no return." It sounded like a plausible story. He wondered if Claudia could tell that he was lying without seeing his eyes.

"So what are you going to do?"

"Collect unemployment while I do some thinking."

"That will be nice for you for a while. You deserve a little vacation."

"I certainly do," he agreed enthusiastically.

"Maybe you'll go back and finish school."

"I'll give it some thought." School was nowhere on his extensive list of leisure-time activities. "So how are you?"

"Not bad."

"Und der Führer?"

"Who knows? He went to a ball game or something."

"How's Maxene and LaVerne?" Old family photos of his mother and two aunts reminded him of the pictures on Claudia's old Andrews Sisters albums.

"Antoinette's still showing her vacation pictures from Hawaii, and Dolores got her hair frosted, the horse's ass."

"That makes her a horse's ass?"

"She let her neighbor do a Clairol job on her and it's in seven shades of orange. She's too cheap to go to the beauty parlor."

"What color are you this week?"

"Still auburn, smart-ass."

"Are you going blond for the summer again?"

"I might. It was almost worth it for the look on your old man's face. Maybe I'll get it done right before his family picnic."

"That would brighten it up. What's new in Cow Town?"

The question was Claudia's cue for a burlesque of painfully weary moans. They became more exaggerated each year, reminding Tory of a Carol Channing performance, though he still enjoyed playing the straight man for her. "This godforsaken hole. Shall I buy you a shoofly pie at the firehouse bake sale? That's the big excitement in town

today. That old redneck Mrs. Kratz had the nerve to ask
me to bake something. I told her my oven was broken."

"You told her the same thing last year," Tory laughed.

"You'd think the old bitch would catch on. She's about
as smart as the rest of them. Hey! I saw Milly Cunningham at the drugstore yesterday. She lost twenty pounds
and found a boyfriend, hasn't looked so well in years."

"It's about time she pulled her act together. She's been
beating that mourning number to death for years."

"Don't be nasty, Tory," she replied patiently. "Look how
long it took for you to get over David, and you were just
a baby with your whole life ahead of you. He was her
only son, and it's rough for a mother to handle something
like that."

"Well, it's about time she got over it. David wouldn't
have wanted her to carry on like she had for all these
years."

"It's almost four now, isn't it?"

"Today."

Tory Bacher had known David Cunningham since pre-
school days. Other children bored him when David was
around; he always knew what to say or do to make everything more exciting and funnier for Tory. It gave him a
pleasantly spooky tingle when they'd say the same thing
at the same moment, and it happened almost everyday.
David's family moved to Massachusetts when they were
eight, and Tory cried for weeks.

They met again at eighteen. Tory came home to Stoltz
Grove after his freshman year and dreaded the coming
summer with a factory job and little to do for entertainment but outrage the locals with his shoulder-length curls
and listen to gossip. One of the hot items was that the
Cunninghams were divorced and David was back in
Sholtz Grove with his mother. The stories said that he
was a theater student in Boston and almost as contamin-
ated by city ways as Tory. Tory wondered how much Da-
vid had changed over the summer and looked forward to their paths crossing over the summer. Whenever he thought of David he
felt the old, vaguely remembered eerie tingle.

He didn't immediately recognize him a few days later
at the community swimming pool. He only melted at
the sight of the tanned Greek god in a skimpy white nylon

swimsuit. Tory melted regularly at eighteen, when sex was still a novelty. He could usually control it, but the bulge in the white nylon kept him from peeling off his jeans and revealing the erection in his own trunks.

They recognized each other at the same moment, and David reintroduced himself with a predatory smile. At first Tory fumbled for conversation, but soon words came easily and it was as if they'd never been apart. They'd changed in the same ways over the ten years, they'd seen the same movies, bought the same books, laughed at the same jokes, ridiculed the same town. And they had the same erotic desires. It became blatantly apparent as they sunbathed side by side on their towels. David positioned himself to give Tory a good view of his body and watched with a sly smile as he tried to avert his riveted eyes. He casually touched himself on the chest or rubbed his thigh while he talked, intently watching Tory the whole time. Tory knew it would be unwise to get involved with anyone while in Stoltz Grove. Gossip was the town's major pastime, and the residents watched their neighbors with unabashed interest. They'd have a field day if the arrogant hippy with the uppity city-slicker mother did something so worthy of their criticism. Tory loved to titillate them, but this would bring him outright ridicule.

It was unwise, but it was beyond his control. He suddenly knew how it must feel to be a bitch in heat. He was no match for the laughing blue eyes and the body that looked ready to pounce on its prey at any moment. He gave in to the first invitation for a ride in David's convertible.

One touch was addictive, and the rest of the summer was tinged with a deliciously uncontainable lust. First love was like a high-grade fever for him, the last of the childhood diseases and one for which he didn't want any medicine. Arranging meetings often frustrated them, because they both lived under parental roof and watchful eye. A desperate urgency occasionally drove them to recklessness. They began to sneak quickies in Tory's bedroom while his parents watched television downstairs. They ducked out of summer jobs for afternoon trysts at David's while his mother worked. They parked on dirt roads for speedy sessions made even more exciting by their furtiveness. They could barely keep their hands off each other in the local movie house or diner, and Tory was sure that people were beginning to suspect.

The inevitable happened in the wee hours of a hot August night. The stairs had creaked when David crept in, and Tory's father swung the bedroom door open in search of a burglar, baseball bat in hand. The memory of the scene that followed still made Tory blush with a nervous giggle. Russell screamed, Mrs. Cunningham cried, only Claudia seemed unsurprised.

September and the city seemed an eternity away, and they made stealthy plans. They rented an off-campus apartment and bought furniture at Goodwill. David transferred from his Boston school to the more prestigious theater department at Philadelphia U. They moved on Labor Day while the Bachers were visiting and Mrs. Cunningham was at the seashore. Russell threatened to disown Tory but continued to pay the tuition bills.

The future troubled Tory on the rare occasions he stopped to think about it. He was happy to let another problem solve itself as they settled into a domestic routine of romantic poverty. He continued with a liberal-arts program for lack of another interest, but school was an afterthought next to being with David. The cheap apartment on the edge of the ghetto became their playhouse. Sometimes Tory felt that he was squandering himself as he experimented in the kitchen or listened to Claudia's household hints over the phone, but David was beside him in the double bed every night and nothing else seemed terribly important.

David quickly established himself in the theater department and won a major part in the season's first production. Tory had fought fiercely for this sort of recognition in high school, but now he realized that he'd been a dilettante while David had true potential. Tory gorged him with moral support and took vicarious pleasure from his success.

The success took other forms. Just as his dorm room had become a haven for the self-styled radically chic, their apartment became a meeting place for the theater department. It was such a pleasure to stop being concerned about Cambodia or oppressed minorities and concentrate on *Variety* headlines or the costumes in *Follies*.

Their new friends were openly gay or uncondemning, and Tory no longer felt like a hypocrite.

He tried not to appear smug, but it was difficult to conceal that he felt he was finally getting what he deserved out of life. He had a man-boy he loved intensely, a sex life that kept him in a perpetual glow, the camaraderie of a sophisticated social circle, reflected glory in David's growing recognition, and a youthfully optimistic vision of a future that promised the glamorous neon of the theater and never-ending bliss. It lasted for eighteen months. Then David was run down by a stolen car and Tory began to wonder if it all had been a tasteless practical joke.

Tory took a long slug of wine before he dialed. He hoped she was at the cemetery or work or anyplace but home. She answered.

"Hi, Mrs. Cunningham. It's Tory Bacher."

The receiver issued a choked-back sob. "Tory! You remembered."

"Don't I always?"

"I can't believe it's been four years."

"Incredible, isn't it?"

"I took flowers to the cemetery this morning."

Tory paused to swallow the lump in his throat. "I knew you would. I've never been able to go back myself, but I wanted you to know I was thinking about you today. And David."

The strained voice on the other end broke into soft sobs. "Oh, Tory, I'm sure his thoughts are always with you."

"I'm sorry. I shouldn't have gotten you upset again." He took a deep breath. "My mother said she saw you yesterday and you're looking fabulous."

"I've been on a diet. And I'm feeling much better lately. How are you? Still at the supermarket?"

"No, I'm retired right now. I might go back to school this summer." He thought she could use an optimistic note.

"Tory! I'm so glad you're finally going to go back. You and I are the ones who suffered most. I guess they were right, though. Time heals all wounds."

Tory laughed. "It took us a long time to buy that one, didn't it?"

Tory still wasn't sure that he bought it. He often thought that the wound seemed to be healed but the scar tissue continued to be sensitive. At first, he'd been hysterical. He'd survived the funeral only with physical support, heavy doses of Valium, and occasional blurred thoughts of Jacqueline Kennedy. He couldn't bear to stay in the apartment they'd shared; he wasn't even happy to be on campus with its myriad memories and sympathetic smiles. Brad found him a small studio apartment in center city.

Tory spent what remained of the spring and most of the summer buried in the apartment. He swallowed three blue Valiums with his morning coffee to control the nervous spasms that racked his body and kept a bottle of yellows with his cigarettes and matches to control any tremors during the day as he watched soap operas or game shows or reread David's favorite plays. Brad came over almost every evening and cajoled him into eating dinner. Tory insisted on wine with his one meal of the day, and afterward they'd play David's old show records while he cried intermittently, finished the wine, and became progressively more incoherent. He disappeared into the bathroom before bed and swallowed two Seconals to ward off nightmares. He avoided his old friends from the theater department and the painful memories they evoked. Claudia appeared every Saturday with cash, groceries, and clean laundry.

He gradually came back to reality. By August, it was apparent that he wouldn't return to school, and his father insisted that he find a job. With either total blindness or cunning foresight, Jack Goldman overlooked his glassy eyes and emaciated body and hired him to work in his supermarket. Tory became part of the customer service department, taking grocery orders over the telephone and helping shoppers in the store. It was therapeutic, and he gradually decreased his intake of sedatives. He lunged at the chance to divert himself, learning the personal quirks and preferences of the affluent Society Hill clientele, and soon had a list of steady customers who would deal only with him. His talent for arranging things resurfaced, and he involved himself in more and more facets of managing the store. As he emerged from his shell, he realized his growing value to the business and forced a grudging Goldman to give him more money. The thought of returning to school didn't appeal to him without David to share it, and the supermarket was a painless way to pass the time.

Tory thought briefly about the long-distance charges on his next bill and dialed anyway. He cursed the switchboard operator for keeping him on hold for an interminable time.

"Mona Brett speaking."

"Oh, please, how professional."

"Tory! I'm flying in next weekend."

"Great! Are you staying with me?"

"No. Dominic."

"Dominic!" he groaned good-naturedly. "I thought your gangster was finished business."

"So did I. Then he mailed me a first-class ticket and a *heavenly* gold bracelet from Caldwell's. What's a woman to do?"

"Deliver the goods, I suppose."

"I prefer to think of his little baubles and beads as tokens of esteem."

"You're going to esteem your poor twat to death."

"Nonsense, *mon cher*. It positively thrives on attention."

"I got fired this morning."

"Tory! Did Goldman finally catch you?"

"*In flagrante delicto,* my dear."

"Whatever will you do?"

"Have a party," he laughed.

"That's a trait I've always admired in you, Tory. Other people try to muster a smile in the face of adversity. You laugh hysterically and draw up a guest list."

"It does no good to dwell on these things. Besides, I have summary sheets that would send the old bastard up the river. I'm getting unemployment and a glowing recommendation."

"How clever of you, you little devil. But how can you possibly get by on unemployment?"

"God only knows. But it's such a relief to be through with the tedium. I feel like school's out for summer."

"Perhaps now you'll listen to my prudent advice and hit those wrinkle bars for a sugardaddy."

Tory shuddered. "I'd sooner have them repossess my Cuisinart."

"Something's bound to turn up," she said brightly. "Perhaps you should treat yourself to something lovely to ward off a depression. Preventive medicine is the rage out here these days."

He laughed at her optimism. "I'm beginning to think we're the only two sensible people left in this world."

Tory had met Mona at the supermarket, and she quickly became his favorite customer. He thought at first that she was a model or someone's mistress. The dark straight hair was perfectly styled, and the deftly professional makeup displayed her striking features to best advantage. Her deep tan in January, a head-turning red fox coat, and gold jewelry in theatrical profusion convinced him that she wasn't a secretary or a housewife. They developed a passing acquaintance as she shopped, and Tory was pleasantly impressed with her outgoing style. She told him in short order that she was a sales representative for a drug company, recently transferred from Houston, divorced from a doctor for two years, not interested in another marriage but always in the market for an attractive man. She frankly studied male shoppers and pumped Tory for details. Tory delighted in divulging all he knew of their reputations, professional standing, financial possibilities, and marital status. Mona's standard question became "But does he have any meat?" Tory found her delightfully outrageous and began to enjoy her shopping trips more than his coffee breaks.

She called the store one afternoon with an air of confidential urgency in her voice. "Tory, you *must* do me a favor."

"Anything, my dear."

"Listen carefully. I'm making dinner for an old friend of my father's tonight. He's the most horrid lecher on the face of the earth but I'm simply *bound* to entertain him when he's in the area. His only redeeming virtue is generosity to a fault. He always brings champagne and absolutely *insists* on paying for the groceries. Pay attention now, this is the strategy. When we come into the store tonight, you'll rush over to me with that sixty-dollar jar of truffles in hand and say in a respectful voice, 'Mrs. Brett, the truffles you ordered have *finally* arrived.' "

"I'm not sure that I can coax twelve syllables out of 'finally.' "

"Practice. I'll thank you graciously and toss them into my cart with a total lack of concern and he'll be too pompous to mention them at the checkout counter. It's the least I deserve for wrestling him off all evening."

Tory thought it sounded like even more fun than helping her cruise customers and looked forward to it with glee. They pulled it off perfectly, and Mona invited him out for dinner on her next free night. Their friendship grew rapidly from there, and Tory gave her truffles for her birthdays and at Christmas.

The reasons for their friendship seemed shallow at first. Tory felt uneasy with men. He had brief affairs or one night stands from the bars, but they all left him feeling either uneasy or unfulfilled. Sex was an occasional necessity, but he always compared the men to his nostalgic memory of David and they never measured up. At the first sign that a date wanted to become more seriously involved, he nervously extricated himself. Men he met as friends sometimes shocked him by turning suddenly romantic. Tory thought it was ironic that a gay man should feel most at ease with a straight woman.

Mona liked Tory, he thought at first, because she didn't have many other friends. Women seemed to take a pathological dislike to her at first sight and reflexively moved closer to their husbands or dates. She usually had four or five men in various stages of involvement in her romantic life, but Tory was the only friend she could confide in.

Their friendship developed new dimensions with time. One night over their third bottle of wine she opened up to him about her past. Tory was stunned to discover such a depth of feeling beneath her frivolous façade. The product of a marriage held together only by social and financial considerations, Mona had had less than a blissful childhood. Her workaholic father was a General Motors vice-president, and her mother devoted her energies to social climbing on her nebulous Chrysler family connections. Mona was raised by a series of mother's helpers and housekeepers, none of whom ever seemed to last more than a year. She wasn't happy, but the thought of rebellion rarely entered her mind. It was inconceivable to her that she could challenge her parents' powerful social milieu, the homes in Grosse Point and Harbor Springs, the memberships at the Little Club, the Caucus Club, the Oakland Hills Country Club, the Detroit Yacht Club. As it had for Tory, school proved Mona's first means of escape.

The world of Bryn Mawr was a pleasant change for her, but not the answer she was looking for. She spent four years indifferently working for a degree in art history, relieved to be removed from the daily routine in Detroit but still at a loss for a world to replace it. She thought she'd finally found the answer in her senior year when she met Robert Brett at a weekend house party.

The marriage made the final break from her family an amicable parting. Robert met all the standards—a good family, a promising future as a doctor, a respectable trust fund. And Mona's parents thought he was pleasant, if a bit ineffectual. Mona's own assessment of him declined as she dutifully tried to play her role of doctor's wife and began to realize that she'd only traded one set of social burdens for another. She sincerely tried to do what was expected of her: the bazaars, the committee luncheons, the thrift shop, the fund drives. She threw her expected share of dinner parties, where the husbands discussed the hospital and the wives discussed their husbands' work.

For some reason not clear to her, she refused to have a baby, the son Robert expected from her to perpetuate the family name. Their discussions became progressively more heated over the subject, forcing Mona to wonder why she was so opposed to the idea. The answer came to her in the middle of an argument one night—she didn't want the baby because she simply didn't want Robert and the life they were leading together. She soon filed for divorce.

The idea of a career didn't actually appeal to her, but it seemed the most reasonable option. Her father offered to help her enter the business world of Detroit, but she refused. She decided instead to put her medical connections to use and landed a respectable position with a drug company in Houston. It was there that she started to live her own life, a thousand miles from family disapproval. She took tentative steps at first, then plunged with abandon into a life she'd never known, a life that gave little thought to "the correct thing to do."

She was relieved to feel so free, but still wasn't happy. After a lifetime of generous allowances, she was genuinely shocked to discover what average people had to cope with to make ends meet. Salary and alimony simply wouldn't cover her expenses, and she frequently had to turn to her parents for help. And the men didn't fill the void in her life. After four years of marriage she returned to dating with superhuman enthusiasm, searching tirelessly for Mr. Right. She'd auditioned close to five hundred men by her own count, but none of them had quite measured up.

She'd almost given up hope, she confided to Tory. Mr. Right just didn't seem to be out there waiting for her, and even the auditions were becoming routine. She'd dated every possible type of man, tried all the positions and most of the toys. There didn't seem to be anything left to excite her. "Except the gifts," she added as an afterthought. Tory was duly curious, and Mona was happy to explain as best she could. They went to her bedroom and she opened her oversized jewelry box. She fondly picked up piece after piece from the huge assortment, offering him a running commentary on the man it came from, the occasion that prompted it, and her delight at having caused such an act of generosity. Tory asked her if she thought her hobby might not be a bit neurotic, but she only shrugged and said that it was infinitely more interesting to her than raising money for a children's wing at her ex-husband's hospital.

Tory found a kindred spirit that evening, a sympathetic ear for his own story, and he surprised himself by telling it. He never discussed David with new acquaintances, feeling he'd cheapen the memory by using it for sympathy. Mona seemed to share his philosophy, that the past was past and it was terribly gauche to burden anyone but the most intimate friends with unhappy thoughts. Another rotten event was probably lurking around the next corner, so life might as well be enjoyed before it happened.

Once they were satisfied that all the proper emotions of true friendship were there, they didn't dwell on them. Life was for fun and games, and they became each other's favorite playmate. Their major topic of conversation became sex. Mona was preoccupied with it as her life's calling, and Tory found he enjoyed talking about it more as he participated in it less. They delighted in shocking each other with explicit details of each encounter. Money and the wonderful things it could do filled much of the rest of their talk. They goaded each other on to greater extravagances and helped each other rationalize away any guilt feelings. Shopping together became a tireless hobby, and they took almost as much interest in each other's wardrobe and home as they did in their own.

They also enjoyed being seen together, aware that they created a head-turning couple. Tory took pleasure in flaunting her in restaurants and clubs, just as he enjoyed displaying his Dupont lighter or his Hermès belt. He loved traveling together best of all; they'd pile up the Vuitton luggage and flash their jewelry and status accouterments, aware that they were drawing attention. Occasionally someone would ask if they were in fashion or entertainment, and Mona would answer cryptically, implying that she'd rather keep their identity a secret to avoid a rush for autographs. They constantly accused each other of being superficial and juvenile, and they enjoyed every minute of it.

Tory was sad when Mona was transferred to Chicago. But she called regularly on her office WATS line, and when she came to visit it was always a special occasion. He looked forward to seeing her on the next weekend. He knew she'd help him celebrate his freedom.

The telephone rang as Tory was about to step into the shower. He tried to be grateful that it hadn't rung a minute later and wondered who was calling with a last-minute cancellation or addition.

"Hello."

"Hello, Tory." Tory gave a surprised giggle at Goldman's voice. "I just put your unemployment forms in the mail."

"Thank you."

"Now, why don't you play ball with me and bring back the summary sheets?"

"You can't be serious."

"It's only fair."

"Fair, my ass. Do you think you're talking to another dumb *shaygetz*? You taught me everything I know."

"You're getting what you want. Why can't you show some human decency and let me sleep peacefully tonight?"

"You'll have to forgive me, but I'm new at this. I haven't learned about honor among thieves yet.'"

"You little prick."

"You needn't lose any sleep over the summary sheets. I have no intention of using them, but I'm insulted that you think I might be stupid enough to give up my insurance. God knows what tricks you might have up your nasty little sleeve."

"I should've never given in to you. I should've pressed charges."

"Wouldn't that have made a charming scene? We could have shared a cell at Allenwood. Except they'd throw away the key if they ever got hold of you."

The grief over David's death gradually waned and left Tory with a smoldering rage. He hid it behind a vacuously frivolous mask, but he felt morally entitled to compensation. Material things didn't fill the void, but they gave transitory pleasure. Like the comic books and the bowl of Campbell's chicken noodle soup that Claudia used to give him when he was in bed with a cold, Tory began to buy little presents to make himself smile again.

Unlike most developing trends in a personality, Tory's consumerism could be traced back to a single event. In the commotion of moving to the new apartment, Brad had taken him out to the telephone office to arrange for service. Brad forced him to go, insisting that he needed fresh air. Being dragged from his cocoon made Tory more irritable than usual, but he spotted a fire-engine-red telephone on display that made him smile with childlike pleasure. Like having a hot line to the White House, he thought.

"May I help you?"

"Yes, I'd like a red telephone, please," he giggled through his Valium haze.

Brad patiently explained to him that colors were several dollars extra and considering his dependence on his father's charity at the time it seemed more sensible to settle for the basic-black model. Tory stubbornly insisted. He had so little to make him happy, and the red telephone made him smile. You owe it to yourself, he thought. Why should *you* have to worry about money?

"You owe it to yourself" became his battle cry when he finally went to work, and he flung himself into the world of conspicuous consumption with gusto. It started slowly with his first few paychecks. Saturday afternoon in the department stores became the highlight of his week. A new shirt, a pair of slacks, a book on the theater, or the latest Broadway album were little treats with which he rewarded himself regularly.

After a few months among the gainfully employed, Tory established credit at some of the stores and discovered the miracle of the revolving charge. Suddenly a two-hundred-dollar suede jacket meant only his signature and ten dollars a month sometime in the future, a future that all the sales clerks apparently assumed would arrive without question. Tory thought of David, so suddenly and so ridiculously dead, and he signed the sales slip with a bright smile. He always thanked the sales clerks with genuine gratitude; it seemed so kind of them to give him so many thoughtful gifts. He began collecting credit cards as he'd once collected stamps, confirming his own exaggerated applications on the supermarket telephone.

Tory watched his affluent customers with a fascinated eye and tried to copy their standards. He unraveled the mysteries of crossed G's on a belt and LV's on a bag. Identifying Gucci loafers on a crowded street became a game, as some of his schoolmates used to identify Plymouths and Fords. He still couldn't tell a Plymouth from a Ford but now he knew a Mercedes 280 from a 450.

The efficiency apartment soon became unsuitable to his escalating life-style. He decided that a Society Hill address would be more impressive, and he found a one-bedroom bi-level with a sundeck view of the evening skyline and a dining area dramatically overlooking the two-story living room, a bargain at four hundred a month. It needed smart furniture to do it justice, and he bought matching velvet sofas, a few oriental carpets, a massive antique walnut bed, a glass-and-chrome dining-room table with Bauhaus chairs, a forest of tropical plants, and an endless list of other comforts.

With such a beautiful apartment, it seemed wasteful not to share its pleasures. Brad was there often, as he'd always been, and Mona visited, alone or with one of the ever-changing escorts. Tory began to select new acquaintances with the same discrimination he had learned to employ in picking his clothes, and an affluent, sophisticated troop paraded through his apartment regularly. It gave him a warm glow to entertain, the same happy glow he used to feel at the family gatherings of his childhood or the parties he gave with David. To recapture that elusive warmth he didn't even think to spare expense. Cooking became a favorite pastime, but hamburger and chicken were replaced with milk-fed veal and backfin crab, sour-cream jars and stainless steel with stemmed crystal and silverplate.

There was so much more he wanted; British sterling and Belgian linen, a summer beach cottage and winter vacations, more domestic help and more imported champagne, fresh flowers daily and silk shirts by the dozen. An endless and always growing shopping list awaited his attention. But somewhere along the line, finances slipped out of control. He'd become a magician with the credit cards when he cared to be bothered, some months borrowing money on Master Charge to pay Visa and juggling the other two dozen accounts with ingenious dexterity. When Brad looked over his bills one evening and told him he'd finally gone into five figures, even Tory became uneasy. He wondered if the sales clerks had inside information and the future was about to come after all.

With unaccustomed resolve, he decided to cut expenses and for two months he took satisfaction in the novel experience of self-discipline. When he saw that all his noble sacrifices barely made a dent in the mountain of debt, he began looking for a more expedient course of action.

Bankruptcy weighed heavily on his mind for several restless nights. He finally managed to convince himself that he'd somehow survive in a less impressive apartment after the stores repossessed his furniture. He was about to call Brad on the bedroom telephone and tell him to begin legal proceedings when the credit-card case on the dresser caught his eye. He glanced back and forth between the telephone and the dresser, barely aware that his legs were slowly carrying him across the room. Once at the dresser, his trembling hand reached out to fondle the leather case. The brass snap yielded easily beneath his thumb and the strip of card-filled pockets cascaded almost to the floor. One by one he fingered the bright cards and tenderly rubbed their smooth, hard plastic faces. Each had its own special memory of an afternoon in a shop or an evening in a restaurant. They'd taken him places and bought him gifts without waiting for the excuse of a birthday or Christmas. They were always there for him, ready to give him everything he wanted. Tory glanced again at the telephone and shuddered. Suddenly he knew he'd never be able to make the call. Embezzlement began to seem like an idea worth consideration.

He'd realized for some time that the supermarket was practically pleading to be plundered. Goldman was expanding into other areas and spent little time at the store, confident of Tory's ability. An unrung carton of cigarettes meant five dollars in his pocket, and a petty-cash slip for stamps or gas went unquestioned. He checked out his own groceries in Goldman's absence, and a few unrung steaks or a bag of coffee did more to cut his food bills than shopping for specials and buying cheaper cuts. The possibilities multiplied as he became more adept at his crimes. Some invoices could be paid more than once and the duplicate checks discreetly cashed. The total from one register could occasionally be overlooked when the daily summary was compiled and the excess cash pocketed. It was risky, but it could mean a windfall. The routine began to seem more familiar, and with familiarity it no longer seemed so wrong. Tory continued to live in his accustomed style and watched the bills plummet pleasingly to five thousand dollars.

Goldman made it easier for him not to feel guilty. Tory didn't think of him as an evil person, but he was certainly not difficult to dislike. His penchant for seizing every chance to stuff his pockets with little regard for employees or customers earned him unanimous dislike in the neighborhood. He raised prices as high as the market would bear, overcharged customers he knew not to check their register tapes, repackaged thawed turbot as fresh flounder, and illegally redeemed coupons from stacks of Sunday newspapers. He also skimmed the state sales tax receipts, entering a fraction of the amount collected on his books. It was a glaringly brazen ploy, but lax enforcement and lucrative returns apparently made it irresistible.

Tory decided that evidence against Goldman would be a sensible precaution as he became more heavily involved in his own illegal activities. He congratulated himself on the rare flash of common sense when Goldman's accountant stumbled over an unexplainable shortage in the deposits. Goldman shrewdly assessed their relative positions and released Tory from his job with full unemployment benefits and a letter of recommendation.

Chapter Two

A week later, the morning sunshine streamed through the floor-to-ceiling windows as Tory pushed the buzzer to unlock the downstairs door. He climbed the spiral staircase to the dining room and moaned theatrically at the anticipated scene with Brad. Judy Garland assured him from the background that life was still a bowl of cherries.

"Tory?"

"Upstairs."

He heard Brad ascending. "Do you buzz everybody in without using the intercom?"

"I was hoping for a rapist," he shouted from the kitchen. "Sit down, coffee will only be a second. Do you want a croissant?"

Tory could hear him settling into his favorite chair at the head of the glass table. "I'm glad to see you're still rich enough for fresh flowers," Brad called with his usual undertone of disapproval.

Tory remembered the arrangement on the table. "Don't jump to conclusions, they're from a gentleman caller."

"I don't see any jonquils."

"They're from Danny, with a nice thank-you note for the party."

"They should be long-stemmed roses, the way he carried on."

"Let's not be unkind. He was unwinding."

"If he unwound any more you could have poured him out the door."

28

"Do you want a croissant or not?"

"No, I've got lunch in two hours with a client." Tory emerged from the kitchen wearing a brightly multi-striped muslin caftan and carrying coffee and croissants on a silver tray. "Is that what you retired folks wear these days?"

"Like it?" Tory smiled. "I got it last month at Bergdorf's in New York. It was marked down to thirty-two dollars."

"I'm so glad you're learning to economize," he smiled in mock enthusiasm.

"Oh, I am," Tory replied in self-admiration as he poured. "I passed up the silk pajamas, so I saved two hundred dollars."

"I straightened out your bills last night."

Tory buttered a croissant and made it a point to look bored. "Goody."

"I don't know how you could run a forty-thousand-dollar-a-week business and let your own finances get into such a mess."

"It's so much easier to be efficient with someone else's money."

"I left it all downstairs on your desk. It's not as awful as I thought. Not great, but it's been worse.'" Brad cleared his throat, obviously preparing to begin a dissertation. "You'll use your Master Charge checks to pay off the small balances at the department and specialty stores— I left you a list. Then you'll just have the Strawbridge account for the carpets, the two Visa accounts, the Master Charge, and the American Express. It's just over five thousand total, and after you pay the American Express your monthly payments will run about one-sixty a month. With rent and utilities about four-twenty, that's five-eighty per month, which is almost exactly your total monthly income from unemployment. If you get a part-time job to cover your other expenses and let me put your cards in my safe-deposit box, you can go on indefinitely without major difficulties."

Tory smiled brightly and patted his hand. "It's so convenient to have a lawyer in the family. I knew you'd straighten everything out."

Brad looked annoyed again. "I'd hardly call it straightened out. You still need some sort of job; without free groceries and cigarettes at the store you'll need at least a hundred a week just to make ends meet."

"Are you sure you don't want a croissant? They're from that marvelous French bakery on Walnut Street. Scrumptious!" Brad's fixed frown told him that the subject had not been closed. "Brad, I really am going to cut back. I realize I have to make some sacrifices or find another job; it's a matter of priorities, and the free time is more important to me right now. I even told Mae I can't afford her anymore. I'm going to do my own housework," Tory said with a selfless valor.

"Did she show you how to turn on the vacuum cleaner?"

"It was a very sad scene. We cried a little and reminisced. She's still going to drop in for coffee and give me free advice," Tory laughed.

"She never did much cleaning anyway."

"But we have such rapport."

Mae was a middle-aged black woman who'd been Tory and David's next-door neighbor. She'd laughed at Tory's domestic helplessness and taken him under her wing, often seeming relieved to escape her daughter and two loud grandchildren. She used to visit practically every day, washing a sinkful of dishes or clearing the clutter when it got on her nerves. She was one of the few welcome visitors after David's death, and when Tory could finally afford it he paid her to come in once a week to clean. She still spent as much time chatting and giving advice as she did cleaning, but Tory enjoyed her company, and any housework that got done was more than he'd do himself.

"That's twenty-five a week you're saving on rapport. What else?"

"I'm living in jeans and Bagatelle T-shirts; all my party frocks and Joan Crawford business suits are collecting dust in the closets. That's about fifteen a week in dry cleaning."

"What else?"

"Almadén Mountain Chablis is now the *vin de maison*," Tory winced. "No more Montrachet."

"That should be a considerable savings," Brad said drily.

"Let's stick to finances. We just did an alcoholism lecture last week."

"OK. What else?"

Tory poured more coffee while he thought. "Isn't that enough?"

"Hardly. You'll have to give up entertaining, no matter what the house wine is."

"I know that."

"No new clothes."

"I can make it through the summer on last year's wardrobe. Perhaps just a few new pairs of espadrilles."

"You could give up cigarettes."

Tory looked offended. "You're getting a sadistic kick out of this, aren't you? Is it because I'm half German and you subconsciously blame me for Anne Frank?"

"I can't picture you goosestepping in khaki." He didn't fall for the diversionary tactic. "No more fancy restaurants twice a week."

Tory batted his eyelashes in burlesque flirtation. "Unless I'm invited."

"No more disco and bar hopping."

"That doesn't cost me much. If I play my cards right."

"You whore," Brad laughed.

"These are troubled times," he said nobly. "One must do what one must do."

"No more twenty-dollar haircuts once a month."

"I can't very well stop my hair from growing."

"No more manicures."

Tory looked as if he'd just been told that Cartier had gone discount. "Now really, Bradley. Austerity is one thing, but a line must be drawn."

"You're hopeless. What are you going to do for a part-time job?"

"No problem. I can be a waiter at Sorenson's whenever I'm ready to start, and the cash is all under the table. I can pick up a hundred in two nights a week."

"If you put out for Sorenson."

"*C'est la vie.*"

"What about school?"

"You must be in secret communication with my mother."

"You only need forty credits. With summer school and

evening classes, you could practically be through by the time unemployment runs out."

"Then I'll have a B.A. in English lit and I can become a management trainee at Gimbel's for two hundred a week. Who the hell needs it?"

"So what do you plan to do with yourself?"

Tory stretched happily. "Well, I'm hoping for an unseasonably warm spring so I can get a head start on my tan. And I have a stack of books I've been meaning to read and a pile of recipes I want to try. Not to mention the trashy affairs and one-night stands I expect to have. I plan to become a fixture at the Allegro and DCA, one of those familiar faces that you see every time you're out and say, 'Jesus Christ, doesn't she ever stay home?' "

"You'll be bored to death within a month."

"You'd be. I won't. Some of us have a talent for leisure."

"Just what are your plans for the future? When unemployment runs out and you have to go back to work?"

Tory burst into a warbly alto. *"Che serà, serà."*

"Spare me, please."

"Perhaps I'll become a chanteuse."

"You'd starve."

"Maybe I'll find a rich husband like Jackie did. I could adjust to a Greek island. And a five-bedroom cooperative overlooking the park."

"I'm sure you could."

"I don't know that I'd want to hunt foxes, though. Maybe I should move to New York. Let's face it, all the action is in the Big Apple. This town is so provincial." It was Tory's favorite way of starting a heated discussion at any gathering. Hard-core Philadelphians seemed to suffer from an inferiority complex and constantly enumerated their city's advantages in an effort to reassure each other that life wasn't passing them by in the boondocks. Tory agreed with them, more or less, but it was always a surefire line to pick up a flagging cocktail-party conversation or change a subject.

"For someone with the hay barely brushed out of his hair, you've got some fancy ideas."

"Sophistication is a state of mind. Can I help it if I was born chic?"

"You're not going to look very chic sitting on the curb with an eviction notice and your Cole Porter songbook."

Tory gave him a suggestive stare. "Perhaps I'll settle for a young Philadelphia lawyer with a promising future."

"I'd murder you within a month.'"

Tory reached under the table and squeezed his knee. "I could make you very happy."

Brad glanced at his watch. "Time to go."

Tory helped him with his trenchcoat and straightened the collar. "Do you want to meet Mona and me for cocktails this afternoon?"

"Is she back in town again?" he muttered.

"I don't know why the two of you can't get along. Perhaps she'll have a bright solution for my financial crisis."

"The last thing you need right now is her bad influence. The two of you together have about as much common sense as the average eight-year-old. She'll probably have her gangster fix you up with a job in an opium den and when you end up in front of the DA you'll scratch your head and say, 'But it seemed so sensible at the time.' "

Mona and Tory paused inside the door of the restaurant and waited to be seated while a scratchy Mario Lanza record played in the background. Tory wore a bright-green cashmere sweater over a pale-gray open-necked silk shirt and charcoal-gray wool slacks, the green suede jacket from a trip to Spain, and black Gucci tassel loafers. Mona wore a simple black wraparound dress dramatically accessorized with abundant gold jewelry and the ever-present emerald earrings, with the full-length red fox draped casually over her shoulders. Their entrance would have drawn casual interest in the best restaurants, but in the South Philadelphia converted rowhouse with plywood paneling, plastic tablecloths, and empty wine bottles interspersed with imitation grapes hanging from the walls, the buzz of conversation stopped for several seconds.

"We're meeting Mr. Santoro for dinner," Mona told the host. "Dominic better be right about the food here or I'll be very displeased with him," she said in an ominous aside to Tory as they were led to a table. She examined the chair closely before she sat. "Can't say I care for the decor."

"Don't say it too loud, they'll have us bumped off. Are you sure this isn't a setup?"

"Stop imagining things, *mon cher*, that was last month and all is forgiven. The poor dear becomes a tad paranoid when he drinks that much brandy, and he thought you were taking liberties with me on the dance floor."

Tory laughed. "Can you imagine?"

"Not in my most libidinous dreams, but you should be flattered that he thinks you're such a stud."

"It's been a curse all my life, I'm just too butch for my own good."

"Oh please. The queen of Society Hill."

"Are you sure this isn't a setup? Check out the fat guy on your left—what's that bulge under his jacket?"

"Check out the bulge in that waiter's pants."

Tory craned his neck wildly. "Where?"

"Calm down. He's absolutely dripping with grease."

"Where's Dominic, anyway?"

"He said he had a business meeting," Mona smirked.

"A pharmaceutical deal, no doubt."

"I don't think he does that. Only the numbers."

"How petty. Why couldn't you find a coke dealer?"

"Wouldn't that be fabulous?" she mused.

A waiter approached for their cocktail order.

"Let's just get a bottle of wine," Tory suggested.

"You get wine. I'd like a Tanqueray martini, up, with a twist."

"How decadent. And a bottle of Bolla Soave, please."

"How ethnic."

"It must be my roots coming out."

"Speaking of roots, I wonder if Germaine can bump someone and give me an appointment tomorrow."

"Not a chance. He's in the Gay Miss Ebony contest tomorrow night and he's spending the day in preparation. I'm going to invite him to be my date for the next high school reunion."

"That should be a hit with the hayseeds. I suppose my tired locks will have to wait until I get back to Chicago."

"When are you leaving?"

"Sunday at cocktail hour. Perhaps we'll brunch before I go."

"I don't want to push my luck."

"I wish you would calm your nerves about Dominic. He was very apologetic, absolutely demanded that I invite you tonight."

"The whole thing was so ridiculous."

"Every time we argue he insists that you and I are having a clandestine affair. I don't think he actually believes it, he's simply jealous of our friendship. It's difficult for him to understand. A relationship between a woman and a gay man is simply not a part of his cultural background."

"A lot of things aren't. You should stick to your lawyers and businessmen. There's such a social gap between the two of you."

"But he's so attentive to my needs."

"He must be quite a man," Tory said with mock primness.

"Oh, he is," she answered dreamily.

"Tell me the story about the sunken bathtub and hot shaving cream again," he begged eagerly, for the benefit of the waiter approaching with their drinks.

"Later. You're right about the social gap. It's almost time for another farewell scene, there are simply too many points of conflict. But it's been a refreshing change from my typical suitor. Dominic is totally in awe of me. He thinks I'm so glamorous."

"And don't you love to hear that?"

"I adore it. But the trivial things are starting to work on my nerves, his grammar and his shady partners. And that annoying streak of plebeian jealousy."

"Just be careful when you break it off. You might wind up in the Delaware with a pair of cement wedgies."

She leaned over the table confidentially. "Don't you dare repeat this, but that's the thing about him that still excites me. There's never a hint of danger with my stodgy lawyers."

Tory laughed with a pleasant shock. "Now, that's perverse."

Mona shrugged. "It's a kick."

Dominic soon arrived, a dark, not unattractive man of about forty in a conservative business suit. He knew the waiters by name and seemed to take pleasure in sending them into flurried activity. He insisted on ordering for Mona and Tory, called the cook out of the kitchen to give him special instructions, and demanded that the owner join them for a cocktail. The food was excellent, and Dominic made an extra effort to be charming throughout the meal. They finished with espresso and Sambucca.

"Nice meal?" Dominic beamed with self-satisfaction.

"Delicious."

"You certainly kept them hopping," Tory said, content to tell him what he wanted to hear.

His smile broadened. "Yeah, this is *my* territory."

"Such an unpretentious ambience," Mona said pleasantly, secretly flashing Tory a look of utter disdain.

Dominic looked puzzled but accepted the remark for a compliment and raised his cordial glass. "A toast to your retirement, Tory."

"God bless the unemployment bureau."

"So what are you going to do with all the free time? Be a bum?"

"For a while. I'll have to get a part-time job eventually to make ends meet. In the meantime I'm enjoying myself, out dancing and prancing every night."

"I might be able to line something up for you in the way of a job," Dominic said with an air of offhand importance.

"He doesn't want that kind of job, Dominic."

"What kind of job?" Tory asked. "I'm open for suggestions."

"Running numbers. Forget it. One hoodlum in my life is enough."

Dominic gave her an offended look. "Running numbers don't make you a hoodlum."

"Forget it. What Tory needs is a nice older gentleman to help him out. I've been telling him so for years."

"Sometimes daily."

"I don't understand why you won't listen to me. There are droves of them out there just waiting for you to come along. They'd enjoy nothing more than to spend their money on you. I don't know how you could let that lovely Norman fellow slip through your fingers last fall."

"I got a weekend in Florida and three Le Bec Fin dinners out of him.'"

"You could have gotten much more."

"And he'd have expected me to be on twenty-four-hour call for blow jobs and companionship. Or worse yet, move in with him." Tory shuddered. "I'd sooner work."

"It would be different with the right man. Perhaps an executive who travels extensively."

"They all want their money's worth. I'd sooner work the streets. The hustlers put out, collect their money, and it's over with."

Dominic smiled importantly once again. "I might have something in that line too."

Tory laughed for lack of a reply.

"Dominic!" Mona exclaimed, more in titillation than disgust.

"I'm not kidding. I know a dame on Rittenhouse Square. She might be interested."

"A madam? You never told me you knew a madam. How lurid!"

"Dominic, I'm not eighteen, you know. I'm getting a little old to be working the streets." Tory hadn't yet sorted out his emotions but was curious to hear more.

"It's got nothing to do with the streets. It's all by appointment. I know a couple of her girls—"

"Dominic!" Mona interrupted excitedly. "You know hookers too?"

"I've talked to them at Duffy's, not intimate acquaintances." He looked at Mona, obviously pleased with her unusual interest in his conversation. "Anyways, they're very classy girls, you'd never take them for hookers."

"But she has men too?"

"I met one. I was in Duffy's one night and ran into Peggy and Debbie. They were at the bar with this guy— tall, good-looking fellow—and we got to talking. I couldn't figure it out, they're always with these older executive types, so when he left, I say, 'What's he got to pay for it for? He could get it for nothing.' And Peggy says, 'You got him on the wrong end, Dom, he's with the service too.'"

"Service?" Mona hooted. "How coy."

"Well, that's what they call it. It's set up as an escort service. Anyways, I say, 'What, they got broads calling up for men these days?' and she says, 'No, he's for the men too.'" He looked at them in surprise. "They got some guys working to take care of the rich fags."

"Don't call them 'fags,' *mon cher*, they're 'gay.' " Mona looked pensive for a moment. "All the minorities are so touchy these days."

"Anyways, the next time I see Ginny—"

"Is Ginny the madam?"

"I don't think she calls herself a madam. Anyways, the next time I see her, I ask her about it and she says she has six or seven guys working for her but they're not steady. They flit off on her all the time. She might be looking for someone new. I can give her a ring and see if you two can work something out."

"How good-looking was this guy you met?" Tory asked.

"I don't know. Good-looking."

"Compared to me."

"I don't know, I'm no expert on men," Dominic replied uncomfortably. "He didn't have nothing on you."

"Mona, do you think I'm handsome enough to be a hustler?"

Mona looked exasperated. "You know you are."

"As handsome as I was three years ago?"

Mona examined him. "I guess so."

Tory sighed. "I need constant reassurance."

Dominic seemed bored by the turn of the conversation. "Well, you want me to give her a ring or not?"

"I don't know," he faltered.

"Tory, what would Claudia say?"

He laughed. "All she says anymore is 'Just so you're happy, dear,' and she doesn't really want to hear the details. And my father thinks I am a total pervert already, this wouldn't shock him any more."

"Could you face yourself in the mirror each morning, knowing that you'd become a fallen woman? A painted strumpet? A brazen harlot? A *fille de joie*? Accepting cash for your favors? Knowing that you were condemned to burn in hell?"

Tory laughed at the tawdry picture she was taking so much pleasure in painting. "It couldn't be any worse than what I've done for three or four margaritas on a bad night."

"You're such trash," she laughed.

"Well, do you want me to call or not?"

"Tory, wouldn't it be sensational to say you'd met a

genuine madam? May I meet her too, Dominic? Oh Tory, why don't you do it? Just for a few giggles?"

He shrugged after a long pause. "What the hell, it will be good for a laugh."

"Oh, Tory, this is so exciting! My dearest friend peddling flesh!"

Chapter Three

As usual, Mona had her way. She called Tory the next afternoon to say that Dominic had arranged a meeting with Ginny for Sunday brunch. Tory began to have unnerving flashes of doubt but he was determined to keep the appointment. He told himself that Sunday brunch was no commitment, no one was going to coerce him into making a promise. There was nothing to lose by meeting the madam; he'd get good mileage out of the story at dinners and cocktail parties. He'd be the only person of his acquaintance ever to have brunched with a madam; dressed up with dramatic details, the anecdote would fascinate folks for months. People had come to expect anecdotes like this from him, something slightly scatterbrained and ingenuously tawdry. And Mona would never let him live it down if he backed out now. She was bound and determined to meet a madam, and if he prevented it, she'd throw it up to him for months. Sometimes it seemed that Brad was right about her being a bad influence. She goaded him on, and he always accepted the dare. It had been that way with some friend or other ever since he could remember; he was always the basically good kid who got into trouble through his choice of company. It had been Nicky Brandt's idea to shoplift at Woolworth's the summer after fifth grade, just for something to do. And at fourteen Tory didn't even enjoy Southern Comfort, but Johnny Rappold thought it would be fun to take a flask to the football game. Tory sometimes wondered if

the people who told him he should grow up might not
have a point.

Yet the idea of getting paid for sex wasn't without its
appeal. It sounded less tedious than waiting on tables
and submitting to Sorenson from time to time. Sex was
no more than a cheap thrill since David was gone, and
it *did* have a certain glamour to it, that men might find
him attractive enough to pay for his body. Strangers sending drinks across a bar and older acquaintances inviting
him to a restaurant had always been a boost to his ego.
Collecting cash on the line would certainly be a laugh
on all those annoying guidance counselors who'd labeled
him an underachiever, someone who was letting his God-
given talents go to waste.

Fortified with his rationalizations and four glasses of
wine, he met Mona and Dominic early Sunday afternoon
in a back booth at Henry's. Mona broke into raucous
laughter at first glimpse of his form-fitting Italian knit
shirt unbuttoned to expose half his chest and the snug,
thin cotton slacks that outlined the lower half of his body
in vivid detail.

"Tory, you look like a hustler already!"

He laughed in embarrassment. "I'm only trying to follow Miss Baker's advice," he replied primly.

"Who the hell's Miss Baker?"

"A teacher at Stoltz Grove High. She always told us
to dress appropriately for a job interview."

"Dear old Stoltz Grove High. If they could see you
now."

Tory thought of his classmates with faint distaste, some
of them now married, with split-levels and budding potbellies, going to the movies on the Saturday nights they
could afford babysitters, gawking in wonder at the neon
lights on their rare trips to the city. On visits home, he
always dressed to the teeth and took vengeful joy in the
stir he created as he emerged theatrically from the train.
He laughed. "Yes. If they could see me now. They go to
the movies to see people like me." He began to feel
slightly less nervous as he asked the waiter for a vodka
gimlet.

"A vodka gimlet!"

"I'm a bit on edge," he explained sheepishly.

"I'm hardly surprised. It's not every Sunday that you

see a lifetime of Christian moral standards go down the tubes."

"You're so supportive, my dear."

"Calm down, Tory. She's going to love you," Dominic said. "You look great."

"Do you think I should button up a bit?"

"Don't worry about it."

"Dominic," Mona asked, "what type of woman is she? Does she have a platinum bouffant and rhinestone earrings? Does she wear tons of black mascara and crack her chewing gum?"

"She's a very classy broad, probably shops in the same stores you do."

"How old is she?"

"Thirty, thirty-two. Takes good care of herself."

"I should suppose she has to," Mona murmured drily.

"Now don't you go and start something with her, Mona."

"Mona always starts something with another woman. It's like watching a cockfight."

"I wonder why they never like me," she mused, not terribly concerned.

"I don't think it's personal. They just realize that it might be foolish to leave their men unattended for more than thirty seconds. I never see women make such quick trips to the powder room as when I'm with you."

She took a quick glance at Dominic and smiled threateningly at Tory. "Why don't we discuss it some other time, *mon cher?*"

He returned the smile and looked up at the ceiling. "They act like there's a condor circling overhead, searching for a fresh kill."

"Well," she said with a kick under the table, trying to change the subject, "I'm going to make every effort to be charming to her."

"Good. Don't hurt Tory's chances."

"When she comes in, I'll smile politely, extend my hand, and say in my most tasteful voice, 'How do you do, madam?' "

Tory laughed. "That wouldn't do."

"Come on, Mona. Straighten out."

"Touchy, touchy."

Dominic didn't have to identify the woman who en-

tered the room fifteen minutes later. Tory knew immediately that it had to be Ginny. There was no single
characteristic that made him aware of her identity, just a
general impression that wasn't ordinary. Tory's first
thought was of her similarity to Mona. They were of
approximately the same age with the same look of having
spared no effort to present a striking image. While Mona
featured a cosmopolitan, slim model look, Ginny worked
for an image of farm girl gone glamorous. Her lustrous
brown hair billowed over her shoulders, its natural thickness accentuated by carefully placed waves to make it
her most noticable aspect. Huge brown eyes were framed
with lashes just slightly too thick and long to be real, her
full lips were set in a half-smile, and her rosy complexion
bespoke fresh air and wholesome exercise. Her figure
was full without being blatantly voluptuous, and she
deemphasized it with a cowl-necked, full-skirted dress
in a warm shade of beige. The brown leather accessories
and sparse jewelry were understated and obviously of
good quality. Only the tawny full-length mink belied her
demure image. Tory thought it wasn't so much the coat
as the authoritative way she wore it. She crossed the
room with complete self-assurance, obviously not missing the convenience of a male escort.

Tory immediately felt more comfortable. He didn't
know quite what sort of woman he'd expected to meet,
but she was certainly not someone he'd be ashamed to
be seen with. She outclassed Dominic easily. There was
no reason to feel ill at ease. She was charming from the
moment she joined the table, even if the charm didn't
seem totally sincere. The perfect-toothed smile looked as
if it came off of a publicity photo, and her manner reminded him of some of the professionally congenial sales
representatives who visited the supermarket.

With a take-charge attitude she discussed mutual acquaintances with Dominic, being sure to include Tory
and Mona in the conversation with amusing anecdotes.
She complimented Mona on her black Rafael suit, and
they launched into a sophisticated discussion of fashion.
She discussed the menu with Tory and coaxed him into
a dissertation on the comparative pleasures of local restaurants which somehow led into entertaining at home,
domestic help, travel, local night life, and New York. He

noticed that his throat was dry by the end of the meal and wondered how he'd managed to talk so much. He thought she'd be a wonderful guest to draw out the wallflowers at a cocktail party.

There was an unnerving quality underneath her charm, though, a toughness that didn't let him forget that she was a businesswoman. It reminded him of watching Lucille Ball on a talk show for the first time; he'd expected a diluted version of her television character and was surprised by a hardcase professional who was obviously not to be dealt with lightly. Ginny was charming, but he didn't think he'd like to see her angry.

As Dominic lingered over his third brandy it became obvious that Ginny had given him more than his allotted time. She glanced at her watch and drummed her manicured nails on the tablecloth. Mona took the hint and convinced Dominic that it was time to drive her to the airport. She made sure Tory saw her respectfully wary glance in Ginny's direction as she kissed him goodbye.

Ginny wasted no time on formalities. "So what makes you think you could be a hustler?"

Tory wondered if the question had been designed to catch him off guard. "I don't know. . . . I've been giving it away for years, I might as well make some money out of it?"

"That's a good reason. What else?"

"I'm tired of punching a time clock."

"Do you think you're ready for this?"

"I had my doubts. But if you're any example of the business, I won't have to feel like the scum of the earth about it."

"We're Philadelphia's finest, Tory. If I hire you, don't ever forget that. You'll have a reputation to uphold. How do you feel about sex?"

Tory shrugged. "It's OK with me."

"Do you have a lover?"

"No."

"Any recent ones?"

"Not in four years."

"Are you looking for one?"

"Not actively."

"That's good. If you're hired, it will make life easier for both of us. I don't want to have to worry about you running off because you think you're in love every two weeks. I've had too many dizzy queens do that to me."

"I'm not interested in getting involved right now. Of course, if Prince Charming comes along and sweeps me off my feet, I might be tempted by a castle."

"Wouldn't we all? How do you feel about older men?"

"How old?"

"Upwards of forty."

"It's not exactly my typical date," he shrugged.

"It's our typical customer. The twenty-two-year-olds don't have to pay for it."

"I can handle it. I find some older men very attractive."

"They usually don't look like Cary Grant either."

"Nobody's perfect."

"What kind of work do you do?"

"Until last week I ran a supermarket."

"How long?"

"Three years."

"Why did you leave?"

"I got tired." Tory didn't think it was necessary to go into detail, and "tired" sounded so close to "fired" that it hardly seemed a lie.

"Do you drink a lot?"

Tory thought of the morning wine, the two gimlets, and the half bottle of Muscadet he'd consumed with brunch and was glad it didn't affect him noticeably. "I'm a social drinker."

"Do you do drugs?"

"A joint now and then. A Valium when I'm extremely upset."

"Ever see a psychiatrist?"

"Years ago, when I was young and confused. Nothing serious."

"I have to watch out for the psychopaths, the ones who are going to take it out on my clients because they're mad at the world for being gay."

"I'm not mad about it," Tory said thoughtfully. "Sometimes I'm downright grateful."

Ginny looked dubious. "Grateful?"

"In a way. If I weren't gay, I might still be back in Stoltz Grove. In the Tuesday-night bowling league."

Ginny brightened. "You're a country boy?"

"Until I was seventeen."

"I grew up in the coal country upstate. It's amazing what this place will do to you. I'd have thought you were a city boy through and through."

"Thank you!" A compliment on his looks was always pleasant, but a reference to his urbanity was treasured for months.

"The clients would like you. I get too many idiots. Sex is the only thing they can do, they're too feeble-minded to hold down a steady job. Some of the clients like to be seen with a young man in elegant places, and your style would be an asset. It helps to be able to hold an intelligent conversation."

Tory was beginning to feel smug. "I adore cocktail chatter."

"I noticed. It's all being taken into consideration."

"You don't miss much, do you?"

"I can't afford to."

"Have you been in business long?"

"Since I was eighteen. Now I just arrange things and let other people do the legwork."

"I love success stories."

"Enough about me. Let me tell you a little bit about the business. We're called the Davis Escort Service."

"Are you the Davis?"

"That's me. We're a legitimate business, listed in the phone book and with the chamber of commerce."

"Times have changed."

"Shut up and listen to me," she chided with a smile. "We do send out legitimate escorts, if that's what the client wants. The catch is that we charge a hundred dollars for the evening. If some fool wants to pay a hundred dollars just for an escort, we're happy to oblige him. Otherwise, the men that call are wise to the setup and it's only a formality. But you have to be careful and make sure that they make the first move if they're not regulars—you never know when the vice squad will get a hair up their ass. We put out good money to keep these things from happening, and usually they're happy to see a clean operation like us take trade away from the trash on the streets, but you never know."

"I get a hundred dollars?"

"You get fifty, if you're hired. The business keeps the

other half for expenses, withholding tax, that sort of thing."

"Withholding tax? I can't work over the table or I'll lose my unemployment."

"No problem. It's a business formality."

"How much can I make in a week?"

"Don't get excited, you're not hired yet. My top man has four regular clients on Saturdays and ten or twelve others during the week. Not everyone can handle that, and you wouldn't get that many assignments to start off with even if you could."

"Four a day?" Tory repeated in wonder. "You must introduce us."

"He'd probably be too tired to do you much good. He usually clears over six hundred a week and probably makes that much more in tips and gifts. He's the exception to the rule, but you can see that there's money to be made."

"What's the average?"

"I have a lot of free-lancers right now who only work when they need the cash, so it's hard to say. It's different from the old days, when I had real professionals who worked at it full-time for twenty a throw. But I've had to change to suit the clientele. For a hundred bucks they want a knockout, but you pretty types don't like to knock yourselves out. You could make three bills a week with no difficulty. It depends on how much time you're willing to put into it. I'd start you off easy, only two or three a week to break you in."

"That would help out the unemployment checks."

"I'm looking for someone to break in on the phones, too. I need somebody with half a mind to arrange appointments while I'm out."

"I think I'd be good at that."

"It's not difficult, just a matter of getting to know the crew and regulars. Alice moved to New York last month —she was with me five years and was an ace at it. Now I have three or four idiots I can call to cover for me, but if I'm out for more than a few hours everything is in complete chaos when I get back. In fact, I dread going back now."

"I used to talk to customers on the phone all day at

the store. We did phone orders and deliveries. It would be the same thing for me, only different merchandise."

"It sounds good. We'll see." She glanced at her watch. "Any questions?"

Tory searched his mind to phrase his words in the least offensive manner. "A few. Do you have many customers that might be considered . . . unusual? I'm not really into kinky sex."

"I have a few. I try to match them up with someone willing to accommodate them. If you're going to feel ill at ease doing what a client wants you to do, chances are you're not going to make him very happy. And that's not good business. Of course, you'd be expected to bend a bit too, to make your client happy, within bounds. That's what it's all about, making the client happy."

"One more question. I'm not turned off by older men, but there are limits. There are men I wouldn't go to bed with for a thousand dollars. What happens if I tell you, 'Forget it, he's not worth it to me'?

"I have no set rules about it. Ideally, I get to know you well and know what you are and aren't willing to do, so there's no problem. We'll discuss the client first. I'll give you all my information and the decision is yours. The one cardinal sin is to meet the client and then refuse. That isn't done."

"That sounds reasonable."

"Of course, you're not going to make it if you're too picky. This is a business, not a dating service. If you make a habit of saying no to me, you won't have a job for long. But that's your option. Fair enough?"

"I think so."

Ginny got up from the table. "Just one more thing. Do you always dress like this?"

Tory laughed in embarrassment as he gazed down at his blatantly provocative outfit. "I just thought you might want to see what you're getting."

Ginny took a gold Cross pen and a business card from her bag and wrote a number on the back. "I'm more concerned with your personality, and that checks out. Call this number tomorrow and set up an appointment with George."

"George?"

"He's one of my top men. He'll give you a little audition, and if you check out with him I'll get back to you and we'll have you working by next weekend."

"OK," Tory smiled uneasily. "I guess."

Ginny cast him a frankly appraising look. "Enjoy it. He's as handsome as you are."

Chapter Four

TORY forced himself to make the call by ten the next morning, before he had the chance for second thoughts. He wondered what he would have done three days before if Dominic had said, "Here's fifty dollars, show that man a good time." It would have been a simple decision based primarily on the man's physical appearance with perhaps a brief afterthought for the question of morality. Sex was rarely more than casual to him, and he could muster no strong distaste for the idea of accepting cash for it. Only his preconceived notion of a hustler's depressing life-style held him back. Even that was beginning to seem less lurid after meeting Ginny. Pros and cons aside, he was excited to be doing something new and out of the ordinary.

Mona called from her office later that morning and wasted no time on civilities. "So what's the dish?"

"It looks like I'm on my way to hell in a handbasket," he answered cheerily.

"What happened with the madam after we left?"

"We had a little business chat."

"Tell me all. Did she hire you?"

"Not yet, but she liked me. I have an appointment with one of her guys at four this afternoon."

"What kind of appointment?"

"Sort of an audition." He was happy to have something shocking to say.

"Tory! How cheap and tawdry! I love it!"

"I guess they can't just hire someone without checking them out first."

"Aren't you nervous?"

It didn't seem chic to own up to it. "Ginny said the guy's gorgeous, so at worst it will be a cheap thrill. I called him this morning to set up a time; he had a nice voice but he didn't sound too interested. It was like setting up a doctor's appointment."

"What did she say to you after we left?"

"She asked a lot of questions, sort of a bizarre job interview. About my romantic life and emotional stability, things like that." Tory giggled. "She wanted to know if I drank a lot."

"Oh God!" Mona gasped. "You didn't tell her the truth?"

"What could I say—the table strewn with empty glasses and bottles at that point. I told her I was a social drinker."

"Very social," she replied drily.

"Have you ever noticed that when we go out to dinner our bar bill is always higher than the food?"

"And that's after we have a few cocktails at home to get in the mood."

"Perhaps we should be concerned."

"Perhaps," Mona replied without concern. "What else did she say?"

"I can make fifty a date. Plus gifts."

"Gifts?" she questioned, with an urgent note in her voice.

"I doubt that I'll get much jewelry," Tory gently replied. "Mostly extra cash, I imagine."

"Oh."

"One nympho clears six hundred a week just in salary."

"That should keep you in Laszlo soap and clean linen."

"I hope so. I was glad you got along with Ginny."

"I was truly surprised. I expected one of Dominic's typical friends. She has style, I'll grant her that. I never saw a barracuda in Jourdan pumps before."

"She's tough. I guess she has to be to run that business."

"Don't be naïve," Mona smirked. "She's just a front for the mob."

"She is?"

"Of course."

"Does this mean I have to join the Mafia?" he asked in mock terror. "What's to become of me?"

"Call it the mob. They only say Mafia on television."

"Becoming quite the gangster's moll, aren't you?"

Mona laughed. "Not for much longer. It's about time to cut anchor. He's testing my nerves to the limit lately."

"They all work on your nerves sooner or later."

"It seems to be an emerging pattern, doesn't it?"

"The same old story. As soon as you're sure they're crazy about you, you can't be bothered."

"Perhaps I need counseling," she said thoughtfully. "What I need is a real man."

"They're all facsimiles these days."

"Too true. Well, I must be going, I have a business luncheon at one. I'm not much good in the office but I'm a wizard at business luncheons. Good luck on the casting couch. I'll call tomorrow for the latest."

Only a sense of adventure kept his nerves from getting out of hand that afternoon. He busied himself with a facial and a pedicure in the bathroom. As other people did housework or needlepoint to relieve tension, Tory immersed himself in grooming. He rarely looked better than in times of turmoil. He searched and re-searched the three closets for the perfect outfit and forced himself to eat a salad, though his only appetite was for several drinks. He limited himself to two glasses of wine, remembering a few occasions in the past when he'd drunk his nerves away and then couldn't perform very well when things turned romantic.

Being in no mood to wait for a bus, he splurged on a cab for the fifteen-block trip to the Locust Towers, a new luxury high-rise in the center of town. As with all matters of status, the posh address wasn't wasted on Tory. It wasn't as chic as his own address in Society Hill, but his image of cheap hustlers living dreary lives was rapidly fading.

Remembering Ginny's remarks about his outfit on Sunday, he dressed carefully in a brown-checked wool Missoni jacket over a tan cashmere sweater and cream cotton shirt, beige wool slacks, and brown Gucci loafers. He wore his only remaining piece of jewelry, a massive gold chain, simple but very impressive. He'd sold the rest, an assortment of light chains, bracelets, and rings, prompted less by financial need than by a dissatisfaction with anything less than first-quality.

He stoically refused to give in to nerves at the last moment and had the doorman announce him. The elevator ride to the twenty-eighth floor seemed to take only a slightly shorter eternity than the wait at the corner apartment after he'd rung the bell marked "Keller." The Germanic name reminded him of his father and the heritage he tried so hard to ignore. It hardly seemed a good omen.

The door finally swung open, and Tory temporarily forgot his nerves in a pleasant shock of surprise. The man before him didn't fit into any of the standard categories of handsomeness; he wasn't the dark, straight-nosed, mustached Marlboro man type, the tanned, curly-haired Latino soccer player type, the T-shirted Marlon Brando in *Streetcar* type, the sun-drenched California surfer type, the Waspy, pretty-boy type, the slickly dark, fine-boned Rudolph Valentino European type, or any of the others. Tory couldn't decide what type he was or why he felt a flutter in his chest and oxygen escaping involuntarily from his lungs. He'd felt this way frequently in his teens, a crystal moment of wonder upon discovering awesome beauty, but time and experience had taken the edge off of his impressionability. It still happened on seeing a truly outstanding male specimen, perhaps once a year, but the feeling had become more aesthetic than sexual.

The man was clad only in faded jeans, snug, but not obscenely so. He had light-brown hair that would probably be frizzy if it weren't closely cropped. The dark-blue eyes were disturbingly bright and somehow familiar as they stared at him without expression. The aquiline nose, tight lips, and square jaw gave an impression of uncompromising masculinity. The impression continued with the body, a "swimmer's body," Tory's mind quickly categorized it, with unobtrusively broad shoulders, pleasantly muscled arms, and a well-defined, almost hairless chest. A wisp of pubic hair began under his navel and disappeared into the low-slung jeans, which covered an absence of hips and long, lean legs.

He looked Tory up and down in expressionless appraisal before stepping aside to motion him in. "Your name's Tory?" he asked in a faintly bored tone.

"Right." Somewhere he found the power of speech.

"Ginny's had such a turnover lately, it's hard to keep the names straight. Have a seat."

He motioned ahead to the living room, starkly furnished in monochromes. Tory thought the lines of the room were like the lines of the man, very spare, nothing superfluous. Three large tan-gray canvas and chrome chairs surrounded a white cube in the center of the room. The parquet floor was bare except for a thin primitive Indian rug in grays and tans under the chairs and table. The rear wall's only decoration was a red-and-blue chrome-framed abstract print which Tory couldn't attribute but noticed that it was numbered and signed. Another wall was filled with a tropical jungle, but not of the standard ficus and spider-plant varieties. The other two walls were floor-to-ceiling windows without curtains or drapes, offering a spectacular panorama of the skyline. Tory searched the room vainly for some characterizing personal effects as he settled into a chair, books or records or knickknacks or photographs. The only signs of human habitation he could find were a blocklike pewter ashtray, a plain white matchbook cover, and a pack of Marlboros on the table. Tory stifled an unexpected nervous laugh as his mind abruptly began to redecorate the room with calico curtains and Rockwell prints. The man slid into an opposite chair, keeping an inscrutable stare on his visitor.

"What are you, about twenty-six?"

"Twenty-four." Tory was still disturbed by his jarring first impression, and the man was doing nothing to put him at ease. He was sure that the remark and the cold expression were meant to keep him uncomfortable. The man continued his piercing stare, and Tory tried to meet it composedly. Like he's considering a new piece of furniture, Tory thought. Not a bad idea, something you could get comfortable in. The staring match finally got to him, and he tried to retreat gracefully by lighting a cigarette. He pulled the Gauloises and Dupont lighter from his breast pocket and noticed the man's face take on a vague sneer of ridicule.

"Where do you live?"

"Society Hill."

The continuing sneer told Tory that it came as no surprise to him. He'd run into the reaction before in certain bars that he rarely frequented, a sneer and a condescending attitude, an unabashed distaste for what he considered glamour and elegance. He found it hard to communicate with the flannel-shirt-and-patched-jeans crowd and often wondered if he wouldn't have been happier in the days of café society.

"You've got a nice face," he said without feeling, giving Tory a brief hope that the meeting would take a turn for the better. "Are you losing some hair?"

Tory maintained a poised expression and after a brief pause answered evenly, "I have a high forehead. It runs in my family." It was almost the truth. But as Tory's annoyance increased, the unease began to subside and he found it easier to defend himself. The man continued to stare through another long pause.

"Plenty of guys who are really good-looking just don't have it. They're like mannequins."

Tory decided to accept this as a compliment of sorts. Not a remark meant to put him at ease, but the adrenaline had begun to flow and he didn't need a kind word at the moment. He was beginning to feel capable of a personality clash without assistance.

"You've got something," he continued without emotion. "Not an actually masculine sex appeal, but it's something. Soft and sensual. Maybe it's the full lips."

Tory tried to stop himself, but the urge was too great. "We can't all be leather queens," he replied demurely. He continued to direct a serene gaze at the blue eyes. "Such blue eyes" flashed through his mind. He crossly banished the thought, not wanting to admit anything about the man was attractive to him.

"Do you work out?"

"No. I'm allergic to exercise." It was one of his stock answers. He'd heard the question so many times in the bars from men admiring his physique. It was usually the opening line of a proposition, and Tory was vaguely pleased.

"Maybe you should. After a certain age you have to pay more attention to these things. The muscle tone starts to deteriorate after adolescence."

"I'll worry about it when it becomes a problem," Tory shot back, allowing the first trace of anger to creep into his voice. The man had scored a point, hitting right on target. There were two or three spare pounds on Tory's frame, and the muscles weren't as firm as they'd been at nineteen. Tory had refused to acknowledge it so far because it was imperceptible except to himself, he thought. It hurt to think about it, where it would all lead as time went on. The man had found a definite chink in the armor of his composure and seemed to sense it.

"Are you hung?" He asked it conversationally, but the undertone was definitely challenging.

"Want me to show you?" Tory didn't think of himself as exhibitionistic by nature but felt confident that he had nothing to be ashamed of. He was rarely so aggressive about it, but his anger goaded him on.

"Yeah, take off your clothes," he replied immediately, meeting the challenge in Tory's eyes.

Without conscious thought, Tory was out of the chair and pulling the sweater over his head. A tinge of nervousness gripped him as he realized what he was doing, but he forced himself to ignore it. He continued with the shirt, slowly and deliberately undoing each button to expose more flesh. He tossed it on the chair, slipped out of his socks and loafers, and continued with the trousers. A shock of amazement flashed through him as he regained an awareness of the situation, but the tingling sensation that was beginning in his crotch told him to continue. He kicked the remaining garments aside, and stood naked, except for the gold chain, before his opponent. It was an uncomfortable situation, but as his cock continued to swell he felt adequate to the challenge. The man showed no sign of being disarmed and continued to stare appraisingly. The tension, disturbingly exciting, seemed to go on for hours before he finally spoke.

"Not bad," he said, giving Tory a short-lived surge of victory. "The streets are full of good bodies. What can you do with it?"

A reckless excitement gripped Tory, a strange surge of confidence that had no rational basis. He felt that he could win, whatever the odds, and returned the stare with defiant calm. "I'm very versatile."

The man leaned farther back into the chair and slid a hand to his crotch. He gave a small smile, the first friendly motion he'd made, and said, "So, entertain me."

Tory noticed himself moving again. He was quickly

between the spread legs and undoing the jeans. They came away easily, and Tory had to suppress a gasp of delight. He always tried to tell himself that size wasn't really important, that finesse and tenderness and an awareness of a partner's desires were what really mattered. Smallness would even have been preferable right now, something more manageable to better display his skills. But logic and reason were far from his mind as he confronted the awesome sight. He automatically began to file away detailed notes on its length, thickness, shape, color, and hardness for Mona's future titillation.

He also appraised the situation quickly and forced himself to proceed with less than the manic enthusiasm he was feeling. He felt a twinge of disgust that he could be so excited by a man with such a rude manner, but he brushed it aside. It seemed an emotion better dealt with at a later time. More important, he knew that the tables were turning and he was in a position to seize control of the encounter. His desire for revenge was almost as great as his lust.

He caressed the throbbing flesh teasingly, with just his warm breath and the tip of his tongue. He worked slowly up and down and from side to side, making excursions over the abdomen and the insides of the thighs, concentrating for a time on the testicles but always returning to home base with maddeningly light flicks at the sensitive underside near the tip. It began to grow an angry shade of pink.

His ministrations finally forced a low moan, the subtle sign of submission that Tory had been waiting for before he'd grant the pleasures to come. He rewarded the moan with his lips and mouth and began to work languorously up and down the shaft, taking careful note of the man's gradually increasing breath rate. His lips, mouth, tongue, and fingertips worked in perfect concert to touch every available nerve ending, but at a torturingly relaxed pace. He listened with satisfied excitement to the heavy pants interspersed with low moans and noted that the huge cock continued to swell. He tried to calculate the exact moment when the stimulation became unbearable, taking expert note of all the vital signs like an ace pilot checking his instrument panel before take-off.

The hips were suddenly thrust forward, and he knew

his moment of victory was at hand. He slowed to a virtual standstill, knowing that each second had become an excruciatingly sensual eternity. Finally, the man let out a deep, despairing moan of total surrender. He lurched forward from the chair and pinned Tory to the carpet on his back. He straddled his face on hands and knees and pumped rapidly, almost immediately reaching climax in shuddering spasms and a desperate cry.

He worked desperately to catch his breath and remained on all fours over Tory's face for a long moment. Tory gave the still-hard cock several final sucks, eliciting a few last uncontrollable shudders, glorying in every moment of his power. The man finally rose and readjusted his jeans, turning to the table to light a cigarette. He remained with his back to Tory's prone figure for a much longer time than it took him to light the cigarette, then turned and exhaled deeply.

"Not bad, kid," he said in his previous noncommittal tone.

Tory was more amused than annoyed to be dismissed so lightly. He was confident that he had achieved showstopping impact. He knew he still had the upper hand and rose, standing aggressively close to the man.

"Anything else, George?" He fought the hope that there would be, but was painfully aware of his own still-hard cock.

George seemed to be caught off-guard by the use of his name. "No, that's it. Ginny will get back to you." He resumed his expressionless stare.

Tory refused to be intimidated by the curt dismissal and replaced his clothes slowly, feeling George's eyes upon him the whole time. He wanted to ask what the decision was, knowing full well that it had to be affirmative but still needing to hear George say so. His pride wouldn't allow him to give George the satisfaction of hearing him ask.

He walked to the door and turned with a huge smile. "Goodbye, George. Nice to have met you."

A half-smile crossed George's lips, and he replied softly, "My pleasure."

Tory slipped into the hall and forced himself to contain his smug giggles until the elevator door closed behind him.

Chapter Five

TORY fumbled blindly for the ringing telephone. He knew it was either on the table or somewhere on the floor beside the bed, but he didn't want to open his eyes. He located it on the fifth ring. "Yeah."

"So tell me all the lurid details."

"Mona, you're such a pervert. Couldn't even wait for a civilized hour to call, could you?"

"Tell me, tell me!"

"I got the job."

"Tory!" she exclaimed with shocked propriety. "You're actually going to go through with it?"

He enjoyed mornings. After two cups of coffee and half a dozen cigarettes, it was one of his favorite times of the day. He tended to be irritable before that point. "Don't sound so scandalized. You pushed me into it."

"Now really, *mon cher*. I simply thought it would be a giggle to meet a madam. I hardly sold you into white slavery."

"Well, I'm still uncomfortable about it, and I'd appreciate some moral support." He located a cigarette, and the first evil-tasting, dry-mouthed drag made him feel slightly more sociable. "Anyway, Ginny called last night. I passed the audition with flying colors, and she's taking me out to dinner tonight. I'll have my first john by the end of the week."

"Do they actually call them johns?"

"I don't know," he laughed sheepishly. "I thought it sounded professional."

"Getting right into it, aren't you?"

"It *is* sort of glamorous. In a divinely decadent way."

"And such a boost for the old ego. Tell me about the audition."

"Handsome guy."

"How handsome?"

"About an eight."

"An eight? That's saying volumes, coming from you. You're so stingy with the numbers."

"Actually, that's for the purely physical. He had this style about him, almost an animal magnetism. All things taken into consideration, he's probably a ten."

"My dear, you must be in love. I've only known you to give four tens in three years, and they were all under duress."

"Forget it. He was a creep."

"Why?"

"His whole attitude, a condescending macho number. Like he was bored to death with the whole thing and doing me a favor."

"Did he?"

"Honey, I was doing all the favors."

"I imagine you were if they hired you."

Tory smiled. "He was impressed with my technique."

"Half of Philadelphia's been impressed with your technique. Strangers accost me on the street and say, 'Your friend Tory Bacher has some technique.'"

"Making love is an art," Tory replied loftily.

"Extensive practice also helps."

"And that's from the mouth of an expert."

"Don't let's start. Tell me more about the gentleman."

Tory knew what was coming and prepared to tease. "About six feet," he drawled.

"Yes."

"Incredible blue eyes."

"Yes."

"Brown hair."

"Yes."

"Beautiful lean build."

"Yes."

He paused. "That's about it."

Mona's long silence was ominous. "Don't make me pump you, Tory."

"What do you mean?" he asked innocently.

"Tell me what I want to hear." Her voice was taking on a throaty tone.

"What's that?"

"You know."

He laughed lecherously. "Say it."

"Tory, my secretary is in here."

"I don't know what you mean," he replied in his most naïve voice.

"You're being less than kind. Leading a poor girl on." She was obviously enjoying her irritation.

"Say it," he rasped. He felt the first signs of his morning erection and rolled over to press it into the mattress.

She whispered urgently, almost inaudibly. "Did he have any meat?"

"What?"

"Tory! Don't do this to me."

"We must have a bad connection."

"How big was it?"

"How big was what?"

"You stop it this instant!" she shouted. "Was he hung?"

Tory arched his back and pressed hard into the mattress. He paused dramatically, then drew out each syllable of his words. "Like a stallion."

She emitted a short shriek.

He was suddenly wide awake. "It was the stuff of dreams."

"Oh!"

"A formidable weapon."

"Oh!"

"A stout member."

"Oh!"

"A phallic feast."

"Oh!"

He paused. "The proverbial massive mauler."

"Tory!"

"More?"

"How big?"

He moaned languorously before he answered. "I'd say about nine inches."

She gasped happily.

"Maybe ten."

"No!"

"Might have been. I could wrap both fists around it and there was still more than a mouthful."

"Omigod! You have such big hands."

"And a big mouth."

Her breath was coming in quick pants. "How thick?"

He chuckled lewdly. "Well, my hand just barely wrapped around it."

"No!" she cried in disbelief.

"Mona, would I lie to you about something so important? You know the twelve-ounce can of Contadina tomato paste?"

"That thick?" she gasped.

He paused significantly. "Somewhere between that and a Pepsi can."

"No!"

"And just as hard."

"Stop!"

He pumped his hips rhythmically. "And great huge balls."

"Please!"

"About the size of jumbo eggs at the farmer's market."

"Tory! I beg of you! No more!"

The line remained silent for close to a minute except for the sounds of Mona catching her breath.

"What a hunk of man. It's a shame he was so rude."

"I could forgive him."

"Forgive him, hell. I got even. I gave him such a blow job he practically had to beg for mercy."

Mona's knowing chuckle told him she was about to turn the tables, and he waited in happy anticipation. "You got off on it, didn't you?"

"What do you mean?"

"His attitude. You get a kick out of a little mistreatment, don't you?"

He laughed uneasily. "Don't be silly."

"I see that masochistic streak come out in you now and then."

"I guess it can be exciting sometimes," he admitted.

"You like them rough and nasty, don't you?"

"Not too rough."

"I can see it all now. Another six months and you'll be begging for whips and chains."

"I hardly think so."

"Leather jackets and cock rings!"

"Please."

"Handcuffed to a stool in an S&M bar!"

"Mona!"

"Spreadeagled over a motorcycle!"

"Oh!"

"Your patched Levi's torn roughly down to your ankles!"

"What else?"

"Bearded men in construction boots, standing in line to have their way with you!"

"Yeah?"

"Huge hard cocks pressing at every orifice!"

"Yeah?"

"Puddles of sperm dripping from your cheeks and chin!"

"Tell me more!"

"I can't. My secretary just overturned the coffee urn. I'll call you later, the poor thing is dripping all over the carpet."

Tory was vaguely troubled by the arousal he felt at her fantasy. Perhaps he did have some masochistic tendencies that kept his thoughts turning back to George. It was one theory to explain his uncharacteristically driven behavior the previous afternoon. He usually enjoyed impersonal sex in an easygoing, take-it-or-leave-it manner, but this had been different, as if there had been a third person in the room directing his actions with uncanny powers, telling him exactly what to do and at exactly which moment. He'd experienced the same feeling before in other circumstances, an intuitive vibration that came rarely and unexpectedly in brief flashes, giving him answers before there had been a question. That he'd had one of these unnerving experiences with George made the man more fascinating to Tory.

Not being one to dwell on the unexplainable, he did his best to brush it from his mind. There were more practical matters to attend to. He called Brad with an excuse to cancel their usual Tuesday-night dinner. He didn't like to lie to Brad, but there was no alternative. The truth was bound to bring on a fresh onslaught of criticism, and he wasn't ready to deal with it until he felt more sure of his own convictions. The idea of prostitution no longer gave him a confused case of nerves; it was becoming more acceptable as it became more familiar. Ginny's operation apparently wasn't without status, and to his mind anything with status couldn't be all wrong. Still, he knew he wasn't yet ready to defend it to Brad. Instead, he daydreamed about the purchases he could make with his projected earnings. He'd almost come to accept the prospect of reduced financial circumstances, and it came as a pleasant surprise that drastic measures might not be necessary. There were so many bills that would be a relief to pay off and still so many things he was convinced he needed desperately. He thought about the outrageously frivolous chinchilla bed throw he'd seen in a decorator's window as he switched the stereo to automatic replay and prepared to listen to Shirley Bassey repeatedly invite big spenders to spend a little time with her.

Preparing for dinner with Ginny also helped him keep his mind off lying to Brad. It took up a major part of the afternoon, and he added this to the asset side of his mental scoreboard. He sometimes had brief twinges of guilt over the amount of time he spent on grooming. Now he could pass it off as a sensible maintenance of business assets. It would be so nice to have such positive feed back on his looks. Cash on the line would speak so much louder than words.

He waited for Ginny at the bar in Astral Plane, pleased that she'd suggested one of his favorite restaurants. Still mindful of her remark about his brunch outfit, he overcompensated with a conservative wool suit and quiet accessories.

"You do run the gamut," she laughed upon seeing him. She was in a simple but glaringly expensive blue silk dress and a mink of the same style as the one she'd worn on their first meeting but several shades darker. "Tonight you look like my stockbroker."

"It's called my pretentiously understated look."

"You're better dressed than some of the clients. A good-looking shirt and slacks will do on most nights. You don't want to frighten them off."

"I just can't seem to please you," he sighed.

"Don't be silly. I'm pleased or we wouldn't be here. Welcome to the Davis Escort Service. Any misgivings?"

"Not really. I had a few but I'm getting over them.'"

"It's to be expected. As you sit by a swimming pool somewhere this summer and think of the cash rolling in for a few hours of your time now and then, it will all start to seem so right."

"I've started that already. I'll have my cleaning lady back and I won't have to peddle pastrami five days a week to pay her. It can't be all wrong."

"It's not exactly a bed of roses either, but for some people it's a logical alternative. If it ever starts to depress you—and it might—don't hesitate to call me and talk it over."

"You do counseling too?"

"Some of the kids need a lot of moral support, and that's also a part of my job. I've got to keep *everyone* happy."

Ginny signaled the maitre d' without moving a muscle below her neck, and he seated them at a good table. Deferential treatment sometimes impressed Tory more than material things, and he noted with respect that Ginny commanded it here. The life-style became more appealing to him by the minute.

"George was impressed with you."

Tory's laugh was almost bitter. "You could have fooled me. If he's that unpleasant on the job you must be losing clients in droves."

Ginny's laugh was patronizing. "Tory, if you had walked into his apartment yesterday and found this handsome man waiting eagerly to drag you off to the bedroom, what would it have proved? Any fool could handle that. You maintained your poise in less than ideal conditions, something you'll have to deal with from time to time on the job, and still performed. Anybody can have sex, it's a biological function. But you're going to be occasionally meeting men you'd just as soon not touch, or men who get their kicks from paying for sex and then using the money to make you jump through hoops. If you couldn't handle a little adversity, you wouldn't have been hired. George was just doing his job."

Tory disliked having his convictions disturbed. Things

were so much simpler in black and white without the various shades of gray. He was already confused about his feelings for George, and now the only definite, that he was an insensitive bastard with a macho complex, was being challenged. Tory was annoyed. "He certainly plays his role well. I was ready to tell him where he could stuff his job."

"But you didn't," Ginny replied with a maddeningly smug smile, "and you're here."

"Well, I think the system leaves a lot to be desired," Tory replied, for lack of a logical expression of his annoyance. "And George is a sadistic bastard."

Ginny smiled. "He isn't exactly Albert Schweitzer."

"He got off on it—it was too real to be an act. I run into it all the time. All these queens in their leather drag trying to convince themselves that they're such butch numbers, they see someone like me with a cashmere sweater and a manicure and they get all bent out of shape. Last winter, I mistakenly stumbled into a leather bar in the Village wearing my raccoon coat, and I almost got killed."

"George isn't into a leather scene."

"He's into some strange scene."

"Whatever it is, it's his own. He's very independent, a loner."

"That's understandable. Who the hell would want to be his friend?"

"Don't take it out on George. He's hard to get to know, but he's actually very kind under the gruff exterior."

"Such hostility. He must have deep emotional problems." It was one of Tory's favorite tactics. Sometimes the most vicious criticism was acceptable under the guise of sympathy.

Ginny shrugged. "He's had his share. A rough childhood, a chip on his shoulder ever since. It's a familiar story. But he's worked for me since I moved the business to Rittenhouse Square, and I wish I had ten more like him. Very dependable, a hard worker, a cool head. And he's bright. He has a degree in finance from Wharton."

"And he hustles?"

"He's not a nine-to-fiver. You can understand that."

"I guess."

"You'll like him once you get to know him."

"I don't know about that."

"I won't put up with another catfight, Tory," she ordered in a tone that left no room for discussion. "I've got enough to worry about without any more infighting. Hustlers are worse than waitresses. They're always at each other's throat, bitching that this one is stealing the other's clients or that one is too lazy and not doing her share of the work. I've got twenty-three girls and eight full-time guys right now and some days half of them aren't on speaking terms. It's like raising a bunch of kids."

"Do we see much of each other?"

"Not unless you choose to. Everything is arranged by phone. But the girls work convention parties, things like that, and sometimes I have to send three or four. That's where most of the problems start. And some of the clients go for ménages or group things now and then, so it helps to get along with your co-workers." Tory was titillated by the decadent thought of it but didn't let it show through his blasé expression.

"If you start hanging out in Duffy's you'll see a lot of the crew. It's their regular watering hole. And I give little parties now and then, just so everybody can get together for some moral support. The arguments that usually start, I sometimes wonder why I bother."

"It sounds like a rough job."

"It's a living. Speaking of making a living, your first client is set for Thursday night."

Tory smiled uncertainly.

"Don't be nervous, he's a lamb. His name is Charles Lawson, as in Lawson Antiques, and he has a beautiful townhouse a block from the store on Pine Street. He calls every week or two and the boys fight over him. You go in, have a cocktail in the parlor, then he takes you upstairs and you just lie back and relax. He doesn't even take off his clothes, you'll be out in an hour."

"Is he a little gray-haired man?"

"Yes."

"I bought a cigarette box from him once. He's sort of cute for an old geezer."

"That's the attitude. Always look for the bright side. And if you can't find one, close your eyes and pretend."

"I'm good at pretending."

"It will come in handy some nights. You'll call me tomorrow for the address and the time. It'll be a piece of cake."

"I'll do my best."

"Eugene will come over the next morning to pick up the company cut."

"Who's Eugene?"

"My driver. He makes the rounds every morning to collect. It keeps traffic in my apartment to a minimum."

"I collect from the client?"

"He'll have an envelope waiting for you. He's a regular, so he knows the system. Another thing I should point out to you: well over half of our business is with regular clients. They might take a liking to you and invite you back, which is fine. Just make sure it's all arranged through me, though the temptation might be there to work out your own deal and skip the middleman. It's not worth it in the long run."

"I think I get the picture."

"Believe me, we find out eventually, and the consequences can be harsh."

Tory thought she looked so pleasant across the candlelit table, but the hardness in her eyes convinced him that she was serious. "Ginny," he whispered, "are we working for the mob?"

She smiled mysteriously. "You work for me. I have certain connections to keep the business running smoothly, but it has nothing to do with you. At least it won't if you play right by me."

"Don't worry. I'm scared to death of guns."

"It's never been that drastic. But stay scared. That way you'll stay unbruised."

Chapter Six

TORY started to prepare for Thursday's cocktail-hour appointment on Wednesday afternoon. He used his last twenty-dollar bill to pay the manicurist and pick up the dry cleaning and hoped that the warm weather would hold so he could wear an open-necked shirt and the Beged-Or jacket instead of a sweater and winter coat. A turtleneck would be out of the question: pulling it off and on would leave his hair a mess. At least the manicure gave him sufficient excuse not to scour the bathtub.

He headed for the bathroom after Thursday-morning coffee to begin preliminary grooming preparations, ready to contentedly settle in for a full day of grooming. He took a long initial glance into the mirror and was as pleased as usual, except that he wished summer would arrive and tan his skin. A few shades of color made such a difference in his outlook.

As he was pondering the seriousness of this problem, Alice from downstairs barged in with problems of her own about her boyfriend, interrupting Tory and Elaine Stritch's duet of "Easy Street." She didn't know if she should ignore his using her telephone for long-distance calls or question him about it and risk making him angry. Tory tried to be sympathetic. He could understand her dilemma, imagining that the man with the mustache and the shoulders might be worth a few overlooked charges on a telephone bill. Alice discussed her problem in detail until four, and Tory was miffed that he was left with only two hours to prepare.

There was no time for a leisurely bath and his usual full regimen. He rushed from the shower to the closets and knew he had to make a snap decision instead of presenting three or four outfits for the mirror's approval. He thought that the black bikini briefs would probably give the man a kick but the Jupiter slacks were so tight the underwear ridges would show through. No underwear would be exciting, but he was trying to get away from the blatantly provocative look that he thought vulgar after extreme youth. The tan Eminence briefs would work, and they coordinated so well with the chocolate slacks and the Lapidus shirt in beige-and-orange stripes.

Tory counted his blessings when he found a cab without walking all the way to Bookbinder's, and he arrived at the Pine Street address only ten minutes after the six o'clock appointment time. The flurry of preparation had kept him from anticipating what was ahead, and he was only slightly on edge when he rapped on the door with the huge brass knocker. He noticed a slight tightness in his stomach and his palms were moist, but it was no worse than going to a new acquaintance's cocktail party. Ginny's reassurances and two glasses of wine made him more confident, and his mind was less occupied with nerves than with being impressed by the house as he waited. He took a passing interest in local status real estate and considering the size and location judged the house to be in the hundred-fifty-thousand range.

A thin grayish man opened the door and smiled tentatively. Tory recognized him as the same little man from the antique store down the street. He went there occasionally to browse. He'd always gotten a kick out of the little man, who always looked at him with thinly veiled interest and made it a point to be courteous and helpful. He wasn't like the lecherous older men who frequented some of the bars and never missed a chance to casually pat a young body or make pointedly sexual compliments. Tory could handle them with poise, but they still made him uneasy. He preferred this sort of older man, who never would be so forward, the kind who would watch him discreetly from the other side of the bar and be deferentially polite if the opportunity for conversation arose.

Sexually, Tory assessed the situation quickly. It was certainly not going to be a treat. The man was at least fifty and looked it, with a slight body and the standard amount of wrinkles, pouty lips, and jowls that reminded Tory of a sleeping pigeon. He searched for good points, deciding to give one to the thinning hair, which was natural and not dyed blond or covered with one of those wigs that reminded Tory of Davey Crockett's cap or a nesting rodent. The man seemed to be accepting his years gracefully instead of trying to deny them, another plus in Tory's mind. Few things made him sadder than some of the older painted queens who were so pathetically oblivious to how ridiculous they appeared. He imagined that coming out in the decades before the sixties must have been a terribly traumatic experience to have taken such a toll.

Tory searched charitably for more good points. The man was no more than five foot six, and it made him think of Mona, how she sometimes dated short men because they made her feel as statuesque as a showgirl. He was willing to look at it her way for the moment. The eyes seemed sensitive, and the smile was kind. He was well-groomed and well-dressed. Tory remembered what Ginny had told him about the sex being totally nonreciprocal, and he managed to keep his smile in place. He thought of how, on lonely nights, a persistent suitor and several drinks could persuade him to relax his standards. They'd never been stretched quite so far before, but he was determined to go through with it. He'd already called Mae to come in and clean the next day, and he'd spent his last money until the unemployment check came in the mail, and Brad had his credit cards under lock and key. He tried to convince himself that dire financial need made it an act of nobility.

"Hello, I'm Tory," he smiled, for lack of a better opening line.

"Yes," the man smiled ingratiatingly and fiddled with his shirt cuffs. "Do come in." Tory stepped into the foyer and thought that the little man seemed more nervous than he was. "My name is Charles. Why don't we step into the parlor and have a cocktail?" Each word seemed to come painfully.

"OK," Tory smiled. He drank in the furnishings, noting the rococo mirror and clock, the abundance of French ormolu, the huge porcelain urns, the orientals. Everything was curved lines and fragile surfaces, a delicate doll-house on human scale. He almost expected to find velvet ropes. "This is even more beautiful than your shop, Charles."

He seemed slightly taken aback, but managed a pleased thank you.

"I guess that's one of the advantages of the business —you can keep the best for yourself."

Charles smiled as if the thought hadn't occurred to him before. "Yes, I suppose it is. Please have a seat and make yourself comfortable. What may I bring you to drink?"

"A little white wine if you have it, please."

"Certainly," he said, and disappeared.

Tory noticed a tray of hor d'oeuvres by the sofa in front of the fireplace and seated himself there. The tray made him smile—the little man was paying him a hundred dollars and still going to this trouble to please him. Charles returned with the wine in a bucket and two crystal goblets on a silver tray. He arranged them next to the hors d'oeuvres and sat on the sofa at a timid distance before pouring.

"Pouilly-Fuissé! You didn't have to open that just for me, Charles." Tory had to suppress a giggle of self-ridicule as he heard his coy tone.

"No trouble at all. It's only appropriate for a young man as handsome as you," he replied with averted eyes. Tory favored him with what seemed like an appropriately flirtatious giggle. "You mustn't come into the shop often or I'm sure I'd remember you." He seemed happy to have a subject to cling to for conversation.

"Not too often. I live in Society Hill and don't get up this way too often. But I bought a small brass box from you about two months ago that I use for cigarettes. You told me it was nineteenth-century Italian. I enjoy it every day." Charles seemed so relieved to have him carry the conversation that he continued. "My mother dabbles in antiques, nothing like your shop of course, but it's given me an interest. And some good buys. She'd be fascinated with your home, so many beautiful things! Is that piece a Sèvres?"

Charles seemed pleasantly surprised to have an audi-ence with knowledge of his favorite subject and began to discuss his treasures. Most of the conversation went over Tory's head, but he managed a pertinent question occasionally and sustained a look of interest, genuinely pleased to put the man at ease. Charles breezed along on the subject for twenty minutes when Tory went into only slightly exaggerated raptures over the homemade pâté. He'd apparently stumbled onto the second great love of Charles' life, and they discussed food and cooking enthusiastically for another twenty minutes.

It became a challenging game to Tory, as if he were going for a Guinness record in keeping a shy man talking non-stop. He was adept at it; he would do it with lonely-looking customers in the supermarket or uneasy guests at friends' parties. It had always seemed like the charitable thing to do, and he was sometimes rewarded with an interesting new acquaintance. All that most of them needed was a smile and an interested expression. It seemed a professional asset worth cultivating. He began to wonder when the conversation would stop and the purpose of the visit would start. He pondered making the first move, thinking it perhaps would be what a shy man like Charles would want, even if he was a paying client. But Charles surprised him.

"Perhaps you'd like to see the antiques in the bedroom," he said with a sly hint of deviltry.

Tory thought of the old cliché about watching out for the shy ones, and he couldn't help laughing as he arose. He was sorry about it immediately when he saw the hurt expression on Charles face. "Oh, I was only laughing because we were so wrapped up in our conversation that I'd almost forgotten what I was here for." He sometimes astounded himself with the lightning quickness of his lies. He was happy to put the skill to such a high-minded purpose, having no ill feelings for the little man and not wanting to cause him any pain.

Charles was obviously pleased. "They always send me such handsome young men from the agency, but you're the first one I've been able to chat with. I'm sorry to have taken so much of your time. I'm sure you're very busy, but it's been so pleasant for me."

The humble kindness touched him. "It's been just as pleasant for me, Charles," he replied, almost sincerely. "Let's see some more antiques."

Tory smiled brightly and walked ahead of him to the

staircase, conscious of the eyes glued on his body. It made him feel like one of the valuable antiques, a costly prize to be handled delicately. But once in the bedroom, Charles grabbed him boldly and kissed him deeply. He wanted to pull away, to repulse the invading tongue. It was so sudden, and he would rather have had time to steel himself for it. He hadn't thought about being kissed. Having his cock sucked was one thing—it was somehow impersonal. A kiss was much more intimate, a reminder of David and the days of innocent discovery of the delights of sex. He maintained his poise only with great effort and by searching desperately until he found a bright side to it. He marveled at how much courage the poor man probably had to muster to make such an audacious move. Somehow, he was proud of him and pleased with himself for provoking it, like a psychologist coaxing the insecure to positive action.

The effort seemed almost too much for Charles. He searched for his breath as he meekly suggested that Tory undress. Tory immediately grasped the dramatic possibilities of the scene and slowly, teasingly disrobed. He felt glamorously theatrical as he assessed the soft light behind him and the different poses he could assume for Charles' view. He maintained total poise except for the thought of becoming aroused, something he was unsure of at the moment. He concentrated on a neighbor's teenaged son he'd seen bicycling that morning in tiny red gym shorts and was rewarded.

Charles seemed incapable of speech as he drank in the sight with awe. He motioned feebly to the bed. Tory flashed a confident smile that reminded him of Ginny and arranged himself on the satin comforter. Charles was quickly beside him in a jerky lurch and again kissed him with urgency. Tory closed his eyes and forced himself to return the kiss, but he sighed inwardly with relief as the mouth worked its way down his neck and shoulder. He kept his eyes closed and began to emit appropriate low moans. He realized that Charles was intent on pleasing him and with closed eyes and the imagined sixteen-year-old body attached to the roving mouth he was able to make his responses seem genuine. It all went easily as Charles worked farther down his body and he could concentrate solely on sex. He finally orgasmed dramatically with his fingers entwined in Charles' thinning hair.

Charles seemed almost embarrassed when it was over. He complimented Tory haltingly on his body, but averted his eyes as he dressed. Tory could only feel relieved to have it over with. Pride seemed out of place, that was an emotion to be felt for something more respectable, but he'd proved himself competent in a new field, completing his first assignment with skill and the ever-important style. He'd successfully pleased his client, his body was now documented to be worth a hundred dollars per orgasm, and he couldn't help but feel proud of himself. He wondered when the disgust and self-hatred were supposed to begin. Feeling more charming than ever as they descended the staircase, Tory was amazed at the brightness of his small talk. A worshipful audience brought out the best in him. Charles disappeared into the kitchen and returned with the expected envelope and a foil-wrapped package.

"A little pâté," he smiled shyly.

"Thank you, Charles. How kind." Tory was almost genuinely touched by the gesture and the thought of the next day's free lunch. There was something to be said for older men if they could make him feel like such a prize.

Charles' original look of extreme nervousness returned before he spoke again. "I'm meeting two friends at the Georgetown Club for dinner. Perhaps you'd care to join us."

An inspired lie didn't pop into Tory's head. It was hard for him to say no to any invitation. Besides, Charles had paid the fee and he was entitled to his company for the evening, though Tory knew that he wouldn't press the point if the offer was refused. He looked at Charles' hopeful eyes and thought of the two friends waiting at the Georgetown, how impressed they'd be and how puffed up Charles would feel to walk in with him at his side. Charitable thoughts aside, a free dinner was a free dinner. Tory favored the little man with his brightest smile. "I'd be delighted."

Charles' face lit up and he became even more attentive. He opened cab doors and lit Tory's cigarettes and checked his coat at the Georgetown. The maître d'

greeted him familiarly and eyed Tory with the hint of a
smirk. Charles grandly informed him that there would be
one more for dinner, and his undertone of cockiness
made Tory smile. Mona's showgirl theory began to make
more sense as they entered the dining room. The Georgetown Club was Philadelphia's oldest private gay restaurant, and Tory imagined most of the evening's guests to
be charter members. Dozens of pairs of bifocaled eyes
focused on him as they crossed the room and he looked
down on Charles with Ginny's publicity-photo smile.

Charles' two wrinkled friends were waiting at the table
and practically overturned it getting up to greet them.
Tory felt his charm oozing from every pore, a superfluous
asset when all he had to do was look young and smile
handsomely. The constant glances from every corner of
the room and the stream of Charles' acquaintances coming up to the table for a few moments' conversation made
him feel more handsome than ever. Lustful looks from
men more than old enough to be his father seemed like a
cheap means of ego massage, but it worked.

Charles looked ready to expire from ecstasy. He ordered more Pouilly-Fuissé; Tory was sure he could ask
for a case of it in a doggie bag and get it. He flashed
Charles an intimate smile and fixed an absorbed eye on
the menu. The crabmeat cocktail and broiled lobster
looked especially appealing. The waiter was a plain-
looking man of about Tory's age who looked at him with
the maître d's subtle smirk. Tory wondered if these
glances were an occupational unpleasantness but decided
not to let it bother him. He was dining at the table and
not waiting on it, as he thought he would be doing just a
few short days ago. Moral scruples were obviously for
the proletariat.

Charles sincerely offered to see him home after the
meal, but Tory graciously declined. He walked the two
blocks to DCA instead, checked his coat and pâté, and
discoed the evening away. He moved so much better when
he felt like a showgirl.

Chapter Seven

TORY felt smugly glamorous the next morning as he lounged in his bedside chaise, drinking coffee, nibbling a brioche, and thumbing through the latest issue of *Gentleman's Quarterly*. He'd looked at the same magazine just a week before with a lack of enthusiasm, almost resigned to having his pleasure in new clothes become vicarious. The glossy pages suddenly looked twice as appealing. He heard the key in the lock and the familiar fortissimo voice singing "Ten Cents a Dance."

"Hi, Mae."

She ambled into the bedroom in her rabbit coat and red turban, taking in the picture of leisure. "Well, if it ain't the Duchess of Windsor." Tory leaned forward with great effort for his kiss. "How's my baby?"

"Just fine."

"Where's the cleaning money coming from? That sure was a short visit at the poorhouse. You find a sugar-daddy?"

"Sort of."

Mae threw her coat over a chair and lowered her bulk onto the bed. "Tell Mae all about it, baby. That 'sort of' sounded mighty peculiar."

"How do you feel about being paid with tainted money?"

"Depends how tainted it is. Did that crazy Mona's gangster fix you up in the rackets? Only a jackass would run numbers, but the money ain't tainted if you're just a runner."

"How about the wages of sin?"

Her eyes widened. "Whoring?"

"If you must be so blunt."

"Get out!" She was stunned into speechlessness, a rare occurrence.

"It's all done very tastefully. I'm not out working the streets like a real hustler, it's all by appointment. Almost like going to a little party. Do you think it's awful?"

"Baby, back when I first met you, back when you and David got your apartment and all the neighbors said, 'Who's these two crazy white kids living practically in the ghetto?' I always told them, 'Maybe a mite crazy but that Tory's got a good head on his shoulders.'" She paused to shake her head in exasperation. "You made me eat my words a thousand times since then. I guess once more won't kill me. I ain't saying I approve but I can see that chin just dying to jut out and it ain't going to do no good to try and talk sense."

"I knew I could count on you, Mae. You always stick by me."

"Makes me wonder sometimes if I got any more sense than you do. I keep telling myself that if I'm around to keep an eye on you, I might keep you out of some real trouble." She shook her head again. "Can't say much for my batting average so far but at least you ain't in a coffin or the slammer. David must be keeping busy up there, trying to explain you to the Lord."

"I'm only trying to keep the wolf from my door."

"Guess I shouldn't be surprised. I knew you weren't going to put up with it for long. Just ain't in your nature to pinch pennies."

"I don't think it's so bad. I met a nice man last night. He was crazy about me."

She raised her eyebrows to show that she understood all too clearly. "I'll bet he was. I'm going to have to talk this one over with the deacon, see what the Lord has to say about all this."

"Is it a sin to spread some joy and happiness in this sad world?"

"It ain't if that's *all* you're spreading."

"I just can't see that it makes me an evil person."

"You remember Serena? No, guess you wouldn't. She lived up the block in the old neighborhood, moved to Norris Street before you got there. Anyway, she was a whore and I'm not saying she was no saint but she took better care of her children than some of those lazy hussies sitting at home waiting for their welfare checks. She died of cancer last year—"

"Cancer?"

"Yeah, baby."

"Are you sure it wasn't consumption?"

"No, cancer of the pancreas, ate her away from the inside out while those fools at the clinic was treating her for ulcers. There was some that says it was a judgment from the Lord, but that ain't what I'm driving at. She was always a good neighbor, always ready to lend a helping hand when you needed it."

"Does this story have a happy ending? Somebody always dies or loses their man in your stories."

"This one's got a moral. I'm just trying to say, don't get mixed up with the lowlifes. You can be a whore without being a hundred percent wicked if you watch your step. How much you make?"

He smiled. "Fifty a night. And dinner."

"My, my, my. To think of the millions you gave away, you're a walking Rockefeller Foundation."

The doorbell rang an hour later. Tory's most strenuous movement had been from *GQ* to *Town and Country* and he called out to Mae in the living room with a trace of grandeur in his voice, "Just ring him in, Mae. It's the man from the service."

She sounded less than pleased to have her spirited rendition of "The Saga of Jenny" interrupted. "Get off your skinny behind and buzz him in yourself. I'm up to my elbows in Mr. Clean."

He somehow found the strength to rise and go to the door. "I'm glad you're here to keep me humble."

"And I don't charge extra for it neither."

He posed expectantly in the doorway, patting his hair and smoothing the pearl-gray robe. He'd heard an extraordinarily heavy tread on the stairs but was still astonished as a fullback-sized black man came into view. His shoulders almost grazed the walls. "Good God, I hope you're Eugene." Tory was relieved when he smiled.

"That's me." He nodded over his shoulder. "I don't know who that guy is but he followed me in."

Tory craned his neck around the man's shoulder to see Brad standing wide-eyed at a safe distance on the landing. Tory's mind flashed him a vague memory of being caught smoking in the high school boys' room, then he decided to try to appreciate the humor of it all. Some coincidences were just too ridiculous to take seriously. "Why, Bradley, what a surprise!" Brad's only reaction was to remain in silent awe of the presence before him.

"I hope you don't have a hundred. Seems like everybody's got hundreds this morning and I'm out of change."

Tory smiled again as Eugene so deftly reduced the possibilities for an alibi. He fished the twenties from his pocket. "Brad, do you have two tens for a twenty?"

Brad fumbled for his wallet, and they completed the transaction. He flattened himself against the wall as Eugene began to descend the stairs, and there was still barely enough room for him to squeeze by.

"Ginny said to stay home till she calls this afternoon," Eugene shouted from the landing. "She's got something lined up for you tonight."

"OK. See you soon." He looked at Brad expressionlessly. "Are you going to stand out here in the hall, or would you like to step inside?"

Brad recovered some of his composure and moved inside. "Who was that man, why were you giving him fifty dollars, who's Ginny, and what does she have lined up for you tonight?"

Mae hooted. "Well, if it ain't Perry Mason."

"Come upstairs for some coffee and I'll tell you all about it," Tory answered calmly. Only a miraculous lie would have worked, and he was relieved to have the whole thing out in the open anyway.

"Just in time for my coffee break! I got to hear you explain this one, baby."

"You've heard it already."

"But this is like reading the book and then seeing the movie. I want to see what gets added and subtracted."

They moved upstairs to the dining area. Brad and Mae took seats while Tory poured coffee. Mae banged her fist on the table. "Court is now in session, the Honorable Mae Wesley presiding. Witness, you may be seated." Tory seated himself primly and folded his hands. "First question. Who was that man?"

"That was Eugene."

"Number two. Why were you giving him fifty dollars? And don't tell us he was from United Fund, we ain't buying."

"He works for the Davis Escort Service and he was collecting the company commission from my appointment last night."

"Very good. Now who is Ginny?"

"The proprietress of the escort service."

"And are we correct in assuming that what she has lined up for you tonight is another appointment?"

"That's correct, your honor."

Mae beamed. "There you go, Bradley boy, nothing to it." She spoke to Tory out of the side of her mouth. "Baby, you just turned *Deep Throat* into a Disney production."

Brad examined Tory in silence for a long moment. "I'm reading between the lines. Tell me I'm wrong."

"OK," Tory happily complied. "You're wrong."

"I don't think so. From what I can gather you're a hundred-dollar-a-night hustler."

"Aren't you impressed that I'm worth a hundred dollars?" Tory replied breezily. "It's a very elegant operation."

"You know what a snob he is," Mae said supportively. "He wouldn't whore for none but the best."

Brad shook his head in despair. "I can't believe it."

Tory decided to try an offensive tack. "You told me I needed a job."

"You know I didn't mean that kind of job."

"It beats waiting on tables."

"Or cleaning houses."

"Don't be flippant about this, Tory. It isn't a joking matter. How long have you been doing it?"

"Last night was my first," he smiled. "My debut."

"Why don't you make it your last?"

Tory sighed with dramatic wistfulness. "Alas, I cannot. The rent will soon be due and the creditors will be pounding at my door." He rose and threw his arms around Mae's neck. "And poor, dear, old, old Mae. She'd starve without me. I'm a victim of bitter circumstance."

"Tory." Brad's tone reminded him of Miss Banks in fourth grade.

"Forced to bend my soul to a sordid role."

"This isn't the time for your little games."

Tory gave him an exasperated sneer and sat down. "Give me a break. No one knows better than you just how desperately in need of money I am. This is the easiest way for me to get it and pay off some of these bills. It's only temporary. God didn't mean for me to wait on tables and get varicose veins. I was born to higher things."

"I wasn't aware of your pedigree."

"Oh yes. My Uncle Joe was practically a nobleman, owned half the valley back in Stoltz Grove. I might be living off a trust fund today if my mother hadn't married beneath her." He wished life could be like the bedtime story of his youth and he didn't have to be concerned with such mundane things as money and morals, just take childlike delight in each new day.

"Uncle Joe would be real proud of you."

"Come off it, Brad. Times have changed. Sex is cheap."

"Ain't the way you're doing it, baby."

Tory ignored her remark. "You go to the baths and suck cock—excuse me, Mae—all night long. I spend a few minutes in a gentleman's bedroom and then get taken out to dinner and treated like visiting royalty. Who's the saint and who's trash?"

"I didn't say I was a saint, but doing it for cash is a different story."

"What of it? Nobody twists these men's arms to call the agency."

"It's still hustling."

"Is that supposed to bother me? I'm twenty-four, Bradley. If I haven't developed many morals by now it's not likely to happen. And if I'd met this guy in a bar and he decided to buy me gifts and take me out to dinner, you'd think it was fine. If I hooked up with a rich doctor, my mother would probably be ecstatic. At least this way isn't hypocritical, we both know exactly where we stand."

"You're oversimplifying the issue, as usual. You're reducing yourself to a piece of merchandise. It's degrading."

"But I'm an expensive piece of merchandise," he mused. "Sort of like the Louis Vuitton of procured sex."

The idea appealed to him. "I fail to see that it's degrading."

"It's going to bring you nothing but misery. Have you ever seen a happy old hustler?"

Tory pondered. "I don't think I've ever seen an old hustler."

Brad pointed his finger victoriously. "Because they're all dead of cirrhosis or living on Skid Row."

Mae hooted. "Or retired to their motels in Florida." She often took Tory's side against Brad even when she didn't agree with him.

"You tell me I'm an alcoholic now anyway, so what's the big deal? Besides, Mae's right. The only hustlers you ever see are the ones who work Spruce Street at three in the morning. They'd be just as scruffy in any other circumstances. I'm working for the best. The people I've met so far live in expensive apartments and dine in fine restaurants and wear beautiful clothes. I imagine they have their share of problems, but who doesn't?"

"You're going to come to hate yourself," Brad said ominously, as if he had inside information.

"That's what they bring us up to believe, and I was half expecting lightning to strike me last night as he handed me the money in a discreet white envelope. But it didn't happen, Brad. I made a lonely man happy last night. He was a gentleman, a kind human being. He was grateful for my company and delighted to pay me. It gives me a glow to think about it, how I brought a smile to his sad face and made his evening a pleasant one." He almost said that it was like doing his Christian duty, but he knew Mae wouldn't approve and might switch sides. He shuddered at the thought of both of them ganging up on him.

Brad shook his head. "You make it sound so noble, like you're doing volunteer work for a nursing home."

The thought of a nursing home brought to mind the image of Charles' desiccated old lips upon his, and he brushed it from his mind nervously. "Except nursing homes don't serve Pouilly-Fuissé."

He watched the wheels turning in Brad's head. "All right, forget the psychological issues. Do you have any idea how dangerous this is? The psychotics you could be dealing with? Who were Jack the Ripper's victims?"

Tory lit a cigarette with a grand flourish. "Cheap tarts.

This is a professional operation. The clients are screened."

"What about the police? How are you going to feel when you have to call me at two o'clock some morning to bail you out?"

Tory laughed with another shudder. "I think I'd rather serve time than put up with your smug but forgiving expression. Besides, it's not likely to happen. Ginny pays off the right people."

"What about the Mafia? Do you realize that you're probably going to be connected with them in one way or another?"

"Oh, I know," he smiled brightly. "Isn't it exciting? My membership card is probably in the mail by now."

"You're beginning to sound like Mona." A look of dawning knowledge swept Brad's face with a frown. "I should have known! She got you into this, didn't she? With her gangster friend."

Sometimes he felt he spent half his life defending Mona to Brad. "So what? Why can't you just accept the fact that you and I don't see things the same way and that I'm going to do things you don't approve of? I enjoy some recklessness in my life, some gambles, some surprises now and then. It keeps the adrenaline flowing. Do I criticize you for leading your careful little life? If debating obscure points in a courtroom and getting a stiff neck over a law tome make you happy, is it my business? We have different temperaments. Why can't you just accept it?"

"Because you never know where to draw the line. I don't want to sound melodramatic, but this time you could be gambling with your life."

Tory gave him the exasperated look of unconcern that he knew to irritate him beyond all reason. "What isn't a gamble? Walking down the street is a gamble."

Brad seemed to sense that he was getting nowhere. He shook his head and sighed. Tory caught the forlorn expression, the one he always wore before trying to play his trump card. He sighed again. "What would David say?"

"That was below the belt, Bradley," Mae answered indignantly. "Besides, David's up there watching over him, making sure he don't do anything too dumb." She looked heavenward with an expression that made it clear she knew the angels on a first-name basis. "I hope."

Tory refused to let Brad upset him. "David would understand. He'd rather see me doing this than scraping up nickels and dimes to pay the rent. He never thought about money unless he had to, but then he was very pragmatic about it. To him, money was a bothersome necessity to enjoy some of the pleasant things. And sex was a driving force in his life, but not one he was above using to his advantage." It hurt him to talk about David in anything but saintly terms, but there was a point to be made. "He didn't get as far as he did in the theater department solely on talent, you know."

Brad searched his face with a new alertness. "I'd heard some talk."

Tory shrugged with a nonchalance he didn't wholly feel. "It was no big deal. I was jealous at first, but there was no reason to be. It had nothing to do with our relationship. It was sex as a bodily function that could bring him closer to some of the things he wanted. In fact, knowing him probably makes it easier for me to do what I'm doing today."

Brad gasped. "That's almost blasphemous."

"If he hadn't gone and died on me, I wouldn't be in this fix at all." He flicked his ash with a cynical smile. "I'd probably be in a co-op on Park Avenue by now. With Angela Lansbury in for cocktails."

Brad studied him for a long moment. "You're saying that facetiously, but I think you mean it. There's still a good deal of bitterness underneath your façade of acceptance, isn't there?"

Brad could be annoying enough without seeing into his mind. Tory refused to show his distress and merely shrugged again. "Could be. I was never big on self-analysis. I deal with things as they come along these days, and this is what I've decided to do for the present. You can either accept it or not; my mind is made up."

Tory's chin jutted out involuntarily, and he knew that Brad realized the subject was closed. He got up to leave and gave him a peck on the cheek. "We'll talk about this later, after you've had time to think it over. In the meantime, just be careful, Tory. Please."

"I'll try."

"And don't worry that I'm going to lose sleep over this every night until you've come to your senses."

Tory smiled in vexation. He admired professionalism in all fields, and Brad was a master at inducing guilt. "Had to get that in, didn't you?"

He only smiled in response. "See you later, Mae. Don't work too hard."

Chapter Eight

TORY ignored his second thoughts and ordered a third glass of Chablis. After years of Brad's lectures on alcoholism, he still felt uneasy about getting a buzz on before lunch. But everyone else at Duffy's seemed to do it, so he thought it must not be all wrong. His co-workers made it all sound so sensible; since they usually didn't work until mid-evening, a few Bloody Marys early in the day were easily canceled out by an afternoon nap. Tory thought it made as much sense as most other rationalizations and he was happy to have an excuse to be sociable with the crew.

Duffy's was little more than a shot-and-beer bar, but it was comfortable. It had a private-club license which allowed it to stay open after the two a.m. Pennsylvania closing time, and its busiest time was after midnight when the upstairs dance floor was open and customers stood three deep at the bar. During the day it was practically a clubhouse for Davis Escort employees and their friends. From his first visit, Tory felt at home there. Carl was behind the bar and knew who he was without an introduction. He worked for Ginny on an off-again, on-again basis and knew all of the crew and most of the gossip. In the best bartender tradition, he introduced Tory to the rest of the crew as they came in and made him feel a part of the inner circle. Tory had taken to dropping in after shopping, and there was always someone to pass the time with, comparing notes on clients, or gossiping about absent co-workers. He especially enjoyed

coming in late at night after an appointment and getting
waited on before the crowds at the bar or sitting in the
big corner booth with the crew and feeling like part of
the privileged elite. Then they'd go over the evening's
assignments and tell funny stories on each other's clients
and drink and laugh until three or four in the morning.
He slid easily into the night people's routine, and there
was less time to entertain old acquaintances at home.

The change didn't bother him. People who had to worry
about getting up for work in the morning seemed dreary
in comparison to his new companions, less spontaneous
about an impromptu pool party in one of the high-rise
apartments or a rowdy breakfast in an all-night diner.
His new friends didn't seem to worry about the mundane
things, and that suited Tory perfectly. After the first
month, he realized that the job was becoming a life-style.

There was always gossip. The forty or fifty crew members and their friends were divided into several factions,
usually not outwardly feuding but always with an under-
current of cattiness. Christine and Theresa and some of
the hard-line professionals, the ones with teased hair
and dangling cigarettes, always found something to criticize in the rest of the girls. Tory was sure they would
come to physical violence if everything wasn't so mysteriously reported back to Ginny. Christine and Theresa were
street hookers who'd worked up to Ginny's operation
only through their looks and resented her stringent in-
sistence on ladylike behavior. It didn't make Tory feel
very chic to know they were all part of the same operation, but he managed to stay cordial. The South Philly
girls made up their own little clique. They were usually
near the dance floor at night, jitterbugging and cracking
gum. Tory thought they also left a lot to be desired class-
wise, but they were younger and friendlier than the pros,
always ready for a party or a joke. Tory's favorite girls
were Doreen and her friends. They were free-lancers who
worked for Ginny between rich boyfriends, the Bal à
Versailles and weekends-in-Aruba group. Tory could
relate to them better, discuss the latest clothes at Nan
Duskin or the newest clubs in New York. They were more
like Ginny without the hard business edge, more like his
idea of a high-priced call girl.

The men were all amateurs and less competitive than

the women. Richard and his friends worked out at the gym all day and drank nothing stronger than beer. They bored Tory with their constant talk of bodybuilding and nutrition, but they were easily ignored. Tom and his friends usually sat in a corner and disappeared occasionally to smoke a joint or pop a pill. They seemed pleasant enough, but it was often difficult to sustain a conversation with them. Tory's favorites were Carl the bartender and his group, the ones with something delightfully malicious to say over drink after drink and little on their minds besides which club to go to next.

George appeared at Duffy's only rarely. Tory had once spotted him across the room alone when he was in the corner booth with a particularly raucous group that was amusing itself by tossing ice cubes at Carl behind the bar. Tory knew they were being obnoxious, but it was so much fun. Another night George came into DCA while Tory was in the middle of an almost obscene dance with Carl's friend Craig. The raised eyebrows had been fun after six hours of steady drinking. He caught George's derisive sneer and ground his hips even harder into Craig's.

In spite of the constant gossip, no one seemed to know much about George. He worked out at the gym, but the jocks knew him only vaguely. Carl said his only real friend in the business besides Ginny was Jimmy, who was in Europe for six weeks with his lover. Tory was curious but tried not to let it show. He took pleasure in having George see that he'd become part of the crowd. Even if George didn't like him, it was apparent that the rest of the crew did. He annoyed himself by hoping they'd strike up a conversation some evening.

The telephone rang while Gloria worked on her third Manhattan and lamented the rising prices in Acapulco.

"Tory, it's for you," Carl shouted after a few seconds' conversation. Tory wondered who could be calling him at Duffy's, though it made him feel more of an insider than ever to get calls at the bar. "It's the boss lady."

"Ginny?"

"That's the only boss lady we've got around here. You better jump, boy. You don't keep Miss Davis waiting."

"I wonder what I did wrong."

"I warned you about stealing tricks' wallets."

Tory wasn't actually nervous. He was sure he'd been

doing a competent job and imagined that she had a rush assignment. "Hi, Gin. What's up?"

"I have some unexpected business to attend to. Can you take care of the phones from two until four or four-thirty this afternoon?"

"All by myself?"

"You're ready. It won't get busy before five today, and I'll leave a number where you can get in touch with me if an emergency comes up."

"OK." Tory had helped Ginny with the telephone six times in the previous four weeks and didn't feel any real apprehension about handling them solo. Compared to the pace at the supermarket during busy periods, it was almost relaxing. He enjoyed sitting at Ginny's Regency desk in her cozy apartment-office, listening to records and reading magazines when the telephones weren't ringing. He also enjoyed flipping through the file boxes of index cards with clients' names and confidential information, discovering names of casual acquaintances or an occasional well-known local business or political figure.

"Are you sober enough to work?" Her tone was brusque, but he'd learned to distinguish it from her hard no-nonsense business tone. "It hasn't taken you long to pick up all the bad habits of the trade."

"I just happened to be passing by on my way home from Bonwit's and thought I'd drop in and say hello. I've only had two glasses of wine."

"Make sure you don't have another, and be here at two on the dot."

"Yes, ma'am."

"She's sure keeping you on a short leash," Carl laughed as Tory handed back the telephone. "It's not everyone she calls to see how much they've had to drink before lunch. If you're nice to me I won't mention that you counted wrong."

"She wasn't checking up on me. She has to go out on unexpected business and she wants me to watch the phones this afternoon."

"You hear that, Gloria?" Carl shouted across the bar. "More 'unexpected business.' "

Gloria raised an eyebrow. "It's got to be a man."

"Or big trouble with Mr. B."

Tory's ears perked at the mention of Mr. B. He was

supposedly the force behind the escort service, the mob boss who actually called all the shots. None of the crew had ever met him, and the mystery made him all the more exciting.

"Let's hope it's a man," Gloria said quietly between sips. "Bitch that she sometimes is, I wouldn't wish trouble with Mr. B. on her."

"She's not really a bitch," Tory replied loyally. "It's a tough job. Would *you* like to manage a group like us?"

"Listen to Goody Two-Shoes." Carl laughed. "You two are getting to be real pals, aren't you?" He looked at Gloria. "Maybe this is the spy in our midst." It was another of their constant games. Ginny always seemed to know everything that they least wanted her to know, and they often speculated over who was the undercover informant.

"Not Tory," Gloria answered sagely. "I still have money riding on that lacquered old witch Christine."

"You never know. He's been over there working the phones every time you turn around lately."

Tory looked heavenward in exasperation. "Can I help it if I'm one of the few of us who can write a phone message in legible English?"

"Linda's getting ready to deck you. Says you're moving in on her beer money."

"I just follow orders."

Gloria smirked. "Linda can't even remember her own phone number half of the time. I'm surprised that Ginny hasn't given her the ax long ago. The only place she knows what she's doing is on her back."

Carl clasped both her hands in his. "Dear old Gloria. Always a kind word for everyone."

She shrugged. "I just call them as I see them. What time do you have to be there, Tory?"

"Two sharp."

"Good. You have time to meet Doreen for lunch at the Garden with me. She's gotten a sudden urge for soft-shell crabs." She sipped her Manhattan thoughtfully. "God, I hope she's not pregnant again. I couldn't put up with her through another abortion."

Tory drank coffee at lunch while Gloria and Doreen polished off three rounds of Manhattans and a bottle of

Chardonnay. He arrived at Ginny's apartment sober and on time. He was more interested in making an impression with the telephones than with the clients. He realized too late that the idea of prostitution was more glamorous than the cold facts of the job. Managing the operation came naturally to him; it was absurdly similar to running a phone-order grocery business, while retaining some of the forbidden-fruit lure he'd been attracted by in the first place.

He could see that there was more money to be made this way than in jumping in and out of beds. Ginny had given him a twenty-dollar bill each of his previous training visits and had promised him fifty dollars for each two or three-hour session when he was ready to work alone. While he was living comfortably, Ginny made him feel destitute by comparison. Her spacious apartment in its prime Rittenhouse Square location had to cost eight hundred dollars a month. Eugene chauffeured her everywhere in the black Lincoln when he wasn't driving on business, and a full-time maid took care of the apartment. Her clothes, jewelry, furniture, and all the other details of her life-style bespoke an income that brought envy even to Tory's jaded eyes.

She opened the door in a red suit that Tory thought was probably a Chanel. It was perfect for a romantic luncheon date, a bit bright for a meeting with a god-father, Tory speculated, but he wouldn't think of asking. Ginny had been kind to him in her brusque way, but she'd drawn a definite line between her business and private lives. She eyed him with her now familiar appraising look. "At least you *look* sober."

"I told you I only had two glasses of wine," he protested innocently.

"Whatever happened to the civilized cocktail hour?" she muttered with the barest hint of a smile. The social moment passed, and she was suddenly all business. "Call Joanna to make sure she's out of bed. She has a four-o'clock appointment in Cherry Hill. And when Eugene comes back from downtown, make sure he remembered to pick up my dry cleaning. And don't let him wander off, I may need him to pick up Mr. Evans at the airport at six. And Mr. Haimes will be calling back, tell him everything is set for tomorrow night."

"Who's available if I get rush orders?"

"The list is on the desk. Send Louise if you get a chance—she's crying about her doctor bills, poor kid. And if a guy named Brandish calls, send him anyone but Jeannie. He sometimes calls for a quickie on Thursday afternoons and they didn't hit it off last time."

"OK. Do I have Charles tomorrow night?"

Ginny smiled. "He insists on no one but you these days."

"He's a lamb."

"I think Richard and Derek are about to scratch your eyes out. Charles used to be their territory."

"Can I help it if he finds me more charming?" Tory asked with a trace of grandeur in his voice. He'd been introduced to Derek at Duffy's two weeks earlier and was almost intimidated by the impressive muscles and blond good looks. But after a fifteen minute conversation which centered on Derek's exercise program and dietary habits, he found Charles' preference understandable.

Tory had seen Charles every Friday night for the past month and was beginning to feel very comfortable with him. The sexual part of their meetings became even easier for him because it never varied and he knew what to expect. Their conversations were becoming longer as Charles relaxed, and he always served vintage wine and elaborate hors d'oeuvres. Tory looked forward to their next meeting and the ego gratification afterward at dinner in the Georgetown Club. He was becoming a near-celebrity there with the older crowd and enjoyed it immensely. He also didn't overlook the impression that Charles' loyalty made on Ginny.

Charles made it easier, a stable, nonthreatening sanctuary in an unpredictable occupation. As Tory's data for comparsion grew, he began to realize that most of the other men were no more attractive and usually much more demanding. Tory wondered if it had all been part of Ginny's plan, to initiate him with Charles to get him involved and then introduce him to the usual order of business. He didn't underestimate Ginny's cleverness and thought she was probably right. Had his first client been one of the more disagreeable men, he doubted that he'd have lasted past the first night. But he was learning to detach himself when he didn't like to think of what he was doing, and sometimes he could almost fantasize that he was a spectator watching his mirror image in an erotic performance. When he couldn't, he tried to dwell on the fact that it would all be over shortly.

It was usually just a matter of an hour or so, and he quickly brushed it from his mind. Once outside the apartment or hotel room he could fondle the hundred dollars in his pocket and convince himself that it was no worse than working an eight-hour day. Then he'd head for Duffy's and search for the amusing parts of the encounter, the parts that would make everyone laugh in sympathy. After a few glasses of wine and some frivolously congenial company, the distateful memories began to fade and he could go home to bed without a Valium.

"Rosen thought you were charming, too," Ginny continued. "He called yesterday and raved about you."

"Oh no! God, is he a troll."

"But he's a regular."

"I have scratch marks on my shoulder and a broken nail to remember him."

"Really?" she asked with concern. "He should know better than that."

"He wasn't trying anything strange, he just got carried away. What an animal. I thought that when they hit forty they slowed down, but he was going at it like a sailor on shore leave. He sure got his hundred dollars' worth."

"They can't all be princes."

"I keep waiting for a prince and all I seem to get are sick queens."

"You've got to take the good with the bad. Wasn't Carmichael's friend nice?"

"I guess. At least someone without a potbelly was a change of pace. I hate to complain, but he wasn't all that exciting in bed."

"*You're* supposed to be the excitement."

Tory sighed. "I try. But sometimes it's like pushing elephants uphill."

"Keeping pushing, kid. I've got a plum for you tonight at nine. Double pay."

His first thought was to wonder if he'd have enough time to prepare on only seven hours' notice. It took a few seconds for the idea of double pay to sink in. "What

do I have to do for it?" he asked warily. "He must really
be disgusting if you charge him two hundred."

"He's very rich and values discretion. Have you ever
heard of Andrew Arledge?"

"As in Arledge Securities and the Main Line Hospital
board of directors?" he asked in shock. "Ginny, he's got
to be ninety!"

"He's seventy-eight, but it doesn't matter. He just likes
to watch."

Tory gave her a confused look. "He's paying two bills
to watch me jerk off?"

She looked at him distastefully. "You're beginning to
sound like the rest of them. And it's not the case, anyway.
He's paying four hundred to watch you perform with
George."

"George!"

Her no-nonsense tone and expression were completely
sincere. "If you still have a grudge against him, get rid
of it immediately. You'll meet him at his apartment at
eight-thirty in full dress and a cooperative mood." A telephone rang in the distance. "And get to work. On the
desk is a number where you can reach me in an emergency. I'll be back by four-thirty."

Chapter Nine

THE afternoon dragged by. There were no more than two dozen calls on the four telephones, resulting in two immediate appointments, seven weekend bookings, and a pile of messages for Ginny. Nothing in *Esquire* or *Viva* held Tory's attention, and his thoughts kept returning to George. He only half accepted Ginny's explanation that George's surly behavior had been for professional reasons. He wished that she'd never explained it, that there were no extenuating circumstances to mitigate his hostile feelings. Not knowing how he should feel annoyed him more than the affront, real or imagined. He'd always been able to accept a mistake in his own judgment more easily than the annoyance of confusion. He wanted to hate George, to deal with a simple emotion. But his memories of the hypnotic blue eyes, the tight-muscled frame, and the eye-widening cock were tinged with an emotion far from hatred. It frustrated him even more, and he tried to banish it from his mind, as he tried to banish all frustrating thoughts.

It was a relief for him to go home and start primping. The bathroom mirror was an escape from all the unpleasant realities, an idyllic world where the most pressing problems were an occasional blemish or uncooperative curls. He was outraged when George invaded even this temple, commandeering his eyes to examine the reflection and having the effrontery to find flaws. It sapped the simple pleasure out of narcissism, and Tory finished his preparations with spiteful thoughts and a fantasy of revenge.

The fantasy had so many satisfying variations, always ending with George begging him for the merest scrap of affection and being refused with Garbo-like cool.

During the cab ride through midtown traffic he vacillated at each red light over which attitude to project. Overtly bitchy? Icily remote? Good-sport conciliatory? He wondered if perhaps it might be best not even to acknowledge any unpleasantness at the last meeting, lest George suspect he'd been brooding over it, then go on to offend his macho pretensions by blithely discussing Mae West movies and Judy Garland records. He couldn't come to a firm decision by the time the cab finally arrived at the Locust Towers, and his self-annoyance intensified when his heartbeat quickened ridiculously before he rang the doorbell.

George appeared, looking conservatively collegiate in a navy blazer and gray slacks. He eyed Tory's cream St. Laurent suit and Ted Lapidus shirt in graduated stripes of blue and pink with a look of total disapproval. "Ginny should have told you to tone down the high fashion. Old Andrew gets crotchety when his boys don't look Waspy and butch."

It was difficult for Tory to hate someone so handsome, no matter what he said. Vengeance was suddenly the last thing on his mind, and he only wished they could be friends. He caught his softening thoughts and tried to recover some of his anger. "Hello, George," he replied with a civil coolness as he swept into the room. "Glad to see you haven't lost any of your charm."

George smiled broadly. "Are you still pissed? Ginny said you had no kind words for me."

Tory felt a twinge of embarrassment to have the subject brought so frankly into the conversation. Suddenly he didn't want to discuss it, to actually speak all the stinging words of his imagined conversations. "She explained that it was all part of the audition."

George looked at him with a roguish grin as he slipped into a chair and lit a joint. "Mostly."

The insulting smile and blunt admission brought back Tory's memory of their first encounter in vivid detail. "I told Ginny you got off on it, you sadistic prick."

George remained annoyingly unperturbed and passed the joint. "I think 'sadistic' is a bit strong. You breezed in here so piss-elegant in your gold chain and ninety-dollar shoes, I thought you could stand to be knocked down a peg or two."

Against his better judgment, Tory sucked deeply on the joint. He occasionally enjoyed smoking at home or with friends where nothing extraordinary was likely to happen. Dope sometimes made it difficult for him to deal with unfamiliar circumstances, and he decided to do only three or four tokes so he could stay in control. Holding in the smoke gave him time to digest George's comment and think of a bitchy retort. He decided that aloof pity would annoy him the most. "It's a shame you have to pick on piss-elegant queens to prove how butch you are. When you were a teenager, did you drive around nights and beat up on faggots in dark alleys?"

It only provoked a grin. "Did you always have a vicious tongue, or did you pick that up from Carl at Duffy's?"

The memory of George's sneer at the flying ice cubes embarrassed him, but he recovered quickly. "I'm not being vicious, I'm only trying to understand your hostility toward me."

"It's not hostility. Maybe you just caught me on a bad day." He flashed Tory a needling smile. "Actually, you're kind of nice for a piss-elegant queen."

"Thanks."

"A little dizzy, but you carry it off with style."

Tory shrugged and tried not to smile at his next malicious thought. "Some of us like to pretend we're John Wayne and some of us like to be ourselves."

"Yourself? I thought you were doing Alexis Smith."

"I'm being a homosexual without apologies."

"And you think I'm apologizing for it?"

"It's your business. But why do you have to take it out on me?"

George gave him another sly grin. It was hard to concentrate on a semi-civilized debate when his lips looked so inviting. "Because I like the way your jaw juts out when you're pissed off. Like a little kid. It's kind of cute." Tory managed to maintain a frown, but he couldn't control a faint blush. He misplaced the insult that had been forming in his mind. "And I'm not apologizing," George continued. "Being gay doesn't mean you have to mince around and smoke fancy French cigarettes."

"A Gauloise will rot out your lungs a lot faster than a Marlboro. Doesn't that make them butch?"

"It makes them stupid. Besides being affected."

Tory made a point of shifting uncomfortably in the canvas chair. "As affected as macho furniture that could cause spinal curvature?"

"I imagine we all play roles to some extent. Some of us are more comfortable with certain ones."

"Are you really comfortable?" Tory noticed his tone changing from bitchy to curious.

"More comfortable than I'd be as a dizzy queen. Besides, why are dizzy queens always hot for truck drivers and construction workers? They try to ignore masculinity in themselves but it's the first thing they look for in another man."

Tory had no quick answer, so he decided to ignore the comment. "But don't you feel you're missing something sometimes? Wouldn't you really rather have a velvet sofa with soft cushions?"

"It's not my style."

"Or a pretty cashmere sweater instead of a CPO jacket?"

"No."

"Some days, instead of working up a sweat at the gym, wouldn't you secretly rather be watching an old Bette Davis movie on television or trying out a new recipe for salmon mousse?"

"Not really," he laughed.

"Can you walk through the main floor of Wanamaker's without slowing down at the cosmetic counters?"

"It never enters my mind."

Tory gave him a perplexed look. "I'm worried about you, George. Perhaps you're a latent heterosexual."

George slowly looked him up and down in unconcealed appraisal. "Not tonight." Tory couldn't contain a titillated smile. "Let's not worry about my psyche anymore. It all worked out for you, anyway. Ginny must be pleased with you to send you to old Andrew, and Derek tells me you've got an exclusive franchise on Charles Lawson these days."

"I've just been trying to do my job well."

George's roguish smile returned, and he looked deeply into Tory's eyes as he leaned unnecessarily close to pass the joint. "You did OK by me."

Tory understood the cat-and-mouse game George was playing and chided himself for letting him win so many rounds. He couldn't stop the embarrassing flash of warmth that suffused his body and barely managed to answer without stuttering. "My pleasure."

George seemed satisfied that he had the upper hand and changed the subject. "Well, we're going to do it again tonight, but somehow it's not quite the same with an old man in an armchair acting like he's watching *Sixty Minutes*. On the other hand, it might turn you on. There's a bit of the exhibitionist in you, isn't there?"

"Only when I'm provoked."

"You better grease up before we go. There's a tube of KY in the bathroom."

The marijuana made the last remark come across as a grotesque non sequitur. "I beg your pardon?" Tory asked in offended disbelief.

"Don't give me that condescending Society Hill queen expression. I'm telling you for your own comfort. Arledge is a very strange old man and the sight of a tube of grease offends him."

"I'm sorry, but it's beginning to sound very bizarre. And I don't know how much poise I can maintain walking up Locust Street like that."

"It's your decision," he shrugged. "We can do it dry if you like."

"Not with that thing we won't," Tory blurted out, immediately regreting it as George's roguish smile returned.

"That's no way for a lady of quality to talk. But don't worry, I'll be gentle," he smiled smugly.

"Where was I when we chose up sides, anyway?"

"With that gorgeous ass I'm sure Arledge will want it that way. Besides, you're going to love it."

"Mother was right," Tory muttered as he walked toward the bathroom, trying to hide his smile. "You're all animals."

The marijuana hit him full force as they began the walk to Cypress Street. He'd had only four tokes but knew he was irretrievably stoned. George explained that it was the best Hawaiian dope and seemed amused at his condition. Tory had to focus all his attention on walking and could only feel vaguely annoyed. When they turned into a tree-lined courtyard and stopped in front of a building that Tory had always assumed was a museum, he had to search his mind to recall why they were there and giggled apprehensively at his disorientation. He prayed that the old man wouldn't be too strange, because he was in no condition to handle anything extraordinary.

A uniformed butler opened the huge double doors and ushered them in. Since moving to the city, Tory had conditioned himself not to act impressed by wealth, but he couldn't suppress a look of wide-eyed wonder as they were led through the palatial hall flanked on each side by a huge, antique-filled room. They continued up the massive staircase dominated by a huge canvas, and it slowly registered that the painting was one of Monet's water-lily series. He could barely fathom how it could actually be hanging anywhere but a museum and gradually began to realize that he was being exposed to wealth beyond even his sophisticated experience. The thought was suddenly frightening. He moved closer to George as a chill swept his body.

They were soon in a second-floor sitting room where an old man was half hidden in the depths of a black leather wing chair. Tory examined the balding, wrinkled head and the frail body lost in the folds of a blue velvet smoking jacket, deciding the nasty-looking old man was too feeble to move. He hoped it was true. The man was as intimidating as the house.

"Good evening, Mr. Arledge," George shouted deferentially in his ear.

The old man gave him a curt nod and looked Tory up and down with a frown. "New one," he mumbled at George.

"This is Tory, sir," he shouted. "John moved to San Francisco, but Miss Davis thinks you'll be pleased with him."

The old man was obviously not pleased with change of any sort. He continued to examine Tory. "Are you Italian, young man?"

"Mostly German, sir," he managed through his haze and unease. He somehow knew that his Italian heritage wouldn't please the old man and was surprised that he'd spotted it so quickly. Tory didn't think he looked particularly Italian. He wondered if the old man's money had brought him frightening powers of discernment.

He didn't seem convinced of Tory's Teutonic ancestry and continued to frown. "You may begin." He motioned to the Aubusson carpet.

Tory foggily followed George's cue and began to undress. His disoriented mind focused on Hansel and Gretel and the old witch, and his fright was almost as strong as the first time he'd been read the story. They piled their clothing neatly on the silk-upholstered sofa and soon stood naked before the wing chair. Until this encounter, Tory had never felt worse than somewhat ridiculous when he exposed his body to clients' gazes. This night, he felt totally ill at ease under the old dragon's unsmiling stare, each twinge of discomfort magnified a hundred times by the powerful Hawaiian dope.

His worst fear was realized when the old man motioned him closer. He remained frozen in his spot until George gave him a nudge. He unwillingly stepped forward and stared down in petrified horror as the withered claw ran slowly down his belly. He needed to concentrate all his strength to keep his crawling flesh from pulling away from the clammy touch. The old talons moved down to his flaccid cock, and it was impossible for him to induce a response out of his fantasies.

As the old man seemed about to bellow his anger and order him to the dungeon, George stepped forward. "Perhaps I can help," he said quickly. With that he folded Tory into his arms and kissed him fervently. Tory gratefully surrendered to a flood of relief and returned the kiss desperately, afraid for it to end, afraid to look at the old man even from the safety of George's arms. George slid his hands gently down Tory's back and began to kiss his neck. The sensual stimulus to his nervous system gradually began to calm him. George seemed to sense that he'd eased Tory's panic and gently pulled him to the carpet, blanketing him with his body. Tory clutched the sheltering flesh with a moan of anguished relief, his hazy mind telling him that it was his only salvation. He refused to look at the old man, tried to blot him completely from his mind and think only of George's searching mouth and hands.

As the old man's quickened wheeze began to abate, George moved around to a sixty-nine position on an angle that assisted the view from the armchair. Tory lunged gratefully at the hard prick above him, taking it deeply into his mouth, making it the focus of his consciousness. The old man continued to wheeze and called George's name in a low voice. Instead of looking up, George took it as a cue and turned them both ninety degrees so that his ass was directly in front of the chair. He pulled his cock from Tory's mouth and replaced it with his balls for a few minutes, gradually working forward until Tory's mouth rested between the mounds of his ass. Tory could only feel relieved to have the old man completely removed from his view, and he continued to work feverishly.

A few more minutes passed and the old man wheezed. "Now, George." George dutifully went on to the next position. He deftly flipped Tory a quarter turn, rolled him over, and raised him to all fours. "Hard, George! One stroke!"

Tory was just beginning to register disbelief at the command as he felt a searing pain and George suddenly close on his back. He gave out a gut-wrenching scream before he could think to stifle it. Tears of pain and humiliation welled up in his eyes.

The old man emitted a sharp gasp and yelled, "Harder, George!" in an agitated voice. Tory suddenly realized with disgust that his tears and pain were the stimulus for the old man's excitement, and with a stoic stubbornness he refused to react to George's thrusts. He bit his lower lip and forced himself into silence.

"Harder, George!" the old man shouted in irritation. "Put some effort into it! And let me see his face."

George again shifted their position and whispered harshly into Tory's ear. "Cry, goddammit. He's getting mean."

"Good," Tory whispered back defiantly. He shrieked in pain a second later as George's teeth sank into his shoulder.

"That's better, George. And you, boy! Look at me!"

The pain of the bite was more emotional than physical.

Tory felt suddenly deserted by his only protection against a terrifying ogre, and he allowed his self-pity to surface. He sobbed pathetically, thinking bitterly of the satisfaction he must be giving the old man but unable to stop and no longer caring.

The performance was soon over, but time seemed irrelevant. The physical pain had become a minor nuisance compared to his despair. Through a haze he heard the old man thanking him politely. Tory gave him a startled look, wondering if he'd just played a piece on the violin for the old man's after-dinner entertainment. He remained lost in his bleak thoughts, barely noticing that they were dressed and being ushered out by the butler.

Once outside, the cool April air filled his lungs and suddenly brought him back into partial touch with reality. He turned to George with an accusing, belligerent look.

"Hey, it's all over. Everything's all right now." George touched his shoulder and looked at him with concern. The pressure on his shoulder reminded Tory of the bite, and he turned away and began to walk.

George followed. "Look, maybe I should have told you more about him, but that's the way he sometimes is. He's a sick man, and we were there to indulge him. It was nothing personal."

Tory didn't want an explanation and he didn't respond. He continued to walk in what he assumed was the right direction. George followed.

"I'm sorry, Tory. I'm sorry I hurt you. But it's all over now, let's forget it. Let me find a cab and take you home."

The fresh air had somewhat restored his senses, and the pain and humiliation swept over him in fresh waves. He looked silently at George as a tear began to form in the corner of his eye.

"Oh Christ, Tory, don't cry again. Please."

Tory was startled by the pleading human note in George's voice. He halted and stared again, wondering if he looked as pathetic as he felt. He searched George's face through blurred eyes, trying to understand that the emotion he saw there was real. Ignoring the bright streetlights and passing traffic, George encircled him in his arms. Tory's nervous system wearily refused to deal with yet another emotion, so he surrendered to frustrated sobs.

"It's all right, Tory. I'm going to get a cab and take you home. It's going to be all right."

He hailed a cab at the corner and shepherded Tory in, sitting with his arm around him throughout the crosstown ride and ignoring the disgusted glances from the driver through the rearview mirror. As they approached the apartment, Tory began to feel that the worst was over. Time and distance were beginning to make it possible for him to push the evening to the back of his mind. His feelings for George were far from settled, but at the moment it was more important to have him there beside him than to question and evaluate his behavior. George guided him into the apartment and into the bedroom. Tory didn't resist as he undressed him and moved to the bed. He hadn't dealt with such an assault of feeling in years, and he accepted the comforting warmth next to him with unquestioning gratitude. The clean smell of fresh sheets and fresh male perspiration told him that everything would be better in the morning.

Chapter Ten

GEORGE was barely out the front door when the telephone rang the next morning. Tory listened to the ringing and wondered what to do. They'd just made love with such an unexpectedly tender passion that he wasn't certain he'd be capable of conversation.

It had taken him by surprise. He'd awakened with a start at the sinewy arm wrapped protectively around his chest and the hard-muscled torso pressed gently against his back. Sex was usually a perfunctory act, with the partner sent off after serving his purpose, and Tory was accustomed to awaking alone. He preferred it that way. He knew exactly the image he wanted to present and that it wasn't visible first thing in the morning, with rumpled hair and a mind incapable of clever conversation. Panic seized him as he suddenly recalled that the man beside him was the person he most wanted to impress with a full display of the image.

But the panic passed. It seemed to disappear under George's fingertips as they began to move over his body, replaced by an erotic heat to which Tory was unaccustomed. He wanted to protest, to wrench himself away from the hands that had taken control of his body. The unfamiliar helplessness they were causing swept over him in growing waves, drowning any remaining vestige of the image. Tory finally realized it was hopeless, and joyfully surrendered.

He was still practically speechless when George pulled him into his arms for a kiss and slipped out the door. The telephone's rings seemed to be sounding from another dimension, and Tory tried to recall what the logical response was to stop them.

He managed a hello, and Mona babbled cheerfully for several minutes before she asked if he was still on the line.

"I'm still here," he replied, fairly certain that he was. "What were you saying?"

"My dear, you rarely make much sense before noon, but this morning you sound like a total zombie. What's wrong with you?"

"I don't know," Tory murmured, then felt his eyes suddenly widen as the answer occurred to him. "Maybe I'm in love."

"Love!" Mona repeated in disbelief.

"I *guess* that's what it is," he vaguely replied, still surprised himself. "It's been a long time, but this is how it feels, if I recall correctly."

"This sounds serious," she stated in shock. "Is he a gentleman of means?"

"No," Tory stammered. "Not really."

"Who is he? What does he do? Give me all of the vital statistics. So far, he sounds less than suitable."

"We work together."

She spoke darkly after a long pause. "I do not approve . . . Tory! Not the one who auditioned you?" He mumbled affirmatively and Mona gasped in utter sorrow. "I was afraid of this. You were always a tad on the kinky side, but this job has pushed you over the edge." She moaned histrionically. "And it's all my fault for goading you into it! Please, Tory, tell me he doesn't wear motorcycle boots."

"Calm down, it's not like that at all. My first impression was off-base. He's not a bastard at all."

"Let's begin at the beginning. This emotional about-face is too rapid to be plausible. When did it all come to pass? Tell me all."

"Last night."

"And you're in love?" she asked with a patronizing patience. "Do you think that perhaps your decision might be a trifle premature?"

"Sometimes you just know. You know?"

"Not personally. But I imagine these things are possible, even if it does smack of adolescence. What were the circumstances?"

"We did a really dreadful trick together last night. One of the Arledges."

"As in the Radnor Arledges?" She was obviously impressed. "Which one?"

Tory searched his mind for an event that seemed to have happened long ago. "The old one. Andrew."

"Andrew!" Mona gasped. "They don't make them any older than that. He must have emigrated as William Penn's cabin boy."

"The man is truly twisted," Tory recalled with a shudder. "He took an immediate dislike to me for some reason and got his jollies watching George do nasty things to my body—"

"Here we go," she said smugly. "I knew it. How nasty?"

"Stop trying to imagine me as totally depraved. Not really nasty, no whips or lit cigarettes, just generally humiliating and debasing."

"Someone was telling me about a gay bar in New York where they have orgies and people pee on each other and things."

"If you're reading that between the lines, forget it."

"Do they actually do that?"

"So I've heard."

"Whatever for?"

"I haven't the vaguest notion."

"I get upset when someone spills wine on my dress."

"There was nothing remotely like that last night."

"And they do impolite things to each other with their fists."

"Fist fucking?"

"I can't imagine how it could be enjoyable."

"Don't ask me," he shrugged.

"Not to mention what it would do to a manicure," she added before recalling the subject at hand. "Anyway, I'm relieved to hear that your neuroses haven't progressed that far. What exactly happened?"

"Nothing truly bizarre. Conventional sex. Done with less than the appropriate tenderness and compassion."

"That can be exciting for a change of pace."

"Up to a point. If I hadn't been so stoned I'm sure I could have dealt with it."

"Did you orgasm?"

"I shouldn't stoop to your vulgar level to answer that, but no, I didn't."

"Don't let's get prissy, *mon cher*. I know you for the trash you truly are. I'm simply trying to ascertain the facts. My interest is purely clinical."

"Pardon me."

"So what happened then?" Mona continued with undaunted enthusiasm.

"I was very stoned on this lethal grass and got very upset, barely functional. It did such a number on me, I can hardly remember the last time I was so out of control."

"You must be editing out the juiciest details," she accused. "You never lose your cosmopolitan poise."

"It was mostly the dope. Anyway, George was beside himself with concern, and he never shows any emotion at all. That unraveled me completely, and he took me home."

"And made passionate love to you?"

"Not until this morning."

"In the same manner as the previous evening?"

"No. The total opposite. It was beyond words."

"Perhaps you're not as ill as I'd feared. When are you seeing him again?"

The first less than ecstatic thought of the day crossed his mind. "I don't know. We didn't discuss it."

"Are you sure it wasn't a hit-and-run?"

"He's crazy about me, I can feel it in my bones."

"Tory, I don't want to sound callous, but if you were so upset perhaps it was only an act of sympathy."

"Last night, perhaps. But not this morning." He sighed contentedly. "Believe me, he's interested."

"And you're in love?"

He paused for a few moments before answering. "I don't know, Mona. It's been so long, I'm not sure I know what love is anymore. And I'm not going to let him get away until I find out exactly what it is."

"I'm worried."

"Why?"

"I've never heard you like this. I hope you're doing the right thing."

"I am." He was so content to stop wavering, to finally make a decision and know it was the right one.

"He's not exactly what I had in mind for you. He's not wealthy, he doesn't treat you with the deference and romantic attention you've come to expect, and so far the relationship seems to be based primarily on masochistic sex."

"We can work out the details later."

"I'll fly in next weekend to see if he's suitable for your hand."

"Maybe we'll hold off on that. You might frighten him off."

"How rude."

"When the right time comes, you'll meet him. For right now, I have to play this very carefully." Tory chuckled at the odd feeling in his stomach. "It's been a long time and I'm out of practice."

"It will all come back to you," she assured him.

"I hope so. What's new with you?"

"I've got to find a man somewhere," she sighed.

"Dominic is definitely a thing of the past?"

"He still calls me once a week, but he's catching on. Clever fellow."

"No new prospects?"

"A few standbys and two in my apartment complex that may have possibilities. I hope it doesn't turn into a dry spell."

"I know single women who would drown in your dry spells."

"Well, keep your eyes peeled. I'm in the market for a racecar driver or a skydiver."

"Still on your danger kick?"

"I need someone who will make the adrenaline flow. He doesn't have to be truly dangerous—a professional gambler would do. I'm open for suggestions. Just no doctors. And no joggers. You can barely drive a car around here without mowing a few down lately. They're trying my patience severely, too."

"I'll stay on patrol. Call me next week."

"I will. I say this with reservations, but good luck with your man."

"Thanks. It will all make sense to you when you meet him."

Tory congratulated himself on his timing, to have his mind occupied with speculative romantic thoughts instead of becoming depressed over the previous evening's work. Nothing put him in a better frame of mind than the memory of sex with the right partner. He smiled at his reflection in the mirror and laughed contentedly as details of the early morning floated through his mind. The comic strips in the morning paper seemed unusually amusing, and he admired Ann Landers' sound advice. The coffee tasted better than usual, and each muscle ached pleasantly as he stretched. Even the pale-pink teeth marks on his shoulder looked attractive, a souvenir to remember a man he knew he couldn't forget. He knew his elation was bordering on insanity when Mae let herself in and her rendition of "It's Delovely" didn't sound off-key. She picked up on his uncharacteristic mood immediately, and he gave her an expurgated explanation.

"Baby, I ain't seen you like this since you know when!" she exclaimed ecstatically. "Even when that painter wanted to take you to Europe you stayed cool as a cucumber. This George must be something else, you're head over heels and don't tell me you're not. I know all the signs. Just ain't seen them on you in a month of blue moons, and you sure do wear them well. And it's about time! You been alone too long, ain't natural for a youngster like you. Don't you let him get away!"

It was the only troubled thought in his mind. Tory hadn't even questioned that there would be a second meeting until Mona brought it up. Everything had been almost perfect, but why hadn't they made arrangements for their next meeting or even mentioned communicating by telephone? He crossly brushed the thought from his mind as neurotically pessimistic and reassured himself with a gut feeling of certainty.

Still, he worried. He had doubts that one night of very strange circumstances necessarily led to an ongoing relationship, even if the feelings displayed in that night were undeniably tender. He even questioned his own feelings, wondering if perhaps they weren't an overreaction due to his agitated state. He quelled his own doubts with no difficulty but wondered if they were also passing through George's head. He thought of how pathetic he must have looked outside Arledge's house. Anyone but a complete misanthrope would have had to respond to him; George would have seen him home out of human decency. But no one forced him to spend the night. And the electrifying morning heat hadn't vaguely resembled an act of charity. He knew instinctively that the next meeting would follow, just as naturally as white sales followed New Year's Day. Everything had seemed so certain when they were so close together; even the differences in style and outlook they'd discussed in George's apartment hadn't mattered. But doubtful thoughts seemed to incubate in the passing hours apart from him.

The telephone seemed to ring continuously. He jumped for it with atypical energy, chastising himself for hoping it was George and being annoyed each time it wasn't. He had to fight an urge to call by midafternoon, Aunt Dolores' admonitions to her daughter on inappropriately aggressive behavior having somehow become ingrained in his mind. The irony of it amused him. Suitable behavior had never stopped his cousin from making her interest known to a man.

At least the bathroom mirror calmed his nerves for a few hours. He wasn't terribly concerned about how smashing he looked for Charles, but the ritual of opening and closing all the comforting jars and bottles and tubes took his mind off his increasingly troubled thoughts. They were once again fading into confusion, just as the heady, lingering scent of lovemaking faded in the shower. Even the pink bite marks were fading to blend with his skin.

He toyed briefly with the idea of inviting Charles to his apartment instead of traveling across town and leaving behind the telephone that was bound to ring at any second. He left for the appointment at the last possible minute, disgusted with himself for accepting such a passive position. His anger almost convinced him to make the call, if only for the sake of establishing where he stood. But other forces held him back. If his worst thoughts were true, he wasn't sure that he wanted them certified just yet. Even uncertainty was preferable to a total emotional plummet. The dreadful scene of the night before and the soaring events of the morning were more than enough emotional stimulation for any twenty-four-hour period.

And perhaps the noncommunication was a sign. He often wondered if certain events in his life were signs from David and the powers beyond. There was rarely strong evidence, but he continued to wonder. Perhaps no word from George meant that they weren't meant to get in-volved.

He arrived at Charles' house still distracted, the ro-mantic quandaries now compounded by mystic ones. His pre-business cocktail chatter was less than spirited, but Charles didn't seem to notice. Tory was far from in a mood for sex but forced himself into a performance. He knew he could probably make up an excuse and Charles would still pay him for the evening, but a perverse honor wouldn't allow him to accept cash without delivering. And he was determined not to leave empty-handed. If all the energy he was expending on troubled thoughts eventually amounted to nothing, he didn't want the additional mem-ory of a lost fifty dollars to bother him and make him feel even sillier than he was beginning to feel. Dinner at the Georgetown Club did little for his ego. Middle-aged men slobbering over him gave no gratification when he knew they should be George.

He left as soon as he felt a polite interval had passed after dinner and took a cab home without a thought for the crowd at Duffy's. The telephone was ringing as he climbed the stairs to the apartment. He practically un-hinged the door getting to it before it had the chance to stop. He tried to sound civilized when Brad said hello and invited him to meet some old school friends for a nightcap. Tory pleaded exhaustion. Besides not being re-motely interested in drinking with suburban former class-mates, he knew Brad would probably notice his distracted mood and interrogate him. He'd finally ceased his con-stant harangue on the escort service, now limiting himself to occasional biting remarks, but Tory was sure he'd have nothing kind to say about George. He took a Valium and drank wine until he began to fade. The telephone didn't ring again, but he was sure he could find a solution to his situation after a good night's sleep.

Chapter Eleven

MAE let herself in and was immediately silenced by the competition of Dinah Washington mourning through "Stormy Weather." Tory heard her footsteps and the closet door opening and closing below but didn't acknowledge it. She jumped back in fright as she climbed the stairs and discovered him at the glass table.

"Hi, Mae."

"What are you doing sitting up here like a spook so quiet and scaring folks into palpitations?" she asked angrily.

"Sorry," he answered flatly and lit another cigarette.

Mae examined him with an unhappy shake of her head. "Still hasn't called?"

"Still hasn't called."

"And you ain't done a thing about it."

"And I ain't done a thing about it."

"Well, what the hell are you waiting for, baby?" she asked crossly. "It's been a full week."

"What's to do?" he countered with a nonchalance he didn't feel. "I guess he isn't interested."

Mae looked exasperatedly toward heaven for guidance. "Look, baby," she began to explain patiently, "whoever this George is—and I wouldn't want to be in his shoes if he runs into me today—he owes you an explanation. He had you so worked up last week, like I ain't seen you in years, and no man has the right to do that to a body and then drop them flat without even a beg-your-pardon."

"It's his life. He doesn't owe me anything. If that's the way he feels about it, it's his business."

"You might as well be talking in tongues, baby, because that don't make no sense at all to me and furthermore you don't believe it neither. You can't sit around smoking cigarettes and drinking coffee and playing sad songs and pining away. Take it from Mae, baby, you got to do something about it. You got to grab the bulls by their horns and get to the bottom of the facts and get it out of your system. You let something like this eat away your insides, it can do you in. I seen it happen, to poor Emma Johnson back on Sedgwater Street. Her old man left her and she kept moping around. Dropped dead six months later."

"Cancer?"

"No sir! Just a fatal case of the empty-bed blues, pure and simple. You got to get it off your chest."

"It's too late. I should have called the first day. If I do it now I'll feel like a fool."

She shook her head again and disappeared into the kitchen. "Better late than never. And we all got to play the fool now and again. You got too much pride, baby. That's your problem."

He knew it was the truth. Many steps in the process of falling in love exasperated him. It demanded an openness that left gaps in his carefully constructed façade of sophistication, leaving him vulnerable and even looking foolish because of another person's whims. The drawbacks of living his life alone had faded to an occasional melancholy that he could ignore or deal with easily. The thought of being vulnerable or looking foolish frightened him much more. He half hoped that time would alter his emotions, that he could stop thinking about George so constantly and go back to the imperfect but comfortable routine of his life. A surprise now and then delighted him, but for a week each day had been a purgatory of mystery. He was beginning to wonder if it was all worth it.

Mae returned with a cup of coffee and sat down. "Besides, how do you know it ain't all just a misunderstanding? Maybe you got your wires crossed and he's waiting for you to call him. Happens all the time, you know, these misunderstandings. Take Thomasina Jones for example—"

"Thomasina Jones?"

"Yeah, she lived with her folks on Butler Street till she

found out what her mama pulled on her five years ago.
Thomasina was wild about her man Lorenzo and her
mama didn't like it one bit. Old Mrs. Jones was a school-
teacher till she retired last year and she thought Lorenzo
was beneath her daughter, but the reason's neither here
nor there. One night Lorenzo came by when Thomasina
was out and her mama told him she was out with her old
boyfriend, the insurance salesman, and they'd patched
everything up so Thomasina would appreciate it if he
wouldn't come around no more. Now old Mrs. Jones
taught drama in high school and Lorenzo ain't too bright
anyway, so she convinced him without much trouble.
Thomasina fretted around a few days and finally she's
going to call Lorenzo and her mama says, 'What, girl?
You're going to crawl on your belly and make a fool of
yourself?' Now Thomasina's a lot like you, real haughty-
like, and it didn't take her mama much convincing. By
the time Thomasina figured it all out Lorenzo was married with two sons and another on the way."

It took Tory a few seconds to remember the last point
in their discussion. "George isn't the kind of man that
would mope around a telephone."

"Didn't think you was neither. Ain't like you to sit
around doing nothing. I think of all the times when doing
nothing might not have been a bad idea and you were
out screwing things up worse than ever, just to have something to do. And here you are with a problem that's just
crying out for a simple phone call and finally you're sitting still and twiddling your thumbs. What's got into you?"

"Maybe I'm scared."

She looked pensive. "Ain't the time to be scared, but
maybe it's a good sign. All the times you was too
simpleminded to be scared when you should've been shaking in your boots, maybe you're finally getting some
sense."

"I have plenty of sense, I just haven't seen anything
worth using it for lately. Losing my job, almost going
bankrupt, becoming a hustler, if they happened they happened. Everything's relative, and those things weren't
really worth losing much sleep, if you stop to think about
it. They weren't going to make me unhappy if they didn't
work out. Just inconvenienced." He stabbed his cigarette
into the overflowing Lalique ashtray. "I have this gut

feeling, Mae, a voice deep inside me. You know what I mean?"

She nodded gravely.

"It's telling me that George could make a difference in my life. And I'm afraid I'll do something wrong to screw it up."

"Listen to your heart and it'll most times give you the right answer. But for some things you got to be practical and think with your head. You got to do *something*!"

Tory smiled. "Mona said I should hire a private detective to trail him. When he spots George in a restaurant or someplace, he can call me and I can stroll in and act surprised to see him."

Mae went through a series of exaggerated disbelieving expressions. "Nice girl, that Mona. Got about as much sense as a can of Green Giant peas, but she's a nice girl."

"Actually, there's some sound logic in there."

"If you say so, baby. I just hope she catches herself another husband soon. Her boss is bound to figure it out any day now that she ain't playing with a full set of jacks."

"But she's right. Not about a detective, but Philadelphia is a small town in a lot of ways. I'm always bumping into people I know. It's just a matter of time before I see him around town."

"Then what?"

"Then we can talk. I'll have plenty to say once I see him. I just don't want him to think I'm chasing after him."

"And until then you're going to sit around and play Billie Holiday records?"

"Maybe."

She shook her head. "Seems to me like you're taking the long way around, but I guess it's better than nothing."

Tory spent more time on the streets than at home the next week. He sometimes ambled into Duffy's three times a day and was out running errands on the flimsiest pretext. He felt alternately mysterious and silly as he ignored the neighborhood stores and traveled fifteen blocks to shop near George's apartment. The doormen at the Locust Towers began to nod to him as he walked by and he got to know a few of the waitresses by name in the coffee shop across the street. He felt truly ridiculous when he began to recognize certain cars that were parked on the street day after day.

Being the pursuer was an unfamiliar role, one he didn't enjoy playing. Everything was so much easier at places like the Georgetown Club, where he never had to reach for his Dupont lighter or a check, where there was never any doubt that he was desirable. Even at the younger bars he could be coyly flirtatious, enjoy the hungry looks and sexy smiles as part of the game. After years of not caring, he was being forced to play by an alien set of rules.

Only his gut feeling of certainty gave him the courage to go on. That, and a gambling instinct that had always given him such an unnerving thrill. He'd been addicted to pinball machines since the age of eight. Carnival wheels, harness racing, and dollar-a-point backgammon followed over the years, and a roulette or blackjack table touched nerves he sometimes forgot he possessed. Gambling gave him a queasy case of the jitters but was strangely invigorating. This time he was gambling for George with his whole image of nonchalant sophistication, the emotional safeguard more valuable to him than any stack of chips. It made it all the more painfully exciting.

But even in the thrill of the game Tory felt that he was cheating the laws of chance. He was being exhilarated by the excitement of anticipation without really taking a risk. The murky voice inside told him that the odds were fixed in his favor, that he was sure to win. He sometimes wondered if hearing voices might not be something to worry about, but he continued to listen.

Tory decided that the voice wasn't a figment of his imagination when he spotted George through the window of a Chestnut Street bookstore. With the hours he'd logged in the streets it was just as likely a triumph of tenacity as a metaphysical phenomenon but he chose to ignore the more mundane explanation. Confident that some power of fate was pulling strings in his favor, he strode into the shop with total poise. He unobtrusively edged himself to a position just out of George's direct line of vision and cleared his throat theatrically. He flashed a caricature of a toothpaste-ad smile and, as George looked up, exclaimed, "Howdy, stranger!" in a shriek of surprise. George's usual composure deserted him, and Tory watched with a mixture of vengeful glee and empathetic discomfort as he searched for a response.

"I was just thinking about you." George seemed to be still collecting his thoughts.

Tory thumbed a novel nonchalantly. "I'm sure my phone was about to ring off the hook any minute now," he replied in a cheerily loud voice that turned several heads.

George looked around the store, obviously not savoring the prospect of a public scene. "Why don't we go for a walk? Let's go to my place for coffee."

Tory deigned to raise his eyebrows a fraction of an inch in assent. He was thoroughly enjoying his domination of the encounter and gossiped about business through the walk as if there were no other reason for conversation. George seemed to be regaining his composure. By the time they sat down to coffee at the butcher block in George's kitchen, Tory knew he no longer had a large advantage. George took the first sip from his mug and looked pensive. "OK, let's talk," he said firmly.

"So talk," Tory smiled politely.

"OK. First of all, I don't think I have to tell you that the last time we saw each other was almost mind-boggling to me."

"How do you mean, 'mind-boggling'?"

George gave him a vexed look. "I didn't take you for the kind to fish for compliments."

Tory laughed in annoyance. "I'm not above it, but I'm not doing it now. I don't understand what you mean by 'mind-boggling.' It can have a good or bad connotation. You could mean that the unseemly way I carried on was a trial to your nerves." He glanced down at his coffee. "Or you could be referring to the more pleasant aspects of the time we spent together."

"You know what I mean, damn it. I could barely drag myself away."

Tory looked up with the hint of a smile. It seemed like an auspicious beginning. "I've been trying to tell myself that I wasn't being conceited to think that, that I wasn't the only one having a marvelous time. But who said that you had to drag yourself away at the crack of dawn? And what I'm even more curious to know, who said you couldn't come back? What did I do wrong? Is it because I don't own a leather jacket?"

George laughed. "You didn't do anything wrong. You did everything so right it was almost frightening."

"I'll buy a leather jacket if it will make you more comfortable with me. I'm willing to compromise."

"Your so goddam dizzy," he smiled. "You'd look like you were going to a Halloween party in a leather jacket, and that's part of your charm. I don't want to change you. You're great the way you are."

Tory quietly filed the compliment away and tried to hide a smug smile. "Then what's the problem?"

"I needed time to think."

He gave George an Orphan Annie stare. "Think about what? Two people get together and find that they do special things for each other, they get together again. It's all very easy."

"Stop trying to sound simpleminded. It fits in with the act, but you can't pull it off. We're not talking about a one-night stand from the bars that you might or might not invite back."

"What exactly are we talking about?"

George paused. "Something with more depth."

It was exactly what he wanted to hear, the words that would tell him they could iron out any minor differences. "We don't have to rush into anything if you're going to be bothered by second thoughts. I can understand that. I haven't been . . . involved . . . for a long time myself, and it's not something to rush into blindly."

"My eyes are wide open. I can see your good and bad points, the things between us that would work out beautifully and the things that might cause some problems."

"I'm sure we could work something out."

"It's a secondary issue."

"Then what's the primary one?" He hoped it was as simple as the first.

George fixed his blue eyes on Tory across the table and paused for an endless ten seconds. "I don't want a commitment in my life right now. I'm not ready for it."

Tory searched for the words to correct the sudden wrong turn their conversation had taken. "Sometimes these things don't run according to our schedules. People have to adjust to accommodate them."

"I can't. I'll be going through a lot of changes over the next two or three years. I've got a lot on my mind."

"Who doesn't?"

"I'm getting out of the escort service, Tory. Another two years and I'll have the cash to set myself up in a comfortable little business and stop worrying about all the shitty things there are to worry about in this business. I'm going to get as far away from it as I can, out in the woods or on a quiet beach where I can forget that I've ever seen a high-rise or a neon sign."

Tory found the thought of a rustic life far from appealing, but he ignored it for the moment. After he had him snagged, he could talk him out of the silly idea. "So? That's two years away. What about the meantime?"

"It's hard to explain."

"I'm a good listener."

George looked pensive through a long pause. "Sometimes I really hate what I'm doing. I come home from a trick, take a shower, go to bed, and sometimes I can't think of one good thing about myself. We all go through it. That's why Joanna is always incoherent on downs and Ruth OD'd last year. And Duffy's is practically our private club because we're all in there drinking our guts out around the clock. I deal with it differently. I guess sometimes I pretend I'm not me. I spend a lot of time at the gym or the library or just driving around out in the country. Nobody knows me and I can let my mind wander and forget for hours at a time that I've got a nine-o'clock appointment waiting for me back in town. Sometimes I go to diners or taprooms in these one-horse towns and sit around, just to be where nobody knows me and I can pretend I'm a traveling salesman or a truckdriver or anything but what I am."

"It's a bit strange, but I guess I can understand it." Tory thought of Stoltz Grove. "Except for the part about the hick towns. Now *that's* really twisted. Anyway, how does it apply to us? You know you don't have to be someone else with me. I'm hardly the one to hold your lax morals against you."

George sipped his coffee with a troubled expression. "This isn't easy for me to say, Tory."

"Try."

"I will." Tory did not like his heavy expression. "You're

incredible. To me, you're the city personified. You make me think of neon lights and posh restaurants and expensive shops. You're a walking billboard for cosmopolitan living."

Tory couldn't contain a gasp and a chill. He'd worked over half his life to hear such words, and George couldn't have thrilled him more except with a declaration of eternal love. He thought his brain had short-circuited from an overload of ecstasy and he didn't even search for a reply.

"But that's the problem, Tory. Sometimes I hate the city. And all the bullshit that goes on behind the bright lights. The crooks with potbellies and three-piece suits, wheeling and dealing and buying bodies for cheap kicks. And Ginny's crew selling it to them without batting an eye, so they'll have cash for another spree at Bonwit's and another night on the town. You knock me out, Tory. But I guess I'm afraid to get involved with you."

Tory had to laugh in spite of himself. The conversation was suddenly absurd. He wished they could go over the part about neon lights and excitement again. "Let me get this one straight. You can't get involved with me because I'm a hustler?"

"It must sound ridiculous coming from me but that's a part of it."

Tory shook his head in disbelief. "Did the Hays Office write this script? I can't have a happy ending because I'm a person of easy virtue? How about if I recognize the error of my ways and get a job with the Salvation Army?"

"It's not that simple. I don't want to get involved with anyone. At least not until I have my own life straightened out."

"Couldn't we sort of play it by ear until then? The Salvation Army was a joke, but I could give up working for Ginny if it would make a difference." He tried to say it offhandedly, to let George think that the job was unimportant and he wasn't actually chasing after him.

"Tory," he said with an uncomfortable expression, "nothing's going to make a difference until I'm out of this business."

"If it's so tough on you, why don't you get out now?" A brilliant flash of inspiration lit up his face. "You can move in with me and be my gigolo!"

George shook his head and laughed. "That's a quality I find fascinating about you. You function under an entirely different code of logic than us earthlings."

"Maybe you're not cut out to be a gigolo. But I'm sure you could do something besides hustling."

"It's either two more years of hustling or thirty-five behind the desk in a bank. I have clients who tip me with hundred-dollar bills and give me fat envelopes at Christmas. Where else can I clear a thousand a week?"

Romance flew out of Tory's head for a split second. "Why don't I see any of these big tippers?"

George smiled. "Seniority. I'll send you mine when I retire."

"When you retire," Tory mused. "Maybe you'll be ready to settle down by then."

"And you're going to sit in a corner with your hands folded and wait for me?"

"No," he smiled smugly, "I'm going to be plotting and scheming to make you come to your senses before then."

"I can see the wheels turning already. You're accepting everything graciously today because you're sure to have things your way tomorrow."

"Maybe not tomorrow," he replied matter-of-factly. "But I'm sure I can wear you down in less than two years."

"You're used to getting what you want, aren't you?"

Tory fixed him with a steady stare. "When I want it badly enough."

"I believe you. And it's unnerving."

Tory smiled as he got up from the table. "No sense laboring the point," he said breezily, relieved to realize that most of his sophistication was still intact. "Don't forget my phone number." He walked to the door and tilted his head into what he hoped was perfect Lauren Bacall position. "If you want me . . ."

Chapter Twelve

Tory and Jimmy cased the men's shop with a professional eye, ignoring the racks they'd examined the week before and zeroing in on new merchandise with radarlike accuracy. Tory had always done his clothes shopping alone or with Mona. It was a serious business to him, and he didn't like to make casual small talk and important decisions at the same time. When Jimmy was faced with a decision on apparel he usually bought both selections in several colors. He respected Tory's solemn attitude and didn't make a nuisance of himself. They struck up a quick acquaintance when Jimmy had returned from Europe and spent the summer making religious rounds of the city's better clothing stores.

"Tory, do you think this is too flashy?"

Tory gave a cursory glance at the blue suede jacket in Jimmy's outstretched hand. "It's a bit bright. You'd be better off with the one you tried on at Gatto's last week. The lines were better." He fingered a seam disgustedly. "And the stitches looked like they wouldn't fall out the first time you wore it. The prices they charge in here, and they probably use the same factory as Penney's."

Jimmy moved on to a pile of sweaters. "Who's Penny?"

Tory shook his head, though he had ceased to be amazed. Whenever Jimmy's wallet looked thin his lover or the trust officer at the bank refilled it, and his shopping habits made Tory feel thrifty by comparison. Besides shopping and socializing, he filled his hours with modeling and occasional dates from the escort service. The income was superfluous but he said he liked to keep busy.

"Penney's, darling. Poor people buy clothing there."

"Oh." It was obviously beyond his realm of knowledge.

"Poor people. They're those sad little Biafrans with the swollen stomachs you see in magazine ads for CARE."

"I could never figure out how they get potbellies if they're so hungry." He turned his attention back to the sweaters. "Well, I don't see anything I'm terribly excited about. I guess I'll just take these two. Aren't you buying anything?"

"It's hard for me to get in the mood for winter clothes when it's still ninety out there. Let's pop over to Dimensions to see if they marked down any more of the Valentinos."

"OK. Will you drive up to New York with me one day next week? We can have lunch at La Grenouille and check out what's new on the Avenue."

"Sure. As soon as this heat wave breaks."

Jimmy sighed despondently. "New York's the last place to be in a heat wave, but I have to find cufflinks for Hal's birthday and there's not a thing in Philadelphia."

"You're so devoted, you poor lamb. I hope that man appreciates all you do for him."

Jimmy had little notion of sarcasm and took the remark at face value. "Any man will begin to take you for granted after five years. I really can't complain, he's very good to me."

Tory had to bite back another sarcastic remark. It was no fun to be bitchily clever with someone who apparently didn't have an unkind bone in his body. It was hard for Tory to understand what Jimmy saw in Hal. He was at least forty and good-looking by only the most charitable standards. His money would have been attractive if Jimmy didn't have his own. Jimmy was obviously driven by the need for a father figure, and that drive led him to date older men from the escort service. Hal was tolerant of his little quirks, overlooking them for his many good points. Jimmy was outrageously handsome with dark Irish features, but almost untouched by the snobbery that often accompanies exceptional looks. His congenial personality made up for the less-than-erudite mentality he brought to extensive business socializing.

They walked out into the damp heat of the sidewalk and headed up Walnut Street. "Do you want to go up Wednesday?" Jimmy asked. "We could catch a matinee."

"Let's go Tuesday. I have an appointment Wednesday night and I want to rest up."

Jimmy gave him a concerned look. "I'm worried about you. You're turning into a workaholic. Just like Hal."

Tory laughed at the grain of truth in his observation. "Not quite like Hal. Four tricks and three or four sessions at Ginny's working the phones doesn't even add up to a forty-hour week. I just need something to get me out of the apartment every day."

And my mind off George, he thought. He'd made no progress with him over the summer and the job helped to occupy his mind, besides providing cash to buy substitutes for the reward he felt he'd been temporarily denied.

"Doesn't it get boring?" Jimmy asked. "I mean, when I go out on a date once or twice a week, it's like a little adventure, something fun to do instead of waiting for Hal to come home. But if I had to do it four nights a week I think I'd get bored."

"The novelty of immoral glamour has begun to wear thin," Tory admitted. "But the longer I do it, the less attention I need to devote to it. It's all becoming so predictable."

"You mean like you know what they'll want before you get there?" Jimmy stared at him as if he'd just met a psychic.

"It's no great feat," Tory laughed. "Some of the regulars haven't changed their routines in years. Christ, with Charles Lawson it's like an *I Love Lucy* rerun. But nowhere near as amusing."

Jimmy's attention was suddenly riveted. "They showed the one yesterday morning where she's stomping grapes," he laughed merrily. "I almost choked on my Cheerios."

"Even the out-of-towners are beginning to seem familiar." Tory replied, ignoring the digression. "They all look alike. Fat. And old. And I can usually size them up in the first five minutes and know what the agenda will be in bed. There are only four or five basic categories."

"Categories? You mean like underwear sniffers?"

"Underwear sniffers!" Tory shouted in surprised laughter as they stopped for a red light, then studiously tried to ignore the stare from the woman on the curb beside him.

"You haven't had Sidney the Sniffer yet?" Jimmy asked conversationally. "I won't take him anymore because he likes you to wear the same pair for three or four days before you come over. Then he slips them over his head and you both jerk off. He's a real easy trick if you're not big on taking showers."

"I guess I've still got a lot to learn."

"There are a few like him around," Jimmy shrugged. "Tell me about your categories."

"Oh, my categories. There are only four or five basic types. Sometimes I'll walk into a hotel room and the guy will shake my hand in a certain way, like he wants to make sure I know right from the start what a man he is. There's never any doubt that he intends to be on top, proving to himself what a stud he is. Then there's the guy that sometimes appears butcher than the first one, but there's a furtive, desperate look about him that screams to you he has a wife and kids in the suburbs and he's disgusted with himself for being there. You know he'll have his legs up in the air almost before he hits the mattress. Then there's a certain type that just *reeks* of sex. Any kind, any way, just so he gets his rocks off, maybe three or four times. You can't stroll into Duffy's after a night with him except after doing major repairs to the coiffure. Then there's the guy with a bottle of vodka on the dresser, ice in one of those laminated buckets, and no mixers. He's got half a load on when you arrive and sex is entirely secondary. He's much more interested in having you there to listen to him be incoherent, hear all about his tragic past and how he's been so mistreated and misunderstood. And finally there's our darling on social security. He wants something pretty to show off to his eighty-year-old friends and he's usually happy to rest his hand on your thigh during dinner. Anything more would bring on a stroke."

"You've got it down to a science."

"Simply trying to do my job," Tory shrugged. "Some of us need jobs for mundane things, like paying rent."

"Don't you cry poor to me, Tory Bacher! I know a lot more about money than people give me credit for. When you're not working the phones you're moving clients faster than the escalators at Bloomingdale's. And still signing up for unemployment every week. You could rent a floor at the Barclay with your money."

Tory couldn't deny that his industriousness was providing him with some appreciated financial benefits. By August he was shocked with his weekly income, usually in excess of five hundred dollars without the annoyance of withheld taxes. He lived comfortably but didn't feel he was being extravagant. It all seemed too good to last, and he continued reducing his indebtness with regular monthly payments. The plastic cards that once had given him so much pleasure remained locked in Brad's safe-deposit box.

It was no hardship. There was always plenty of cash. He kept a pair of hundred-dollar bills tucked in the back of his wallet for emergencies and another five hundred tucked away in *Gone with the Wind*. He replenished his wallet from the tens and twenties in the porcelain bowl on his dresser, and the singles that ruined the line of his clothes with an unsightly bulge seemed to multiply in a desk drawer.

It cost little to run the apartment, since he was so rarely there. At-home entertaining consisted of occasional cocktails with the crew before a night out or early-morning omelets after the clubs closed. He spent more money at the liquor store than at the A&P. Mae agreed to come in an extra day a week, though she thought it ridiculous for a one-bedroom apartment. Tory was happy to have the linens changed twice a week and the ashtrays emptied before they overflowed, and he luxuriated in being lazier than ever. He dined in restaurants more often than at home, but someone else usually picked up the check. Cocktails were a major budget item. He liked to buy a round once in a while to let his friends know that he appreciated them. It was apparently traditional for his social group to leave bartenders generous tips, and Tory didn't resent it. He knew so many of them by name, and it seemed only right, besides assuring him special service.

He bought clothing with enthusiasm, but his brush with poverty had made an impression. Instead of shopping frenetically and impulsively as in his credit-card days, he now bought things meant to be worn and worn frequently and not languish away in the corners of the closets. He was proud of his new practicality, and it extended beyond clothes. He bought a Chinese garden seat and painted screen from Charles, at wholesale prices, and they gave him equal pleasure as investments and as additions to his decor.

"I have a lot of expenses, Jimmy. I've whittled the charge accounts down to three grand. Brad's very proud of me."

"Was he that funny little man you introduced me to at DCA last week when Vincent kept shoving poppers up my nose?"

Tory laughed. " 'Funny little man'?"

"I didn't mean funny-looking. You know what I mean, sort of fidgety, like he was expecting a raid any minute. His eyes kept darting around the room. Don't get me wrong, I'm sure he's a nice person. But frankly, I was getting jumpy myself just talking to you for five minutes. Maybe you should shoot him up with some morphine, calm the boy down."

"That's an idea."

"He looks like he'd be a hot number in bed, though. All that nervous energy. I bet he goes on for hours."

Tory raised his eyebrows questioningly. "I wouldn't know."

"Really?"

"Why do you look surprised? We're just friends, known each other since college."

"It's just things you've said about him, how he bullies you about spending your money and complains about the escort service. Since he's not taking care of your wallet, I thought maybe he was taking care of something else."

"No. It's hard to explain. He *is* a pain in the ass, but only because he cares about me. And sometimes he's right. I can get carried away, and he talks me out of some of the more impulsive things I consider doing."

"But no romance, huh?"

"No. Hell, I hardly have time to see him as a friend anymore."

"You don't see much of anybody you knew before you joined the service, do you?"

"Not really. I'm no longer received in respectable social circles."

Jimmy looked at him askance. "Did you really used to hang out with people like that?"

"Just kidding," he smiled. "I doubt that it would bother many of them very much. I'd probably be more uncomfortable about it than they would. There's just nothing to say to them anymore. They're all wrapped up in their little nine-to-five worlds, and I'm rarely out of bed before noon. I was never particularly close with any of them anyway, besides Brad and Mona and Mae."

"When's Mona coming to visit? I'm dying to meet her."

"She's been tied up with business lately. I really wish she could move back," he said wistfully. "Maybe she'll make it for Gloria's surprise party. Have you talked to Doreen lately?"

"Not since last week."

"We had lunch yesterday. She's gone completely bananas with the party, decided her apartment was too small for the crowd and rented the second floor at Elliott's."

"It must be costing her a fortune," Jimmy speculated.

"You're such an innocent." Tory smirked fondly. "Would Doreen spend her own money on something like that?"

"Oh," Jimmy replied after a long pause. "I get it."

"And she's hiring a band and getting a dozen cases of champagne, besides an open bar, and she's running all over the city looking for a bakery to make a cake big enough for dippy Derek to jump out of nude. Won't it be a hoot?"

"I can't wait!"

"And Gloria will probably walk in and not be a bit surprised, just give the crowd one of her exasperated looks and dish anyone who's out of earshot."

"I hope not. I love surprise parties! They're so . . . surprising!"

Tory shook his head again. Most of his new friends didn't seem exceedingly bright about anything not connected with having a good time, but Jimmy made him feel like a Rhodes scholar. At least he was amusing and didn't have a thousand personal problems to unload. In many ways he was a perfect companion for Tory, always ready to shop or sunbathe or gossip over a lunch with no demands for anything but a pleasant time. Tory's only complaint was over his stunning looks, which sometimes made him feel drab by comparison.

"Did she set a date yet?" Jimmy asked. "I hope it's not on a Saturday. Hal always has people in on Saturdays when we stay in town."

"It's the Friday a week before Labor Day. I'll have to ditch old Charles early so I have time to go home and change."

"Poor Charles."

"He's getting out of hand. I'm expecting him to propose any week now."

"You must be giving him what he wants."

"Apparently," Tory answered with a vaguely puzzled look. "It's some part of neurotic compulsion to place me on a pedestal. Sometimes I catch him looking at me with an expression that I've only seen on him when he talks about his Chippendale highboy."

"It must be love."

"It's ridiculous," Tory frowned. "I've always tried to give him his money's worth but I've never done anything to lead him to believe it was anything but a business relationship. Honestly, it has me so distraught I can barely accept gifts from him anymore."

"What did you get last Friday?" Jimmy smiled.

"Another piece of that Indian brass I can't stand. I keep talking antique sterling until I'm sick of hearing it and he comes up with brass."

"What are you going to do with it?"

Tory shrugged. "I just accept everything with a smile and then put the ugly pieces away in the closet. They'll be easy enough to sell, the next time I come upon hard times."

"You're so practical sometimes."

"Sometimes."

"Did you find out any more about your trick in the Franklin last week?"

Tory shrugged again. "I went over his file at Ginny's with a fine-tooth comb and asked everyone I know about him. Nobody noticed anything unusual. I guess a person can travel with a gun and not be a psychopath. I would have never known it was there if I hadn't been looking for matches in the night table while he was in the bathroom."

"I don't know if I could keep it up with a gun two feet away from me."

"It was one of my more challenging performances. Brad's been driving me absolutely paranoid about something like that happening and I was almost ready to make a mad dash for the door."

"Nothing like that's ever happened to me."

"He was actually pretty nice. God knows, I've had ones without guns who were a lot stranger."

"Richard said your baseball player is a sickie."

"He is not!" Tory shouted. "Richard's pissed because I got him on this home stand. Believe me, there was nothing wrong with that man. Hell, I'd have paid *him*."

"Hal showed me his picture on the sports page. Why does someone that handsome have to call the service?"

"Because people know him, Jimmy," he explained patiently. "He can't go out and cruise the bars. If only they could all be like him."

"He's the type that really turns you on?"

"Definitely. I thought I'd smother under all those muscles. What a way to go." He smiled at the memory. "That couple on the Parkway wasn't bad either. Did I tell you about my ménage?"

"Yes."

"Oh." He paused. "Want me to tell you again?"

"If you'd like," Jimmy answered with a vacuously good-natured smile that reminded Tory of Billie Burke in *The Wizard of Oz*. "But I think I remember the story. They were the handsome ones with the cocaine, weren't they?"

"Yes, Jimmy."

"Why don't we stop at Stanley's for a Campari? My throat is positively parched."

"That's a good idea."

"I'm pretty smart sometimes, aren't I?"

"Yes, Jimmy."

They greeted the owner, the bartender, and three other patrons, then settled happily onto barstools. Stanley's was a change of scenery from Duffy's, a place where they were more likely to run into clients than crew. Tory didn't mind being charming to them, though he sometimes resented doing it gratis.

"Shall we get my car from the garage and drive out

to Saks after we do Dimensions? I haven't been there in weeks."

"I can't. I'm relieving Ginny at four."

"Again?"

"You can come and keep me company if you'd like."

"No thanks. Ginny's still mad because I wouldn't do Morrison last week, and I don't want to see her until she cools off." Jimmy gave him a perplexed look. "She's always mad at me."

"The way you turn clients down, I'm not surprised."

"Morrison's no fun." He turned to frown accusingly at Tory. "And you're not much fun either when you're on the phones. You get that efficient look on your face and sound just like Ginny."

"I enjoy being efficient now and then. I could never go back to a job like my last one, but sometimes I miss it a little bit, especially the mass public contact. When I'm in the right mood there's nothing I'd rather do than pick up a telephone and make charming small talk with a client. Besides, it keeps my mind from falling apart, getting myself organized enough to learn a new business routine. It's good to know I can still do it."

"Doesn't Ginny get you nervous?"

"Not so much anymore. She's a tough cookie, but not nearly as tough as she'd have you believe. Besides, lately she seems so grateful just for a chance to get out of the apartment."

"Do you think it's a boyfriend?" Jimmy asked, bringing up one of the latest hot topics among the crowd at Duffy's.

Tory shrugged. "You know as much as I do. She's opening up to me lately about some things. She'll sit around and dish dirt about business. But never much about her private life."

"There's probably enough dirt there to bury half of the respectable family men in Philadelphia," Jimmy speculated with a mischievous laugh.

"I don't think that's it. Ginny's a total professional. She draws a definite line between her business and social lives, and that's all there is to it. She's probably good company away from the service, once she loosens up."

"She likes you a lot. They get catty about it in Duffy's

sometimes, how you seem to be getting more than your share of the good tricks lately."

"There are a few fringes," Tory admitted without much concern for talk at Duffy's. "Last week when I was ready to leave her place and it was raining, she had Eugene drive me home in the Lincoln. I sat in the back seat and tried to look bored for all the curious pedestrians." He laughed. "I could adjust to chauffeured limousines quite easily."

"Are you going home to your family for Labor Day?" Jimmy asked out of the blue.

Tory gave him a blank stare. "Whatever gave you that preposterous idea?" It was part of his image to discuss the family and Stoltz Gove as if they were in a foreign land, with nothing at all to do with a glittering sophisticate such as himself.

"I just thought you might," Jimmy shrugged. "Holidays and all that."

"I'd sooner spend it in the Franklin with that man and his gun."

"What do you tell Claudia you're doing to support yourself?"

"As little as possible. I've always had to edit out some of the more indelicate details of my life in the wicked city from our conversations, but lately there's hardly one thing I can tell her."

"She *must* be suspicious."

"She was down last month and gave the Chinese screen such a look. She knows something about that stuff and that I couldn't have picked it up with my unemployment checks. I told her it was a gift from a guy I was seeing."

"What did she say to that?" Jimmy smiled.

"She said, 'Oh,'" Tory laughed. "Like she was dying to hear more but wasn't really sure if she wanted to. Then the dry cleaner delivered, with a heavy week's worth of clothes plus four pair of slacks I had altered. The bill was about fifty dollars and she just raised her eyebrows as I paid. She knows something is going on, but she won't ask."

"You're probably doing her a favor letting her think you have a rich boyfriend."

"Instead of four or five a week," Tory giggled.

"Well, if you're not going home, why don't you come to our place in Ventnor for the weekend?"

"That would be nice. I'll probably have to come Sunday, though. I imagine I'll be working Saturday night."

"OK. We're doing a Sunday brunch for two of Hal's clients. I'll invite some neighbors in. There's a gorgeous man in the next block, about thirty-five, blond, well-to-do-and unattached as of two weeks ago. You'll like him."

"Oh please," Tory muttered.

Jimmy gave him a frustrated frown. "Don't be so negative, Tory. You haven't even met him."

"A holiday is supposed to be a change from the normal routine. This is like inviting Duncan Hines for coffee and cake."

"What you do to earn a living and coming to my house to meet a nice man are two different things. This isn't just sex, this could be romance."

"Who the hell needs it?"

"Sometimes you're so cynical I don't know what's wrong with you."

Tory exhaled smoke with a total lack of concern. "I've just had it up to my earlobes with men."

Jimmy sipped his drink through a long pause. "Guess who I had a drink with yesterday."

"Who?"

"George Keller."

Tory fixed him with a frown. "That was unkind and not at all like you, James."

"It's for your own good. I've known George since I flunked out of art school, and I don't like to see you wasting your time. If he said he's not interested he means it."

"But he *is* interested. He's just being silly about it."

"I agree with you. He needs someone like you so he won't always walk around with that nasty scowl on his face. I tried to reason with him——"

"You didn't!"

"Of course I did. We're old friends."

"Now I can crawl under the floorboards the next time he shows up at Duffy's. How could you do this to me?"

"Don't be a dumbbell. We had a friendly little chat and I made you sound like a saint. He agreed with me completely, but he just isn't interested in getting involved, never has been. And when his mind is made up there's no sense trying to be logical with him."

"What did he say about me?"

"Oh, just tons of wonderful things! But it doesn't make any difference. He's not going to change. I called you the other day when you were out and had a long talk with Mae. She's absolutely right. You've got to stop moping around and try to get interested in someone else."

Tory didn't actually mope about George. The first few weeks had been saturated in self-pity, but that came as no surprise to him. Knowing where he stood and responding with a logical set of emotions was more therapeutic than the weeks of uncertainty. After he'd made Mae and Mona sufficiently miserable with his problem, he was able to cope with it better.

Besides, he was nowhere near to writing the whole thing off. George had left him room for a small ray of hope, and with Tory's powers of rationalization, it soon became a matter of ironing out a few kinks that stood in their way. He was confident that George would eventually see things in their proper perspective, and he was always ready to give the process a gentle nudge. Tory knew the places they were most likely to bump into each other, and he adjusted his schedule to be there more frequently, always carefully groomed and with attractive company. On the occasions when his hunch was correct, he gave George a cordial but casual greeting, hoping his mere presence was as maddeningly tempting to George as George's was to him. As he began to spend more time at Ginny's, he sometimes had reason to call George and set up an appointment. It gave him a special satisfaction to play the upper hand in an employer-employee relationship. He didn't know if George's discomfort at these times was helping or hurting his cause but it was a small release for his frustration.

If life wasn't perfect, at least it wasn't beyond hope. Tory still had plenty of hope, and a patient determination refueled it constantly. It made the pain of a failed romance unnecessary and gave him something to strive for, a project to exercise his wits. Sometimes when he was extremely tired or a sentimental memory of David took him unaware, he lapsed into a depression. But it quickly passed. And it gave him another tool to cope

with the bad moments, the intuitive notion that someday soon it would all be like the old days.

"Who's moping?" Tory asked. "I never had so much
fun."

"I thought you were having fun too, but Mae explained
it to me. 'Having fun and being happy are two different
things.'" Jimmy lapsed into profound thought. "It makes
me wonder if I'm happy myself."

Tory patted his hand. "Don't worry about it, dear.
Ignorance is bliss."

"What's that mean?"

Chapter Thirteen

THE telephones were quiet that afternoon except for the usual four-o'clock rush. July and August were slow months in general, with so many of the regular clients out of town. Tory kept himself entertained with calls to Doreen and Carl, and one incoming business call that he completed as Ginny returned from the beauty salon.

"Ginny! What a beautiful job he did on your hair!" Tory enthused from the Regency desk.

"Thanks," she replied warily. "It's the same thing he's done for the past month."

"And that dress! So chic! You certainly do have flawless taste."

"It's one of the old rags I always wear to the hairdresser."

"And those shoes!"

"All right," she said in an unkidding tone as she reached for her messages. "Skip the shit and get to the point. What the hell do you want?"

"An assignment."

"Your baseball player gets a different boy each visit unless he asked for you again."

"The team's in Cincinnati, it's someone else. His name's Michael Weiss."

Ginny thumbed through the messages and appointment card. "Michael's back in town?" she asked with half a mind. "He's a gem. If only he'd stay put here."

"Can I have him?"

138

"Didn't he ask for George? They were a fairly steady thing last time he was in town."

"He wants George but he needs someone for his friend too."

"A little double date?" she smirked. "Wouldn't that be cozy? Why don't you give up and stop chasing that poor man?"

"I'm not chasing him," Tory sniffed. "I'm just letting him know I'm available."

"The point's been made."

"He's crazy about me. Just a bit jumpy about getting tied down. He needs a little encouragement to come to his senses. Wouldn't it give you a warm glow to help the course of true love?"

"Not particularly."

"Wouldn't we make a beautiful couple?"

"It's enough to drive a woman to homicide at the waste of it all."

"Please, Ginny." He used the unhappy-little-boy expression that could sometimes work wonders. "Give me this assignment and I'll never complain about a troll again."

She tried to sound harder than usual. "I'm going to check with George before I give you a definite yes. If you're going to make him uncomfortable, the clients are the ones who will suffer."

"What are you going to say to him? Don't make it sound like I'm being aggressive."

Ginny raised her eyebrows disdainfully. "Who the hell do I look like, Helen Hayes? He's going to see through whatever I say."

"Tell him that everyone else is booked."

"It's as good an excuse as any," she shrugged. "Is it for a weekend night?"

"Yes. The last one in September."

Ginny quickly glanced up from her messages with a knowing look. "What are you neglecting to tell me?"

"What's to tell?" he asked innocently.

"Is this one of Michael's Caribbean jaunts?"

"Didn't I mention that?" he replied guiltily. "Three days in Freeport."

"Forget it," she commanded. "I promised the next trip to Derek."

"Derek!" Tory sputtered. "Mr. Weiss doesn't want Derek. Would *you* like to spend three days with Derek?"

"God forbid. But I stuck him with a string of trolls last February when everyone was out with the flu and he wheedled it out of me. I can't go back on a promise."

"How about if he breaks his leg?"

"Just forget the whole thing."

Tory had no intention of forgetting the whole thing and racked his brain in impotent rage for the remainder of the day. It all seemed so unfair, his perfect chance arbitrarily snatched away. All because of empty-headed, egotistical, boring Derek with his wheat germ and barbells.

Several solutions crossed his mind, but they all seemed too drastic. His flippant remark about Derek breaking a bone could be brought to reality with a few phone calls and a few hundred dollars. It could be done humanely, a simple fracture to put him in a cast for a few weeks. Or with a bit of fieldwork, he could arrange for one of Derek's tricks to give him the clap. The timing would be important, but it seemed more humane than a broken limb and something he was sure that Derek had coped with many times before. Then there was the Haitian woman he'd heard of from Mae who could put a spell on him, give him migraine headaches or a rash. He didn't doubt Mae's word but it seemed risky nonetheless.

Tory was still speculating over how low he was willing to sink when he joined Jimmy at the Society Hill Swim Club the next afternoon. He'd expected no more than sympathetic words from Jimmy and was astounded when he came up with a constructive idea.

"I know Michael Weiss," he said with an offhand naïveté. "Hal rents him some warehouses. He imports wine."

Tory's eyes widened hungrily. "How well do you know him?"

"We entertain him almost everytime he's in town," Jimmy answered blithely. "He's a lot of fun. I have nothing against Derek, but he's definitely not Michael's type."

"What type is he? Have you balled him?"

"No. That's where Hal draws the line. He thinks it's bad enough that I have this strange hobby, but if his clients were also my clients . . . "

A spark of hope began to rekindle in Tory's mind. "Do you think he'd be more *my* type?"

"Heavens, yes," Jimmy replied. "He says the funniest things and likes someone who can laugh and have a good time. You'd be perfect for him."

"Can you introduce us?"

"Sure," Jimmy answered brightly. "I'll have Hal invite him for dinner."

"OK," Tory replied thoughtfully.

"What's wrong?"

Tory pondered while he applied Bain de Soleil. "I don't doubt that I can make him find me attractive, but I'll have to be dazzling to persuade him to change Ginny's plans to send Derek on the trip."

"I'll invite Derek too. Michael will spend fifteen minutes with him and beg you to take his place. They're really not cut out for each other."

"That would look too obvious." The more devious wheels of Tory's mind began to spin. "Don't invite Derek. And don't mention a word about the trip to Michael."

"OK," Jimmy agreed pleasantly.

"And don't invite anyone else who will hold his attention for long. Have some of Hal's more tedious friends over."

"OK."

"Let's keep it under ten. And let's make it a barbecue on the terrace so I can wear something informal and revealing."

"OK." Jimmy looked confused but readily agreed.

Jimmy launched into his new project with happy enthusiasm. He arranged the party for the week after Labor Day and called Tory several times a day with progress reports and pointers on charming Mr. Weiss. The other guests were meticulously chosen for their dull natures, costuming was discussed at length, and the doorman was instructed to send Tory upstairs at Jimmy's signal. Jimmy said it was almost as much fun as Gloria's surprise party.

They synchronized their Cartiers on the day of the party and Tory had to wait only a few minutes in the lobby for the buzz that signaled the first lull. He swept into the room on a cloud of poise and vivacity, created by equal parts of his own personality and Ritalin. He would have been a focal point of the gathering without theatrics, the balmy September evening being a good excuse for thin linen slacks and a Danskin tank top. An open silk shirt that hung loosely from his shoulders saved the outfit from total obviousness. It was carefully put together to provide occasional glimpses of more than a proper amount of glowing tan flesh, more eye-catching than if he'd come shirtless.

Mr. Weiss quickly and willingly took him captive on a sofa. Tory was pleasantly surprised by him. He'd heard that he was an attractive man but discounted that as Ginny's usual pep-talk exaggeration and Jimmy's unorthodox taste. He judged him to be slightly under forty and aging well. Despite a very prominent nose and a thickening jawline, he had a pleasing, masculine face. A small roll of fat around his middle and muscles that had begun to go to flab didn't completely obscure a broad-shouldered, well-proportioned frame. By Tory's professional standards, he was a prize. By his personal standards, he was definitely not beyond consideration. His personality quickly erased any minor reservations. He seemed as intent on charming Tory as Tory was on charming him, a perfect encouragement to his wit and vivacity. Tory thrived on it. Within an hour he was sure he had him mesmerized and was pleasantly shocked to realize that he'd enjoyed himself in the process. When Mr. Weiss invited him home for the evening he accepted with no more hesitation than seemed appropriate. He insisted only that they stop first for a drink at Duffy's, so he could give an important message to a friend.

They took a booth at Duffy's and Mr. Weiss ordered Dom Pérignon, insisting that as an importer of fine wines he had a moral obligation to drink only the best. Tory didn't object too strenuously. The friend who was to receive the message mysteriously never appeared, but Derek was on his usual stool at the bar drinking grapefruit juice. Tory decided that it was only polite to invite him to their booth, and good manners dictated that he encourage him in conversation. Derek needed little encouragement and began his usual monologue on nutrition and bodybuilding. Tory launched into a defense of the vitamins in fine wine and watched Mr. Weiss keep a polite silence as Derek criticized his argument roundly.

They left when Tory decided that his elusive friend wasn't going to show, much to his escort's relief. Tory generously defended Derek, allowing that he might be somewhat egotistical but had compensating good qualities. He couldn't give a specific example but he said that Ginny must think highly of him or she wouldn't be sending him to Freeport with a very important client. He was overcome with surprise when Mr. Weiss explained he was that client. When he suggested later that night that the arrangement with Ginny could be altered, Tory managed a mild protest about hurting his friend Derek's feelings.

Tory took a deep breath before answering the telephone the next afternoon.

"Where have you been?" Jimmy shouted excitedly. "I've been trying to get you all day!"

"Please," he sighed in six syllables. "If you only knew what I've been through today. It's enough to make me break out."

"You were doing fine last night. What happened?"

"Michael had to rush off for an appointment this morning, so I stopped at the Latimer for coffee on my way home," he began to explain.

"You spent the night?"

"How could you doubt it, my child?"

"I didn't. The way you two were carrying on, I was expecting you to do it on the sofa."

"He's crazy about me. Though I almost lost him when you were making faces at me from across the room. I practically cracked up in the middle of a sentence."

"I couldn't believe my eyes," Jimmy replied in awe. "I've watched professionals work before, but you were amazing."

"Yes," Tory agreed complacently. "Anyway, I was walking down Walnut after coffee and Eugene drove by. He said I better not let Ginny find me this morning or she'd tear me apart with her bare hands. I said, 'Why, whatever for?' in my most innocent Mary Pickford voice. I really didn't think anything could have happened while I was having coffee, but apparently Michael got on the phone right after I left and insisted that Ginny send me to Freeport instead of Derek."

"You're incredible."

"I couldn't have done it without your help."

"It was the most fun I've had in ages! I felt like we were Lucy and Ethel trying to pull one over on Ricky. And it worked!"

"Of course it did. Anyway, I got home and the phone was ringing off the hook. I knew it had to be Ginny, the rings had an angry tone to them."

"What did she say?"

"I wasn't about to answer. At least not until I'd had a couple Bloody Marys. It kept ringing every fifteen minutes. Finally around one I picked it up."

"Was she really evil?"

"You'd have thought I'd kidnapped the Lindbergh baby. She was truly unkind, like I've never heard her."

"I could have told you that. You haven't seen mean until you do something that she doesn't like. Take it from me."

"I didn't expect her to take it so seriously. Honestly, what's the big deal? Michael decided he'd rather take *me* to Freeport. It's his prerogative, isn't it?"

"Not the way she sees it."

"She got incredibly nasty. Called me all sorts of rude names, told me I was despicable and a brazen bitch."

"You'll get over it."

"Yes, but that was just the beginning. Then she threatened me, said I stole a client from the service and could be dealt with severely. You know what that means," he said ominously.

"She wouldn't." He paused. "Would she? I mean it wasn't like you did her out of a commission."

"That's what *I* said. Is it my fault that my social life includes some of her clients? And why shouldn't I do it free? He's an attractive man."

"Isn't he?"

"A prince. Attractive, witty, charming, generous. He sprang for Dom Pérignon at Duffy's."

"He always does. I think he gets a commission."

"And not bad in bed. Not bad at all."

"He has that look about him. Those are definitely bedroom eyes."

"That's not the only feature of his anatomy that says 'bedroom.' "

"Big?"

Tory sighed contentedly. "I can't wait to tell Mona."

"Ginny's not really going to have you roughed up, is she?"

"No. She said she wouldn't be surprised if Derek throws a few punches, though. I guess I'll steer clear of Duffy's for a while. But get this. She says that what I did was the same as stealing money from Derek's pocket, and she's going to make it up to him out of my pay."

"I think you'd rather be roughed up." Jimmy laughed.

"And besides that, I'm on troll duty for the rest of the month."

"You knew that would happen. Is it worth it? It means at least three nights with Mr. Softee."

"Don't remind me," Tory said darkly. "He wouldn't be so bad if he'd just accept it as a fact of life. But you have to give it the old college try for a couple of hours before he'll give up. It's got to be the most boring thing in the world."

"And you'll have Pearson at least twice."

"He's even worse," Tory moaned. "With him it's up but it just won't come. And you have to keep working on it until your jaw's ready to dislocate. And he's just as bad the other way around. I swear, he must have his incisors sharpened."

"Ginny's probably happy to have an excuse to shove them all off on somebody."

"I don't think she knows that you had anything to do with it, so you're safe."

"What can she do to me?" Jimmy laughed. "She knows I don't need the job."

"Just the father figures." ·

"What are they?"

"Forget it," Tory laughed.

Jimmy readily acquiesced and changed the subject. "So was it all worth it? After all this, you better come home from Freeport with George on a leash."

"I don't know. I must be wearing him down, though. I'm so ubiquitous."

"Maybe you should concentrate on Michael. He'd treat you so well. You could get an apartment in our building and we could go to Saks every day."

"Wouldn't that be fun? Like a couple of JAPs. Get our hair done twice a week and bitch about our maids."

"Redecorate every two years."

"Do charity luncheons."

"Join a country club."

"Have affairs with younger men."

"Winters in Florida."

"Weekends in New York."

"You really ought to give it some thought."

"I should."

"You won't, though. You know," Jimmy said, impressed with his insight, "as cynical as you try to be, you're a dyed-in-the-wool romantic."

"One more try, Jimmy. If it doesn't work this time, I'll give up and go for the big bucks. But it's going to work."

Chapter Fourteen

TORY took small but regular sips of his vodka martini at the airport bar. Flying didn't actually terrify him, but it wasn't something he looked forward to. He knew that his sense of imminent disaster upon takeoff was ridiculous, but the thought was with him on every flight. He tried to concentrate on the bright side. At least he was getting a vacation, always a good reason to plan a set of outfits, pack them all in the Vuitton luggage, and feel more glamorous and sophisticated than usual. Flying first-class also helped him deal with his foreboding, expecially since it wasn't costing him a cent. And George was on the stool next to him and would hardly be out of his sight for three days, reason to risk far more than two hours unnaturally suspended in the stratosphere. He drained the second glass with a grimace and immediately signaled the bartender for a refill. Another advantage of the fear of flying was that it made insobriety more socially acceptable.

"One more and I think I'll be able to save you the embarrassment of a hysterical scene with the stewardess."

George smiled indulgently. "You should be more worried about Derek coming in here swinging a barbell. He still has a few minutes."

"He's getting over it. God knows, I've paid him back with interest. He's gotten all my decent tricks for the past three weeks."

"Serves you right."

Tory flashed him a martyred look. "I only did it for you, George. I'm just too soft-hearted. I couldn't bear the thought of you having to put up with Derek for an entire weekend. This trip means nothing to me. You should thank me instead of casting stones and aspersions with the rest of them."

"I *am* grateful," he laughed. "You may be unprincipled and cruel and deceitful and despicable and ruthless and all the other things everyone agrees that you are, but at least you're entertaining."

"Thanks," Tory said drily, then leaned closer and lowered his voice seductively. "But aren't you afraid I'll compromise you?"

George remained unruffled. "Michael and his friend will keep us too busy for anything to happen."

His lips turned up slowly in a smug smile. "Then it *is* a temptation?"

George pressed his knee to Tory's in reply. "You're shameless."

"Michael won't be down until seven. Do you think you can hold out that long?"

"I think I'll make it."

Tory disgustedly lit another Gauloise. "You could have at least pretended to think it over before answering. Such moral resolve isn't very fashionable, you know. What's Michael doing in New York, anyway?"

"Something about a possible dock strike. He had to make contingency arrangements for air freight from Marseilles, so he'll catch the afternoon flight from New York."

"Industrious little devil, isn't he?"

"That's how he can afford to pop down to Freeport for the weekend with a couple of hustlers."

"Speak for yourself," Tory replied loftily. "I've decided to refer to myself as a courtesan."

"You're a latter-day Madame Du Barry," George agreed sardonically.

"Yes."

"They guillotined her, you know."

"Poor dear."

"Drink up. It's time to go."

Tory relaxed after takeoff. If he didn't look out the window he could almost forget that he was airborne. The cloth napkins and glasses that weren't sharp-edged plastic ones helped to reduce his discomfort, as did the thought of the claustrophobic coach seats thankfully behind a curtain.

"Talk to me, George. Tell me something fascinating so I'll forget we're flying."

"I'm fresh out of fascinating stories."

"Tell me about yourself."

"That's not very fascinating."

"Tell me anyway. I want to know all about you." George gave him a wary glance. "Don't be shy," Tory coaxed playfully. "Tell me all about your unhappy childhood."

"What makes you think it was unhappy?"

"Wasn't everyone's?"

"Was yours?"

"I guess it was fair as childhoods go. Tedious, but not terribly traumatic."

"Mine could have been worse."

"Were you born and raised in the city?"

"Mostly in New Jersey. In and around Trenton. We moved a lot."

"Do you have brothers and sisters?"

"No," he replied thoughtfully. "But I used to have a Doberman."

"We had a cocker spaniel once but my mother didn't like dog hair on the furniture."

"Mine didn't mind the hair but my old man got pissed when Mickey bit him. Sent him to the ASPCA."

"Why did Mickey bite him?"

"He came home in the middle of a bad drunk one night and started beating up on my mother."

"Sounds like a charming fellow."

George smiled pensively. "He was. Most times. Every now and then he'd go on a bourbon binge and lose his paycheck in a card game. I learned to stay out of his way when it happened."

"Do you see much of him?"

"Not since my mother died. He took off. I used to get letters, but not in a couple of years."

"How old were you when your mother died?"

"Fifteen. Old enough to deal with it."

"Was she Irish and beautiful?"

"How did you know that?" George smiled in faint surprise.

"It's written all over your face. So you were without parents at fifteen. What did you do?"

"My grandmother put me in boarding school."

"That sounds depressing. Were you a problem child?"

"Not at all. I was quiet, studious, always did my homework on time."

"Were you on the football team? I had a crush on Stoltz Grove High's first and second strings. For several years running."

"I wrestled and played soccer."

"A macho even back then."

"You really have a grudge against masculine gays, don't you?"

"I guess I do. I've decided that you're not faking it, but some of those denim queens remind me of Ava Gardner trying to pass for white in *Showboat*."

"I'm for real," George laughed. "But I can understand what you're talking about. Some of them would probably be happier if they let themselves camp it up and swish a little. Like you."

Tory fixed him with a disdainful stare. "I may not be Clint Eastwood but I do *not* swish."

"You know what I mean. You don't repress your unmasculine side. It takes a certain amount of balls to do that, and I admire you for it."

"It's not balls. Men like to think that manliness is the only real virtue, but most true strength is feminine."

George gave him a long, puzzled look before replying, "That's either totally absurd or too deep for me to comprehend."

Tory gave him a blank stare. "Me too. Sometimes I say these things off the top of my head and with the right intonation they sound so profound. Let's talk about your sex life instead."

"It's only a two-hour flight."

"When did you start?"

"The usual fooling around during puberty, I guess. After school with some buddies, that sort of thing."

"I had a cousin who made me do nasty things in the woods." Tory smiled dreamily. "How I loved those family picnics."

"It must have been nice to grow up in an affectionate family."

"They had their moments," he laughed. "I hardly see them anymore, just for an occasional wedding or funeral. But back then we'd all go to Uncle Joe's farm for holidays, about a thousand aunts and uncles and a couple battalions of cousins. It used to look like they evacuated South Philly and sent them all upstate."

"That's your mother's side of the family?"

"The deLucas," Tory said with a trace of pride. "Stoltz Grove has never recovered."

"Why the hell did they settle up there?"

"I don't know," Tory shrugged. "Uncle Joe was my grandmother's oldest brother, and somehow he had money. Everyone's always been very vague about where it came from, but I have my suspicions. God knows why he decided to settle up there, but he did. He bought a huge farm and the family just flocked there, like they were the serfs and peasants and he was a medieval baron. He scared me to death."

"What did he do to scare you?"

"Nothing, really. He was basically a warm-hearted man, a benevolent dictator, as far as I can recall him. But he used to sit in a big chair at the end of this huge living room. When we'd visit, which was about once a month, I had to go up to him and give him a kiss. Then he'd pinch my ear and look in his hand and say he found a quarter behind it. That was always the inducement that gave me the nerve to go up and give him the kiss."

"A hustler even back then," George laughed.

Tory looked at him thoughtfully. "I never considered that angle of it. Interesting. Until I was about four, I had a strong suspicion that he was actually God."

"Is he still alive?"

"No. He died when I was in second grade. The funeral was like a De Mille production," Tory laughed. "A cast of thousands. Then as soon as they had him in the ground they started fighting over the money and sold the farm to a developer. Now all that's left to remember him is deLuca Drive, with split-levels on each side."

"It's hard to picture you out there with the cows and chickens."

"Gingham didn't become me," Tory deadpanned as he sipped his wine. "Tell me more about you. So you were a brilliant student and a star on the wrestling team and then went on to get a degree in finance?"

George smiled. "Why talk about it? It looks like you have all the answers."

"Sometimes Jimmy's memory isn't too reliable. I want to be sure I have all the facts straight. After you graduated, you went to work at the bank and were on your way to a successful career when one day you just up and quit. Did a teller say something annoying?"

"Every day for a year someone said something annoying. Or shot me an evil glance if they thought the pattern of my tie was too loud, that sort of thing. This was back when those things were still important. Then my grandmother died and all of a sudden I had six thousand dollars. It seemed a fortune at the time, enough to open a restaurant anyway."

"I never heard this part of the story."

"I'm appalled at your sloppy research. I got a partner with big ideas and plenty of enthusiasm. Between the two of us we had three summers of busboy experience. But who needs experience when you're a young genius? To make a long story short, we ran it into the ground at the speed of light and almost murdered each other in the process."

"And there you were, no family to turn to and up to your handsome Adam's apple in debt. You had no alternative but to sell your innocent young flesh."

"The circumstances weren't quite that pathetic. I managed to salvage a couple thousand dollars out of it, and I could have gone back to work easily enough. But I didn't want to. The restaurant was a total fiasco, but it opened my eyes, made me realize exactly how much I hated the nine-to-five grind. And the ass-kissing to get ahead. I discovered that I liked calling the shots. I got a job as a bartender at the Cellar. With the tips and no taxes I was doing better than at the bank. And as soon as they got on my nerves at the Cellar I told them to go fuck themselves and became a waiter at Morgan's. Then I was a maitre d', then a bartender again, then I went to Mexico and drank Dos Equis for a summer. It's not a bad life if you don't mind the instability."

"Where does Gary fit into all of this?"

George laughed. "You didn't miss that part, did you?

Gary was around back then. You'd have liked him. He switched jobs more than I did—we used to have a lot of fun. We lived together for a while until he floated off to New Orleans. I still hear from him now and then."

"Tell me the rest of it," Tory demanded. "I heard from Carl that it was a hot affair and when he left you were heartbroken and haven't had a serious affair since."

George gave him an irked frown. "That's ridiculous. We were good friends back then, that's all. We slept together sometimes but it was never more than horniness. There were no broken hearts."

"Never?"

"Not unless you want to count a broken engagement when I was a junior in college," he laughed.

"You were engaged?"

"Yeah."

"To a girl?"

"That's the way it's usually done."

"I'd like to scratch her eyes out, leading on a foolish young lad like you. How could you do something so perverse?"

"It still happens under the right circumstances."

"I don't care to hear about it," Tory sniffed.

"She was a sweet little thing, old Mary Ann. I'm sure she found a bright young executive and she's out there in the suburbs going to PTA meetings."

"A fate worse than death," Tory shuddered.

"Not for her. And at the time, I thought it was what I wanted too."

"How did you escape?"

"I guess we realized in time that it wouldn't work out."

"So there's no sad affair in your past that has ruined you for the romantic schemes of an eligible young single person such as myself?"

"Sorry."

"So am I, it was a convenient excuse. So when did you meet Ginny?"

"A million years ago," George laughed. "Back when I was bartending I was out every night after work, partying it up just like you. Ginny was a party girl too, except she was getting cash for it. But she always had that mind up there just clicking away. When she opened the escort service and offered me a job I took it."

"Just like that?"

"You're shocked by my morals?" George asked with a hint of sarcasm. "It wasn't really a big step. I'd been free-lancing once in a while, things I stumbled into at the bars. So when Ginny opened up it was no big thing for me to go pro."

"What's made you decide to retire?"

"I'm no chicken anymore," he shrugged as he lit a Marlboro. "It's time to go back and see what's happening in the real world."

"The real world," Tory spat. "Who needs it? Give me parties and neon lights."

"The novelty will wear off soon enough," he replied wearily. "You'll find out. Because you've got a mind in there somewhere. The party life is fine for most of the crowd at Duffy's. Because it's about all they're equipped to handle. You're not really one of them."

Tory looked bereft. "I hope you're wrong. The night I can't enjoy a party is the night I throw in the towel."

"There are other things."

He lowered his eyes and attempted to look demure. "I guess I wouldn't miss the parties so much if I had someone to come home to."

"You don't need someone else. Enjoy your own company."

"How isolationist. I'm a social creature. I don't want to be a hermit."

"Like me?"

Tory searched for the words to express himself without offending George. "I can see the benefits of being self-sufficient, but it has its drawbacks too. The more a person depends upon himself, the less open he is to outside stimuli. I love peace and quiet when I get up in the mornings, and I can enjoy an afternoon with a good book. But I'd get lonely not being around people most of the time." He looked at George in puzzlement. "What do you do with yourself all day long?"

He shrugged. "I keep busy."

"You go to the gym. You read a lot. You take long rides in your Volvo. What else do you do?"

"Ski. Swim. Ride my bicycle."

"You're exhausting me just talking about it."

"And I'm not always alone. I play tennis. And fly."

"Airplanes?"

"And helicopters. They're even more fun, in a way. You can just hover around up there like a big dragonfly. I'll take you for a ride sometime."

"Thanks, but I'll wave to you from the observation deck. If God had meant for us to fly He wouldn't have given us Henry Ford and the QE2." He sighed wistfully. "If only parlor cars would come back into vogue."

"I saw one for sale last month. Someone could make it into a great little restaurant."

"Is that what you're going to do when you leave Ginny?"

"Another two years and I'll have the cash to do it in style. An elegant little place out in the country."

"Perhaps you should consider a field other than restaurants," Tory suggested with a vaguely caustic gentleness.

"Bull-headed, aren't I? But I've worked them since then. I know what makes a restaurant tick now. And I've still got to be my own boss. I could never go back to a bank."

Tory's eyelashes batted with abandon. "Do you need a charming maître d'?"

"No thanks."

"There must be an easier way to get rich," he sighed.

"Being born poor cuts down the alternatives. People like us who don't get breaks can be either rich or respectable."

Tory examined his new gold signet ring from Van Cleef and Arpels. "Respectability never did anything nice for me."

"It's an acquired taste," George replied smugly.

"There must be a way to have them both. How much do you think I'd need to retire?"

"And just live off the interest? In the style to which you've so quickly become accustomed? You might be able to make ends meet on half a million in tax-free municipals."

Tory frowned.

"That's only ten thousand more tricks," George calculated rapidly. "Start doing six a day and save it all, you can retire in five years."

"If it didn't kill me."

"It will drive you crazy before it kills you. You've

been at it almost six months now—the glamour will start to fade soon."

"And one day I'll be sipping wine in first-class on the way to the Bahamas and throw back my hands in surrender and say, 'I can't go on, it's just too, too dreary'?"

"No. You'll wake up one morning after a bad trick and look in the mirror and realize that thirty is just around the corner. If you wise up before then, you'll have started to stash some money away and be able to get out with some dignity."

"Maybe Jimmy is right. Maybe I should give up on you and find a rich man to take me away from all this."

"Charles Lawson would grab you in a minute."

"He's only affluent," Tory smirked. "I want someone who's filthy rich. Jackie O is my role model."

"You're incorrigible," George laughed. "Wise up and start saving your money instead of putting it all on your back. In a few years you can be giving the orders."

"The only orders I want to give are to my shirtmaker. 'I'll take six of these in linen and a dozen of those in silk.'"

George shook his head in dismay. "If you weren't so goddam dizzy I'd probably fall for you in a minute."

The customs line moved smoothly, a quick formality that didn't give Tory a chance to become impatient. He spent the fifteen-minute wait secretly enjoying the other passengers' curious glances at his signature luggage and linen suit. Besides, the status of an additional stamp in the back of his passport made it time well spent. He was slightly perturbed with himself for finding fault with the balmy air and cloudless sky. It seemed something of a waste with the temperature at home still hovering in the seventies. He began to hope for a similar run of luck with a client in the dead of the coming winter.

He maintained his unimpressed demeanor when a waiting driver whisked their luggage into a Cadillac and drove them to the hotel while the other vacationers milled about waiting for their tour guides to organize them. They arrived at the hotel in a few minutes, a standard commercial establishment designed with the typical middle-class American tourist in mind. Tory assumed that he'd be comfortable, but after a few stays at the Pierre in New

York, he was unimpressed. He quickly cased the lobby shops and the other guests while George took care of formalities at the desk.

George joined him a few minutes later, a puzzled smile on his face, room keys and an open envelope in his hand. "You're not going to believe this."

Tory's mind refused to allow anything to spoil what had so far been a pleasant day. "If it's bad news, I don't want to hear it."

"Michael's tied up in New York for the weekend. He and his friend canceled."

"Derek must have kidnaped them," he replied with a total lack of concern. "I don't care. Let's stay. I have my American Express."

George surreptitiously exposed the corners of the five one-hundred-dollar bills in the envelope. "The note says that this should cover anything we can't charge to the suite and credit has been arranged at the casino for us."

Tory laughed, not terribly surprised. "I knew that man was a gentleman." His mind raced with thoughts of how far he could safely abuse the carte blanche. "Let's go to the room and order champagne. Michael would want it that way."

He was so occupied with gleefully greedy thoughts of the windfall that it wasn't until the elevator door closed behind them that he realized he'd be alone with George for three days. The thought was strangely unnerving, coming as unexpectedly as it did. Events were proceeding at a pace beyond his hopes, a pace he wasn't prepared to cope with. An abrupt nervousness gripped him as he glanced at George from the corner of his eye. His expression was serene and inscrutable. Either George didn't grasp the nuances of the situation yet, or he grasped them and didn't find them a problem, or he understood them completely and was looking forward to them with predatory anticipation. Tory read each interpretation at least twice during the eight-floor ride.

The bellhop led them to a corner suite with a sitting room and two bedrooms. It wasn't necessary to order champagne. A bottle of Dom Pérignon was waiting for them, along with flowers and hors d'oeuvres. Tory tried to camouflage his edginess with the motions of filling two glasses.

"I think I can cope with this for a few days," he speculated with what he hoped would pass for a nonchalent tone. "I won't know how to act, though," he added absentmindedly as he held out a glass, "without having to ball for all of it." He felt the blood rush to his face as he caught George's wisp of a lustful smile. He no longer had any doubt as to how to interpret the inscrutable expression.

George's hand lingered on his for an unnecessarily long moment as he took the glass, an unnervingly devilish glint in his blue eyes. Tory was relieved to have the glass removed from his hand, which was beginning to shake, and he held his breath in anticipation, helplessly trying to brace himself for the next step of his undoubtedly approaching seduction. George sipped calmly without speaking, and Tory turned away with mixed feelings of frustration and adolescent panic. He sank into the sofa unsteadily, momentarily concentrating on the champagne and smoked salmon to avoid George's eyes. He looked up when he thought he'd collected himself sufficiently, but George was still standing in the same position, the same alarming gaze in his eyes over the upraised glass.

"Well? Are you going to stand there all day?" He hoped his voice projected a calmness and sophistication he didn't feel. "Sit down. Relax. Have some Nova."

George moved slowly and deliberately to the sofa, arranging his bent leg on the cushion within inches of Tory's thigh. Tory knew that the heat bridging the short distance must be a product of his imagination.

"Try the pâté, it's delicious."

"No thanks," George replied evenly, without removing his eyes from Tory's.

"Oh, go ahead. There's plenty of time before dinner." Dinner seemed like an excellent topic to change the subject he wasn't sure he wanted changed. He couldn't understand how he could have worked for weeks to create a situation and then resist it when it finally came to pass. It seemed completely without logic, but his behavior often confused him. "Let's go to the restaurant on the far side of the lobby. I looked over the menu while you were checking in, and it seems decent." He moved to the telephone on the desk. "I'll make a reservation. What time do you want to go?"

George's self-assured shadow of a smile was becoming almost as annoying as it was unnerving. "Late."

Watching George remove his shoes and jacket as he dialed, Tory cursed himself for becoming even more on edge. He was sure that he sounded totally scatterbrained as he tried to get connected to the nameless restaurant and drained his glass nervously as he waited. George glided to his side with the same deliberate movement, the champagne bottle in hand. Tory tried not to notice the crotch so excruciatingly close to his shoulder as the champagne was poured. He needed several moments to remember the purpose of the call when a voice finally answered and another moment to remember the name for the reservation.

"I made it for nine," he said as he hung up the telephone. He didn't understand why he was repeating something he'd said audibly on the phone seconds before, but there were a number of things he didn't understand at the moment.

George had returned to the sofa. He patted the cushion next to him and fixed Tory with a steady stare. "Come over here so you don't have to shout."

Tory couldn't suppress a startled smile as he spilled champagne on his slacks. "My nerves must still be shook up from the flight." He knew it was a feeble excuse but felt that he had to make one for his mortifying lack of poise.

George smiled back, obviously enjoying the reaction he was evoking. It was the same cat-and-mouse game of their previous encounters, the one George always seemed to win. "I never realized how high-strung you are."

"It must be jet lag. Maybe I'll feel better after I unpack." The sudden idea seemed inspired, an escape from a situation where he felt so unstylishly uncomposed. He walked quickly toward the bedrooms, noticed his luggage in the room on the left, and called over his shoulder, "Did you want the room with the view of the pool or the one with the beach?" He jumped at George's unexpected breath on the back of his neck.

"The one with you in the bed," he whispered. There was nothing flirtatious in his tone. It was a simple, matter-of-fact directive that left no room for discussion.

Tory's heartbeat shifted into an unfamiliarly high gear

and the underlying exhilaration was becoming unbearable. He no longer cared if he looked foolish, unsophisticated, totally bereft of urbanity. It didn't matter, as long as he could have the man who was standing so breathlessly close to him. He made a last valiant stab at bravado before his final surrender. "I thought you weren't going to give in to temptation."

"I've got plenty of discipline, but I can't fight Fate." George spoke to the pores on the back of Tory's neck. "Especially when there's a demon manipulating it."

"A demon?" Tory murmured with a nervous laugh. "I feel more like Silly Putty."

George turned him, slowly and deliberately, gently holding him at arm's length. Their eyes met, George's calmly demanding, Tory's on the verge of panic. George closed his eyes and leaned forward, pressing his lips firmly to Tory's and meeting no resistance to his probing tongue. The kiss was unquestionably sexual, done with a self-assurance that Tory supposed should offend him for its arrogance. But the white flashes of heat, illogically ending in icy chills as they reached his skin, left no room for offended thoughts.

Chapter Fifteen

"I hope you realize the full extent of your moral obligations now that you've robbed me of my virtue." Tory stretched languorously against the body next to him, running his hand lightly over George's taut midriff.

"But I'm not a gentleman."

"We could do this every day," he tempted.

"It might be too much of a good thing."

"Was it good?" Tory tried to sound playful, but he wanted a serious answer.

George yawned. "It was OK."

"Tell me the truth."

"You know it was good."

Tory paused. "How good?"

George ran his fingertips down Tory's back, erupting him into spasms of goosebumps. "Pretty good."

"Is that all?"

"About a B-plus."

"What can I do for extra credit?"

George nuzzled the crook between his neck and shoulder. "We'll think of something."

Tory leaned over him to light a Gauloise and sip some champagne through a long hushed pause. "George?"

"Hmm?"

"Really only a B-plus?"

He responded with a short, humorless laugh.

"Tell me."

"Do you know how annoying that is? All right, goddammit, you're the best! Are you happy now? The best

I've ever had or ever hope to have again if I live forever. It was almost unbearable, it was so good. OK?"

Tory tried not to smile too smugly. "I thought so."

"Jesus Christ." He took the Gauloise from Tory's fingers.

"I'm not trying to brag. It's just that it was so special. Let's face it. We've both been around. Good sex is one thing, but once in a blue moon you can really connect, and it goes beyond physical pleasure. I've been waiting years for it to happen again. And we've got it together." He paused, deep in thought. "I guess you could almost call it magic."

"Let's not get carried away."

Tory clicked his tongue in disgust. "Why don't you want to talk about it? I feel like I just won the lottery, I can't hold it in."

"Some things are too difficult to verbalize."

Tory ruminated for a few seconds. "I can sort of understand that. Like it's almost a little bit frightening. Like the first big hill on the roller coaster. Is that it?"

"Magnified a couple thousand times."

"But don't you feel great when you get off? They always used to have to drag me off, I wanted to do it again and again."

"I used to get sick."

"That's not very butch."

George laughed. "I guess that's why I don't ride them."

"Let's talk about something else. This analogy took a wrong turn somewhere."

"Good idea. What time is it?"

Tory glanced at his Cartier on the night table. "Seven-thirty. You bastard, you made me miss a whole day of prime suntan weather."

"You weren't tied to the bed."

"That sounds sort of kicky. Call room service and order another bottle of champagne and a clothesline. Or we could do it with ties. It would be much more elegant with Sulka ties."

"You're depraved."

"Maybe I'm just delirious from love."

"Let's limit the conversation to afterglow civilities."

Tory lit another Gauloise. "The afterglow must be over. Rude old George is back. You know, if you could be as open and affectionate in the rest of your life as you are in bed, you'd be a much happier person."

"The only happy people are the ones who are too stupid to know any better."

"Then what's so good about being smart?"

"It was a statement, not a value judgment."

"I think you're wrong. In fact, I think your attitude sucks."

"Don't talk dirty, you'll get me excited again."

"Does that turn you on?"

"Just kidding."

"It's amazing how many people are into it."

"Like Mr. Kramer."

"I wish someone had told me about him beforehand. He started whispering these raunchy things in my ear and I cracked up. He wasn't pleased."

"He takes it very seriously."

"So I discovered. I played along after that and it was kind of fun. It took a certain amount of creativity."

"Not for him. He alternates the same three or four phrases."

"That's OK for him, but I *do* have my professional standards to uphold. If he asks for me again, I'm going to rehearse."

"You should talk to Carl for pointers. We did a ménage once and he started with the talk. It was amazing. Almost poetic."

"I had a South American last month at the Latham. He did it in Spanish and it was much more romantic. I assume he was talking dirty but for all I know he could have been telling me about the wife and kids back in Caracas. Everything sounds better in Spanish."

"Olé."

He collapsed onto George's chest. "I'm yours."

"We better get cracking if you want dinner. I'm sure you need at least two hours to prepare."

"We could cancel and have room service send it up."

"Let's go downstairs."

"How gallant."

"It was a compliment. I don't trust myself alone with you."

"The gypsy love potion must be working. She guaran-

teed that you'd be a slave at my feet before the weekend
was through."

George propped himself up and looked at Tory with a
vaguely uneasy smile. "I think I liked it better when you
were stuttering on the telephone and spilling champagne."

"You have to be always calling the shots, don't you?"

"Always." He got up and unzipped a suitcase. "You
need a jacket to get in the casino here."

"Damn. I was going to wear my day-glo blue leisure
suit. With the white vinyl belt. And matching shoes."

"Don't get sarcastic, I was trying to be helpful. It's more
formal here than in Las Vagas."

"I know."

"Are you a gambler?"

Tory exhaled smoke with a giggle. "Not until I sit down
at a table. Then the next thing I know it's four in the
morning. I adore bad habits."

"I'll keep an eye on you."

"A lustful eye?"

"That too."

Tory had forgotten how a casino affected him. He recalled enjoying long hours immersed in blackjack on two
trips to Nevada, but the intensity of the feeling had faded
with time. As they entered the tightly packed, cavernous
room, the feeling slowly came over him, and he shivered.
Whirring wheels, ringing slot machines, and boisterous
shouts from the crap tables assaulted his ears with an un-
melodic but riveting rhythm. He stood transfixed as players moved trancelike from table to table, people tapped
their feet impatiently at the glassed windows, and short-
skirted girls picked their way through the maze with trays
of cocktails while pit bosses and security men darted their
eyes wildly in apparent omniscience. A dark-suited man
absentmindedly shook a handful of chips as he squeezed
past Tory, and the sharp clicking noises gave him a
Pavlovian chill.

He grabbed George's forearm and didn't know why he
was whispering. "Let's get some chips."

George gave him a puzzled smile, and they threaded
their way across the room to the cashier's window. Tory
watched a roulette wheel intently while George handled

the transaction and returned with a look of bemused amazement.

"The sport left us two thousand. Can you believe it? We should quit while we're ahead." He was confused by Tory's vacant expression. "I got you two hundred in chips for tonight. Don't go wild and you can go home with a nice profit on Sunday." He searched Tory's face with concern as he handed him the chips. "Are you OK?"

"I'm fine," he murmured vaguely.

George didn't seem to believe him. "Let's stick to the five-dollar blackjack tables. That's all the money you're getting tonight."

Tory fingered the two black chips with an unimpressed smile. He thought back over the events of the day, and it seemed like a dream, one happy surprise after another. That a man he barely knew should leave two thousand dollars for his gambling pleasure seemed a logical part of an emerging pattern, a pattern that would be immorally underfacilitated at a five-dollar table.

George followed him impatiently as he looked into the various dealers' eyes until he found one who satisfied some urge within him. When George peevishly asked him to explain why they were waiting at a full table when there were two vacant seats behind them, Tory shushed him with a quiet urgency and concentrated on the back of a seated woman. She suddenly decided to move on to another table with her husband in tow, and Tory offered George the vacant chair with an enigmatic smile.

They each exchanged a black chip for two stacks of red. Tory scrutinized the dealer, assessed the other players, and stared blankly at the pile of cards in their holder while his left hand idly dropped the chips on top of each other. He listened closely to their steady clink, trying to interpret their message. As if following their advice, he moved half of one pile to the green felt rectangle before him. He caught George's stony stare from the corner of his eye and brought his hand back with all but two of the chips. The dealer laid the cards in a graceful arc, a king of spades and an ace of spades in front of Tory. He laid three red chips beside Tory's original two before revealing his eight and nine and collecting the other player's cards.

Tory pushed one chip toward the dealer and doubled the pile on the felt, pointedly avoiding George's gaze. The next deal gave him two black tens, which he placed side by side, along with a matching pile of four red chips. He met the dealer's eyes, and the trace of a smile seemed to match his own in an eerie understanding. A black king and queen joined his two tens, while the dealer accumulated four cards totaling twenty-three. Their eyes met again as the dealer matched each stack from his tray.

Tory rattled the pile three times, stopped, then repeated the motion. He hesitantly removed all but one chip from the felt. He refused an additional card for his red nine and black six. George took it, a seven of clubs, which gave him twenty-one, and he was rewarded with a red chip to match the one before him.

Tory flashed him an indulgent smile as the dealer gave himself nineteen.

It continued for several hands in the same manner. Four chips, then six, eight, or ten chips, seemed by sheer force of their number to intimidate the deck into a steady flow of aces, tens, and face cards. Tory listened to the vibrations of the rattling chips as they asked each other how many of their number should make the next trip to the felt. He tried to follow their advice, but it wasn't always possible. He felt obligated to move at least one chip forward even when none volunteered. On other hands they begged him to let them go en masse, but George's set frown frightened most of them into immobility. Still, they seemed to Tory a cheerful group as they were joined by a growing number of their brothers in haphazard piles, then several of their stylish green cousins and even two of their stately black uncles.

The dealer's eyes bade Tory a secret farewell when it came time for him to change tables. Tory scrutinized the new man unhappily and felt heartless as he pushed his red friends forward in neat piles of ten. He averted his eyes as they returned to the tray and were replaced with three blacks. He gathered them in his fist with several greens and the other two blacks and got up from the table. George gave him an annoyed look, but gathered his meager pile and followed. Tory realized with a start that George was still with him. Then he remembered the occasional pleasant pressure of the leg against his own under the table and recalled that they had been side by side for over an hour.

"Are you enjoying yourself?" he asked guiltily.

"Not as much as you are," George smiled strangely. "How much did you win?"

Tory somnambulantly held out the fistful of chips. George gripped his wrist firmly in a quick motion and extracted them all. He handed back the greens and a few stray reds, slipping the five blacks into his jacket pocket.

"I'll hold these for you. You'll thank me when we get home."

Reality rudely interrupted Tory's trancelike calm and evoked an angry response. "Give them back! They're mine!"

"Don't you even *think* about throwing a tantrum in here," George hissed threateningly. "You have a hundred fifty-eight in your hand and a hundred in your pocket. It's more than a crazed idiot should be trusted with."

Tory gasped. "I'm not a crazed idiot, you tightass. I'm hot!"

"If you're so hot, two-fifty-eight should be plenty," he replied impassively.

Something deep inside advised him to try to preserve the calm equilibrium in his mind. "You're right," he smiled. "I don't need them. See you later." He walked off toward the roulette wheels.

"When you lose them, don't try to get any more from the cashier," George shouted. "They're in my name."

Tory ignored the voice from ten feet behind him and the startled laughter from several upturned heads. He fixed his mind on croupiers' faces, determined to ignore the indignation in the back of his mind. He calmed himself with positive thoughts; he still had plenty of chips and the argument could be ironed out later. He knew it would do nothing but harm to dwell on it now.

Chapter Sixteen

TORY half-opened one eye and tried to identify the unfamiliar bed. The pervasive aroma of hamburger and enthusiastic chewing noises behind him were not helpful clues, but he remembered the answer in spite of them. Contentment at solving the mystery was short-lived as he wincingly remembered his parting with George the night before. He'd managed to slip into the bed unnoticed around four, but the consequences couldn't be put off forever.

It was an affront to have to deal with such a weighty issue before coffee, but better to assess it while he could feign sleep than to jump into it defenseless. He cursed silently as even this option was denied him. George had apparently noticed a change in his breathing and now was gently rubbing his bare shoulder.

"Time to wake up. The tropic sun is calling your name."

Tory grunted in response, encouraged by the pleasant tone. George nibbled his ear and moved slowly down to his shoulder. "You've got to maintain this delicious shade of golden brown."

Tory turned and buried his face against George's chest, pleasantly aroused by the caresses but not ready to expose his matted curls and puffy eyes. He knew it was probably a silly attitude, but it seemed too early in the relationship to take chances.

George seemed to read his thoughts. "You don't have

to hide. I've had all morning to look at your crow's-feet. I love you anyway."

Tory bolted for the bathroom. He locked the door to George's laughter and had to laugh at himself for being so transparent. He wondered if all the other men had seen through him so easily, the ones he'd left in the wee hours of the morning after sex was finished. He'd always said it was because he couldn't sleep in an unfamiliar bed, but vanity was the real reason. David had been the only man he'd ever felt at ease with in the morning, and even then Tory tried to wake up first to make himself presentable. Morning dishabille did not fit in with his self-image. But he was incapable of facing the full morning grooming regimen without coffee and cigarettes, so he decided to listen to the part of his mind that told him he was being silly and returned to the bed after only essential repairs.

"Your eyes are still bloodshot," George teased.

Tory leaned over him for coffee from the cart and searched the night table for a Gauloise. "I don't care, you said you love me."

George pulled Tory down on top of him for a kiss. Tory tried to balance the coffee cup still in his hand. "You need two witnesses."

"The way one of those goons was watching me at the roulette table, I wouldn't be surprised if the room is bugged." He felt the muscles in George's arms tense almost imperceptibly and wondered how he could have been so stupid as to bring the subject up.

"Why was he watching you?"

"Probably because I was winning," he replied lightly. "I guess it made him nervous."

"Or he thought you were a psychopath getting ready to flip out."

The "crazed idiot" remark drifted back through Tory's mind. He kissed George lightly and carefully rolled off his chest to sip the coffee. "Why don't we forget about last night for a while?"

"I wish we could," George answered flatly. "I saw a side of you last night that I never suspected. I knew you were a little on the eccentric side, which is charming in small doses. But last night . . . do you have any idea how strange you were?"

"I wasn't strange," he answered indignantly. "I was getting vibrations."

"By most standards, talking to a pile of chips is strange."

Tory couldn't cover a fleeting look of guilt. "I wasn't talking to them."

"Not out loud. But I saw you doing it under your breath. So did the blackjack dealer you were flirting with. He was probably never so relieved to rotate tables."

Tory felt confused and slightly hurt. The first dealer had seemed so kind and so in tune with his vibrations. He wondered if the man had really thought he was strange or if George was imagining it. He couldn't know for sure. His night in the casino seemed a light-year away. "People talk to dice. Why can't I talk to chips?"

"Because they were answering you."

Tory's tan took on a rosy tone. "And who was the big winner at that table?" he replied defensively. "Maybe more people should talk to their chips."

"Why stop with chips?" George smirked with a ridiculing laugh. "Why not have a chat with your coffee cup? Ask the ashtray to tell us a joke."

"One comedian per bed is more than ample," Tory glared in what he hoped was a withering stare. "How can you ridicule me when the evidence is right there on the dresser?"

George glanced at the pile of green and black chips across the room. "Hi, fellas! Sleep well?"

"Go ahead and make jokes. That's six hundred dollars you're laughing at. Is that so funny?"

George paused before answering. "I'll admit that your luck was impressive."

"It was not luck," Tory replied with a smug, secret expression.

"Come off it."

"How about that lady in the red dress? How long did it take me to psych her out of her seat?"

"It was a coincidence," he answered uncertainly.

"You know you don't really believe that."

"It *was* uncanny," he grudgingly admitted.

"I rarely discuss it, but sometimes I *do* have certain powers."

"You have an imagination that's gone haywire," George snorted.

"Tell me you didn't sense it in bed yesterday," Tory challenged. George's frozen expression told Tory he'd scored a point. He hadn't discussed it at length, but he knew, and he knew that George knew, that it had gone beyond the coincidence of good sex. "I'm not saying I'm a psychic. But I get flashes sometimes, little intuitive messages. They don't actually tell me what's going to happen but they tell me what I should do without a logical reason."

George made it a point to barely suppress a smile. "You hear voices?"

"Not really voices. Just vibrations. I think everyone gets them but some of us are more aware. I didn't even know what they were until a few years ago, and they've been happening all my life. Sometimes they're years apart and sometimes they come in clusters, three or four of them in a month. Sometimes they last a fraction of a second and sometimes, like last night, they go on for hours. It's not something I can control or explain, but I'd be foolish to deny it."

"I don't deny that these things might exist. And maybe you *do* have some sort of communication. But it's unnerving to watch you whether it's real or imagined."

"Like yesterday when we were talking about the roller coaster?"

George looked totally and uncharacteristically uncomfortable. "I guess."

"You can't call all the shots in your life, George. Some things are just beyond our control. Remember how they used to tell you in church to accept God on blind faith? That someday you might have a revelation and know without a doubt that it was true? That's how I feel about the vibrations, that certain things are predetermined for us and it's absurd to go against them. You should realize it too. You have it inside you just as much as I do."

"Not me. I only believe in hard evidence. And I question that."

"You have it, even if you refuse to acknowledge it to yourself. I know you bring it out in me. I've been having flashes right and left since the day I met you."

"Maybe I'm a carrier."

Tory refused to respond to his ridicule. "What do you think about reincarnation?"

"Very little."

He paused significantly. "Don't you ever get the feeling that you've known me before?"

George's look asked him if he could possibly be serious. "Go talk to your chips."

"You know, if you weren't so cynical you might be more in touch with your feelings—and a much happier person."

"This is becoming inane. If you were so tuned in last night, why didn't you break the bank?"

"It's your fault."

"Why not?" he shrugged with a sly smile. "Who am I to argue with the Oracle of Delphi?"

"My mind has to be clear and relaxed to pick up the vibrations. After you pulled your big bully act with the chips, I couldn't hold onto them. They came and went for about an hour afterward, then I kept getting thoughts about you and the signals faded out completely."

"You don't need a psychiatrist. You just need your antenna adjusted."

"You're only making jokes because it makes you uncomfortable to admit that there's something beyond your control. But before the vibrations faded out, I sat at the roulette wheel and willed three sevens in five spins. I was almost four thousand ahead!"

"So why didn't you quit then?"

"That's the problem. I couldn't tell for sure that the vibrations had stopped until later. I still felt . . . unearthly . . . but I had myself so revved up that I was just imagining it toward the end."

"Hindsight's a wonderful thing."

"It was such a beautiful rush while it lasted," Tory murmured. "Better than snorting coke. It happened once before with gambling when I was in Vegas two years ago with my friend Mona. I got the vibrations but I wouldn't let myself go with them, I stuck to the cheap tables. I didn't understand exactly what was going on back then. Just these strange, brilliant white flashes, so short I didn't notice them until I concentrated. But last night was different, partly because I knew what to expect and partly because of the earlier events of the day." He looked at

George significantly. "Yesterday just had 'Fate' written all over it. Anyway, the vibrations were so incredibly strong last night it would have been impossible to have missed them. The first time in Vegas was like a flashlight battery blinking on and off, just gentle little sensations. But last night," he whispered, awed at the memory of it, "I could have lit the Manhattan skyline. It was unreal. I could concentrate on the cards or the roulette wheel and make things happen."

"Why don't you tell it to Gamblers Anonymous when we get back?"

Tory was about to explode in a fit of anger, but as he played the line back through his mind he couldn't detect a trace of sarcasm. With only a slight pique in his voice, he replied. "It's not a problem, George. It's a gift, a talent. I never gamble at home, except for some dollar-a-point backgammon. And that's just to be sociable. Gambling's not a major influence in my life."

"My father probably said the same thing when he was young. By the time I was twelve, we were eating cold cereal for dinner some nights and changing apartments every few months because he blew the rent money on the horses or a poker game. Sometimes he'd hit a streak and walk around for days with that glassy-eyed stare you had on last night. Then we'd get new clothes and go out for Sunday dinner. But it never lasted."

Tory was startled by the emotion in his voice and tried to answer gently. "That's a very sad story, but you're missing an important point. I was playing with found money."

The point didn't seem to impress him. "And we're going to keep it that way. You have six hundred on the dresser, which will be plenty to piss away for the next two nights. I'm holding five hundred for you, and we'll split the sixteen we still have on credit. You'll see it when we get back to Philadelphia. Then you can blow it on bingo at St. Bonaventure's for all I care. I won't feel responsible."

Tory listened in growing indignation and wondered if George had suddenly become a ventriloquist's dummy for Brad at his most maddening. But even Brad never did more than suggest or complain. The final decision had always been Tory's, and he was infuriated to have the prerogative denied to him. "So who said you were responsible for me? I'm a big boy, George. I can take care of myself."

"That remains to be seen."

"Nobody's forcing you to stick around to see it." Tory regretted the words as they spilled from his mouth. Sometimes he wished he could manage his conversation like courtroom testimony and have phrases stricken from the stenographer's notes. He couldn't decide if he was too angry or too stubborn to apologize.

George glared at him for an interminable moment with eyes that suddenly seemed a glacial blue. "If I thought you were serious, we could make an issue out of it."

Tory fumbled with another cigarette to avoid the accusing stare, then moved to the bathroom through the heavy silence. George finally spoke, a trivial question about the swimming pool, and Tory clutched at it like a life preserver. The explosive situation was defused, but the strain was far from totally relieved.

Chapter Seventeen

MONA entered the living room with a deliberate stride and a haughty stare, pausing to pose grandly before the fireplace. "Do I look sufficiently chic?"

With a wry smile Tory inspected her from his sofa. Her usual bangs were pulled back in a tight French bun, revealing formidable diamond studs in each earlobe instead of the usual emeralds. A severely tailored and obviously expensive black wool suit covered her primly from neck to mid-calf, relieved only by a patch of white silk blouse at her throat demurely pinned with a circular diamond brooch. An oval diamond pavé dinner ring and an imposing solitaire sparkled on her carefully posed hands.

"Are you supposed to be a golddigger with pretensions or a spinster schoolmarm gone wrong?"

Her studied expression turned into an annoyed frown. "I'm supposed to be an intimidating matron."

"Don't you get nervous wearing all that glitter at once?"

"I pray they'll be stolen so I can collect the insurance. They were all Grandmother Benson's, except for the solitaire from the drone, and Mother would crucify me if I sold them."

"Why would you want to sell them?"

"I've never been a fanatic for diamonds."

Tory crossed himself hastily.

"I much prefer emeralds. They do such lovely things for my green eyes."

"How do you manage to cope with such problems?"

"Life has never been easy for me," she sighed.

Tory moved to the impromptu bar set up on the Korean brass chest in the corner, his birthday present from Charles. "Let me make you a martini to help you forget, poor dear."

"What a clever idea. Actually, most intimidating matrons I've met drink sherry, but I think we can bend the rules a smidgin."

"Who are you planning to intimidate?"

"Your gentleman, of course. Your parents would want it that way. A pity they couldn't be with us tonight."

"Pity," Tory repeated drily.

"Someone must act *in loco parentis* to see that this young man is suitable. I'll examine his manners and family background and Brad will take him into the study after dinner to discuss his financial prospects."

"I don't have a study."

Mona obviously wasn't in the mood to be ruffled by details. "I suppose we'll be forced to improvise. Have you planned a festive menu?"

"Rib roast, parsleyed potatoes, asparagus, chocolate cake and whatever else strikes Mae's fancy."

"Rib roast," Mona repeated without expression. "How mundane."

"George is pretty much a meat-and-potatoes person."

"That's not a very encouraging sign. Are you quite sure that you should be getting involved with a man who will want to take you to Beef 'n' Brew?"

"He has other qualities."

Mona's disdainfully raised brows said she realized what one of the other qualities was and they wouldn't discuss it while she was in an intimidating-matron frame of mind. "Of course we'll call the *Inquirer*'s society editor to announce the engagement. Passé, but it must be done. Have you registered your china pattern at Caldwell's yet?"

"I haven't even seen my engagement ring yet," he deadpanned.

"Very remiss of him. I hope you're not planning on anything too ostentatiously large."

"I have my eye on a little twelve-carat number at Cooper's."

"That won't do at all. A stone of more than five carats is inappropriate before the age of thirty."

"I'll have to call Mr. Cooper and have him take it out of layaway."

"I presume your young man is Presbyterian or a member of one of the other acceptable denominations."

"We've never actually discussed it."

"Very unthinking of you. But with a solid surname like Keller, I don't suppose he could be totally beneath consideration. Unless of course he's an Irish Keller, and that wouldn't do at all."

"He's of the New Jersey Kellers, you know."

"I'll have to check my social register. I was thinking of a May wedding and a small reception at the Barclay. Nothing too garish."

"May? I'm sure to be showing by then."

"We can do marvelous things with an Empire bodice. In a subtle shade of cream, I should think."

Tory sighed despondently and slipped out of his role without warning. "If only all this were true."

"What's wrong?"

"I don't know," he shrugged. "But something is. It's just not working out."

"I thought it was going rather well. You've been seeing him steadily for two months."

"That's what I've been trying to tell myself, but it isn't so. On the surface, everything seems fine since we came back from Freeport. Off nights we go out for dinner or a show. He stays over when our schedules don't conflict. We talk on the phone almost every day. He even took me to New York for my birthday."

"From what you've told me before, the problem couldn't be with sex, could it?"

Tory thought of their first day in Freeport, and it seemed like a dream. Their lovemaking since had been satisfying and not without a special quality, but the ethereal spark that had ignited them had not returned. He'd wondered ever since if he was being greedy to expect it again.

"Everything is fine in that department," he replied, trying to believe it was true.

"Do you have many arguments?"

Their one real argument flashed back to him vividly,

never far enough out of his mind that it needed to be consciously recalled. A few careless words, spoken to express irritation, and nothing had been quite the same since. He couldn't comprehend how something so trivial could make such a difference.

"We argue all the time, but never seriously. Only once were we actually angry. And it blew over in minutes."

"I'm sorry, but the problem eludes me."

"He's trying to get out. I can sense it. Part of him doesn't want to, he's crazy about me. And I'm not imagining that. People who have known him for years are amazed, they say he's like a different person when he's with me. Jimmy's known him forever and says he's never seen him smile more than a dozen times until he met me. But sometimes he'll just clam up in the middle of a sentence for no explainable reason, like he's catching himself from letting too much escape out of the shell."

Mona mulled his words silently. "Tory, some men are like that. Perennial bachelors. They get involved up to a certain point and then they get cold feet. They're incapable of emotional commitment. Perhaps George is one of them. What kind of track record does he have?"

"None, as far as I can gather. He was engaged once while still in college, but was apparently more relieved than hurt when it was broken off."

"Engaged?"

"To a woman."

"Perhaps *that's* his problem! An unresolved sexual-identity crisis. Perhaps he subconsciously needs a woman."

"I'll murder the first one who lays a hand on him."

"That's not very openminded. You sound like a big-oted yokel from Stoltz Grove in reverse."

"I could deal with another guy. The competition might even be fun. But a woman? How could I fight back?"

"It's quite chic to be bisexual these days."

"You're on your own this time, dearie. We've been through platform heels and permanent waves together, but I think I'll sit this one out."

"I wasn't speaking for myself. As far as I'm concerned, men will always be in fashion. Like good pearls and basic black."

Mae's voice reverberated over the upper-level balcony, distance and the closed kitchen door not seriously impairing her audibility. "Baby, come up here and slice these mushrooms."

"I can't. I'm entertaining."

Her threatening face soon appeared at the balcony. "You get your skinny-behind self up here this minute! If you'd've gone out for the romaine this morning like I told you to when I called, I wouldn't be running late." She disappeared without waiting for a reply.

"Come upstairs with me. God, she gets touchy when she cooks."

They gathered their drinks and cigarettes and climbed the stairs. "Why aren't you cooking?" Mona asked. "It used to be one of your big productions."

"I still do when I'm in the mood. I enjoy it even more now that it's an option and not a necessity. But I'll have to be a full-time referee tonight, with you and Brad in the same room."

"He picks on me."

"You always manage to defend yourself admirably."

"Who's the sixth person?"

"My friend Jimmy McBride. I told you about him. His grandfather made the family fortune in bootlegging and his lover is Hal Bergman, as in Bergman Realty. He hustles as a hobby."

"How droll."

"He's not playing with a full deck, but fortunately for him he was dealt a royal flush at birth. You'll like him, he's a lot of fun. And drop-dead gorgeous. Sometimes I want to smack him, he's so handsome. And he'll make George feel more comfortable. Poor George. Between you and Brad I'm afraid he's going to think that I've invited him to the Spanish Inquisition."

They entered the kitchen, a jumble of utensils, dishes, and food in various stages of preparation. Mae didn't look up from her involvement at the range.

"Put on an apron, baby. You'll stain that pretty sweater."

"With mushrooms?"

"You never know what might come your way when I get rolling." She caught Mona from the corner of her eye and turned around. "Well, if it ain't Princess Grace! Honey, you are looking sharp! Diamonds and the works!"

"She's trying to scare George."

"Now why you want to go and do that to my lover man?"

" 'Lover man'?" Mona was obviously impressed. Mae's names of endearment were arranged on a strict scale, "honey," "sweetheart," and "sugar" thrown out indiscriminately to mailmen, trolley drivers, and anyone else who crossed her path. "Baby" was reserved for Tory and occasionally her daughter when they were on good terms. Mona had worked her way up after several years to a sporadic "love bug" or "sugar lump," and she seemed slightly miffed that George should be so quickly honored.

"Mae's crazy about him."

"Honey, he is one hunk of man. If I was twenty years younger . . . my, my, my."

"If only he had money," Mona mused ruefully,

"He don't need it. He'd still be a dreamboat on the welfare line. Not that looks is everything. I've known gangs of beautiful men in my day—"

"How do you mean that?" Tory asked.

"Just slice your mushrooms and never you mind—and nine times out of ten they wasn't worth a plug nickel, too busy looking into mirrors to worry about anybody but themselves. But my George is different, he's beautiful inside and out. And the way he lights up my baby's eyes, it's something else. Just between you and me, it's let me breathe a sigh of relief. He's been so picky all these years, and he ain't getting any younger."

"That's for sure," Mona agreed with unnecessary enthusiasm.

Tory tried to ignore the familiar bait loftily and concentrate on the mushrooms, but as usual he couldn't resist. "Nonsense. I'm barely over puberty. And watch your step, Mona. I've seen your driver's license."

"How'd you get your hands on that?" Mae asked, obviously shocked.

"The time she accidentally put in a second diaphragm and they got stuck. She insisted that I rush her to the hospital and I stumbled across it looking for her Blue Cross card while she was with the doctor."

"Stumbled," Mona spat. "There I was at death's door and you were muckraking through my purse. Besides, it's only a counterfeit that I use to get served in the bars."

Mae peered over Tory's shoulder as she turned back to

the stove. "Slice them thinner, baby. They sop up more butter that way."

"Is there anything I can do to help, Mae?"

"It's sweet of you to offer, sugar lump, but the last time you was in this kitchen I scraped frappéd strawberries off the wallpaper for two weeks."

"Tory's Cuisinart is obviously defective."

"I noticed that, too," she replied sympathetically. "It don't have sense enough to screw on its top before it starts churning. But just the same, you cross your legs and drink your martini. We'll manage without you somehow."

Mona's protest was cut short by the doorbell. "There's something more in your line," Tory said. "You can answer the door. It's probably Brad, so practice being polite on your way down."

She returned alone a few moments later. To answer the question on Tory's face, she replied, "You were right. It was Brad."

"Well, what did you do with him?"

"He was barely in the door before he said it was nice to see me dressing my age and gave my drink a pointed stare, so I suggested that he wait in the linen closet until dinner."

Mae took the finished mushrooms from Tory and muttered, "Just so she don't start dropping macadamia nuts on his head from the balcony again. That was almost as much fun as the strawberries."

"She only does that after her eighth martini." Brad entered the room as he spoke.

"Do you think the two of you can pretend to be civilized for one night?"

"Don't tell me, tell her. Hello, Mae."

"Well, if it ain't old Bradley. You didn't wrinkle any pillow cases in there, did you?" Her question evoked a hoot from Mona.

"Don't encourage them, Mae." Tory faced Mona and Brad with what he hoped was an authoritative expression. "I'm serious. I'd like this dinner to make a good impression, which will be very difficult if two of my best friends look like they're on the verge of going ten rounds after dessert. I'd appreciate it very much if you could call an evening's truce."

"I'll try, but he started it."

"I didn't threaten to lock you in a closet."

"You started with your snide remarks before you had your coat off."

Tory sighed. "Also, it would be pleasant if the dinner conversation could be raised to a slightly more mature level."

They agreed to try, but Tory was far from optimistic. They'd taken an immediate dislike to each other on their first meeting three years before. Brad told him that Mona was pretentious, superficial, mercenary, erratic and promiscuous. Tory agreed that all of his adjectives were to some degree accurate but somehow they all managed to seem charming when applied to her. Mona considered Brad tedious, narrow-minded, interfering, self-righteous and uncomfortably reminiscent of her ex-husband. Tory found it equally difficult to defend him except to say that his irritating ways were endurable because they were underscored with sincere affection and concern.

He attempted a few more meetings between them, hoping that time would show them each other's good qualities. But Mona cheerfully painted Brad an outrageous self-portrait, measuring her enjoyment by the number of shocked looks and stifled gasps she could coax from him in the course of an evening. Tory finally shelved the project and arranged to keep them in separate parts of his life, but as the memory of each meeting faded his optimism grew. It had become something of a pattern. Approximately every six months he invited them both to dinner, then soon remembered why he didn't do it more often.

His hopes for the evening grew as his words seemed to be having some effect. Mae evicted them from the kitchen and they went downstairs, where the conversation remained comparatively polite while they waited for George and Jimmy to arrive. Tory hoped that the additional two faces would divert Brad's and Mona's attention from each other, and he answered the anticipated chime with relief. George's embrace was warmly intimate, the kind of gesture that had confused Tory for two months, telling him that everything was perfect between them. Fervently wishing he could believe it, he introduced George to Brad and Mona, confident that they could find no fault.

Mona gave George and Jimmy a reflexive once-over,

temporarily forgetting her intimidating-matron role, while Brad's eyes darted nervously from one man to the other. Tory gave little thought to ice-breaking conversational openers. He'd often been amused by Mona's proclivity to engage total strangers instantly, not letting complete ignorance of a subject hold her back. And Jimmy was as poised as he was handsome, after years of entertaining his lover's extensive business contacts. There was no hint of an awkward silence as Tory devoted himself to mixing drinks.

Things were proceeding so well that he felt almost left out after he finished serving drinks and hors d'oeuvres. Jimmy had given Brad greetings from a lawyer acquaintance who was apparently a subject for extended talk. Mona told George anecdotes about Chicago on the opposite sofa. Her dramatic flair made even a recap of ordinary events vividly interesting. Tory sat on the cane chair between the sofas awaiting an opening in either conversation. He waited five minutes before deciding to check progress with Mae in the kitchen.

Jimmy and Brad were in the middle of discussing a new restaurant when he returned. It was a topic he could discuss with expertise, but his attention was constantly diverted to the other sofa. Mona's anecdotes had migrated to Mexico, and George seemed riveted. In the intensity of her narration, Mona had turned to face George directly with her legs tucked under her and her face unnecessarily close to his. Had she been anyone but his best friend, it might have given Tory cause for concern. His attention was drawn back by a question about the evening's menu, which led to a discussion of butchers and the Italian market. He cut short an anecdote on his first experience with a soufflé to freshen Mona's half-empty martini glass, a pretext to remind her that there were other guests present. He was beginning to understand why certain hostesses didn't invite her more often. Mona interrupted her monologue long enough for a "Thank you, *mon cher*" and continued on in the same breath about an eccentric friend in Atlanta. Tory mentally rearranged the furniture into one conversational setting as he returned to secondhand gossip about a notorious restaurateur.

As he donated his well-informed opinion on the restaurateur's marital arrangement, he quickly glanced across the room to hear Mona laugh. After countless hours in her company, he recognized subtleties in her manner that were indiscernible to most. She possessed at least six styles of laughter, each with a distinct meaning. This had been the soft, slightly contrived laugh with a trace of shared intimacy, the one she reserved for prospective suitors in the early stages of seduction. He reexamined her body language with suspect results. He was willing to allow her all benefits of doubt but still decided it would be a good idea to consult Mae.

"Would she do that to me?" he asked after giving Mae a quick rundown. Mae surreptitiously peered over the balcony and came back to the kitchen with her forehead furrowed.

"My first thought is to say that she wouldn't do that to someone she loves like a brother. But on the other hand, she's a woman with a lot of urges, if you know what I mean. And I could tell you a story about what my second cousin Regina did to her stepsister that would straighten your curls. All for a man. Them old urges can make a body do some funny things. I'd stay on my toes if I was you, baby."

"What shall I do?"

"For starters, light the candles. I'll hurry dinner out in two minutes and you make sure you're between them at the table. Maybe they just need a change of geography."

Tory announced dinner from the balcony and Brad, Jimmy, and George ascended. He reserved the ends of the table for himself and Mae, George and Brad were to his left, and Jimmy was directly to his right, leaving the chair next to Mae for Mona. Jimmy went into the kitchen to offer his assistance to Mae as Mona swept up the staircase and commandeered his chair across from George.

"Isn't it hot up here?" she asked rhetorically, explaining her missing jacket and the formerly demure silk blouse unbuttoned to display a hint of cleavage.

Tory turned his head to obscure his threatening expression from George. "So turn off your oven," he hissed in a softly vicious voice.

Dinner progressed more to Tory's satisfaction. His threat to Mona seemed to have little effect; she continued to direct her conversation toward George, who did nothing to discourage her. But Tory's position between them allowed him to influence the conversation and put Mona's possible designs in neutral gear. Mae valiantly tried to lend a hand with loud demands for Mona's attention.

Tory held his ground when they moved downstairs for coffee, outmaneuvering Mona for the sofa seat next to George. She was at a definite disadvantage on the opposite sofa but continued to campaign doggedly. When Mae joined them later, Mona somehow got her in her seat and took the corner of the sofa next to George in a tactical move that Tory was sure would have impressed any West Point cadet. But he was ready for the challenge and held his territory for the rest of the evening, squelching Mona's attempts to dominate the conversation with uncustomary aggressiveness. He was almost relieved to see George and the other guests depart at two, leaving him alone with his houseguest.

"Lovely little party, *mon cher,*" she said evenly. "And George is a treasure."

"I was so happy to see you get along with him so well," Tory replied, adrenaline beginning to constrict his voice.

"We found an immediate rapport."

"About this much more rapport and you'd be in traction," he replied through clenched teeth.

"Tory!"

"Skip the theatrics. Remember who you're talking to, someone who knows you inside out. Or at least I thought I did. I never thought you could be this way with *me.*"

"The thought is reciprocal! That you could even suspect such a thing is devastating!"

"Come off it, Mona. I have eyes. So did everyone else in the room. Mae noticed it right away, and Brad kept giving me 'I told you so' looks. Helen Keller could have picked up on it. You weren't exactly subtle."

Mona dropped all pretenses. "Was it that obvious?"

"Worse." Tory's anger began to subside with her admission. He could deal with almost anything better than her dishonesty.

"Honest to God, Tory, I started out with nothing but good intentions."

"I can't believe it, but I believe it."

"Honestly. Remember our discussion before dinner, my theory about an unresolved sexual thing? I decided to check it out, send out some signals and see if they got an answer."

"The FCC has regulations about that volume of kilowatts."

"The point is, they came back loud and clear. I didn't know what I was stepping into. But what's a woman with a healthy libido to do? It caught me by surprise and I couldn't simply push a button and turn it off."

"He came in that strong?"

"Tory, I hate to be the one to say it, but better that it comes from a friend. I could have definitely had that man. In fact, I could barely avoid it except for your vigilance."

"Did I hold my own?"

"Better than most wives I run up against," she answered with a trace of pique in her voice. "I truly had little control over it, Tory. He is one hell of an attractive man. There's something almost animal there."

"Take it from me, honey, there is."

"Tell me no more. I'm about to climb the walls as it is."

"So I was right," he sighed with a trace of melodrama in his voice. "I'm losing him."

"I don't know. I caught him watching you across the room once, with one of those four-year-old lost-little-boy looks that makes you want to rip out your heart and hand it to him. No man looks like that unless there's something there."

"So where do I stand?"

"I'm not sure. Something is amiss. I think you can hook him. But you may have to share him."

"You can bet your emerald earbobs that *you'll* never set eyes on him again."

"How parsimonious," she sniffed.

Chapter Eighteen

TORY sipped his after-dinner espresso with little pleasure, which was unusual for him in La Panetière. The cognoscenti agreed that its food couldn't seriously compete with that of Le Bec-Fin, but Tory thought that the stately main dining salon with its flawless service and painstaking attention to elegant detail more than compensated for any gastronomical deficiencies. A dinner there was part of the diminishing list of things he still found hedonistically impressive.

George had surprised him with the invitation two weeks after his dinner party. It was totally unexpected and Tory hadn't had time to become suspicious until George was uncharacteristically ruffled over pre-dinner cocktails. Tory saw Damocles' sword clearly and he chattered nervously throughout the meal, hoping to keep it suspended through the sheer force of his garrulity.

George finally fixed him with a portentous stare, and he knew that his efforts were in vain. He trailed off into silence and met George's somber eyes, the following hush seeming to be politely arranged for him to brace himself.

"You must be wondering why we're here."

"When I get an invitation to La Panetière, I don't ask questions." Tory was determined to maintain an off-hand grace through whatever ensued.

"This is sort of a going-away party."

Only a tightening of his jaw betrayed Tory's composed mask. His eyes patiently awaited a further explanation.

"I'm moving to Bucks County. I have a restaurant."

A glimmer of hope reappeared in Tory's mind. He could understand a restaurant, the object of George's ambition. And Bucks County was only an hour's drive away. He hoped that he'd blown things out of proportion.

"That's wonderful," he smiled tentatively, recalling George's outline of his plans on the flight to Freeport. "You're about two years ahead of schedule."

"It's not happening quite the way I planned it. I have a partner." He paused and continued slowly, carefully weighing each word. "I'd always planned to do it on my own, but she made an offer that's impossible to turn down. We're taking over the Oaks. Lock, stock, and barrel. It's impossible to do anything but make money there, it's been a tradition for over a hundred years."

Tory's mind raced with questions that he refused to ask. Why did George sound so grim about something that he'd wanted so badly? What kind of terms were involved to make him undertake something clearly beyond his own means? Most important, who was the mysterious woman who'd made the offer?

"It must have been quite an offer."

"I'm putting up the cash I have and all my time. She's making up the difference and we split it down the middle. I'm signing the papers tomorrow."

Tory laughed nervously. "She sounds like she was sent from heaven."

"You've met her," George replied uncomfortably. "Janice Barton." Tory looked blank. "She comes to Duffy's now and then."

Tory's mind searched for Janices at Duffy's. He didn't want to believe that the only one he recalled could be George's Janice. She was a suburban executive's wife with a bad marriage and a teenage son constantly in trouble with the police over drugs, a textbook study of the American Dream gone wrong. When she couldn't cope with her problems, she'd drive into town for a binge and a crying jag. Tory avoided her when he could. She seemed to him a basically kind person, but her tearful grievances soon became boringly repetitious.

"I can only think of a Janice from New Hope who burns cigarette holes in the upholstery and drinks vodka in a tumbler, up with a twist, and calls them martinis."

"That's Janice," George laughed uneasily.

Tory was shocked but determined to remain nonchalant. "Perhaps a project like this will help with her problems."

"Don't play naïve, Tory," he replied irritably. "It's everything it appears to be. Her husband left her, and all she has left is her booze and her cash. She's buying me with the restaurant to have round-the-clock attention and live-in stud service when she's sober enough to care."

Mona's warning about a woman ran through his head, but it didn't seem to apply. Janice was too pathetic to arouse jealousy. He could only feel disbelief that George would allow himself to get involved with the woman on any level.

"George, it's not worth it. Not for ten restaurants."

"I've thought it through." His aloof tone said he didn't care to discuss it.

"You couldn't have. It's too ridiculous for words. Even *I* wouldn't do something this ludicrous. And it's completely inconsistent with what you've said before, how your own business would let you get out of the escort service and be respectable and independent. What kind of respect can you have for yourself with her? I'm hardly the one to lecture on morality, but it seems to me that you can keep more integrity by jumping into bed for a hundred-dollar bill than by preying on an alcoholic's neuroses."

"Disgusting, isn't it?" he replied without intonation.

"More sad than disgusting," Tory murmured quietly. "And totally out of character. It's not like you, George."

"Don't you dare patronize me," he almost shouted. "And don't give me any more bullshit about my integrity. As if you cared. You see me slipping off your leash and suddenly you're concerned with integrity."

"Off my leash?" Tory could only repeat the words through his incredulity. The shock of George's news had prevented him from yet considering how the change would affect himself or what part he had played in bringing it on. The phrase added a new facet to the picture, shedding a dim light on George's unfathomable decision. "I didn't realize that I made you feel so constrained."

George seemed to regret his outburst, and his face became unreadable. "Constrained," he repeated softly. "I guess that's an appropriate description."

Tory knew that George was ambitious in his own way, but moving in with Janice Barton had to be an act of desperation, a last-ditch attempt at escape. He'd sensed that things hadn't been perfect between them sometimes, that George was uncomfortable in their deepening relationship. It hurt to realize just how intent he must be upon disentangling himself.

"Don't you think that perhaps you're overreacting? If you don't want to see me anymore, you can just say so. I wouldn't be happy about it, but you don't have to leave town because of me." He laughed mirthlessly. "Perhaps I should be flattered."

"Don't let your head swell too much. This is a business opportunity and I'd be a fool to pass it up. Don't think that I'm doing it because of you."

"George." Tory leveled him with a stare that said he saw through him. "I know you. Not completely, but I know enough. You're ambitious but you're not greedy. And most of all, you're not a fool. Which you'd have to be to move in with that woman." Tory's mind grabbed desperately for tactics to help him reverse George's decision, and he found the solid standby, guilt. "You must really hate me if I can make you think so irrationally."

"You know I don't hate you," he replied quietly.

"Then why are you doing this to me? Doing this to us?"

It was painful to watch George's troubled expression through the long pause. "I guess I feel I'm getting too involved and I have to get away from you."

"Then why don't we just break it off? There's no need for melodramatic gestures." Tory felt a sudden swell of pride at his valiance. "Stay here. I promise that I won't bother you, I won't try to get you back, if that's the way you want it to be. I'd rather give you up without a fight than watch you do this to yourself."

"You'd stick to your word for about a week. Then you'd start laying traps again." George smiled gently. "And most likely I'd fall right into every one of them. I feel the need for some distance between us, a change of scenery."

"So move to San Francisco! Or Timbuktu or the Fiji Islands! Is being tied down to a neurotic lush an improvement over feeling tied down to me?"

"They're two distinct sets of circumstances. It's different with Janice. She just needs one ear and half a mind. I'm still in the driver's seat."

Everything began to fall into place with his last remark, and Tory's face took on a disgusted smile. "That's the whole thing in a tidy little package, isn't it? Always have to be calling the shots, don't you? It makes you a big strong man."

George shrugged exhaustedly. "It's the way I am."

Tory's more noble emotions were rapidly giving way to anger and a desire to hurt, to sting with vicious words. "You should never have broken off that engagement, George," he began in a venomous tone. "You belong in the suburbs with meek little Mary Ann and a flock of adoring children. They'd play along with you, feed your fragile little male ego, tell you every night when you came home from the safe little bank what a great big virile pillar of a man you are." He paused to blow cigarette smoke rudely across the table. "And you're probably right about us. We don't belong together. I want to be a partner, an equal. You have to be the lord and master. It would never have worked. Someday I'll probably thank you for letting me out of this dead end before much more time was wasted."

Tory felt a sickeningly triumphant chill as he watched George's head snap back as if from a blow. His face turned an angry red and his features contorted with pain. Tory began to regret his words as he watched the transformation. He'd hoped for the anger but he hadn't fully considered the pain.

"Goddammit, Tory! I was willing to meet you halfway." The waver in his modulation was so uncharacteristic. "There's nothing I wanted more. I've tried but it can't be done. You don't know how I've tried."

Tory listened to the torment in his voice and immediately hated himself for his horrid words. He came to the verge of panic when he noticed a glisten in George's eyes; the revenge he'd lashed out for was now anything but satisfying. He desperately didn't want to see him cry, knowing the humiliation it would make George feel.

"I'm sorry," he said in growing alarm. He was willing to say anything to help George preserve his pride. "I didn't mean what I said. I was being childish and dreadful and disgusting. I'm sorry."

"I *have* tried, Tory." He sounded like a sad little boy, and Tory wished himself dead of shame.

"I know you've tried. It's all my fault."

"It's not your fault." He paused and seemed to be collecting himself. "It is your fault, but you have no control over it. I could be totally happy to have a fifty-fifty relationship with you, but I can't do it. Some nights I've left you and felt like a nonentity, like I need you with me to make me feel I exist. At first I thought it was just the novelty of being involved, in love. But the feeling gets stronger the more I see you, and I can't live like that, so totally dependent on another person. I have to get away from you while I still have some control."

Tory was transfixed into open-mouthed, totally confused speechlessness.

"Don't look so surprised. You know you've done everything in your power to bring this about."

"No!" It was all he could coax from his vocal chords.

"And maybe a few things beyond your power." The tone wasn't insincere.

Tory's mind flashed back to the first magical day in Freeport. It truly *had* seemed the product of a greater power: a business trip suddenly transformed into a romantic rendezvous as if by an incantation, cerebrally powered roulette wheels and enchanted chips with voices, heights of sensual and sexual awareness beyond the grasp of mere mortals. Tory hadn't understood it all, merely accepted it with primitive awe. He began to remember George's reactions. They were tinged with an element of distrust and perhaps even outright fear.

"We've joked about it, but I truly do frighten you, don't I?"

"It's never been a joke to me. You made one in Freeport about a gypsy love potion. Sometimes it hasn't seemed funny at all. You make me feel things sometimes that are beyond my control."

"You do the same things to me, George. Honest. I'm not pulling the strings."

"Yes you are," George smiled jokingly but not really laughing. "You're a demon. You can make chips talk."

"Demon or not, these things you feel with me, don't they feel good?"

"Beyond words."

"Then why fight it?"

"Because I'm afraid it will do me in. One moment it's there and we're off to another dimension or wherever it is you take me. Then you turn it off and I'm back in a catatonic trance. I used to lead a fairly sensible life. Not always overwhelmingly exciting, but there was a comfort in its predictability. With you, it's one surprise after another. They're beautiful surprises, but after a point it becomes too much for the standard human nervous system."

Everything was suddenly clearer, and with understanding fear diminished. Tory accepted his words and realized that for the moment, at least, George really did need to get away from him. He didn't yet know how to bring him back, but at least he understood the problem. "Recognizing the problem is half the solution," the nebulous voice of a vaguely remembered high school math teacher told him, and he could feel an optimism beginning to grow. He couldn't doubt his ability to win back a man whose biggest problem was apparently that he loved him too much. As problems go, it seemed a pleasant one to deal with.

"So you're going to hide out in Bucks County with that woman to get away from me. It's not going to work, you know. It's not going to make you happy."

George shrugged, apparently not sure of the future himself. "I'm beginning to think it's not in my chromosomes to be happy. It's an overrated emotion anyway. I'll have security, and peace and quiet, and a nice little business to occupy my mind. It's not such a bad deal."

"You'll regret it."

"I regret most everything, sooner or later."

Tory decided that they'd exhausted the topic for one evening. George needed time to think, to come to his senses. He decided to give him something more to think about. "You can't escape from me that easily, George," he hissed ominously. "Perhaps I really am a demon. And maybe I wasn't joking about the gypsies and the love potion. Magic spells are very powerful things, you know. Bucks County isn't far enough away to weaken them."

He leaned forward over the table and noticed George involuntarily draw back. "I'm going to visit you in your dreams, George, and haunt your every thought. I'm going to torment you night and day until you surrender." He arose from the chair for dramatic emphasis and leaned over the table, bringing his face within inches of George's alarmed eyes. "Mark my words, George," he whispered eerily from deep in his throat, drawing out each syllable, "I'll have you back." Without benefit of a column of smoke to make him disappear, Tory strode out of the restaurant in what he hoped was a memorably chilling exit.

Chapter Nineteen

TORY glanced at his Cartier as he paid the cabdriver, satisfied that he was exactly twenty minutes late for dinner with Brad. He could have easily been on time but promptness would have deprived Brad of one of his less annoying peeves. Tory always arrived to meet him between fifteen and thirty minutes late, so Brad could shake his head and frown at his watch, briefly flashing a put-upon expression to make sure Tory realized how mature and patient he was being.

The restaurant was a familiar one, Victor's, in South Philadelphia. They often met there for dinner. It appealed to Brad's frugality, and Tory liked its casual atmosphere as a change of pace, besides delighting in the spaghetti sauce, which was the next best thing to Grandmother deLuca's. The hostess led him to a familiar table in the rear dining room, and he threw his raccoon coat over a chair with calculated carelessness while he watched Brad shake his head and silently frown at his watch. The waiter appeared unbidden with the usual carafe of Chablis.

"So how are you?"

Brad's standard opening question sounded more officious and proprietary than usual the past three months, ever since Tory's depression over George. He'd expected his other close friends to be sympathetic, but Brad's unusual compassion constantly convinced him that he'd lost a true gem. He couldn't recall Brad approving of any of his men since David.

"OK," he answered, with a smile that was supposed to say that he really was.

And he *was* OK, most of the time. He hadn't expected to go through what he had, but after three months things were bearable. He'd taken to his bed immediately after the dinner with George, as he often did when faced with a problem. A long afternoon nap or a ten-hour night buried in goosedown and satin usually acted as a tonic. What seemed insurmountable the night before customarily looked brighter with the morning sun. His mind was at its most acute after a good night's sleep and three cups of coffee.

This time, the morning after had come as a cruel shock. He'd done so well during the confrontation with George, keeping a calm demeanor, analyzing motives, listing alternatives, finally settling on a course of action that would surely correct everything in due time. He'd been so optimistically involved in the solution that it wasn't until his morning clarity that he fully comprehended the problem. He was certain that he'd get George back eventually, if it took six months, a year, even longer. Depression didn't set in until he'd begun to think about the six months, the year, even longer, and what he was to do alone during that period. He'd had a good laugh at the idiosyncrasies of his mind before his spirits had plummeted.

As depressions go, Tory knew that it could have been worse. It wasn't a light depression that he could sometimes find enjoyable, the kind that would pass dependably but give him reason for sympathy-producing tears, overlooked antisocial behavior, and general self-indulgence while it lasted. Nor was it a debilitating breakdown that made it impossible to sustain a thought for more than a few seconds or perform the most routine functions without great effort, the kind that he dreaded more than the flu or pneumonia. This depression had fallen somewhere in between, a joyless purgatory with no visible end. It had given him no satisfaction to discuss it. He'd been irritated to even think about it. The only relief came from a busy mind. He'd gone through a similar period after his acute grief over David had passed, where being busy at the supermarket helped him not to dwell on things. This time keeping busy was a way to channel his anger away from destructive activities.

"Are you *really* OK, Tory?"

Tory cursed in exasperation and took a long swig of wine. Sometimes it seemed to him that Brad loved him best when he was at his worst, when he was absolutely beset by Brobdingnagian crises. Tory imagined that it was something of a vicarious thrill for him and tried to be understanding.

"Please believe me," he implored in overdone distraction. "The crisis stage passed after I managed to stumble through Christmas and New Year's. It's February now. We've milked it for all it was worth. Let's move on to something else."

Brad refused to let it die. "You're still not your old self, Tory," he said sadly. "You've changed."

"Of course I've changed," he replied irritably. "We all change. Wouldn't life get a bit repetitive if we didn't? Besides, you should be proud of me lately instead of worrying so much. Haven't the changes been for the better? Aren't you impressed over how efficient and organized I am these days?" He looked at the ceiling in utter boredom. "I even balanced my own checkbook today. And I hadn't forgotten to enter one check. How's that for organization?"

Properly channeled, the depression had become constructive. He'd replaced his usual relaxed personal habits with a manic quest for order, attacking drawers and cupboards and closets, organizing the jumble of winter and summer clothing, kitchen utensils, old correspondence, canceled checks. He'd alphabetized the record albums, matched the odd socks, sorted through the clipped magazine articles, rearranged the furniture several times, and written detailed lists for every conceivable purpose. He had to bite his tongue with Mae, barely able to keep from mentioning discolored grout in the bathroom tiles and brass drawer pulls that were looking tarnished.

"You've been amazing," Brad admitted grudgingly. "Even the electric bill gets paid without me reminding you." A look of optimism briefly flashed across his face. "But you never cook dinner anymore. We always go out. I wish you'd start cooking again. Nobody cooks like you do when you're in the mood." His voice was becoming irritably close to a whine.

Tory eyed the middle-aged couple across the room and

wished that he could join them, anything to escape Brad's maddening remarks. "I'm too busy to organize dinner parties."

"You always found time before, even when you were working overtime at the supermarket."

"OK. You win." He took another long slug of wine. "I don't cook anymore because I'm sick and tired of it. I've had it up to my Braggi-bronzed cheekbones with cooking and staying home. I like to be out, see people, get out of the apartment once in a while."

"Once in a while?" Brad repeated in delighted accusation. "I'll bet you haven't eaten one dinner at home in the past month."

It was true. He rarely went near the range for anything but his morning coffee. He couldn't poach an egg without wanting to smash it against the wall. Cooking made him think of George for some reason, how he should be contentedly stirring a saucepan, whipping something up for the two of them, instead of eating alone or with friends who affronted him for being only friends. Sometimes his bitterness frightened him.

"Who has time to eat at home?" he asked calmly. "I work nights, you know." He hoped his remark would divert Brad's mind from the domesticity issue and set him off on his favorite criticism.

"You certainly do," he replied drily. "And afternoons too."

Tory shook his finger primly. "An idle mind is the devil's workshop."

"I don't think that applies in your case."

"Don't you think it's better for me to concentrate on my appointments instead of sitting around feeling sorry for myself?"

"There's a limit."

"Someone had to pick up the slack after George moved and left all his regulars stranded."

"And you volunteered for every one of them."

"Not quite," he replied matter-of-factly. "But there were some aces there that I'd have been a fool to pass up. Opportunity was pounding at the door."

"How can you have sex with two men a day?"

"They used to do four shows a day in vaudeville," Tory shrugged. "I'm just an old trouper at heart. And two a day is nothing with a few hours' rest in between. Ed does three a day, two or three times a week. And Anthony manages to press it into service for four regulars every Saturday."

"Quality must suffer," Brad said thoughtfully.

"So call for an early appointment."

"You know I didn't mean it that way," he sputtered.

"It's not true anyway. You learn to pace yourself, gear your energy toward performances. It's almost like being an athlete in training."

"You're turning into quite a pro, aren't you?"

"Maybe I should write a manual."

"Where would you find the time? Or the energy? If you keep using your sex drive on business you'll never even have the energy to look for another man."

He tried not to snap. "So who's looking?"

"You're not going to give up on him, are you?"

It was the truth, but Tory wasn't going to admit it. "I didn't say that. Right now I don't want any involvements. That's understandable, isn't it?"

"Just so it doesn't turn into a repeat of what you did to yourself after David."

"They're two different men, two different situations. You don't see me wandering around in a daze, do you?"

Brad examined him for a long moment. "Sometimes the new you worries me more. You're getting more and more like that Ginny."

"So what's wrong with that? I should be so successful."

"You're developing dollar signs for eyes."

Tory fixed him with an unkidding imitation of Ginny's hardest expression. "That's where it's at, kid. Money talks."

Ginny had become something of a role model for him since George left. He knew that she'd never let a man upset *her*, and he watched her carefully for pointers. He was sure that someday soon he'd have George back and he could be himself again, but in the meantime he patterned parts of himself after Ginny and concentrated on being professional and making money.

His new industriousness had put him fully back in her good graces. She'd milked his Freeport transgression for months, but that was all in the past. With her absences from the telephone becoming mysteriously more frequent, she depended on Tory more and more.

Tory found the perfect outlet for his frustrated energies in the telephone. Every memorized name, address, telephone number, time schedule, and personal preference filled a brain cell that might otherwise be looking for trouble. The supply of information was inexhaustible, but Tory tried to memorize it all, wondering if he could saturate his brain and turn into a computer, replacing memories and feelings with names and numbers.

"I have as much respect for money as anyone," Brad said after a pause. "But there are other things in life."

"I know there are," he replied with an annoyed frown. "I still see my friends. I still go to Duffy's almost every night."

"Duffy's isn't the answer. You need something like George to keep you *out* of Duffy's."

"I don't want a man, goddammit!" He glanced at the couple across the room again. They seemed to be having such a pleasant, quiet meal. "I've had it with men for a while. I'm on sabbatical."

"I don't mean you need another grand passion. Just someone nice and stable to keep you company, help you fill the hours. And who knows? Something might develop and you'll be happy it happened. You've got to keep an open mind. How about that Charles you see on Fridays? He sounds nice."

"Charles!" he shrieked with laughter. "If only you could meet him and see how ridiculous that is."

"I didn't mean you should fall in love with him."

"Love? I can't even respect him anymore." Tory grimaced as he toyed with a breadstick. "He reminds me of the dog we had when I was a kid. Claudia had him put to sleep when I was eight. He was old and decrepit as far back as I can remember, just sat around looking sad and waiting for someone to pat his head or scratch his neck. Charles moves me the same way. I pat his head, listen to him rattle on about his dusty old antiques, act young and flirty with his dusty old friends at the Georgetown, and he's happy." He lost interest in the breadstick and lit another cigarette. "He bores me to tears."

"Then how can you take gifts from him like you do?"

Tory shrugged with indifference, secretly delighted

with the note of scandal in Brad's voice. "He enjoys giving me things. Who am I to deny him that pleasure?"

"That's not right, Tory. It wouldn't be right if you liked him, but this makes it disgusting."

"I don't even have to settle for potluck anymore," he continued as if not hearing. "He has three friends with shops in his block. I can just go in to browse and casually admire something. The next Friday it's waiting on the nelly little French bombé in his foyer."

"You're worse than Mona."

"She'd never make it in the big leagues. She gets too sentimental about her men."

"Do you feel so cynical about all of them? It's been a little easier for me to accept you doing what you do, to think that at least you enjoyed some of it, that it wasn't all so cut and dried."

"I like plenty of my clients," Tory answered offendedly. "I'm seeing one of my favorites after dinner tonight. Michael Weiss."

"Isn't he the one who sent you to Freeport and sends you the champagne every month?"

"That's my Michael," he smiled. "If I wanted to think about getting involved, he'd be the one. He meets all the requirements."

"Just what are your requirements these days?"

"A fat cock and a fat wallet." He was disappointed when Brad didn't choke on his water. "Just kidding, though he has both and they're very handy things to have. He's also sophisticated, considerate, amusing, generous—he tips me with hundred-dollar bills besides the Dom—and he's out of town a lot, which is sometimes the most important attribute of all. On top of that, he's an animal in bed." Tory grinned dreamily. "I'm getting hot just thinking about tonight."

Brad looked skeptical. "What's such a prize need with a hustler?"

"Demimondaine, if you don't mind," he said with disdainfully arched brows. "Hustlers are those tasteless blue-collar people on street corners."

"Pardon me."

"To answer your question, I didn't understand it myself at first. There's no earthly reason for him to pay for a young man's company. But a hundred dollars means very little to him, so I'm a convenience. Just like guys in New York, San Francisco, Paris, and a dozen other cities are to him. He doesn't have time for all the bullshit of picking someone up in a bar, all the civilities and polite getting-to-know-you business." Tory looked puzzled. "And I don't think he really wants to get to know any of us anyway. It's strictly fun and games, a lot of laughs and straight, simple sex. He doesn't want to get emotional about it."

"Which suits you fine."

"Almost a match made in heaven," he mused. "I should take Jimmy to lunch tomorrow for introducing us."

"How's Jimmy doing?"

"I'm so glad you like at least *one* of my friends."

"He's adorable. Not a brain in his head, but he's adorable."

"Jimmy's not all that dumb," Tory said with respect. "We went to Victor-Sacks yesterday for a fitting. He's getting an eight-thousand-dollar lynx. It's just not fair."

"Jealous."

"Who needs a lynx anyway? They shed all over everything after the first year, and after three, they're absolutely shot. But I suppose I shouldn't cast stones." He nodded to his coat on the chair. "The old coon's starting to show its age." He ignored Brad's wary stare. "I saw the cutest little mink jacket at Saks last week, only twenty-seven hundred. It should be on sale next month."

"I guess I shouldn't criticize," Brad allowed. "From where the charge accounts have been, twenty-seven hundred is no big deal."

"You know, I was very upset when Duskin's and Bloomingdale's didn't call to inquire after my health. This is the first time I haven't owed either of them money since I was in kindergarten, and they haven't even sent a note."

"I must admit, you've done a hell of a job with your financial situation."

Tory smiled ingenuously. "There's a lot to be said for the wages of sin." He knew that Brad found it difficult not to admire his success in reducing his debts, no matter how it was accomplished, and he couldn't stop himself from throwing a few jabs now and then. "I wouldn't charge the jacket anyway. I've got close to two thousand in the apartment now, counting my rainy-day money."

"You keep that kind of money lying around?" Brad sputtered. "You? Who can't even remember to lock the front door half the time?"

Tory threw a hand to his forehead in bewilderment. "Isn't it awful? I just can't seem to spend it fast enough anymore. And God knows, I've tried. I go shopping at the drop of a hat, I throw it around the bars like it's confetti, I blew close to a thousand with Mona in Chicago that weekend I flew out. It just keeps piling up, Bradley. I don't know what to do with it."

"That building two blocks down Second Street from your apartment is called a bank."

"Sure," Tory muttered, suddenly serious. "I can just put it all in a safe little account and wait for the IRS to come around with snide remarks about no visible means of support."

"Good point."

"How do I open a Swiss account?"

"You don't. At least not until you have a hundred thousand to make it worth the trouble. But you can't keep that kind of money in the apartment. We'll get you a safe-deposit box tomorrow."

Tory gave him a bored look. "That hardly carries the same panache."

"You'll have to make do."

He slumped in his seat with a tragic sigh. "My life is one compromise after another.'"

Chapter Twenty

"AIN'T you got nothing else to do but cruise around the streets bugging folks for money?" Tory heard Mae demand at the door below. "Every time I answer this bell you're back for more, just bleeding us dry."

"We got to pay the man, Mae," Eugene's unperturbed voice answered.

"And pay him and pay him," Mae wailed dramatically. "You got juicy news today? If you do, I got fresh raspberries and cream."

"Not too juicy, but it's big."

Mae shrieked happily and led him upstairs. She had come to look forward to Eugene's tales of the escort service with more interest than she paid to *General Hospital*. With her indefatigable pumping and Eugene's willingness to talk at length, she caught more of the trade gossip than many of the people directly involved.

Tory was never averse to a scandalous story about a co-worker or a client and enjoyed Eugene's tales when he had time to stay and listen. He looked up from his Shirley Temple bowl filled with raspberries and the silver dessert spoon swiped from Claridge's to give Eugene a stern look. "This better be good, Eugene. We don't share our raspberries with just anyone."

His initial awe of Eugene's terrifying massiveness had quickly faded after he'd discovered the man's nonviolent nature. Tory hadn't yet seen any reason for violence in the business, but he imagined the darkly threatening look that Eugene sometimes practiced on pedestrians or parking-lot attendants would probably be an adequate deterrent. He seemed more at home drinking coffee and passing on stories, something his casual attitude toward Ginny's schedules always allowed.

Eugene busied himself with settling in the chair and stirring his coffee before he spoke, obviously relishing the suspense. He examined the raspberries at length, then cleared his throat importantly. "Ginny's leaving on a vacation next Friday," he announced.

Mae stopped ladling and slammed down the spoon with a threatening clang. "You call that big?" she asked in incredulous disgust. "I want to hear dirt!"

Tory was more interested. "Ginny on a vacation? I didn't think she knew the meaning of the word."

"Hasn't had one in two years and that one was only for female troubles. This time she's flying the coop to Florida with that old fart she's been seeing."

Mae suddenly perked up. "The lady's getting serious about him," she stated smugly. "Told you all along.'"

"He's old enough to be her father," Eugene grumbled with proprietary offense.

Tory could understand Eugene's negative feelings. James Kirk wasn't exceedingly likable. Tory had met him a few times when he'd picked Ginny up at her apartment for dinner or cocktails, and his attitude conveyed a definite distaste for Ginny's livelihood. Tory didn't give him much thought, though he didn't understand what Ginny saw in him besides several million dollars.

"It's good that she's giving herself a vacation. The phones seem to be getting to her lately."

Eugene's martyred expression said that he agreed heartily. "You said a mouthful. I thought it was her time of the month, but it's been going on for six weeks now. She's been so jumpy. I'll be glad to get her out of my hair for a week, be a vacation for me too."

"And I guess you don't give her no reason to be jumpy," Mae hooted. "If I was running that business, brother, you'd've been out on the curb months ago. Sitting around drinking coffee and shooting the breeze when you should be out working."

Eugene maintained his lazy half-smile. Few things ever changed it. "If you were running the business, we'd *all* be out on the curb. But that reminds me of the big part." He looked at Tory through an exaggeratedly significant pause. "Guess who's going to be running things while the Queen Bee's gone."

Mae shrieked in delight and got up to clutch Tory to her bosom. "My baby's getting a promotion!" she screeched at the head buried in her cleavage. "I'm so proud!"

Tory recovered from his surprise after a few moments, and was left with mixed feelings of pride and apprehension. He knew that Ginny had been pleased with his efficient work, and it was gratifying to receive such concrete recognition of her approval. On the other hand, there was a huge gap between babysitting the telephones for a few hours and being responsible for the entire operation. Any uncertainty he felt in the course of a short session could be dealt with by delaying a decision until Ginny's return. He felt he had the competence to make the right move usually, but there were still times when he was relieved to abdicate his temporary authority. Also, the thought of being responsible for cash receipts that had to run into thousands of dollars daily was somewhat unnerving.

"Don't look nervous," Eugene comforted. "I'll be there to help you."

"That's some comfort," Mae replied with a derisive laugh.

Eugene ignored her. "And they're putting Linda on the phones for extra time. Not that that should make you feel better. She can barely find her way to the Square some days, all those babies screaming at home and boyfriends moving in and out. But you'll do OK."

Tory thought of Linda and hoped that next week would be one of her better ones. When her home life was running smoothly she was fairly dependable, despite a mind that seemed sometimes to be operating on a foreign voltage. But she seemed to cultivate personal crises with a green thumb, and in the midst of one she was less than effective at business.

Another problem suddenly crossed Tory's mind. "But what about my clients? I'm almost booked up for next week."

"Ginny's getting Howard from New Jersey to come out of retirement for a week. He was before your time, opened a bar in Atlantic City about two years ago. Used to turn tricks like a conveyor belt, couple dozen a week without batting an eye."

Mae gave a respectful whistle. "He must have been a gold mine."

A wistful faraway look came into Eugene's eyes. "It used to be a tough business before we moved to Rittenhouse Square and got classy. The girls used to turn ten, twelve tricks a day. Every year there's more and more free-lancers and amateurs, working when the spirit moves them." He shook his head and sighed. "There's just no professional pride anymore, not like in the old days."

Tory ignored the familiar lament. "I hope she's planning to pay me well." The thought of money was rarely far from his mind anymore. "I can't afford to give up my trick money for a week."

"Shit," Eugene smirked. "You must have a million stashed in your mattress."

"How can we have any money when you come and take it all?" Mae demanded in her continuing complaint over the fifty-percent commission. "And Tory's got better hiding places than the mattress."

"I'm glad I've got no secrets to hide with you around." Tory sighed resignedly.

"Mae knows all, baby," she said without shame, obviously considering full disclosure her due.

"Don't worry about the money. Ginny's mean, but I've never seen her stingy. She'll take good care of you."

"When is she planning to let me in on all this? Friday is barely a week away."

"She just made the plans last night when the old fart came over. I guess she'll tell you today when you go in. Just try to act surprised." Eugene leaned forward confidentially. "Don't let on that I told you. She thinks I talk too much sometimes. And another thing, she's going to introduce you to Mr. B."

"Oh, baby!" Mae whispered in extravagant awe. "You're going to meet the godfather!"

"Ginny thinks it's only fitting that you should meet him, since you're going to be running the show. I don't think he really gives a damn, to tell you the truth. Our operation is small change to him."

Tory felt a curious titillation at the prospect of finally meeting the mysterious Mr. B. As he became more familiar with the business, he began to realize that Ginny flourished only through his grace. No one from the business but Ginny and Eugene had ever met him, and he was the subject of a considerable mythology among the crew. Meeting him would undoubtedly make Tory the star of several evenings' conversation at Duffy's.

"He's no big deal," Eugene announced with studied offhandedness. "Just a little gray-haired man with tinted glasses. Looks a lot like Ginny's old fart, come to think of it." He laughed suddenly. "Except if you get *him* mad, it only happens once."

Tory concentrated on maintaining his bored expression in the back seat of the Lincoln as it pulled away from the curb. He thought that the three of them would make an interesting impression at red lights; stodgy old James Kirk with his patrician profile, Ginny looking expensively glamorous in masses of mink, and the handsome young man with so much poise and style. He hoped for a big crowd at the airport when the luggage was unloaded and he bade them farewell. It would be a fond farewell, but not overly fond. After all, it was only a jaunt to Palm Beach, and people who rode in chauffeured cars wouldn't show inordinate excitement over that.

Ginny prevented him from developing the fantasy any further with a constant barrage of nervous last-minute instructions. She didn't mention anything that she hadn't advised him on during the previous week of intensive training, and the words seemed to tumble out involuntarily. Her escort punctuated her sentences with annoyed clicks of the tongue and exasperated sighs, finally grumbling that it wasn't going to be much of a vacation if she was going to worry about business all the while, "business" enunciated with unmistakable distaste. Ginny flashed him her movie-star smile and patted his camel-coated arm, reassuring him in sugary tones that brought a nauseated sigh from Eugene in the front seat. The parting scene wasn't quite as smashing as the picture in Tory's mind, but after the stressful ride he was more relieved to be rid of the couple than disappointed at its shortcomings.

"Doesn't seem like much of a vacation," Eugene complained half to himself as they began the return trip. "Putting up with that old fart for a week."

Tory couldn't help laughing at how aptly Eugene had read his thoughts. "I guess she was really desperate for a vacation."

"I'm beginning to think Mae's right. She's going to sink her meathooks into this sucker and marry him."

Tory dismissed the thought with a laugh. "Mae doesn't miss much, but I don't think she can read minds of people she's never met."

"She might have a point, though," Eugene replied thoughtfully. "If Ginny really wanted a rest, why would she bother herself with that old thing looking like a dill pickle for a week? She's got the cash to take a vacation to the North Pole, she doesn't need him for that. And you know how skittish she's been lately, like she's on pins and needles waiting to play four aces. And she's been drilling you for the past week like she's going on a two-year cruise."

Eugene's reasons were disturbingly logical, though the idea still seemed farfetched. "What's she need with him? She's too independent to put up with being a wife, even for *his* money."

"That's where you're wrong," Eugene replied with certainty. "She's playing for big stakes this time. That old fart's got money his great-grandfather stashed in the vault and forgot about. What he's got she couldn't hope to make on her own even if she worked without another vacation till she was eighty."

Tory wasn't completely convinced. "How could she get up every morning and listen to that nasal Main Line whine?"

"She just flashes him those caps and twitches her ass and he's like a puppet on a string. Besides, he's got to be the world's oldest man." Eugene chuckled. "It's not like it would be a long-term commitment."

"He's not all that old. Maybe sixty-four."

"But a year with Ginny would most likely finish him off. Then she's a comely young widow with the deed to half of Chester County in her hip pocket. We're talking millions, man. Shit, she's going to be richer than Mr. B."

The name brought a cross thought to Tory's mind. "I don't want to hear about Mr. B. I brag to anyone who will listen at Duffy's that I'm on my way to meet him at Ginny's and he cancels two minutes after I get there. If I ever *do* meet him, you can bet I'll give him a piece of my mind."

Eugene turned around to give him a disdainful grin. "I'll put some cash on that. Even let you call your own odds. Nobody gives Mr. B. a piece of their mind unless they're asked. And then they tell him what he wants to hear."

"Well," Tory capitulated, "maybe I wouldn't give him a piece of my mind. But I can't say much for his manners."

Ginny had laughed when he'd brought two suitcases along for the week's stay in her apartment. She said he might not breathe fresh air again until she returned, and an extensive wardrobe was ridiculous. Tory didn't mind. He was surprised to be so happy to be out of his own apartment for a week. There was something vaguely gloomy about it, so many memories of George. He'd glance at a piece of furniture and remember that George had once sat there or notice a print on the wall and recall that George had once admired it. The bed absolutely outraged him some nights. He'd run his hand over the intricately carved birds on the towering walnut headboard and wish he owned an ax so he could hack out their doleful eyes and all they had seen.

Ginny's huge bed with its sleekly modern lines and Porthault sheets suited him fine, the first night because it held no memories and on the following nights because it was empty. It wasn't something he'd thought about before the week began, but it was a relief, almost a luxury, not to have sex. As he climbed into bed on the second night he realized with a laugh that since George had gone, his cock had been little more than a business asset, something for an accountant to list under Property, Plant, and Equipment on a balance sheet and depreciate on a tax return. He was slightly alarmed at his total lack of interest in sex but chalked it up to his immersion in the business at hand and assumed that it would return when he rejoined the crew.

The telephones gave him little time to worry about it. As long as he remained devotedly conscientious, he seemed to be able to resolve any problem before it got out of hand. And he was completely determined not to let anything get out of hand. Ginny, the crew, the steady clients, and probably even Mr. B. were watching him with curious interest. It was critical to remain coolly efficient and project that same poise he always strived for in any situation.

The weekend was typically sluggish except for the gay trade, with so many of the straight regulars committed to their wives and families on Saturdays and Sundays and several of them on extended winter vacations. It gave Tory a chance to get his bearings and establish a rhythm, before he was faced with the midweek rush. He had expected any problems he had to come from missed appointments and revised schedules. With total concentration and meticulous care there proved to be no difficulties.

The telephones seemed to ring at five-minute intervals from noon until nine or ten in the evening. He thumbed through the files and telephoned out assignments between incoming calls, trying to remain calmly organized when the blue slips piled up during busy periods. Linda helped every afternoon, and Tory was relieved that it was one of her better weeks. She was totally bewildered by the complex paperwork and seemed relieved to have Tory give her orders and make all the decisions. The calls tapered off over the evening, and the business lines could be shut off from one until ten the next morning. Tory managed to pull himself together for an appearance at Duffy's on two nights, but he was usually too mentally exhausted to do anything but collapse into bed.

Dealing with the crew was his only real cause for alarm. Most of them were as interested as Tory was in filling their schedules and making money, but a few seemed to consider Ginny's vacation their cue to relax. They called every day with dire illnesses, urgent personal business that couldn't be postponed, client preferences that they indignantly swore Ginny always honored, and complaints about co-workers that shrieked to be righted immediately. The problem causers were a minority, but exceedingly vocal and time-consuming. They put Tory in no real difficulty during the early part of his substitution, when an absent employee could be easily replaced with an idle body. It was simpler to give in to their demands and schedule around them than to have a time-wasting confrontation. By Tuesday, when the mid-week rush began in earnest, Tory had no alternative to poor management but a display of authority. Since he was on friendly terms with the male crew, except Derek, for understandable reasons, and Eric, who was a suspected schizophrenic, he was able to cajole and plead for their sympathy in any tight situation. But he barely knew some of the women, and they had few charitable feelings for his position. When it seemed necessary, he used what he hoped was his subtly threatening tone and it met with growing success as he practiced it. When that didn't work, he'd make dark references to Ginny's imminent return and the dire consequences that were sure to follow. When voiced with the right mixture of sincerity and vicious vindictiveness, they usually solved the problem. His worst moment was with a woman named Cheryl whom he'd never met. She absolutely refused a Thursday-morning appointment through his complete cycle of tactics, and he finally slammed down the telephone after telling her that the six remaining appointments for the week were canceled. He was on the verge of panic and defeatedly ready to call Ginny at her emergency number in Florida when Cheryl called back and gave in. Tory tried to hide his relief beneath a chilly politeness.

Mr. B. called in twice to check on things. Tory doubted that he'd have any practical advice and imagined that he was only calling to make his presence known. He had a pleasantly gravelly voice and his conversation consisted of polite questions and kind words of encouragement. He sounded more like someone's next-door neighbor or the friendly town pharmacist than an underworld boss, and Tory was more curious than frightened. Aside from Mr. B.'s image, there was nothing for Tory to be frightened of. He'd sent Eugene downtown each afternoon with a healthy deposit.

Chapter Twenty-one

TORY was on the verge of being perturbed as Eugene threaded the Lincoln through the narrow South Philadelphia streets. Luxe transportation was still enough of a novelty to be a pleasure for him but his preoccupied mind prevented him from enjoying it. He couldn't help but be annoyed with the faceless Mr. B., inviting him to supper with all the charm of an officer issuing a subpoena. His call at eight with a summons for ten had sent Tory into a flurry of activity, locating Eugene and the car, threateningly demanding Linda's presence for incoming calls, deciding on appropriate attire, plagued the entire time by the unremitting ringing of telephones.

But he was finally going to meet Mr. B. After months of conjecture at Duffy's, vague descriptions from Eugene and Ginny, and two intriguing telephone conversations, he was finally on his way to meet the legend. He couldn't help but expect it to be anticlimactic after the buildup, like coming face to face with a movie star unenhanced by wide-screen Technicolor. From all the accounts he'd gathered, he could expect to meet an even-tempered, unalarming man. On the surface, not the typical movie gangster who had clawed his way to control of a small but lucrative empire that took in not only Ginny's escort service but also a numbers operation, miscellaneous gambling concerns, cocaine traffic, and legitimate investments in real estate and business. Ginny seemed proud of the fact that he wasn't involved in loan-sharking and other more violent aspects of the city's unacknowledged commerce,

but Eugene ominously assured him that Mr. B. wouldn't
be holding his own against the competition without some
element of enforcement power. The danger made him all
the more intriguing to Tory.

Eugene halted the Lincoln at a shabby rowhouse with
a bright-red door and Tory suddenly wondered if perhaps he wasn't about to meet a small-time hoodlum with
a good PR man. A tarnished plaque identified the buildings as the Congress Club, goading Tory into a derisive
laugh.

He was on the sidewalk watching the car disappear
before he wondered how he was to recognize a man he'd
never seen, and what a Society Hill resident in a cashmere
suit was doing in such a questionable neighborhood in
the first place. His doubts multiplied by the second, but
with no alternative he allowed his sense of adventure to
push him through the door.

A dark-suited desk man nodded politely and motioned
him toward the stairs before Tory had a chance to inquire
after Mr. B. He led him over the worn red carpet to a
closed door on the second floor and knocked softly. On
the count of three he opened the door and half nodded,
half bowed for Tory to enter. Tory couldn't suppress a
nervous laugh at his bizarrely silent deference. His smile
lingered as he entered the dimly lit room and just avoided
tripping over an immense bodyguard seated at the door.
His eyes slowly adjusted to reveal a dining room furnished
in sharp contrast to the exterior and the hall. A pair of
silver candelabra flickered softly on the polished sideboard, matching the pair on the linen-covered table across
the room. They cast shadows that eerily outlined the form
at the head of the table, a small-boned, gray-haired man
with a faint smile.

"Tory." It was the same pleasantly gravelly voice from
the telephone. "We finally meet." The man motioned to
the closest of the eight chairs with a regal beneficence.
"Sit down."

Tory approached him slowly, unsure of his bearings
and knowing innately that a clumsy mistake would offend.
He tried not to stare as he seated himself, but his curiosity was difficult to control. He had the feeling of a theater, a stage carefully set and lighted to evoke a throne
room. He was certain that the desired effect was intimida-

tion, yet there was a quality about the man at the head
of the table that made him feel safe and protected.

Settled in his chair, he looked up to find Mr. B. examin-
ing him expressionlessly. Something drew Tory's eyes to
meet the steady stare, and the unidentifiable familiarity
he felt mitigated any discomfort. They stared at each
other for a long moment, and Tory vaguely wondered why
thoughts of his childhood were flashing through his mind.
It was no specific memory, just a feeling of innocent
happiness. He didn't know why this man should provoke
it, but it finally made him break into an ingenuous smile.

Mr. B. smiled back faintly before averting his eyes,
then made a small motion toward the door across the
room. A waiter immediately appeared with a wine bucket
and filled their glasses with Dom Pérignon. Tory didn't
understand why something so removed from his childhood as Dom Pérignon should reinforce the weird *déjà
vu* he was experiencing, but he emitted a tiny whoop of
innocent delight.

Mr. B. seemed happy to produce a reaction. "I hear
you bathe in it."

Tory wondered if he should be unsettled by a stranger's
knowledge of his personal preferences. It didn't seem terribly important to him at the moment. Santa Claus had
always known exactly what he wanted, too.

"How thoughtful," he smiled brightly.

Mr. B.'s smile diminished by a fraction of an inch before he spoke. "You've been doing a fine job."

"Thank you," Tory beamed in delight. He wondered
if he was beginning to look idiotic with his constant smile
and insipid conversation, but he was too contentedly
mesmerized to behave otherwise.

The waiter reappeared with one serving of a dish that
Tory's senses recognized from five paces as oysters in
a tarragon and cream sauce, his favorite appetizer at
La Panetière. It reminded him of long-ago birthday dinners when Claudia would make his favorite dish of roast
chicken and rice drowning in rich gravy. There was hardly
room afterward for the magical cheesecake that did
something supernatural to the tastebuds, something no
chocolate cake could ever hope to do. Tory shrieked in
uninhibited joy and attacked the dish with enthusiasm.

"That's from your favorite restaurant."

"I know, I know," he managed to moan through his possessed tastebuds. Tory imagined that this knowledge of his personal tastes was meant to be intimidating also, but he couldn't find it in himself to be intimidated by a man who treated him so well.

"It's attention to detail," Mr. B. almost shouted, perhaps in irritation that his audience wasn't properly impressed. "Too many businessmen lose sight of it, but it's crucial."

Most of Tory's brain cells were occupied with the oysters, but he felt a tinge of amusement to hear Mr. B. refer to himself as a businessman. He nodded in enthusiastic agreement anyway, too contentedly involved to take it seriously.

"It takes a special mind to remember these things. When I find one, I respect it."

Tory wasn't sure if the statement was a general observation or a compliment. Either way, it was apparently very important to Mr. B., and he tried to give him a portion of his attention. If a man in his position wanted to throw pearls of business wisdom his way it seemed only polite to appear interested, though the subtle nuances of tarragon and oyster liquor in heavy cream were infinitely more interesting.

"I try to surround myself with these people. People like Ginny."

"She's a smart cookie," Tory replied, trying half-heartedly to appear observant. He wiped his mouth with the linen napkin and pushed the demolished dish aside.

Mr. B. leaned forward to examine the dish. "You ate everything but the pattern off the plate," he deadpanned. "You want some more?"

"No thanks. After that, anything would be downhill." Tory wondered if he sounded rude, but somehow it didn't matter. "Just coffee, please. Espresso if you have it." A sudden inspiration struck him. "Unless you have raspberries, with a little whipped cream. My Uncle Joe always had raspberries on the farm."

Tory's eyes widened and his head reflexively snapped to Mr. B. as he listened to his own words. The mystery was suddenly solved. Uncle Joe, and the family farm.

As imposing to the boy Tory as any Sun King at Versailles. Uncle Joe, the benevolent patriarch who provided for all, and in return demanded only total subservience. Tory remembered the visits to the farm, when Claudia would take him into the parlor and Uncle Joe would be seated in his huge wing chair at the far end of the cavernous room. Claudia would push him forward unwillingly, frozen as he was with fright at the imposing old man. But there was no alternative. He had no choice but to approach the chair and proffer the expected kiss. He never questioned the kiss, no matter how frightened he felt about it. It was a part of the ritual that couldn't be eliminated, not even by a three-year-old's tantrum.

Tory remembered the holiday dinners. Uncle Joe would preside at the head of the table that seemed to seat hundreds. It groaned with food, food from Uncle Joe's fields and barns. Everyone would eat until it was impossible to go on. After the meal, Uncle Joe would examine the children's plates and bellow a frightening disapproval at any uneaten morsels. Tory always cleaned his plate, no matter what it cost his young stomach. Then Uncle Joe would smile benignly and tell him to make a muscle and shout words of praise and make everyone at the huge table laugh. The waves of laughter and approval would sweep over Tory, and chills of excitement and happiness would make him shudder. It was all worth the effort of cleaning his plate.

One summer afternoon when everyone was out in the fields or busy in the kitchen or the barns, Uncle Joe took him for a walk in the woods to pick raspberries. They picked them from the bushes along the shaded paths, and Uncle Joe laughed because Tory ate more than he put in the basket. Uncle Joe was frightening, almost petrifying, but from that moment on Tory knew that he'd always protect him.

"Sorry, kid," Mr. B. answered with a puzzled smile. "No raspberries. How about some Grand Marnier soufflé?"

The voice jolted Tory back to reality. "No thanks. But maybe a little cognac with the coffee." He sipped his champagne thirstily.

"You're right about Ginny. She's a smart cookie."

Tory fought to remember. The picked-up conversation seemed from light-years away.

"Maybe too smart." Mr. B. paused dramatically. "She's marrying Kirk."

Tory laughed for lack of another response.

"Do you think you can fill her shoes?"

Tory's eyes widened, and an exhilaration threatened to burst his chest apart. He suddenly knew that it was one of his moments that was fated to be. He thought of roulette wheels and clicking chips. All the gambling devices in the room were invisible, but the unmistakable feeling was there, the vibrations were flashing through his mind like spinning white klieg lights. Uncle Joe wouldn't let him lose. There was no need to consider the quirks of chance.

Knowing his number was bound to come up, he searched for ways to place extra chips on the felt before the "No more bets" call. "I'd need some extra help. Some of the straight men want a sultry voice to talk to."

"No problem."

"I have just the person for you. Her name's Mona Brett. She's an account executive with Pearson Pharmaceutical in Chicago, but she'd be willing to relocate for the right price."

"I've got plenty of girls in the organization. I'll give you one of them."

Tory assessed his position and knew he had room to push. "I can't do it with one of Ginny's dumb blondes like Linda. I need someone on the ball who can make decisions, a professional who can make her presence known. I know Mona and I know I can trust her."

"Forget it," he answered without much interest. "I need someone I can trust."

Tory remembered his hundred-dollar chip on zero-double zero in Freeport and felt the same exquisite nervousness. "Mr. B., I've got a lot more to lose than you do. The escort service is just one egg in the basket to you. To me, it's all or nothing. I can't take chances." He sipped his cognac thoughtfully through a pause. "I'm sorry, but if we can't do it my way, I'll have to decline your offer." He ignored Mr. B.'s penetrating eyes and concentrated on the espresso, calmly squeezing lemon peel through the oppressive silence.

Mr. B. finally sighed. "You've got balls, kid. Bring your friend Mona in and I'll see what I can do."

Tory tried to hide his gambler's shakes.

Mr. B. examined him for another long moment. "I like your style." He paused significantly. "Just don't get too cocky."

"Yes sir," he answered demurely.

Chapter Twenty-two

GINNY swept into her apartment trailed by Eugene and her luggage, a serene smile on her lightly tanned face. In lieu of a greeting to Tory she held out her bejeweled left hand, the pear-shaped diamond providing full justification for her tranquil expression. Its brilliance seemed powered by nuclear batteries, and it was of a bulk that one rarely encounters except in the company of armed guards and thick plate glass.

Tory approached her and reverentially knelt as he kissed the gem. "Jesus Christ," he gasped in religious awe. "Did you mug Liz Taylor?"

She slapped him playfully. "That's no way to talk to a Main Line matron."

Tory gave her a dubious stare as he arose. "You're not really going to get into that number, are you?"

"Not really." She hung her coat in the foyer closet and stepped out of her shoes before sinking wearily into a chair. Tory settled into the opposite chair, curious of her plans. "We'll have to be in Radnor from time to time for Jim's obligations, but I have no plans to try to crash blue-blood society." She examined her ring with an amused smirk. "Even if I wanted to social-climb, I'd never make it out there with this vulgar thing."

"Some conservative folk might say that it *is* a bit flashy."

Her serene smile returned. "Unless it's on *their* finger. Then somehow it looks different."

"What will you do with yourself? I can't imagine you without something challenging to fill your time."

Ginny hooted. "Just watch me. I've had my fill of challenges for a while. Now I'm going to make a career out of being a respectable lady of leisure. I've got a condominium to decorate in Boca Raton, vacations to plan, Jim's business associates and less stuffy social contacts to entertain. Maybe a little charity work." She paused thoughtfully. "And I'm getting the urge to have a boat. A big one. Something comfortable for knocking around the Mediterranean."

"Sounds like a rough life. Are you having a big wedding?"

She rolled her eyes at the thought of it. "Very smart. Very quiet. Jim's family isn't exactly crazy about me."

"How snobbish of them," Tory sniffed.

"It's not surprising," Ginny shrugged. "They were expecting him to die a widower. It's thrown a monkey wrench into their trust funds, the greedy bastards. At any rate, the wedding will be very discreet. Two weeks from tomorrow." Ginny's expression changed to a more familiar one of cool efficiency. "That gives us some time to smooth your rough edges for the transition. But from what Mr. B. tells me, you don't need much more instruction."

She amazed Tory. He admired professionalism in any field, the type that provided total self-confidence and commanded absolute respect. Ginny had it in abundance. Nothing short of serious illness would prevent her from executing her duties, not even a brilliant match that made the escort service look like a trivial detail that no longer warranted thought. It amazed Tory that she could still bring herself to bother, and he knew the effort must come from an immense store of professional integrity and pride.

The only thing that detracted from his admiration was her coolness. He understood that remaining calmly efficient at all times was part of her professionalism, but wondered where it left off. Her marriage sounded like a calculated business deal that only a pro could pull off. He could detect no emotion in it, nor in any other area of Ginny's life. She wasn't an unkind person. Tory didn't doubt that she was fond of him and Eugene and a few of the other members of the crew. But business always came first. If she had to make a decision between affection and expediency, Tory felt sure that expediency would win soundly. He wondered if the trait was innate or if it had been created by the business; if it came from the business, would the business do the same thing to him?

If it was going to change him, he couldn't muster many strong feelings of regret. He was ready for some changes in his life, a different image that might speed George's return to him. Almost four months had passed, without notable progress. All accounts reported George energetically involved in his restaurant, devoting himself to it to the virtual exclusion of all else but Janice's needs. Tory wondered if George would be more fascinated with a coolly professional entrepreneur than with an impulsive hustler. He thought it worth a try. And if it didn't work, at least he'd have a chance to achieve Ginny's prestige and financial success, a sure salve for his wounds. He was eager to follow her lead and discuss business.

"I thought the tough part would be all the bookwork, but that's easy compared to dealing with the prima donnas."

"Did they give you a lot of trouble? You don't know how many times I almost called to see how you were doing, but I forced myself to hold off. You had my number if anything drastic happened, but I couldn't help worrying. And it was good practice for you to have it all on yourself and take care of the problems. I'm proud of you." The cold glint that came to her eyes gave Tory a frightening excitement. "It might be a good time to weed out some of the deadwood and lay down a sound establishment for your authority."

"I never realized how much authority was involved. You always made it look so easy. You told everybody what to do and there was never a question."

"That's only natural," she replied with unquestioning self-assurance. "There was never a question because they knew what they could expect from me—either the job was done the way I wanted it done or they'd get their walking papers. The guidelines are clearly defined with me. With you, they don't know yet. And they're going to put you through a certain amount of testing to see how much they can get away with." She pointed casually to Eugene as he emerged from the bedroom hall after depositing the luggage, wearing his usual unconcerned air. There's a prime example. He's going to walk all over you if you let him. He needs constant attention. But you can use him as a yardstick. If you don't find reason to scream your head off at him at least three times a day, you'll know you're being too soft."

Eugene huffed indignantly. "The day you only scream at me three times is the day I call the doctor." It was a bold remark for Eugene to make to her face, but he seemed to sense a lame-duck administration. Tory spent a second in braced expectation, but Ginny only laughed good-naturedly. She seemed to sense her changing position too.

"When was the last time you had that car washed?" she demanded. "Not since I've been gone, I'll bet."

"No ma'am. I've had my hands full helping the new boss get organized."

"I think he can manage without you for an hour. Do it now. And be back before six."

Eugene looked at the ceiling in exasperation before making his exit. Ginny shook her head as he left. "It's not all a cut-and-dried business. There's no logical reason why I didn't fire him years ago." She turned her disapproving gaze to Tory. "But you're going to have to change your ways. You don't have to become a monster, but you'll have to stop being a silly faggot and crack down."

Tory managed to hold his reaction to a slightly disdainful laugh.

"You know what I mean. I'm not worried about scheduling and that part of the business that takes brains and know-how. You've got the brain. You'll be able to do that blindfolded in a matter of weeks. I'm talking about management, dealing with personnel. Your whole attitude has got to change. You can either be a boss or you can be one of the crew. You can't have it both ways, Tory. You can't be carrying on in the corner booth at Duffy's one night and handing out troll assignments the next afternoon. There's got to be some distance between you and the crew."

Tory shifted in his chair. "I can see your point." He could say it without a deep sense of loss. He still enjoyed the camaraderie of the crew on some nights, but George had been right, the novelty was beginning to wear thin.

Ginny didn't seem convinced that he understood the

full import of her words. "It doesn't stop with Duffy's. You're going to have to change your whole attitude. You're the boss, not a friend. You're no longer an equal with those people."

"I can't just pretend that I never knew them," he balked. "They'd hate me for it." The thought upset him deeply, but he found a logical cover for it. "I can't be very effective with a crew that hates me."

"We'll find you a happy medium. You can still be friendly," she ruminated. "You just can't be friends. No more lunches with Doreen and Gloria. No more carrying on in the clubs with Carl and that group. No more drunken partying until five in the morning. That's all got to change."

"What about Jimmy?" he asked in sudden alarm. "I can't just cut off my friendship with him. We're more than party pals."

Ginny shrugged with a frown. "It doesn't make much difference with him. He's always done as he pleased anyway—there are no threats to hold over his head. He'd have never lasted a month with me if he didn't have a following."

Tory tried to cover his relief. He was willing to make sacrifices and attempt to become a cold professional, but his few close friends were the only pleasure that remained for him.

Ginny's frown deepened. "And how you ever talked Mr. B. into hiring your friend Mona—"

"Don't worry about Mona," Tory snapped. "She'll do just fine."

"Not if she's still running with cheap hoods like that Santoro who set up your interview with me. The likes of him are bad news, Tory. You had two strikes against you when I met you, just by your company."

"That was over between them months ago. And you have to admit that I need a woman to help handle the straight clientele. You know what tight-asses some of them are."

"You're putting yourself in a touchy position. If she doesn't work out, Mr. B.'s finger is going to be pointing right at you."

She'd struck a nerve. Tory was beginning to entertain second thoughts about taking Mona into the business. Perhaps it *was* a mistake. But when Mona put her mind to it, she was a competent businessperson, or she wouldn't have attained the executive position in Chicago that she was so happy to give up. Her outgoing personality would certainly be an asset with clients. Most important of all, it would be such fun for Tory to see her daily again. He hoped it was worth the risk.

"Don't worry about it, Ginny. Believe me, Mona will be great."

"I have my doubts, but I guess Mr. B. knows what he's doing. He's seldom wrong." She examined Tory with a respectful stare. "You made quite an impression on him, you know."

Tory lit a Gauloise and tried to put casualness into his shrug. "It was like going to visit the Wizard of Oz. Behind all the smoke and racket there was just a sweet little old man with glasses."

Ginny emitted a shocked laugh at his blasphemy. "Don't you believe that for one minute or you'll be in for a rude awakening someday. The smoke and racket aren't phony. He'll treat you well because you're going to do your job well, but don't get carried away with yourself."

"Speaking of treating me well, when do we talk money?" He tried to say it with his usual unconcern, but the thought had haunted him since supper at the Congress Club.

Ginny's look was patronizingly smug. "That's a big plus for you on this job. Greed is a great motivator."

Tory's eyes focused involuntarily on her new diamond, but he managed to hold his tongue. "How much is in this for me, Ginny?"

Her long silence was maddening. "I really don't know what to tell you, Tory. You'll get the apartment and the car and Eugene. And you'll get an envelope every Thursday. Some weeks there will be more, some weeks less. It all depends on how Mr. B. feels about you at the moment. I can't tell you anything definite. Just that you'll be doing much better than you are now."

" 'Much better'?"

"Definitely."

"Twice as much?" His tone made it clear that greed had won out over nonchalance.

"Maybe. Maybe more. Whatever he gives you, you'll

take it and you'll like it. If you're good to him, he'll be very generous with you."

Tory's thoughts went back to Uncle Joe at the head of the table. "As long as I clean my plate," he mumbled.

Tory slept poorly during the next two weeks. Waiting was his least favorite activity. Christmas, lines at the A&P, furniture deliveries from Bloomingdale's, first cocktails in busy restaurants, they all annoyed him acutely. Waiting for a new apartment, the prestige of a new position, practically waiting for a new life, was the worst torture he could imagine.

But it diverted his mind from George. The intervals between thoughts of him could be measured now in hours instead of minutes, about the same time Tory spent thinking about David. At least he could think of David now without bitterness, just a pleasant, vaguely melancholy memory here and there. He imagined he could feel the same way about George eventually, if it had to be that way.

It was a pleasure to spend most of each day with Ginny. She remained every inch the boss until the day before her wedding, but she mellowed. She reminded Tory of his elementary school teachers a few weeks before summer vacation, when they'd let pass minor infractions. Ginny reminisced fondly about her years with the service, years that transformed her from a streetwalker to a millionaire's wife. Tory could forgive her an occasional trace of smugness.

She was obviously not in love, but she seemed to have some sort of affection for her fiancé. Tory sometimes caught her giving him a small gesture or an occasional smile that seemed sincere. It made him happier for her and less worried about himself in a few years. It gave him hope that he could survive the business without becoming a monster after all.

The mechanics of the business no longer worried him constantly. There were still details to pick up, but he knew they'd come with time. He was confident he could handle things adequately, if not with Ginny's total expertise. With intense concentration no longer crucial for the mechanics, he could devote more attention to the psychology of management. He listened in as Ginny called each of the crew members to inform them of the new arrangements. When she felt it was necessary, she emphasized his total authority, even telling Cheryl and a few of the other problem employees that she and Tory were seriously considering replacing them. Tory tried to pick up all her subtle inflections and mannerisms and adapt them to his own use. He couldn't pin down her aura of command to any single quality. It just seemed to permeate her personality. She was at a loss to explain it to him, except to say that she never doubted for a minute that she was in charge of every situation. She couldn't recall ever being less than aggressive but allowed that the business had honed the characteristic to a sharp edge.

Tory hoped the trait could be developed, since he knew it wasn't a natural quality that he possessed in abundance. He knew he was too easygoing to make an issue of the smallest shortcomings or tie his stomach in knots over routine problems, but he began to try. He practiced using a firm tone on the telephone and eliminated any unnecessary laughter and gossip with the crew. It was a difficult task. He'd always been able to find something amusing in even the darkest situations. It was one of the qualities he admired most in himself and it was a sad task to give it up.

He fought to keep it from depressing him, but without complete success. A dark thought would creep into his mind occasionally and then he'd wonder if perhaps he wasn't cut out for the position, if it was better suited to someone with a more somber frame of mind. He wondered if Ginny had many friends. Everyone in her life seemed either a client or an employee.

The coming changes created so many worries, but there were so many potential rewards. The cash would be welcome, of course, along with the perquisites of the position. Anyone with credit cards and pretensions could acquire the status symbols he'd so far accumulated, but the luxury apartment and the chauffeured Lincoln were definitely a move into rarefied heights. People weren't simply going to notice him anymore, they were going to stare and be envious.

With his new self-esteem, the novelty of the empty bed began to wear thin. His relief at no longer serving clients became wholly mental, and the physical reflexes returned in full force. Another fringe benefit of the position filled his needs. An addition to the crew was necessary to replace him, and handsome young men arrived for auditions with nervous hopes of pleasing him. Tory tried to keep his arrogance to a minimum, but the turned tables did not go unsavored.

Tory wondered if eventually he would command Ginny's professional respect. The crew wasn't overly fond of her, but they held her in a certain esteem. The clients thought highly of her, many of them being businessmen themselves and keenly aware of her position and its responsibilities. He'd felt a certain glamour in being an expensive hustler but the new position's status was definitely more rewarding.

He was certain that George would have to take notice. He'd have to realize what a mistake he was making. He hadn't spurned just another dizzy queen, he'd spurned someone with position, a success. Men were going to pursue him now for more than just his body. He'd be in a position to follow Ginny's example and set his sights for the top. Nothing would attract success like success. When the local social climbers of the night people gathered to swap stories, his would be a name to flaunt. "Almost like Cartier or Baccarat," he mused. It brought to mind his mother's long-ago warning, "If you eat one more of these Fudgsicles you're going to turn into one!" He wondered if perhaps he'd finally abused his penchant for status symbols to that ultimate point. But it seemed a blissful way to go.

Chapter Twenty-three

TORY indulged himself in another chill of pleasure as he handed the coats to the attendant and took another glance at Ginny. He'd never seen her more stunning. The sequined apricot Norell gown seemed to have been designed with her coloring and stature in mind. The older diamonds lost some of their sparkle in the shadow of her latest acquisition, but the total picture was nothing short of breathtaking.

But it was her smile that overshadowed all else. It wasn't her trademark display of perfect teeth that appeared and departed on cue. It seemed to originate in her eyes and overflow onto the rest of her face. Tory wondered if there might not also be the beginning of a tear in her eyes, though it was difficult to imagine Ginny in tears, even tears of happiness.

"Are you ready to face your waiting public?" Tory had to blink back the first warning of a tear himself.

She fidgeted with her evening bag and looked embarrassed about her nervous state. "I can't believe this is happening."

Tory saw no reason why it shouldn't be happening. A grand farewell party seemed in perfect order. For someone who organized parties at the flimsiest excuse, to let an event of such magnitude go uncelebrated would be sinfully wasteful. Approaching the project with such moral zeal, it hadn't been difficult for him to enlist Mr. B.'s aid. He'd been at a loss for words at first but Tory's enthusiasm won him over. He was footing all the bills and even making an unprecedented appearance at dinner.

Ginny had protested wildly at first. She refused to spend her pre-wedding night in such a fashion and was totally aghast at the telephones going unanswered for an entire evening. But the caterer and orchestra had already been engaged, the hotel ballroom rented, the invitations engraved. She couldn't insult Mr. B. by turning down his magnanimous gesture. For once she wasn't in control of a situation.

Tory gave the mirror a last pleased glance and extended his tuxedoed arm. Ginny took a deep breath as if to inhale her lost composure, then swept grandly into the main room. Only the viselike grip on Tory's arm betrayed her.

The spotlight picked them up on cue and the orchestra began a snappy rendition of "Auld Lang Syne." The three hundred guests applauded as the spotlight followed them across the room. The applause was for Ginny, but Tory couldn't deny the electric chill that it seemed to impart to every nerve ending in his body.

The bright illumination ceased abruptly as they reached the dais. They had to feel blindly for their chairs on either side of Mr. B., and Tory cursed the lack of candles. But Mr. B. had insisted upon it. He was the focal point of the room even in dim light, and he seemed less than pleased with all the attention.

Tory knew that Ginny was being credited with the coup of unveiling the legend. It was frustrating, since the whole thing had been his idea, but Mr. B.'s attention to him would make its mark. If seeing him in the flesh didn't damage the legend severely, Tory felt sure that the evening would give him a new authority that would help him to manage the service smoothly.

There had been no introductions as they'd taken their seats, but he recognized a city councilman and two prominent businessmen. The others looked as if they might be Mr. B.'s relatives, but Tory could find no definite family resemblance on closer examination. They all shared a slight attitude of complacency about their presence at the head table and patriarchal respect for the man in the center. Tory wondered if he was imagining their hostility toward him, but he decided not to worry about it.

The smaller tables bordered the dance floor at a bizarre distance from the dais, something that Mr. B. had also insisted upon. Tory had to squint to make out faces in the back of the room as he mentally took attendance. He noted with satisfaction that there were no empty seats and that the crew and special clients were turned out in their finest. They obviously understood the significance of the evening.

Mona and Jimmy seemed to be enjoying themselves. Tory was amazed that she could look so vibrant after the efforts of moving halfway across the country and starting a crash course on a new job, but she was her usual stylish self in a backless black Halston and an oversized white feather boa. She seemed engrossed in her conversation with George.

Tory had spent days wondering if George would show. He told himself that he'd be sure to appear, after the years he had spent with Ginny. The night would have been ruined for Tory without him. He desperately wanted him to see how far he had come, how much further he was going to go, what a success he was going to be. If it didn't bring him back, at least the smugness Tory could indulge himself in would be some reward.

He looked more attractive than ever to Tory's bitter eyes. Tory had wondered if the same combustible feeling would still be there when he finally saw him again or if time would have drained away some of it. He had his answer with one look. Four months hadn't dimmed his feelings, and he had to struggle to control his mask of calm. Janice's presence at George's side was an affront. She looked as bleary and bloated as ever, and Tory's mind searched for slurs to shout silently at her.

Ginny began a last nervous business discussion that lasted through the appetizer and main course, going over unnecessary details and reiterating points that had been made perfectly clear days before. She didn't seem to want to relinquish control. The conversation bored Tory, but he imagined they must look formidable from a distance. Ginny, Mr. B., and he were huddled at the center of the table, and Tory was sure they appeared to be passing on to him the most confidential secrets of the business. He fixed his face in a gravely interested expression for the benefit of the crowd.

Mr. B. decided to have Mona presented to him between the main course and dessert. He sent the ever present hulking bodyguard to summon her to the dais, examined Mona politely but without much interest, and she was dismissed. She turned to Tory before she left and motioned him closer.

"Three seats in on the other side of the table," she whispered with a nod. "Get me a rundown."

Tory examined the far end of the dais with a subtle glance. He didn't need to count seats to spot the object of her interest, a dark, powerful-looking man with a strange hawklike handsomeness. The dark eyes were decidedly sinister, and Tory quickly decided that of all the people on the dais, this was the man who looked most like a criminal, the one most capable of committing murder without the least twinge of conscience. Tory shuddered, wondering if his unexpected chill was one of fear or one of excitement, or if perhaps they were the same emotion.

Mr. B. rose to leave as soon as he finished his coffee. He gave Ginny a fatherly kiss and slipped her a small oblong box before turning to wave goodbye to the dais, like the Pope giving a benediction. His exit with three members of the table trailing him and bodyguards holding doors made a final impression that brought the crowd to complete silence. Tory immediately decided that his legend would be helped rather than harmed by the evening. The man's presence at a dimly lit distance made him more familiar, just familiar enough to start a new wave of speculation, speculation that would recall Tory's presence at his side. He was certain the remembered images in their minds would be useful when he had to make unpopular decisions in the escort service.

The orchestra played, and Tory led Ginny out for the first dance to another round of applause. The councilman cut in after the first dance, and Tory went over to Jimmy who was hopping between tables.

"Is everybody happy?" he asked.

Jimmy took his cue well. "We're all stunned," he gasped. "Carl said it was like being ringside for the Last Supper."

Tory felt a surge of satisfaction and knew the reaction was general. "George is looking well," he said without intonation.

Jimmy smiled sympathetically. "He seems to be OK. He's so wrapped up in that restaurant, like a sixteen-year-old with his first car. He converted one of the dining rooms into a dance floor with live music on weekends, made a big hit out in the wilderness. Next he's landscaping the slope to the river for an outdoor cafe. It's good to see him involved." Jimmy sighed. "With something."

Tory ignored the sigh. It wasn't a night to accept sympathy. "Mr. B. thought we should find roller skates for that poor waiter to keep Janice in martinis." Mr. B. had said no such thing, but Tory was experimenting with ways to exploit his acquaintance with the man.

"At least she's not on a crying jag tonight. And she's letting them use vermouth for a change." Jimmy glanced to examine her at the table across the room. "God knows, we've seen her worse."

Mona glided by on her way from the powder room. "All right," she demanded. "Who is he?"

Tory relayed his information from Ginny. "Victor Brattaglia," he whispered ominously. "Number-two man in local cocaine, armed and extremely dangerous."

"He wants me," she rasped.

"Be careful, dearie. We're in the big leagues tonight."

"The bigger the better." Mona's expression said she wasn't thinking in abstracts.

"And that lovely lady to his right is his wife."

She was totally uninterested in the last piece of information. "Cocaine," she mused. "He must be loaded."

"So is his gun."

Mona flicked her lips. "I'll bet it is." She commandeered Jimmy's arm. "Let's take a little fox-trot past the dais," she ordered. "Follow my lead but be subtle about it."

Tory shook his head resignedly and began a tour of the tables, a host's chore he had looked forward to during the meal. His new authority was immediately apparent. He felt that each of his greetings was an honor, a few seconds of his social chatter cause for pride. When he sat down with Gloria and Doreen, he noticed them glance around the room to see who had taken notice. Derek looked on the verge of bolting fearfully for the door as Tory approached his table. Tory exercised his new prerogative of mercy and gave him an aloof but polite greeting. Everything had changed. He could sense it as he moved through the tables; eyes at the next table would await him and conversation would halt. The exchanges were no longer casual; people silently rehearsed their words before they spoke. Tory knew he'd never again be just one of the crew, and he had no regrets. He tried to hide his exhilaration. It became a superhuman feat as he came closer and closer to George's table.

Finally he was there, having made sure his retreat from the last table had been emphatically spirited. He flashed George his imitation of Ginny's business smile and kissed Janice on the cheek.

"Are you enjoying yourselves?" he asked graciously.

George smiled enigmatically and looked directly into his eyes while Janice babbled on incoherently.

"I hear the restuarant is doing well." His hand rested lightly on Janice's shoulder, but his eyes were solely for George.

"It's doing OK," George shrugged. He smiled as he looked about the room, acknowledging Tory's success. "Not as well as you."

He'd acknowledged it, but somehow the feeling of revenge wasn't very satisfying. All that mattered was the riveting blue eyes focused so intently upon him, and the lean muscles that should be beside him when the evening was over.

Tory made a small bored motion to take in the room. "Oh, this." He yawned. "I needed a little hobby to fill in my free time." One of the most satisfying parts of success was tossing it off lightly.

"Another hobby?" George gave him his quiet, knowing smile, the one that always made Tory sigh helplessly. "I should think that witchcraft would be taking up all of your free time."

Tory's eyes widened at the allusion to their last evening together at La Panetière, how he'd promised to haunt him night and day. That George should remember this was more important than acknowledging his success. He hadn't forgotten. He'd all but admitted that he couldn't erase him from his mind. Tory wondered how much longer he could hold out. The hungry blue eyes told him that each second was an effort.

The success of the evening gave Tory a new patience,

a new certainty that everything would work out. He suddenly felt immortal. He could wait as long as George could hold out. He checked the table's candles for the lighting of his features, then brushed the hem of his jacket to create the slightest sensation against George's arm as he moved away. "Sweet dreams," he murmured, then crossed the room to reascend the dais.

Chapter Twenty-four

TORY hung up the telephone on the Regency desk, reached behind him, and pulled the plug from the outlet with a self-righteous sigh. Another day was successfully over, another day of uncounted calls answered, another day of clients served, another day of receipts earned for the Davis Escort Service and Mr. B. And himself. The two months since his promotion had been almost absurdly rewarding.

Ginny had left him the Regency desk along with her bed, three sofas, several chairs, and assorted other furniture. With her husband's Radnor estate crammed with the accumulation of generations and her wedding gift of a Boca Raton condominium being freshly decorated in off-whites and sands, she could afford to be generous. Tory was sincerely grateful. The furniture from his old apartment might have filled just the living room of the new one, leaving bare the two bedrooms, dining room, den and office. He had money to buy furniture, but lately it gave him more pleasure in neat growing piles in the safety-deposit box.

Tory lit another cigarette from the crumpled pack on the desk, which was either his second or third of the day. He had risen to go to the kitchen to pour himself a well-deserved glass of wine when he heard two sharp kicks at the office door. With no idea of what could be on the other side but prepared to be unsurprised by anything, he strode to the door and threw it open. He saw the top of Jimmy's head behind a pile of Côte d'Azur bags and boxes.

"Now *that's* dedication," Tory greeted him seriously. "Only a true clotheshorse could convince Cote d'Azur to stay open until one in the morning."

"Help me!" Jimmy demanded. "Between you and Mae and the doorman making jokes, I've about had it with good deeds for today."

Tory struggled with half of Jimmy's burden and threw the packages on the sofa. Jimmy dropped the rest on the floor.

"The cute gray-haired salesman let me take them out on approval this afternoon. You can try them on and send Eugene back with what you don't want on Monday."

"You darling!" Tory shrieked, genuinely touched. "With these phones tying me down like a set of quadruplets, I thought I'd soon have to turn to the Sears catalogue out of sheer desperation."

Jimmy laughed at the preposterous idea as he untied a hat box. "You should be able to find a few things you like in this batch. But you can't start trying them on now or we'll never make it to the clubs." He pulled out a wide-brimmed gray felt hat and adjusted it on Tory's head, then stepped back to examine it as Tory happily posed. "You were meant to wear hats," he said with certainty. "Few men can carry them off."

Tory admired himself in the dimly lit mirror over the sofa. "You're right. I look smashing. This definitely calls for a bottle of Michael's champagne."

"What doesn't these days?"

Tory moved to the desk and buzzed Mae on the house phone. She eventually answered and took the request with her usual "Why don't you get it yourself and stop bothering me?" tone. She'd moved into the extra bedroom, delighted to be with her daughter and grandchildren on a less than daily basis. Tory didn't know how he could manage without full-time help anymore, though Mae considered herself more of a helpful houseguest than a domestic.

Tory returned to the packages, the delight of Christmas

morning on his face. "I have time to look over a few things. We have to wait for Brad anyway."

"Brad's coming out with us?" Jimmy asked incredulously.

"It seems he should be respectably tucked into his bed at this hour, or at least in his jammies studying a law brief over a cup of cocoa. But he's coming from an after-theater supper and decided to make a totally decadent evening out of it." Tory sighed as he pulled a cashmere cardigan from the tissue paper. "He says I never have time for him anymore."

"Well, you *have* been a busy little bee."

"Speaking of busy, are you in the mood for a few extra assignments next week? I let Eric go today."

Jimmy looked up from a handful of belts in exaggerated wide-eyed fright. "Whatever you say boss. I want to keep my job."

"You knew Eric's days were numbered," Tory almost snapped. "I can't have him scaring off clients with his fantasies about the CIA. He's getting worse, you know. He really needs professional help."

"Was he number six or seven? I've lost track."

"Six," Tory answered quietly. "I don't enjoy firing people, you know."

"*I* know it. But the word at Duffy's is that you're having a ball."

He laughed mirthlessly. "Let them think what they want. Just so they stay on their toes." Tory tried not to let his plummeting popularity with the crew bother him. It was logical resentment, he told himself. One week he was drinking and gossiping with them and the next week inspecting them with a proprietary eye.

"They're on their toes, all right. I'm not going to mention names, but last night someone spotted you coming into Duffy's with Mona in her black mantilla. He yelled, 'Heads up! It's Mildred Pierce and the Black Widow on patrol!'"

Tory couldn't stop himself from laughing. "It had to be Carl. It's certainly too clever for Derek."

"I'm not naming names. Poor Derek thinks he's living on borrowed time."

Tory exhaled smoke disgustedly and brushed fallen ashes from a pair of Cacharel slacks. "Do they think this is a personal vendetta? Derek's doing his job. I have plenty of clients who go for brawny idiots, and he's perfect for them. In fact, I'm going to ask him if he has any friends from the gym who want to work. I'd rather have his type than some of the lushes and junkies I have now."

" 'Lushes and junkies,' " Jimmy repeated with a laugh. "That's a little strong, You can't have forgotten so soon. Some nights, a couple stiff drinks or a 'lude are all that will do."

"A line must be drawn," Tory replied loftily. "One bad night with the wrong client makes the whole organization look bad. Do you know any more models like Cindy? She's working out very well, just the type I'm looking for. She's fresh. She doesn't have the hard edges some of the other girls have."

Jimmy shrugged. "Hard edges come with the job."

"Exactly. That's why I'm looking for more freelancers like Cindy, nonprofessionals who can hustle for pin money. She won't get hard. When it gets to her she'll get out."

"If she's lucky enough to see it coming." Jimmy intently examined a white silk scarf. "With some people, it seems to creep up on them."

"Room service," Mae boomed as she trudged into the room with champagne and a tray of sandwiches. She set everything down on the desk and examined the hat on Tory's head. "Ain't that pretty! Look at your new things when you're done eating, baby. You don't want to drip mayonnaise on them."

Tory looked up and noticed the tray of sandwiches. He ignored them as he crossed the room to pour champagne.

"Don't you go sticking your nose up at that food," Mae threatened. "You ain't ate a thing since that bitty chicken leg this afternoon. You can't be out drinking and carousing till four in the morning on an empty stomach."

He stamped his foot and tried to look seriously angry. "I'm not hungry!"

Mae wasn't impressed. "Just look at you. Don't know why you're bothering with new clothes. Pretty soon they're just going to hang on you like a scarecrow. You're beginning to look like Loony Larry Loames."

Tory and Jimmy both stopped their glasses in mid-motion to stare at her.

"What did *he* die of?" Tory asked.

"Malnutrition, most likely. Didn't have folks that cared, lived all by himself on cream soda and Tastykake Jelly Krimpets. That boy had bones sticking out on him like a coat rack, just like you're starting to look."

"Oh, please," Tory sighed impatiently as he sipped champagne. "I've only lost five pounds."

"You didn't have five pounds to spare in the first place."

"I'm no skinnier than Jimmy," he answered in defense. Jimmy shifted uncomfortably, obviously not wanting to be involved in a confrontation with Mae.

"Jimmy's got a skinny frame. Some people was born to be skinny, but you ain't one of them. You come from sturdy farmer's stock. You were meant to have some meat on your bones."

Tory was at a loss for words, his head spinning indignantly from the reference to his humble origins.

"And sleeping four, five hours a night ain't helping either. You're out in those hellholes every night checking up on your floozies and scouting for new business, then you're on the phones every morning at the crack of ten o'clock. A body can't go on like that."

"I have a lot of nervous energy lately."

Mae engaged him in a short staring match as the bell rang and she moved to the doorway. She shook her head as Tory's chin jutted out. "Baby," she pleaded, "do it for Mae. Just one little sandwich before you pour all that liquor into your belly." Her sad eyes sent out almost visible waves of guilt. "I'll sleep so much better if you do."

Tory crushed out his cigarette with a frown and crammed half a roast beef sandwich into his mouth as Mae left the room. He truly wanted to eat, but with the knots that resided in his stomach there didn't seem to be room for food. He tried to fire people and give lectures and tongue-lashings with Ginny's inanimate coolness, but it didn't come easily to him. Every day was a trial to his nervous system. He didn't believe Mae's exaggerations but realized that the stress would eventually take its toll.

Brad entered the room a few seconds later to take in the picture of Tory and Jimmy in a sea of strewn clothing, bags, and boxes.

"Bradley," Tory gasped. "You have the audacity to arrive empty-handed on my birthday?" He brushed a pile of St. Laurent shirts from a chair. "You may stay anyway. We'll be ready after one more glass of champagne. Want some?"

Brad shook his head negatively as he sat down. "I had wine at supper. Any more and I'll pay for it in the morning."

Tory sipped thoughtfully. "I don't want to sound like a bigot, but do you think there's any truth to my theory that Jews have congenitally weak stomachs? So few of you make good drinkers."

Brad looked at him with a slightly superior air. "It's not one of our cultural traditions."

"I'm glad I can't say the same," Jimmy giggled as he got up to refill his glass.

"We both come from drinking cultures," Tory muttered. "Lace-curtain Irish and sturdy Italian peasant. Though you should be proud of me, Brad. This is only my second drink today."

"I'm beginning to wonder if some people aren't better off as functional alcoholics," he answered. "Where are we going, anyway?"

"The usual haunts. Duffy's for a quick one to make my presence known. DCA. Maybe Second Story. And I should stop at La Roma to say hello to some clients. There's a huge potential market down there for new business. Do you mind if we stop there, Jimmy?"

"I'd love to! All those gangsters and thugs make it almost like going to the movies."

"You might enjoy it, Brad. If we're lucky we may even bump into Mona with her new beau."

"Wouldn't that be a joy," Brad muttered. "Are you getting along with her again?"

Tory fixed him with an annoyed look. "I wasn't ever *not* getting along with her. It was just that one time when she scheduled Rose for back-to-back appointments in Elkins Park and Cherry Hill. I snapped out on her but it all blew over in a few days. She realized I had a lot on my mind. Besides, she's picked up the business and doesn't make stupid mistakes anymore. I can even leave her here and get out at cocktail hour now to drum up business. I'd be a wreck without her to help me."

Brad examined his fingernails. "I guess you shouldn't be surprised that she's competent at her job. It's not like she came into the business a rank amateur."

Jimmy whooped delightedly. "I can't wait to repeat that one to her. It's sure to set her off, and she's such a hoot when she cuts you up."

"I'm sure she is," Brad replied tersely.

"Jimmy, can we take your car tonight? I had a fight with Eugene and sent him home."

"OK."

"You have a lot of fights with Eugene these days."

"They don't mean anything. He just likes to provoke me."

"Tory has fights with everyone these days." Jimmy smiled ingenuously. "He gave the ax to another one today."

Brad looked at Tory with a worried frown.

"A budding schizo," Tory announced in a deliberately casual tone as he adjusted his hat. "I think I'll wear my black coat. That should work with the chapeau."

"How many more are you going to fire, Tory?"

"What the hell do you care?" he snapped at Brad. "Its my business."

"I care because every time you fire one you go on Valium for a couple days. Don't tell me you don't. I remember that slur you get in your voice all too well from the summer after David died. You're letting this job get to you."

Tory almost closed the discussion with a curt remark, something he'd started to do frequently with those around him. He caught himself as his conscience chided him once again for his impatience, and he decided to offer an explanation instead.

"I have three or four more slobs to get rid of and replace, then I think I'll have the business closer to what I want it to be. It's no picnic, but it has to be done."

"Who's next?" Jimmy asked in sudden alertness.

"I'm not saying. You gossip too much. But you could probably guess from the direction in which things have been moving."

"Which direction is that?" Brad asked.

"From mercenary professional to young innocent."

Jimmy jumped out of his seat. "Christine and Theresa are next! Wait till I tell Gloria. She'll gloat for days."

Tory pointed his finger threateningly, a gesture he was becoming adept at. "Not word one!"

"Then I'm right?"

"Yes," he answered quietly.

"Christine's going to try to scratch your eyes out."

"That's why she's going. She's a beautiful woman, but she belongs on the streets. I see things from a different perspective than Ginny did. Christine came up from the streets with her, and Ginny never quite realized how hard and mercenary she is. The clients don't want that, at least not from my crew. They'd rather think that it's all good company and animal lust, that the money is an afterthought. Christine's been at it too long to ever project that attitude. But there are plenty of people who can. Models and secretaries and sales clerks and waiters —the ones I'm hiring are sophisticated and cosmopolitan but they still have an innocence about these things that's a breath of fresh air. They need closer supervision, and their part-time schedules screw up the bookwork until *I* can barely understand it. But it's worth it. The feedback from clients has been good. And most important of all, Mr. B. is impressed because the weekly gross is starting to climb."

Brad gave him a familiar frown. "It's not worth it if it's going to drive you back to Valium and booze."

Tory gave him a chillingly serene smile in return. The prospect didn't worry him, not since the night of Ginny's farewell party. It seemed that some of her strength had been transferred to him through the catalyst of Mr. B. that night, the strength to face the business crises and personal pressures, even the strength to put George in the back of his mind for the present. The exhilaration of that evening had never totally deserted him, and it was the power behind every effort. It had made him an entity in

his own right, something more than another body, someone not to be dealt with lightly. It made the burden of
his position so much more bearable.

"It won't happen, Brad. I'm a different person now. I
can deal with it." He lit another Gauloise. "I can deal
with just about anything these days."

Chapter Twenty-five

TORY threw his hat and coat on a foyer chair and entered his living room to find Mona prostrate on the sofa with a martini and a pile of schedules. Her white silk blouse and billowing black slacks were dramatically accented with a huge red rose behind her left ear.

"What's up, Juanita?"

She chose not to acknowledge his greeting. "Your new space cadet forgot her client's Chestnut Hill address. She blithely arrived at 247 instead of 742 and confused the hell out of two spinsters."

Tory picked up some schedules and appointment cards from the coffee table, peeved as usual that Mona chose to work in the living room instead of the office but holding his tongue. "Did you straighten it out?"

"I called 742 and explained that there would be a slight delay. He hasn't called back so I assume that it all worked out. Where did you find that girl? Disney World?"

"She's in art school," Tory smiled as he settled into a chair. "A sculptress. Sweet little thing, isn't she?"

"Adorable," Mona answered flatly. "We must send her on a ménage with the ballerina, surprise some fortunate stiff with a fine-arts festival." She sat up to page through the call sheets. "I had a run of last-minute-rush calls. It must be the breath of spring in the air. And about two dozen bookings for midweek. I left the doubtfuls open for you to schedule. Will Janine be suitable for Anson Ferst?"

"No. How about Ruth?"

"Ruth . . . Ruth . . ." she muttered as she paged. "Wednesday at nine . . . booked. How about Charlotte?"

"She'll do."

"Just what are the criteria in this case?"

"Ferst just wants his cock sucked, and Janine can't suck cock worth a damn. Ruth, on the other hand, has true talent. But Charlotte's no slouch either."

Mona arched her brows. "I assume you know all of this through word of mouth, so to speak. Or is there a Standard and Poor's Fellatio Index that you've neglected to show me?"

"Believe me," he said distastefully, "it's not firsthand knowledge. Men are all basically little boys, and there's nothing they'd rather do than brag about their last lay. Especially to me, for some strange reason. If their last orgasm happened to be with one of my crew, you can be sure that I listen carefully and pump for vivid details."

"Is that what you talk about with those men when you go off into a corner at the Lombard Club?"

"A successful merchant must know his stock," he replied smugly.

"You never rest. All this time I thought you were trying to seduce them."

Tory riveted her interest with a series of facial contortions. "Those trolls? Your estimation of my taste appalls me, my dear."

"I have eyes, *mon cher.* Don't try to tell me that you don't play up to any number of those men."

"Some of them, of course I do," he replied matter-of-factly. "I leave the irretrievably strait-laced and the uncomfortably latent alone. I'm too much of a threat to them except on a strict business basis. But most men aren't averse to my suggestive remarks or double entendres, as long as they're done in a jocular manner. They all enjoy a compliment. They're no different in that way from you and me. And it gives them something to laugh about with their friends—'That faggot who runs the escort sevice has the hots for me!' Talk is good for business." He shrugged. "So I give them something to talk about now and then."

"There's something coldly perverse about it."

"It helps to bring in the bucks. That's the bottom line with Mr. B."

"Dear Mr. B.," Mona trilled sarcastically. "How was supper with the godfather tonight? Does he send his warmest regards?"

Mr. B. hadn't had one kind word for Mona in the three months since the farewell party when she'd trapped her quarry on the dance floor. She'd slipped him her telephone number, he'd called the next morning, and they'd seen each other steadily since.

"He sends his usual cordial message. 'Tell that home-wrecker to leave Victor Brattaglia alone!' Victor's wife was in to see him again. She dropped in at the office unannounced with the two bambinos in tow and wept pathetically."

Mona cast a martyred expression toward heaven. "I wish she'd give me a break. Does she think I'm *coercing* her husband to be unfaithful? Besides, it's traditional for Latin husbands to keep mistresses. Has that woman no ethnic pride?"

"From what I can gather, her father was once quite high up in the scheme of things. I don't think Mr. B. would give a damn otherwise, but being who she is, he has to make a token display of disapproval. Probably the only way that Victor got to where he is in the organization was by marrying her." He tried to hide a catty smile behind the motions of lighting a cigarette. "I have my suspicions that he didn't get there on brains and clever repartee."

Mona ignored the unkind remarks and smiled as she stretched languorously. "He has other good qualities."

"Oh Christ," he muttered. "Now you're going to tell me how big it is again."

"Tory," she moaned, "it's gargantuan! And tireless! Last night . . ." She held up a full hand of fingers and sighed ecstatically.

"Does he want a job?"

"I'm not sharing," she answered dreamily. "It never gets soft."

"It's from snorting all that coke. He'll burn himself out before he's forty."

"But what a way to go. Shall I get you some? I can

have all I want as long as it's not for commercial purposes."

"Whatever happened to candy and flowers?"

"Keep them. I'm working on emeralds. They come from the same general vicinity as cocaine, you know. As long as he has connections in South America anyway I don't think it's asking too much of him to pick up a few gems." She jumped as the doorbell rang. "That must be he. Will you answer while I freshen? Mae went to bed eons ago."

"He's here? In my apartment?"

"We have a date. You didn't expect me to take a cab, did you?"

"You could have at least warned me so I had a chance to lock the drawers and hide the silver," he hissed at her disappearing form.

Tory had decided that the Mona-Victor issue wasn't worth pressing. It would be a convenience if she'd find a quiet tycoon and put an end to Mr. B.'s constant harangue, but the affair looked as if it would soon burn itself out. It didn't seem possible that they could sustain such a state of heat forever, and with that would disappear their only bond. Tory had watched several of her affairs from the sidelines, and they all fell into the same pattern. He'd never seen her quite so fanatically sexual, but the emotional attachment looked far less than usual. Victor seemed like a continuation of the fad that had started with Dominic. She was concentrating on unsavory Latin types as she had once dated a string of car dealers and, before that, gone through a stockbroker phase. She said that the hint of danger was the main attraction, a new twist to stimulate her nervous system.

Victor had money, sex appeal, and good looks, but he had no style, the most important quality of all. Mona couldn't possibly feel at ease being seen with him in posh restaurants or exclusive shops. Tory knew without a doubt that it must bother her, because they were so much alike in that respect. They might spend an evening in the Village on a weekend in New York, but they always gravitated back to the East Fifties with a hint of relief. They toured the dives of Torremolinos when on the Costa del Sol, but were always drawn back to the Marbella Club. Victor's South Philly was a colorful change of scenery, but Mona was instinctively Rittenhouse Square.

Mr. B. didn't seem concerned enough to make demands. He mentioned the affair in annoyance at every meeting but delivered no ultimata. Tory conjectured that he'd go directly to Victor if the situation truly concerned him.

Tory braced himself as he opened the door. He'd seen Victor only twice since Ginny's party, but it had been enough to confirm his first impression. Something about the man still gave him a chill, though the air of brutal sexuality that surrounded him was undeniably exciting.

"Hello, Victor." He forced himself to smile.

"Hey!" Victor shouted as he thrust out a hand. "Wonder boy! How the hell are you?"

"Fine. Come on in and have a drink while Mona finishes primping and preening." He couldn't help admiring himself as he led Victor to the living room, remaining so graciously poised even though a predatory beast had been thrust upon him without notice. "What will you have?"

"Johnny Walker Black on the rocks," he almost commanded as he examined the room with an appraising eye. "Nice little place you got here."

"Thank you," Tory managed to reply as he set down the drink and seated himself across the table in the far corner of the sofa. For some reason the thought of Sherman burning his way across Georgia came to his mind.

"You're really shaking up some people downtown with your ideas, you know. Ginora told me that everytime he calls up for a girl lately, he gets a new face."

"What's wrong with that? I should think he'd be pleased."

Victor ignored the question. "And every one of them an amateur."

"Young and fresh, perhaps. But not complete amateurs. It's our new image. There's something to be said for the professionals. You have to admire their efficiency. But their time has passed, at least with *my* clientele."

"I hear Christine was shopping around for someone to rough you up for canning her." Victor's smile had an unnerving resemblance to an animal baring its teeth for attack. "You better watch out. She's a tough chick to cross."

Tory was sure that it was a fabrication meant to upset him. Christine was unquestionably vicious, but street-wise enough to know that, with Tory's connections, that such a move would be bound to backfire. "I'll keep an eye out for her, Victor. Thanks for warning me."

"Hell," he smiled in an imitation of humility, "it's the least I could do for a friend of Mona's." He took a swallow of his drink. "I wouldn't worry too much about her. She's small change compared to some of the other shins you've been kicking."

"Indeed?" Tory's tone was coolly civil. He straightened his back and primly folded his hands before fixing Victor with an uncompromising stare. He suspected that some of Victor's hostility was due to their social differences and decided to give him something to be hostile about. "I'm not sure as to what, exactly, you are referring, although I assume that there has been idle talk about some of my innovations. Change often meets with friction, especially among the less informed." He managed to convey his vague distaste even through a slight smile. "I suppose some of my ideas are difficult for the downtown mentality to grasp at first, but I'd hardly call it kicking shins."

Victor's tightly collared neck turned two shades brighter, but he managed to control himself. "I'm not talking ideas, pal, I'm talking dollars and cents. I hear you've got twenty grand on the streets in charge accounts. You may be the boss' golden boy but you won't be for long with that kind of money floating around. This is just friendly advice—you better watch your step."

Tory couldn't suppress a smile of enlightenment as he heard himself described as Mr. B.'s golden boy. Victor's hostility apparently had little to do with social differences. It looked more like a case of pure and simple jealousy. Suddenly he didn't seem quite so frightening.

"Oh, Victor," he laughed artificially, "don't be such a twit. These aren't the dark ages, at least they aren't this far uptown. Credit is the American Way. I have more than twenty thousand outstanding, fifteen of which represents new business. The day I started the system I got a call from Alan Lohrmann of Geddes, Lohrmann, Smith to open an account that's been bringing in a minimum of five hundred a week ever since. And he's one of several. As long as they had to pay cash on the line they weren't interested more than occasionally. Now that they can write a check to pay a bill on Davis Escort stationery, it's a legitimate entertainment-account tax deduction for them and their clients. It's extra bookwork for me, but the business it brings in makes it worth the trouble."

Victor flashed his teeth-baring smile. "It's a good thing you're bringing in some extra cash. I hear payoffs have gone sky-high since you took over and became the town character."

Tory couldn't argue the point, except to say that sky-high was a bit of an exaggeration. His growing visibility was undoubtedly the cause for the increase. His usual stylishness had begun to show a trace of theater with the adoption of constant wide-brimmed hats, boutonnieres, flowing scarves, and other eye-catching accouterments. Mr. B. usually turned to the subject after he finished lecturing on Mona and Victor, banging his fist and complaining that the service's discretion and the amount of his weekly payoffs had a direct correlation and that each of Tory's new hats cost him several hundred dollars. Tory countered that his growing celebrity meant new clients and the hats paid for themselves with interest. He felt safe as long as the figures backed him up.

It sounded like a valid argument, though Tory realized that the primary reason was his ego. He secretly enjoyed the buzz of conversation that his entrances provoked lately and the growing number of people who knew him by name. It may have been clever public relations but it wasn't without personal motivation.

"Don't worry too much about my business, Victor. I appreciate your interest but I'm quite capable of taking care of myself."

Mona appeared in the doorway. "Come on, Victor, we're late," she said with a trace of peevishness, as if it were his fault. "*Adieu, mon cher.* Until the morrow."

Victor arose and flashed Tory another smile. "Just be careful, pal. If you pull another stunt like the one with Fumo, you might not have to worry either. About anything. Ever again."

Tory returned the smile as he blew Mona a kiss. "It was a pleasure to see you, Victor. We must do it again soon."

Tory poured a glass of wine as the front door closed.

After two weeks the mention of Fumo still brought a knot to his stomach, and he drank thirstily. He had regular heated discussions, even arguments, with Mr. B. About Mona and Victor, about his growing flamboyance, about his new ideas. But the argument over Fumo was still a shock to his system.

Mr. B. often used the service to reward an underling or please an associate. It was more of an inconvenience to Tory than a real problem, except for Fumo. The girls complained about him constantly. Tory had learned to brush off most of their complaints, but he couldn't ignore Lenore's black eye. The next time Mr. B. wanted Fumo entertained, Tory refused. Mr. B. screamed on the telephone and made vague but nevertheless unsettling threats. Tory held his ground, and Mr. B. finally hung up on him in a rage. He wondered if he'd finally gone too far and waited apprehensively the rest of the day for an armed thug to appear and do him in. He barely slept or ate in anticipation of their next meeting, but when it finally came not a word was mentioned.

Tory began to understand Mona's flirtations with danger after this incident. He knew Mr. B. would overlook things from him that few others could get away with. It became almost a game, to see how far he could push. The rewards were gratifying. People were amazed and treated him with a certain awe because of it. The risks were vague but undoubtedly great. It was like putting his head into a lion's mouth, something to make the adrenaline flow. And with George out of his life, it was a welcome titillation.

Chapter Twenty-six

TORY was happy for the unseasonably cool June evening, perfect weather for his new opera cape lined in red silk. He contentedly noticed the contrast between the black cashmere and the cream paint of the Mercedes, his latest acquisition. The lease had run out on the black Lincoln and he'd decided that he needed something less funereal. A cream Mercedes was just the thing, so many points higher on the status scale. His constant cry of "Public relations!" to Mr. B. was providing manifold rewards.

He frowned at Eugene in his usual corduroy jacket. The new chauffeur livery that picked up the shade of the paint and the chocolate upholstery would make the picture perfect. Even if Mona insisted that it was glaringly vulgar, it made a head-turning impression. Except for running the escort service, turning heads had become his major preoccupation. But Eugene could be convinced to wear the outfit only under the greatest duress, and Tory was often too busy to argue with him. There were infinitely more pressing matters to consider this evening.

The car halted at the curb, and he swept into the Congress Club with his usual condescending smile for the doorman. The employees here jumped for him as they jumped for only ten or twelve other visitors, another reassuring sign of his burgeoning status. He ascended to the second-floor dining room and tossed his cape at the ever-present bodyguard with an offhand flourish. Mr. B. gave the gesture his usual derisive smile from the head of the table, but Tory suspected that he secretly enjoyed the ostentation.

"What's new, Beau Brummell?"

Tory's plans for a casual approach to his new project flew out of his head. He didn't want Mr. B. to realize exactly how much he wanted it, but he could barely contain himself as he took his seat. "There's an apartment building I want you to buy."

Mr. B. maintained his smile, apparently looking forward to being amused by yet another outlandish scheme. "And then what?"

Tory took a sharp breath. "Then you give me the top floor for a brothel."

The benign smile erupted into a hearty laugh. "You've been wearing your hats too tight."

"Be serious and listen to me," Tory commanded sharply. He felt a familiar quickening of his pulse as he used his arrogant tone, the one that might just push him too far with Mr. B. It was more exciting than roulette. "It's a stupendous idea. This town is crying out for a brothel! I must have a hundred men on my files who have to rent a hotel room or wait for their wives to go out of town before they call me. And I know of at least a dozen men who go to New York for it because it's not available here. It would all be extra cash on top of the telephone trade."

Mr. B. stopped laughing and took on a fondly paternal expression. "It could never work, Tory. The overhead would eat up any extra profits." His tone was patronizingly patient, the voice of experience explaining fundamental principles to a novice. "I admire your ambition, but it's just not feasible."

Tory tilted his head downward to keep his chin from assuming a provoking angle. "Why not?"

Mr. B. leaned forward in his chair, obviously pleased to impart some of his wisdom. "With the telephones, who are you bothering? No one. The only people who know you're there are the people who are interested. There are no complaints, and payoffs are minimal." He looked askance at Tory's boutonniere. "At least they *were*. But a whorehouse is a sitting duck, Tory. The neighborhood would be in an uproar and the payoffs would at least triple." He paused to listen to his words, and the thought seemed to cause him physical pain. "Instead of greasing a few palms in the vice squad, I'd have to pay everybody from the commissioner on down to each cop on the beat. I'm not saying that it couldn't be done, but you'd have to price yourself right out of the market. The only place a whorehouse can operate anymore is out in the country with good connections and a couple of acres for insulation."

Tory was far from defeated. He'd expected to meet opposition, but he'd planned a logical set of arguments. "How about at Twentieth and Birch?" He paused to let the location sink in. "Think about it. Six blocks from the center of town. But on the east, you have the art school. On the north, a business school and office buildings. There are six blocks of textile factories behind it to the south. The neighborhood turns into a tomb after dark. The only residential area starts with this building on the corner and continues with three blocks of old rowhouses until it runs into the park. Those places are all rundown and subdivided; most of the tenants are students and transients who aren't going to start a block committee to complain about neighborhood standards."

Mr. B.'s expression changed into a respectful frown. "I know the neighborhood. If a whorehouse could make it in this city you'd have a perfect location. But it's still too risky, anywhere in Philadelphia. It's not like the old days when you could buy the mayor and the council. There's too much interference from the media." A dark expression clouded his eyes. "Everybody's a crusader these days."

Tory kept his calm demeanor. He still had plenty of ammunition, and already he'd changed Mr. B.'s attitude from ridicule to passing interest. "Let me tell you about the building. Ten floors, sixty units. It's starting to look shabby, but it's structurally sound. And it's going for a bargain. We can get rid of the present tenants and rent to the crew and people who aren't going to complain. I could fill it in a month. The tenth floor would be for business, and I'll take the ninth for myself and the escort service for some extra insulation. We can put in our own doormen and some surveillance equipment—we can even convert one of the elevators into a private entrance. No one would get past the front door without an invitation."

"It's a fascinating idea," Mr. B. replied after a thoughtful pause. He gave Tory a fond smile and patted his hand. "I'm glad I met you, kid. It's almost like having Scheherazade come up to tell me stories once a week. You keep my mind from getting rusty."

"But you're not convinced."

"No," he answered firmly. "The way you've laid it out, it might have a fighting chance. It's economically feasible. I could set it up with a legitimate front and write off a fortune in taxes. With the location and proper security, payoffs wouldn't ruin your profit structure."

"Then where's the problem?"

"It's a big investment, Tory. I could use something like this to put some idle cash to work, but it's still a risk. One bad break and we've got big problems."

Tory stared confidently at Mr. B. and sipped his champagne. It was time to play the trump card. "Not if you buy me a club license and we sell memberships."

The idea seemed to strike Mr. B.'s sense of the absurd. "Memberships to a whorehouse," he chuckled. "Where do you come up with these ideas?"

"You're not using your business insight, Mr. B.," Tory chided gently. "It's basically the same principle that's made the service a success. I'm carrying Ginny's idea a step further. We stay out of trouble now because we don't solicit—they come to us and we accommodate them if they've got references. This is the same thing, except we can exercise even tighter control on references as a private club." He paused to light a cigarette. "And I'll level with you. What I have in mind would be just as much a club as a brothel. I want to open something competitive with the other clubs in town. The girls would be an added attraction, eight or ten of them tucked discreetly away in boudoirs in a corner."

Mr. B. didn't speak for a long moment. Tory couldn't decide if the blank expression meant he was unconvinced or thoughtful. The suspense gave him a familiar heart-quickening sensation.

"A club." He didn't speak for several seconds. "You just might have something, kid. I have two dives down here, but an operating base uptown raises some interesting possibilities."

The last remark didn't make an impression through the

exhilaration that Tory felt surging in him. He tried to remain calm and businesslike, finally deciding that a few more persuasive points might help seal the deal. "I'm glad you like the club idea, because what I actually envision would have the girls as little more than part of the atmosphere, an added touch that would give the place something of a 'forbidden fruit' ambience. I know the big money is in the prostitution, and I could still run that for you. But with proper backing I think I can make you a good profit in a club, too."

"The accent would *have* to be on the club," Mr. B. mused. "Even with the best security money can buy. The girls couldn't be more than a convenience for your special members. In fact, they'd have to operate independently, no connection with the club at all, a separate set of books and maybe even a separate entrance." He smiled strangely at Tory. "So you think you'd like to get into the club business?"

Tory didn't want to lose him now. "I'd enjoy it, and I think I could make it work for you. I know I'm asking you to take a big risk, but I'm not planning anything too outlandish. What I have in mind would be small, but totally elegant. There'd be a bar, of course, something paneled and comfortable like the Oak Room at the Plaza on a much smaller scale. And a tiny restaurant operation, maybe three or four private dining rooms like this room. I know a lot of businessmen who would use it for luncheons, things like that. And a miniature health club with a sauna and a steam room. And a game room. We can pick up money there with backgammon tournaments, some very discreet high-stake card games, that sort of thing. And maybe after we get rolling we could even put in a little supper-club operation with a piano and a simple menu." Tory tried to stop himself as he realized that his sensible points had somehow turned to reveal some of his more grandiose plans, enough to frighten off any backer. But Mr. B. hadn't made any of his familiar gestures of disapproval. "Nothing too grand, but all done in good taste with a hint of decadence to it. I'm getting a reputation around town as the most decadent thing to hit the streets since the fall of Rome. We might be able to capitalize on it. I realize I'm asking you to gamble a lot of money on me, Mr. B., but I sincerely feel that I could make it worth your while."

Mr. B. waved the thought of money off disdainfully, still deep in his own thoughts. "That's the least of my worries about this thing. Let me think on it for a couple of days. I'll have the lawyers and tax people check out the property, and I'll get back to you. It's crazy. Even for you, it's crazy. But you just might have something, kid." The strange smile returned to his face. "Something more than you imagine."

Chapter Twenty-seven

TORY moved quickly from the car to the office building, checked the directory for Steven Sachs, Public Relations, and waited impatiently for the elevator. He smoothed his uncharacteristically conservative business suit as the elevator ascended, annoyed by the slight touch of intimidation he felt. He hadn't been intimidated by anyone in months, and it was an unfamiliar feeling. But Steven Sachs was supposed to be the best in the business. Only Tory's connections through clients and Mr. B.'s generous expense account had gotten him the first appointment, and Sachs had seemed uncertain even then, wondering aloud if he should stoop to something so inconsequential as a private club. Tory had been incensed, but Mr. B. insisted that he hire only the best talent, so he'd held his tongue.

He announced himself to the receptionist and prepared to be unimpressed with the completed project. With the buildup the man had given himself, Tory decided to let nothing short of sheer genius bring an approving smile to his face. But he hoped desperately for sheer genius. His modest plans for a small club seemed to expand everyday. Even more unnerving, each new idea met with unwavering approval from Mr. B. The vastness of it all was beginning to overwhelm him, but he couldn't let it show.

Sachs emerged from his office promptly and showed Tory in, a sign of deferential courtesy that did not go unnoted. Tory's thoughts were completely on business but he couldn't help appreciating the man's looks. He was somewhere near thirty-five, dark-haired, almost swarthy, a wiry build. Tory's professional eye judged him to be a bundle of energy in bed.

"Have a seat, Tory. We've got plenty to talk about." He motioned to a plush leather chair in front of his sleekly modern desk. "May I offer you a drink?"

"Something dry in a white wine would be pleasant," he answered distantly. He thought it might sound pretentious to ask for Dom Pérignon, even though it had become his usual beverage. "Well, have you put together a package that's going to sweep Philadelphia off its feet, Steven?"

Steven handed him the drink and slouched into his chair with an uninterested smirk. "Clubs are pretty routine stuff. I have it all outlined, a few gimmicks and variations of the usual novelties to grab people's attention. You can look it over later." He gave Tory an arrogantly familiar smile. "What I really want to talk about is you."

Tory wondered if it was the opening line for a proposition, despite the wife and two kids out in Penn Valley. He was prepared to be flattered, but it almost panicked him to think that Steven's mind might be anywhere but on business. "Steven, I'd rather talk about the club."

"They're one and the same." He paused portentously. "Your name will be above the front door."

"What!" Tory screamed in ridiculing laughter. "I thought you were going to cook up something with 'Dionysus' or 'Bacchanalia.' Something decadent."

Steven made a face of bored disapproval. "Too trite. We're going to coin a new synonym for 'decadent' instead." He moved his hands to convey the idea of flashing neon lights. "'Tory's.'"

Tory lit a Gauloise and tried to look imposingly unimpressed. "You're bananas." But the idea of his name in neon wasn't without a certain attraction.

"I'm a genius. It will all make sense in a few minutes." He leaned forward conspiratorially. "But first I'd like to ask you a personal question."

Tory's suddenly racing mind prevented him from being offended. "So ask."

"It really doesn't matter if this club turns a profit or not, does it?"

"What do you mean?"

"Don't play innocent." The smirk was a familiar one,

the same one he'd often seen on waiters and cabdrivers when he was in the company of an older client. "What started out as a modestly elegant little club has turned into an MGM extravaganza. You've got big money behind you. Mafia money, if the rumors can be believed. This whole thing is just a huge tax write-off, isn't it?"

Tory roused himself into a semblance of offended propriety and stared haughtily at Sachs over his up-raised jaw. "Where the funds are coming from is hardly your concern. Unless the absurdly large check I gave you didn't clear the bank." Tory paused and decided that he didn't like his own tone. He didn't mind sounding snobbishly arrogant when it rang true, but all he could discern in his voice now was pretense. "Look, Steven, the money's obviously not mine. And I really don't know what the financial setup is. All I know is that I'm author-ized to spend whatever is necessary to get the best. I know that, and I know that my reputation is at stake." The thought gave him nightmares. "Whatever my backer or backers want from this, the club has got to take off and be a smash to preserve my own fragile ego. There are too many jealous people watching me and hoping that I'll fall flat on my face."

"Don't worry about that, babe." His protective tone was annoyingly alluring. "Everything's going to work out fine. I've got what you need to get it off the ground."

"I'm listening."

"OK." He clapped his hands together and sat upright, suddenly enthusiastic. "Let's start with our basic premise. You run the escort service now. What makes you so suc-cessful at it?"

Tory gave him a brittle laugh. "I'm the meanest son of a bitch in the business."

"That keeps things running smoothly. But what brings in the new clients?"

"Public contact. I'm out there working the bars every night drumming up new business."

"And how do you do that?"

"What the hell is this, twenty questions? I'm paying *you* for answers."

"All right, I'll give them to you," he smiled smugly. "When you're not so intent on being a tycoon, Tory, you've got real charm. The genuine thing. People like you.

You make them laugh and feel at ease. It's an important quality for what you're getting into. But you've got something more."

"What's that?" Tory asked, happy to discuss his favorite subject.

"You've got a flamboyance about you, a style, a touch of the theater."

Tory resisted the urge to beam and shout, "Tell me more!" Instead, he said, "I suppose I turn a few heads."

"And you love it," Steven laughed familiarly. "You're a natural. You know how to put it to work for you. Anyone who gets out on the town occasionally has caught your act. The chauffeured Mercedes, the hats, the clothes. And you really look like you're enjoying it all, like it's all a perpetual party. It makes people feel good."

"Making people feel good is my business."

"But you've just touched the tip of the iceberg. You worry too much about running things with an iron hand. It doesn't fit in with the party image."

Tory fixed him with one of Ginny's piercing stares. "If I weren't running things with an iron hand there wouldn't be a party to go to."

Steven continued, unimpressed. "Those days are ending. You're going to have professionals to take care of details and discipline for you now. Anyone with an aggressive personality and the proper training can run a business. Your talents are more important as the host. Your personality can set the tone for the whole operation if you follow my advice."

"So what exactly do you want me to do?" Tory grudgingly asked. He'd fallen out of the habit of listening to advice from anyone.

"I want you to give the public what it wants. You can be the draw there, Tory. As much of a draw as the names in the supper club."

Tory burst into torrents of laughter, then batted his eyes. "Oh, Mr. Sachs," he asked breathlessly, "are you going to make me a star?"

"Something along those lines," he answered seriously. "But we're going to have to make a few changes in your image first."

"Like what?" Tory asked suspiciously.

"First of all, I want you out of active operation of the escort service. As soon as possible."

"Easy enough. We're breaking in new people now, so I can devote most of my time to setting up the club. They'll be ready by the end of the month and I'll just have to oversee things."

"I don't even want it to be known that you're still overseeing. You're to be strictly ornamental now. Nothing but fun and laughter and good times."

"Ornamental?" Tory gasped in disbelief. The idea was almost blasphemous to him after he'd worked so hard to become anything but an ornament. He flinched to think what Mr. B. would say. Mr. B. wanted someone who rolled up his sleeves and got results, a go-getter. He thought of Ginny and felt a blush. She'd passed on the business to him like a sacred trust because she had faith that he could become an efficient machine like herself. George came to his mind. How ironically amusing it would all appear to him. Wouldn't he laugh to see all the qualities he'd always ridiculed resurface with even greater force? He'd surely lose any chance of George's ever returning. But on the other hand, he didn't seem to be making much romantic progress with the tough business image. "Fun and laughter and good times? If I didn't bust my ass seven days a week I wouldn't be in the position to talk to you about a fancy PR campaign today. I didn't get here by being an ornament, you know."

Steven gave him another unimpressed look. "And you won't go much further playing Simon Legree."

Tory glared haughtily in hopes of intimidating him. After months of practice it worked like a charm on the crew, but Steven didn't respond.

"Face the facts. You're building a smart club. Smarter than anything in the city. You've got the money and the talent at your disposal to do it up right. But you're out there at Twentieth and Birch in the middle of nowhere. What's going to bring people out there?"

"Snob appeal," Tory answered with a trace of uncertainty. "I know the right people from promoting the escort service. The trend setters, the big spenders, the party people. They'll come, and the public will follow. It's going to be a limited membership, an exclusive place where the right people will go to see and be seen. They'll come."

"Perhaps. But you're dealing with a touchy commodity. The fickle public. You need insurance, and there's no better insurance than a name."

"So what's that have to do with being an ornament? I'm a name already."

Steven flashed him a sympathetically pained expression. "Are you aware of some of the names you're called?"

Tory had uncomfortable suspicions that he'd rather not have confirmed. Only a perversely compelling need drove him to ask, "What do you mean?"

Steven shrugged with a sad frown. "There's nothing to accomplish by repeating slurs. But they're all due to the business. That part of you just doesn't jibe with the rest of the image. People get a kick out of you, but somewhere in the backs of their minds they're thinking, 'This pervert's the biggest pimp in the city. He's rotten to the core.' Your success in business gives you a sinister shadow, one that people would rather not see. They want to see 'naughty,' not 'evil.' "

Tory thought of the dozens of people he'd seen the night before and wondered how many of them had such unkind things to say about him when he'd moved on to the next table. "So you want me to be an ornament."

"People are crazy for that part of you! The car, the clothes, the champagne. It gives them a vicarious kick. They see your life as one party after another. At least they try to see it that way when they can forget that you're up to your neck in business. In a minor way, you fulfill their fantasies just as the movies did for people in the Depression. We've got to capitalize on that part of you."

Tory moved absent-mindedly to the window and looked down on the street thirty floors below. The trash and backed-up traffic and the press of lunch-hour pedestrians were thankfully distant. "OK. You win. I'm an ornament."

"Point two," Steven continued quickly. "With the business image we also dispose of your present image as a homosexual."

Tory crossed the room and sank back resignedly into the chair. "Now what?"

"We're dealing with a very liberal-minded portion of the public. They're urban, they're affluent, they're sophisticated, they're in tune with the latest trends. Homosexuality is in vogue. These people are willing to bend over backward to prove how sophisticated they are, just as they did with black people in the sixties." He smiled slyly. "They're crying out for a homosexual to call their very own."

"What more do you want me to do?" Tory asked in exasperation. "I've hardly made a secret of it."

"You flaunt it, but not in a friendly way. What you think you're projecting is 'Look at me, hip establishment heterosexuals. I'm living, breathing proof that a homosexual can also be a human being. Not all of us cruise men's rooms and molest children and live depressing, disgusting lives. I'm no different from you regular folks except that I prefer to consort sexually with members of my own gender.' "

"I say that?"

"But your whole attitude has an arrogance about it, a 'Check me out, motherfuckers. I'm a faggot and I've got a silk shirt and a chauffeur and a successful business. I live a life of guiltless hedonism that you transplanted suburbanities haven't even fantasized about yet. What do you think of that?' "

"Goddam," Tory murmured without intonation. "I never realized that my face was so expressive."

"Either way, it's not what the public wants to hear."

Tory laughed in anticipation, vaguely resenting his interest. "What is it they want to hear, Steven?"

"They want 'Hi! I'm Tory the dizzy queen! I don't have a brain in my head and all I want to do is go to parties and buy new clothes and have a good time. I'm not all that bright but sometimes I say the cleverest things.' "

"He sounds like a gay Stepin Fetchit."

Steven shrugged. "It worked for him."

"So you want me to camp outrageously and wear rouge and tell stories about the big cock I sucked last night?"

"No!" he almost screamed. "There's a definite line to be drawn. I want you to be a little bit outrageous, a little bit larger than life, but never, under any circumstances, can you be a sexual threat or make people feel uncomfortable. I want you to exaggerate your wardrobe another step or two, but don't go anywhere near drag. You're a handsome man, and the public wants to see that too. I want you to camp, but don't get too campy. There's a lot in gay humor that isn't amusing to the straight world, only incomprehensible and vaguely disgusting. I want you to be frankly interested in men, but never in anything but a joking way. A coy flirtation with a customer is about the limit, and preferably when he's with his wife so they know you're not serious."

Tory sighed as he crushed out his cigarette. "It's a good thing I never bothered to join the Gay Activist Alliance."

"Just let yourself relax and you'll carry it off with flying colors. We'll go over all of this in detail next week when I start to plant blurbs about you with the local columnists. You're going to be surprised at some of the idiotically clever things you've said. When we get closer to the opening, I'll line up some interviews and all that garbage. In the meantime, concentrate on being less efficient and more frivolous."

Tory thought back to the days before he became a boss, the silly parties and idle gossip and drunken laughter and carefree friends. The days when he was one of the crowd and everyone liked him. The memories weren't without their appeal. They made him think that Steven's ideas might not be so hard to execute after all. "Frivolous," he repeated distractedly. "I used to be good at that."

Chapter Twenty-eight

"GOING once! Going twice!" The gavel fell with a thud of finality. "Sold to number twenty-nine."

Tory felt his stomach plummet, an increasingly familiar sensation. The chandelier would be perfect for one of the dining rooms, but sixty-five hundred dollars wasn't a sum to spend lightly, even if it *was* Mr. B.'s money. Brad had tried to explain to him that with Mr. B.'s interlocking quasi-legitimate businesses and so much illegal money waiting to be laundered, each dollar Tory spent for the club could probably be manipulated by the accountants into a full refund. He still felt as if every move was a gamble, and he was receiving few vibrations to guide him. Taking over from Ginny had been a nerve-wracking experience, but he'd never seriously doubted his ability to do a competent job. A small private club with a bar and a few rooms would have been a pleasant challenge but not a large risk. As Tory had recklessly pushed the project on to new heights and Mr. B. had alarmingly assented to each addition, he'd begun to feel overwhelmed.

He had to give himself pep talks constantly. Hadn't he proved himself with the escort service? The administrative ability was obviously there. Wasn't he a minor celebrity, even mentioned twice in the past week by local columnists as an outlandish star of the city's night-life? He had the name to pull in guests. And would such an astute man as Mr. B. trust a loser with a project of such magnitude? He prayed that the man actually had the business savvy with which he was credited.

He'd hired the best talent Mr. B.'s money could buy, that was reassuring. The architects and engineers and design consultants knew what they were doing and how to set things in motion. The army of carpenters and plumbers and electricians knew their business, and the old building was beginning to look exactly as the blueprints and sketches had promised it would. There was a professional agent to book the supper club, a chef from Quo Vadis to oversee the four menus, a food and beverage manager from the St. Regis to operate the five bars, and a general manager from the Fairmont organization to supervise them all. Both masseurs and the masseuse were professionally trained. The dealers and croupiers were amateurs, but the pit boss from Harrah's would see that things ran smoothly in the casino. Mona and the two new assistants could handle the escort service with the help of the new electronic data system and a minimum of supervision. There wouldn't be much for Tory to do when they opened except look amusingly handsome and act eccentrically charming. The idea of shucking responsibility and living a sybaritic life had steadily grown more appealing over the months of making gargantuan decisions about the club. Tory looked forward to it as a well-earned vacation.

It was an awesome responsibility nonetheless. The explosion would be ear-splitting if the club turned out to be a bomb, and Tory's name was on the side of the building in twelve-foot-high neon letters. There would be over a hundred employees in an operation that could accommodate over a thousand guests at capacity, at a cost that had long since run into seven figures. Sometimes it seemed as if he'd spent that much to furnish it, his tongue-in-cheek vision of a Hollywood brothel not coming cheap. The sixty-foot mahogany bar cost almost as much to transport and assemble as he'd paid for it. The plush red carpeting and flocked red-and-gold wallpaper ran into tens of thousands for the vast space, and the warren of rooms seemed to swallow up gilt mirrors and crystal chandeliers by the dozens. Each private dining room needed special touches to make it the sanctuary of status that it was meant to be, and the ten boudoirs needed an imaginative use of money to make each one distinctive.

The expenditures were endless, but Tory met them from an apparently bottomless expense account.

He'd waited nervously the first few weeks for Mr. B. to complain about the bills, but not a word was ever spoken. Tory thought he could surely rouse a reaction with twenty-eight thousand dollars for a pair of George II giltwood side tables, but none came. He hadn't seriously planned on keeping them. They had been a test of the limits he was certain he'd exceeded. When his shock over Mr. B.'s silence subsided, he felt a sense of irresponsibility at exposing such precious antiques to the constant traffic of a club. He had them removed to the safety of his apartment's entrance hall.

Rescuing George II gave him the warm glow of a good deed done. He'd found a humanitarian calling, not unlike taking in stray dogs, and proceeded to rescue Queen Anne chairs, Hepplewhite tables, Sèvres porcelain, and Georgian silver from the clutches of antique stores and auction houses. His twelve-room apartment, now situated on the eighth floor since the club had expanded to two full floors, seemed to provide ample asylum at first. But it soon reached the saturation point.

Tory rented the remaining forty-two apartments to the crew and their friends. The eighth floor remained his sprawling private domain, with apartments for Mona, Mae, and Eugene, two guests suites, and an office for the escort service. Mr. B. installed his own employees as doormen and a building manager whom Tory could treat as his personal concierge. Mae informed him that the new apartment would be just too much for her to handle, especially with all the new knickknacks, and she began interviewing for a full-time maid and a twice-a-week houseman. It was all too ludicrously lavish to be true.

As he initialed the auction ticket he caught Jimmy's impressed stare from the corner of his eye. Things were definitely changing if he could cause Jimmy to take notice of prodigality.

"The Lillian Russell Room cried out for it," he explained nonchalantly as he handed back the ticket.

"You're keeping Lillian Russell? I thought she was iffy."

"She was, but we decided some Art Nouveau would be good for the mix. I just kept egging those decorators

on about the chicness of the twenties until they were
ready to smother the whole restaurant operation in a fit
of Deco frenzy. Fortunately, we've all given it some more
thought and decided to go for an eclectic balance."

"So what's the latest news?"

"Well," Tory happily enumerated, "the blue-and-silver
Cole Porter Room and the silver-on-silver Noel Coward
Room are definite. I need someplace to escape from all
that red velvet."

"Is Ruby Keeler staying?"

"I think so. It should be quite striking, all that ruby-
red enamel against a background of Busby Berkeley
black-and-white."

"How about Harlow?"

"Probably. We can do something dramatic with
platinum-blond paint and white satin walls."

"Jayne Mansfield?" Jimmy asked doubtfully.

"She's definitely in, despite all of the opposition I've
had to deal with. I can see it now," Tory whispered, peer-
ing off into the distance, "everything in the room heart-
shaped and pink. It will be a whole different slant on
poor taste. I'm going to reserve it only for the people I
detest the most."

"Any word on Blanche DuBois?"

"I'm afraid the poor dear won't make it," he sighed.
"There's just no way to do a room in paper lanterns and
have it turn out anything but depressing. Even with all
that charming New Orleans wrought iron."

"So who's going to replace her? Any new ideas?"

"Oh yes," Tory enthused as he offhandedly placed a
bid on a cloisonné jardinière. "I'm brimming over with
ideas these days."

"You certainly are," Jimmy agreed emphatically.
"You're so much more fun since you dropped all that
Mildred Pierce business."

"What do you think of a Scarlett O'Hara Room?"

"All in green, like her eyes?"

"With the earthy red accents of Georgia clay. I'm
looking at marble pillars next Thursday."

"How will you get them up to the ninth floor?"

Tory gave him a vaguely amused look. "I'm sure the
engineers will think of something. Or someone else will.

It's certainly not *my* problem—I just buy the stuff. And how about a Johnny Weissmuller Room?"

"With a jungle and hanging vines?"

"Of course. And waiters in loinclothes."

"And a chimpanzee?" Jimmy asked hopefully.

"I don't think so. They're totally lacking in table manners."

"I can think of some guests who wouldn't notice."

"Too true. And how about an Esther Williams Room?"

"Sounds soggy."

"It could be done. Just a tiny waterfall in the corner and a reflecting pool. And do you want to hear something truly twisted?"

"Need you ask?"

"I was toying with the idea of a room after my heroine, Jackie O."

"That doesn't sound so twisted."

"When I mentioned it to that sick decorator from Jersey, he said, 'But of course, darling. We'll do it all in Dallas pink and Arlington black!' "

"That's dreadful! Even by our standards. Remind me not to hire him when we move."

"You better get Hal on the ball or you won't have a place to move to. I can't hold that apartment forever, you know."

"Give me another week. He'll come around. He's crazy about the layout and the extra space, I just have to convince him about the neighborhood. You know how older people are about neighborhoods."

"Christ, with Mr. B's thugs on the doors and enough electronic gadgets and cameras to open a television station, it's going to be like living in Fort Knox."

"And he's still not convinced about your connections. I keep showing him all your classy ads in the papers but he still thinks he'll be living in a whorehouse."

"I'm going to phone him as soon as we get out of here," Tory snapped. "How much more do I have to spend on PR before people will believe I've gone legit?"

"He'll come around. Especially since you knocked two hundred off the rent."

"Doreen's braving the workmen and moving in over Thanksgiving weekend. And Carl's set for the first. Next month should look like homecoming week at Duffy's, all the old, familiar faces pulling up in Mayflower vans."

"Won't it be fun?" Jimmy gurgled. "All of us under one roof. It will be like a fraternity party every night. Have you set a date for your moving men yet?"

"I'm more concerned about being in shape upstairs for a grand opening on New Year's Eve. It's hard to believe that everything will be done, but they insist that it will. If everything goes according to schedule I can move the week before Christmas. But there's still so much work to be done on the eighth floor. Now the plumbers tell me that they have to wait for the carpenters to reinforce the bathroom floor before they can install the tub."

Jimmy laughed at the mention of the absurdly oversized sunken tub. "If you put sunlamps on the ceiling you could sell memberships to your bathroom as a pool club."

Tory raised his brows suggestively. "It will be for the pleasure of only very special guests. Besides, I might put a pool on the roof next spring. Wouldn't that be fun?"

"Everything's so much fun since you stopped worrying about money."

"Why should I worry?" Tory asked as he made another motion at the auctioneer. "It's not mine."

All of his money went straight to the safety-deposit box in the sometimes-unopened envelopes from Mr. B. There was no rent to pay and there were no transportation expenses to worry about. He managed to put Mae on the club payroll along with any other help she might hire. Nights on the town were a business undertaking, with gourmet meals, drinks for the house, and generous tips as public-relations expenses. With the new apartment, there would be a French chef and his staff in the restaurant kitchen upstairs to supply his private dinner parties and a few borrowed waiters to serve them. Even clothing had become a public-relations expense, since he was dressing to please his audience and not his own whims. There was nothing to do with the weekly envelope but stash it away.

The safety-deposit box began to look crowded after the first thirty thousand, and the sight of so much idle money began to irritate him. He thought it should be out working for him as so many people were. He discussed the

Swiss-bank idea with Brad again, who still thought it was inconvenient though no longer absurd. He suggested a bank in the Bahamas instead, which would serve the same purpose with the advantage of being several hours closer. Tory remembered Freeport with an angry frown, but agreed. Brad was happy to take care of it for him in exchange for air fare and a few nights' accommodation, and every time the deposit box looked cluttered they'd repeat the operation.

Chapter Twenty-nine

"BEGGING your pardon, m'lady, but if you'd stop fidgeting I could get these damn things in," Germaine complained in polite exasperation as he struggled with the diamond shirt studs, Tory's opening-night present to himself. He'd decided to go elegantly conservative the first night and then build momentum with progressively more conspicuous outfits through the first few months. Steven Sachs even wanted him to hire a designer, a move Tory didn't know if he was quite ready for. Everything had happened so quickly, and it wasn't a simple matter to adjust. With opening-night jitters to contend with, it was a relief to feel confident of his appearance in the tuxedo. The diamonds gave it just the right touch of theater, and they sparkled even brighter when he remembered they were purchased with club funds. Germaine sighed with accomplishment as he fastened the final stud. "There we go. Now let's do your tie and jacket and you'll be ready to face your adoring public."

Tory glanced into one of the twelve mirrored closet doors of his dressing room and frowned. "I look like a Korean War orphan."

"Nonsense, darling," Germaine trilled with annoying encouragement. "You may look a bit piqued, but it's understandable with what you've put yourself through to open this establishment. Besides, with your hair so beautifully coiffed, who's going to notice a few hollowed cheeks?" He stepped back to study his handiwork. "It's an interesting look anyway. It brings to mind pre–World War Two German decadence."

"I still think the rinse was a bit much," Tory complained as his tie was fastened.

Germaine extended his hand dramatically. "Not one more protestation! The rinse brings out your natural auburn highlights perfectly. And with your color from the sunlamp, you can tell everyone that you've only recently returned from Rio." He helped him into the jacket. "With the black of the tuxedo and the crisp white of the shirt, not to mention the sparkle of diamonds, the contrast of your hair will cause breathless gasps of admiration."

Tory smirked, unconvinced. "I'll give them all your number."

Germaine was available after salon hours for comb-outs and shampoos in exchange for a free apartment on the fourth floor. Tory had installed a barber's chair and sink behind a Japanese screen in the dressing room to accommodate him, and he'd proved a convenience. Besides pampering Tory's hair, he seemed happy to help out with shirt studs and bowties. Tory imagined that he was just as interested in publicity for his salon as in doing an act of kindness for a friend, but he didn't mind. He savored such personal service as an unquestionable status symbol of Old World charm.

Germaine made one last adjustment to the bowtie. "Well, I'm off to the party. If I don't catch you in the mad crush, have a marvelous New Year."

"You're priceless, Germaine. Thank you." He waved him out and sipped more champagne.

He wondered nervously about the crowd upstairs and knew it would be a New Year's Eve to remember, one way or another. The club would be packed to capacity, no great feat on New Year's Eve with the offer of an open bar. It was simple to fill the rooms with party-goers, another matter to sell them five-hundred-dollar memberships. Steven had insisted on the high fee even though other clubs in the city were selling memberships for ten or twenty dollars, a formality to comply with state club regulations. Steven said it would establish a tone of arrogant status from the start, giving the members a common bond of privilege and nonmembers the bitter taste of envy. They'd sold only six hundred through December, though sales had quickened the week after Christmas. The figure was leaked to the press as nine hundred, with less than a hundred charter memberships still available. Steven calmly assured him that a successful opening night and the press coverage he planned for it would convince prospective members not to miss a rare chance to join the cognoscenti. He had no doubts that by the end of January they'd sell two thousand of the green-and-silver cards, the magic number that would keep the ninth floor packed nightly with members and their guests.

The two hundred and fifty green-and-gold membership cards had been surprisingly snapped up at two thousand dollars each. They entitled the holder to deferential treatment on the ninth floor as well as admission to the casino, health club, and boudoirs above. Tory sold them easily to clients of the escort service with whispered promises of pleasure beyond words. His fading business image came in handy for the task. The reputation promised them that he'd deliver.

Propped against the back of a chair so as not to ruin the crease in his trousers, Tory sipped his champagne. He was grateful the crease was one of his major concerns. With the staff shaping up and the wizards that the personnel consultants had hired to operate the club, all he had to worry about was being a charming host. The new responsibilities appealed more and more to him. It was such a relief to stop worrying about the mundane but crucial details of daily operation. He'd invited the old crowd upstairs to the club every night of the previous week to give the staff a chance to rehearse, and it had been a pleasure to find that his months of tough efficiency hadn't irreparably damaged his rapport with them. They were still wary, still alert to his power. But his new casual attitude told them to relax, and some of the old camaraderie began to return.

Mae entered the room with all the dignity of Queen Victoria approaching her throne. She wore a powder-blue gown with a fringed silk shawl, showing ample décolletage. Her accessories included a floral arrangement under each arm.

"I feel like Gertrude Lawrence's dresser on opening night of *Lady in the Dark*," she complained with a laugh. "Here's one from Stan Jackson and one from Jack and

Helene and the kids, whoever they are. If they're coming, I hope they left the kids at home. It don't look like that kind of party."

"Have you been up?" Tory asked anxiously.

"Just to check on the kitchen," she replied importantly. "They can barely keep the buffet tables filled. Those people are up there eating like the New Year's going to come in with seven years of famine."

"Is it full?"

"Jam-packed, baby. I seen you throw some parties in your time, but this one's a real humdinger. Where'd you find all those folks?"

"Each and every one is an intimate friend," he smirked. "Did you happen to go past the cashier's window?"

She beamed brightly. "Lined up, baby. Slapping down hundred-dollar bills like nobody's business. Your pal Steven's wearing a grin from ear to ear."

"That's encouraging."

"Speaking of Steven, did you read what you told that fat lady from the *Post*?"

Tory braced himself. "What did I say now?"

"That one of the main reasons you was opening a club a floor above your apartment was because it was so inconvenient to go outdoors on rainy nights."

"That's not so bad."

"And now you won't have to worry about checking your coat. You expect the club to save you a bundle on clothes because you misplaced two mink coats in the past month."

"Please," he grimaced. "Tell me no more."

"Now who's going to believe a fool thing like that?" she asked disgustedly. "You might not have the *most* common sense in the world but you never go around losing fur coats."

"The most disgusting part is that people are so ready to believe that it's all true. That man is turning me into a cartoon."

"I guess you got to give a little to get a little," Mae sighed philosophically. "You about ready to go up?"

"I'm waiting for Mona. Go enjoy yourself." He glanced at her cleavage. "Just don't steal any clients from the girls."

She came closer to give him a kiss on her way out. "Happy New Year, baby," she said quietly. "I hope it brings you the one thing you're missing."

He tried not to wince at her words. The one thing he was missing would so soon be so close. Tory studied his reflection in one of the mirrors, wondering if George would still find him attractive. The skipped meals and sleepless nights were beginning to show. Germaine's skills had minimized the dark circles and gaunt cheeks, but Tory knew he wasn't the physical specimen George had last seen. He scrutinized the image and demoted himself from a solid nine to a borderline eight on his ten-point scale, wondering nervously if George would still look the same. He considered it briefly, then cursed himself, knowing he'd have the same weak knees and fluttering heart no matter how George looked. And with Janice clinging tightly to George, any reaction would be useless.

They'd confirmed their invitation, along with practically everyone else on the carefully compiled guest list. With all the publicity and superb refreshments, it would undoubtedly be the party of the season. Tory wondered nervously if his guests were also coming to gawk, to ridicule the heralded lavishness of the club and its dizzy-queen host, half hoping to see them both fall on their faces. He was fairly confident that the morbidly curious would be disappointed. After months of uncertainty, it finally looked as though they might have pulled it off.

His eyes concentrated once again on the reflection, and the tuxedo gave his mind some comfort. If he was no longer stunning, he at least looked successful. He hoped it would impress George, give him second thoughts over what he'd given up. His rustic little restaurant was successful, but the club's grandeur would make it look like a hot-dog stand. Tory laughed as he studied the reflected diamond studs, thinking how ironic it was that all of the qualities George had most ridiculed were to be the same ones, exaggerated through the magnifying glass of the media, that would make him a success. Even if most of the success was the product of luck and circumstance and public relations, George was still bound to be impressed.

Tory gave the mirror a defiant stare and halfheartedly jutted out his chin. He told himself that George didn't matter, with so many men ready to fall at his feet.

They were thrilled to be invited to his party, to be singled out for a few minutes' conversation. He decided to be polite to George but tried to convince himself that the days of patient pining were over. He tried to summon Ginny's toughest feelings and make himself believe that someone who could get his name in twelve-foot neon letters was certainly capable of forgetting a man.

The night maid appeared at the door. Mae had decided that the day maid wasn't enough, with the frequent late-night socializing.

"Mrs. Brett is here."

"Show her in, Mildred," Tory replied, amused at the grandeur in his tone. "She's a special friend. You needn't ever keep her waiting in the hall. And bring another bottle of champagne, please."

Mona appeared at the door a moment later in a black sequined vintage Mainbocher gown with a dramatically slashed V-neck. She stared in disbelief at Mildred's disappearing form. "How efficient."

"She better be if she wants to keep her job. Mae's a tough boss."

"Just what does Mae do these days?" Mona wondered vaguely. "She's got more help than most of the heiresses I've met."

"She keeps busy," Tory smiled in Mae's defense. "She brings me my coffee and newspaper every morning on a tray with a white rose. Then she yells at Eugene and the day maid and the houseman. Then she goes upstairs to tell the chef what was wrong with last night's dinner. On Mondays and Thursdays she tells the laundress she's putting too much fabric softener in the sheets and on Tuesdays and Fridays she tells her she's not putting enough starch in the tablecloths. Then she watches her afternoon soap operas. Then she gets all the daily gossip on floor-by-floor rounds. After that, she's too exhausted for much else besides giving me advice on running the business and how to get George back."

"He's here."

"Who needs him?"

"Who invited him?" she replied automatically with a knowing look. "Janice looked almost sober on the elevator, but she was foaming at the mouth for a cocktail. And Bradley's upstairs in a corner with Hal, smiling intently at a potential account for his office. I really think you should say something to him." She sniffed as she accepted champagne from Mildred. "This is supposed to be a party, not a business conference."

"How can I tell him that without sounding like a hypocrite? This is just one big business conference for me too."

"Now, now," she chided with a warble. "That's not the attitude we've been coached to project. Don't let's slip back into our dismal executive frame of mind."

"Sorry," he smiled. "It's hard to break the habit. But if tonight is the success it's supposed to be, I think I'll truly be able to forget about business for the most part and relax."

"I certainly hope so. Face the facts, *mon cher*. You can do anything you set your mind to, but you weren't born and bred to cultivate ulcers. It may take time to reacclimate yourself, but you'll be ever so much happier for it. Just think of it," she murmured ethereally. "Luxury and glamour and a party every night. If you're lacking an ingredient for the perfect life, excepting the one that we rarely discuss because it's too dreary to dwell upon, I fear that it eludes me."

"I hope you're right. We'll have a chance to find out if I pull it off tonight."

"What could go wrong? You've memorized your new anecdotes, haven't you?"

"Of course. The only hitch will be in keeping my stomach from turning as I tell them." He put down his glass and looked at Mona anxiously. "What did it look like at the cashier's window?"

"The poor woman in that cage hasn't had a moment's rest. Steven said they'd sold two hundred memberships in the first two hours and it shows no signs of abating. Relax."

"Is Ginny here yet?" he asked with a trace of discomfort. He was sure she wouldn't approve of the new image.

"Yes. She even brought her relic in from Radnor. She's in rubies and ingenue pink."

"How about Victor?" he asked with distaste.

"Dancing with the Mafia princess. She's in matronly mauve. So rude of her to leave me unescorted on New Year's Eve."

"But you have me, my dear. The star."

"And I shall share in the adulation of the masses. It's all been arranged. Steven has rehearsed the waiters and the crew to burst into spontaneous applause upon your entrance."

Tory laughed with a touch of embarrassment. "I'd prefer strewn roses, but it will do."

"Don't fret. You'll still give George a banquet for thought."

Chapter Thirty

THE grand opening had given George and hundreds of other people a banquet for thought. It could never have lived up to Tory's highest expectations, but it made its mark. The applause for his entrance had sounded genuine after the crowd had picked up the rehearsed staff's cue. There had even been a few photographers waiting for him, and the flashing bulbs added a certain element of electricity to the events. He could sense the crowd's mood changing with the flashing bulbs, a new excitement filling the air. He could feel the atmosphere subtly shifting from "party" to "event," and the following week's media coverage confirmed his feeling.

"Tory's" reached its goal of two thousand memberships well before the end of January. The general membership rooms were crowded every night. Dinner reservations had to be made two weeks in advance, and the supper-club acts were immediately sold out into the spring. Members were even forced to make reservations on weekends to get into the Mahogany Room, the main lounge with the sixty-foot bar. People grumbled about paying five hundred dollars for a membership card and then not being able to use it at their convenience. The manager offered them refunds, but few accepted.

In contrast to the lower floor's perpetual pandemonium, the upper floor was a sanctuary of storybook splendor. It often bustled but there were never three-deep crowds at the bar. The gold card should have carried infinitely greater status than the general-membership silver card, but few people knew of its existence. The excitingly clandestine atmosphere upstairs was intoxicatingly different, one of certain knowledge that the slightest whim would be filled instantly.

The upper floor was Tory's fantasy turned into fact, his visualization of heaven fashioned into a reality. Magical powers were always available in the upstairs hideaway to fulfill every desire. . . . A little plate of Scotch salmon to nibble with your cocktail, sir? Certainly, sir. We have a gourmet kitchen at your disposal. A massage for your weary muscles? Just through the double doors, sir. There's a professional staff waiting to pamper you. Some soft music to soothe your nerves? Just give me your request, sir. Kay will be happy to play it for you. A little excitement for your libido? The girls are all waiting to please you, sir. Unless perhaps you're in the mood for a boy tonight. A little excitement for your mind? The casino is to your right, sir. I'll fetch you some chips. You forgot your wallet? Money doesn't exist up here, sir. Everything will be discreetly billed.

Tory lounged at the roulette table and negligently tossed a hundred-dollar chip on twenty-four as the pianist in the background ran through "La Vie en Rose" for the fourth time. His fantasy world wasn't quite as believable in the sober summer sunlight when his name wasn't flashing in neon letters, but it was still amusing to him. Mona and Eugene seemed to feel something coming in the teens. They'd been betting them heavily for several spins. Jimmy and Ginny were playing conservative side bets with little success while Mae was cleaning up on eights and thirteens. Xavier spun the wheel and they all waited in hushed anticipation.

"Thirteen again!" Mae hooted as the ball stopped. "I got it today, folks!"

"If only we got to cash in the chips," Mona mused.

"Speak for yourself, sugarlump. You wasn't singing that tune last week when you dropped ten grand. If this was real money, Tory'd be wearing your emeralds by now."

"It wouldn't surprise me," she replied without concern. "He's just about exhausted the publicity value of fedoras and ice-cream suits. You're going to have to find a new gimmick, Tory."

"I'm working on it," he replied complacently between sips of champagne.

There were few other pressing thoughts to occupy his mind. He spent only a few hours a week with the escort service. The competent staff and the computer made even that time unnecessary, but he liked to keep in touch. The sprawling club's routine operation was in the hands of experts. He didn't have to check for wilting flowers in the dining rooms or worry about a bartender out with a cold. He discussed details with his managers, but only to let them know that he was watching. Being physically present was his main function in the day-to-day operation of the place, a subtle reminder to everyone that he was still ultimately in charge. He knew he was a figurehead, that the workings would come unglued without professional supervision. But it seemed like a wise idea to keep everyone vaguely aware of his dormant power.

His position was that of a glorified social director. He stopped at tables to ask if dinner was up to its usual standards. He introduced the acts in the supper club. He chatted gaily with people at the bars. He congratulated big winners in the casino. It was a pleasant set of tasks for someone who loved parties, and every night was now a huge party at which he was the beaming host. With no need to worry about the club's success, he'd learned to enjoy the job.

He was a status symbol, a creation of public relations. If he joined a table for a drink, he knew he would provide name-dropping opportunities for weeks. His clever remarks and outrageous anecdotes were repeated, and he was credited with some that Steven hadn't even written. The public sometimes seemed to labor for his image as much as he did.

Clothes were a major part of it. He'd gone past the point of wearing something slightly outlandish just to please himself. It was expected of him now. His public wanted a foppish gay clown to make them laugh and feel sophisticatedly open-minded. They wanted a slightly scatterbrained, exceedingly flashy, always ebullient faggot to entertain them. Then they could make condescending jokes about him and feel witty.

Tory had come to accept his role philosophically and hoped he was playing it well. He hoped the value of his image wasn't being overrated, or if it was, that Mr. B. wouldn't realize it. He hoped the masquerade wouldn't suddenly end and take away his absurd salary and the personal services at his disposal that few people since the Industrial Revolution had been able to enjoy.

The ball ended another circuit on twenty-five. There were no winners.

"It figures," Mona muttered with a glance at the door. "Look who just walked in."

"Lady Luck!" Tory shouted at Brad's approaching figure. "Come have a seat on Mona's shoulder and tell us who unchained you from the office at one-thirty on a Thursday afternoon."

"I'm meeting Hal and your friend for lunch downstairs."

"Hal?" Jimmy questioned, suddenly diverting his attention from building a tower of black chips.

Tory patted his hand kindly. "Don't worry, dear. I'm sure it's just business." He cast a bored glance at Brad. "Some people are still involved in that, I'm told."

"He's signing the contract with Ivan today," Brad said with a trace of excitement.

"Ivan?" Ginny raised her eyebrows. "Gussdorfer?"

"The one and only," Tory responded. "Will you collect a fat fee, Bradley?"

"I'll make out," he answered uncomfortably.

"I want a cut. Ivan doesn't generally trust his business with young whippersnappers, you know. It was only my charm that got you the business."

"Oh, Tory," Jimmy protested mildly. "You don't know what to do with all the money you have as it is."

"Don't you believe it," Ginny advised sagely. "It won't go bad on you. It can sit in a bank and collect interest from now until Doomsday."

"And that's from the mouth of an expert." Eugene smiled in devilment.

Ginny only smiled back at him. He could no longer goad her into an ill-tempered retort, and he seemed to miss it. Many things that once brought on an aggressive display of her personality were now met complacently. Tory thought she seemed a bit bored at times, but she was relaxed. She used the same discipline she'd once exercised in business to play her new role of wealthy matron. The home in Florida and the yacht filled much of her time. They were gracious settings in which to entertain her husband when he could join her on weekends. Occasionally she'd come North for a midweek visit when he was in need of a hostess. Tory looked forward to her Philadelphia jaunts. She was good company at the club in her new relaxed state of mind. She was also an old face that didn't require a constant display of the image.

"You keep piling it up, kid. You never know."

He *was* piling it up, but he wasn't serious about a cut from Brad. It gave him a certain amount of pleasure to be even peripherally involved in a financial deal, to still be vaguely in touch with the world of real business. He tried to play it down. People didn't want to remember that part of him, how he'd once run a business competently. It didn't fit in with the frivolous image. He promoted his new image with all the calculation and efficiency he'd once devoted to the escort service, but recognition for that would be self-defeating. When someone made a joke about his dizziness, he chided himself for being silently annoyed. With all the advantages it had provided, it seemed silly to let it bother him.

Mae gave the croupier an impatient frown. "Let's go there, Xavier, spin that wheel. Time is money."

Xavier complied, and all attention was drawn to the blur of red-and-black spokes.

"It just keeps going around in circles all day long," Jimmy announced somberly, obviously impressed with his observation.

"And we sit here like idiots and watch it." Ginny laughed.

"You're absolutely right," Mona agreed. "We should all be out in the fresh air augmenting our wardrobes or doing something equally constructive."

Her words roused Jimmy's guilty conscience. "Tory, do you want to pop out to Saks with me before cocktail hour?" he asked as the ball halted on six and Xavier raked in the chips.

"I can't today," he answered calmly. "I've got a baton lesson at three."

"Baton lesson?" Brad asked, threatening disapproval.

"Didn't I tell you about that?" he inquired brightly. "For my Fourth of July party. You're sworn to silence, of course, but I'm making my entrance as Uncle Sam in red, white, and blue bugle beads with flaming batons to 'Yankee Doodle Dandy.' At least the batons will be flaming if I get in enough practice. My technique needs to improve drastically or I may go down in history with Mrs. O'Leary's cow."

"You might *need* a fire to top your last party." Eugene laughed.

"It's getting so that I dread holidays now," Tory lamented in a semi-serious tone. "Each act has got to be more ridiculous than the last, and I don't know where the next idea is coming from. I thought I was adorable on Valentine's Day with the little diaper and the bow and arrow. The crowd always goes for a little flesh. And everyone loved me as a leprechaun on St. Patrick's Day, even though those green eyelashes stayed with me for days afterward. The sequin sailor suit for Memorial Day was effective, if not in the best of taste. But I've got all of the fall and winter holidays coming up," he moaned before another sip of champagne. "Whatever am I to do?"

"Don't worry, baby. Steven'll come up with something."

"You could do Yom Kippur as a demented Arab," Mona suggested with a sweet smile for Brad's benefit.

"That's an idea," Tory said thoughtfully. "I'll toss it out to Steven at our next tryst."

"Tryst?" Brad repeated.

"Oh yes, my dear," he replied brightly. "You miss so much succulent gossip being among the employed. It was a classic case of the *My Fair Lady* syndrome. He simply became enamored of his creation."

"It must be nifty to have an affair that follows the plot of a show you've seen," Jimmy conjectured. "That way you know how things are going to turn out."

"Yes, darling," Tory replied fondly. "My life is just one long musical comedy."

"Ain't no comedy to be messing with a married man," Mae scowled.

"No one forces these husbands to adulterate at gunpoint," Mona retorted testily in Tory's defense.

"Thank you, my love. I knew I could count on you to

come to my aid. And well she should on the subject of married men," Tory confided to the rest of the room. "She's caused so many divorces, lawyers pay *her* a retainer."

"All this sinning's going to come home to roost some day," Mae predicted ominously as the ball completed another circular journey.

"Sweet sixteen!" Mona shrieked. "It's about time my luck changed. Perhaps it's an omen that I'll pick up Claude Terrell tonight."

"Who's Claude Terrell?" Ginny asked.

"The new singer. He's in the Rialto Room until tomorrow night, and I've done everything within the bounds of propriety to let my interest be known. It must be the language barrier."

"Forget it, lovebug," Mae advised, her moral mood quickly passing at the prospect of imparting fresh gossip. "Didn't you see him eyeing that waiter last night?"

"You're making that up to spite me," Mona accused.

"You know I ain't that way. Besides, I'd *like* to see you fixed up with somebody new, get that Victor snake out of my face."

She was still suspicious. "Which waiter?"

"Frankie. The little blond one. It was plain as the nose in front of you."

"She's right, Mona," Jimmy agreed with an innocent but smug certainty.

Mona gasped at Jimmy accusingly. "You didn't!"

"What could I do?" he answered apologetically. "He threw himself at me."

"That little son of a bitch." She looked to Ginny for sympathy. "One simply cannot tell in these troubled times. He's the picture of healthy heterosexuality, complete with a little wife waiting for him back in Quebec."

Ginny couldn't resist a trace of cattiness. "Maybe you're losing your touch, kiddo."

"Too long with the snake," Mae concurred.

"Does this mean you don't want to come to my dinner party tonight?" Tory asked. "Dee Dee Donner would kiss my ass for months to have your seat. She's doing an article on him."

"Forget it," Mona commanded. "I'd come in a respirator before I'd do a favor for that fawning bitch. Besides, I want to see old Pantages for the scoop on fall couture."

The dinner parties were one of the brightest spots of Tory's new life. With everything on such a grand scale, it was a pleasure to sit down in his own dining room with just seven other people for a relaxed meal. The entertainers performing upstairs were usually interesting guests, and occasionally he could snag the star of a pre-Broadway tryout or a headliner at the Music Fair. The celebrities gave him another lever to win points on the social scale, and he manipulated his advantage ruthlessly. Invitations were issued with all the importance of royal decorations, and the grateful guests could be pumped afterward for an infinite variety of favors.

He summoned the restaurant's chef to his apartment the day before a party to plan the menu, always looking for something that guests weren't apt to find upstairs. It was served on the china too precious to be used in the club dining rooms and eaten with the antique sterling that even his gold-card members might be tempted to pocket. Two waiters and an assistant chef were rescheduled to his apartment on these evenings, and the picture of elegant luxury it all created in his dining room gave him a nostalgically warm glow. He often thought of David at his dinner parties. He hoped that David was watching him from heaven at these times, to see him entertaining celebrities they'd once admired together and living the glittering life they'd only dreamed about. It wasn't the same without David here to enjoy it with him, or without George to fill the void. But Tory often had the smug thought that it beat working in a supermarket.

"Thirteen again!" Mae shrieked after the next spin and looked conspiratorially toward heaven. "Thank you, Lord."

"If those folks in the House of Prayer could see you now," Eugene said.

"Ain't nothing wrong with this," Mae shot back nervously. "It ain't real money. I'm a Christian woman."

"A Christian woman at the gates of hell," Tory mused.

"Executive housekeeper to Jezebel," Mona added.

Mae glared at her self-righteously. "And if I wasn't here to look after him, no telling how much more sinning he'd do."

"Some chaperon you've been," Tory laughed. "If I've missed breaking any of the Ten Commandments it's only been due to lack of interest."

Mae raised her finger and paused significantly. " 'Thou shalt not kill,' baby. As long as you don't break that one, things ain't past hope."

"This luck is killing *me*," Eugene muttered.

Mae's attention was drawn back to him. "And if I wasn't here, if I was still back on Baltimore Avenue doing day work, how much money do you think there'd be in the Church Scholarship Fund? I'm taking the taint out of some of this money, putting it to work for the Lord."

"You stroll into that church in your mink stole and those deacons jump these days," Eugene laughed.

Tory turned to Ginny. "She hit Mr. B. for the choir fund last week. He gave her a hundred."

"He's always been charitable. He practically built St. Jerome's."

"Speaking of charity," Mae remembered, "you got those kidney folks coming tomorrow."

"I remember," Tory sighed. "God, they're dreary. The ballet and the museum people are much more entertaining."

"How do you put up with those committeewomen?" Mona grimaced as she pulled an emerald-and-diamond pin from her Vuitton satchel and attached it to her black silk pajama top.

Brad leaned over the table to stare incredulously at the assortment of emerald jewelry in her bag. "Do you always walk around with all that loot from Victor in your pocketbook?"

"Of course," Mona replied, unconcerned. "I never know when the urge may strike to slip on another bracelet." She turned her attention back to Tory. "Attending endless luncheons with those dismal doctors' wives has to be one of the ten dreariest memories of my life."

"But it's good business, my dear."

The charity work actually *was* good for business. Mr. B. saw the sense of it, done with the proper publicity, and he agreed to Tory's philanthropy. Tory had no strong personal feelings for the field, though it was pleasant to help a worthy cause. As long as the money didn't come out of his pocket, he was happy to take credit for giving it away.

It took him to places he otherwise wouldn't be welcomed. The complacent committee women and the Social Register set didn't think kindly of him. He was a local celebrity but he was still far from respectable. The charity didn't buy him into their cliques, nor did he want it to. But it gave him a perverse pleasure to see them force themselves to be ingratiating. He could barely control his hysteria at the Orchestra Ball when his white satin tuxedo received good-natured compliments instead of ridicule.

The ball stopped again and there were no winners. Eugene lost his last three thousand on red.

"Shit. I can find better ways to entertain myself than this."

"Don't get lost on me again," Tory told him as he rose from the table. "You have to go to the airport at four."

"I'll be in 603," he grinned with a flick of his tongue.

"You stay out of 603!" Mona commanded. "She's on call tonight."

"Give me a break," he pleaded. "She's been bothering me for it all week. Let me get her off my back."

"You stay off *her* back," Tory replied darkly, taking pleasure in a rare opportunity to exercise his authority. "Go bother someone who's not working tonight."

"All right," he sniffed as he left.

"Tory," Ginny frowned, "do you let him fool around with the girls?" Her old personality seemed to resurface fleetingly on its own volition.

"It's their business," he shrugged. "As long as it doesn't interfere with mine."

She shook her head and seemed to will herself not to be critical. "Times certainly have changed," was all she said.

It was one of Tory's favorite changes. With the move from administrator to figurehead, he found he could relax in certain areas. There were managers to worry about discipline now. Of course, he couldn't be one of the crew again, nor did he wish to be. The in-between position suited him perfectly. He had respect because of his authority, but since he didn't have to display it he could once again enjoy some of the camaraderie. He liked being liked almost as much as he liked being a success.

"Who's at the airport?" Mona asked.

"Michael Weiss."

"A little quickie before dinner?" she smirked.

"I have needs too," he answered demurely.

"Why do you still see him when you can have your pick of the crew?"

"That's why *you're* playing with *his* chips, Mona," Ginny blurted out. "It's not good business."

"I can understand that. But why Michael? Every night there's another gorgeous young trick throwing himself at you in the club."

"Celebrity fuckers," Tory sneered indifferently.

"Nothing like a positive self-image," Brad laughed.

Tory gave him an affronted look. "I'm not bragging. I'm calling a spade a spade. I'm a name. At one time, I made a few hundred a week with my body, and after that I did even better using my brain. But this present embarrassment of riches is all the gift of public relations. It will last only as long as the public can believe I'm a little bit larger than life. And if they get too close, they'll see it's all a fake. Every one of those gorgeous young tricks I could take home for a roll in the hay would leave with a little piece of the mask, like a souvenir. And if I lose the mask, I lose the works."

"A prisoner of fame," Mona lamented.

"What do you have against Michael, anyway? Besides being dynamite sex with no repercussions or attachments, I think he's kind of cute. I sort of like love handles."

"He is cute. I was only speaking comparatively."

"He's a gentleman," Mae approved.

"And he has other good points," Jimmy smiled suggestively.

"And no matter how rich you are," Ginny announced authoritatively, "a monthly case of Dom Pérignon is nothing to sneeze at."

"That reminds me," Mae said as she got up and stacked her chips, "I better check that they sent down the right wine for dinner tonight."

"You push yourself too hard, Mae."

"Darden's the one that needs pushing," she replied, obviously not catching the intended sarcasm. "We got those magazine people in on Saturday and the place is a mess."

"What magazine people?" Jimmy asked absently as Mae left the casino.

"I told you about it. *Metro* is doing a spread on the apartment. The publicity will be good for the club."

"I'm getting fed up with hearing how everything is good for the club," Mona muttered good naturedly. "You know you love all the glitter."

"I do," he cheerfully admitted. "But the club makes it all legitimate. It was like finding Ali Baba's cave."

"The IRS might be interested to see all of your antiques in *Metro*," Brad worried. "Even with what you declare, they'll be prone to wonder."

"I'll tell them the place came furnished," Tory blithely replied. "Anyway, Jimmy, *Metro* is doing a six-page spread on the apartment and an interview with me. I plan to be ever so gracious about it, like Jackie doing the White House tour. Everything will be terribly tasteful. They're going to use the picture of me emerging from the Mercedes in tuxedo and sable at the mayor's testimonial."

"That's one of the best pictures of you," Jimmy stated.

"I know," Tory happily agreed. "Flashing teeth for days. I look like I'm on my way to the Academy Awards."

Mona gave him a knowing glance. "If that doesn't bring George back, nothing will."

"Who needs him?" Tory asked without conviction.

Chapter Thirty-one

THE dinner had gone well the previous evening despite Mona's pointed remarks to the French Canadian singer. Zoltan Pantages had entertained everyone with stories of his latest European buying trip, which had included a party for St. Laurent, and the food had been up to its usual standards.

The meal just completed was on a much smaller scale, only Tory and Mr. B. with broiled flounder and the ever-present Nick on guard duty in the corner. Mr. B. had switched their weekly meetings from the Congress Club to Tory's dining room, quipping that he might as well enjoy the bounty he was providing. He always asked detailed questions about the club. He seemed almost fascinated. But he hadn't set foot in it since the night before the opening.

Image barred the door to him, Tory had no doubt. The practical experience of building his own image gave him an insight into Mr. B.'s machinations, and he admired him for the flawless campaign he'd run. He admired him and he respected him, but he didn't fear him. The image of awesomely dangerous power had never rung true to him. To Tory's eyes, Mr. B. was still his terrible but merciful Uncle Joe, the stern but benevolent patriarch at the head of the table.

His gut feeling was reinforced with his position. Through some quirk of laughable fate, he was receiving full credit and ludicrous financial rewards for the club that bore his name in glaring neon. He had a sound case for speaking his mind without fear of retribution, and he used it as yet another measure of his prestige. He no longer obeyed orders, he considered suggestions and honored requests. He sometimes amazed himself with his arrogance.

They finished their weekly discussion of Mona and Victor as Mr. B. spooned sugar into his coffee. There was a brief silence, and as he spoke again he uncharacteristically looked down at the table. "We're having problems with the numbers operation on Tasker Street. I'm moving it up here."

Tory's expression plainly stated that the idea was too ridiculous to be outraged over, but Mr. B. couldn't see it with his eyes still on the tablecloth, as if he were embarrassed to have mentioned it. Tory sipped his espresso in disdainful calm before he answered. "Forget it. Tory's is a class operation. Keep your dirty laundry downtown where it belongs."

Mr. B.'s shoulders seemed to sink in a sigh of defeat. He didn't look up and he didn't speak. He didn't react at all except for a small motion of his forefinger.

Tory caught a movement from the corner of his eye. For some reason, Nick was suddenly beside him. Then there was the mammoth open palm approaching his face. Its speed precluded a reaction. It connected with his cheek in a sudden white flash. Before he could fully digest the situation, he was sprawled in front of the sideboard with a nauseating pain coursing through the left side of his face. He heard the demitasse cup crash with a delicate tinkle against the wall and watched the espresso dripping down the plum enamel finish to the molding. The inevitable stain absurdly held his attention until he could think to locate Nick and avoid another blow. But Nick was immobile beside the overturned chair, and Tory could concentrate on the pain, abating now but still acute.

As the shock subsided and released some of his brain cells for other functions, he assessed the situation. The violence seemed to be over. Relieved at this, he could indulge a feeling of outraged dignity. He rose from the carpet with what grace he could muster. Nick stood only a few feet from his most direct path to the door, but Tory didn't think he looked vicious enough to do more than obstruct the way. There was an outside chance that he was wrong, but it seemed minimal and worth the risk of the haughty gesture. He took two steps and Nick blocked the way with his bulk, as expected.

"Sit down, Tory," the heavy-hearted voice behind him commanded.

He had no options. He felt fortunate to have a vestige of dignity. He hoped he could continue to project it, if only to keep from being overwhelmed by his fear. He looked down at the overturned chair and then frowned imperiously at Nick. After a glance at Mr. B. Nick looked apologetic and quickly righted the chair. Tory seated himself with a dim ray of optimism.

"Don't bleed on your fancy silk shirt," Mr. B. ordered with a brusque concern. He pushed a linen napkin toward him.

Tory dabbed dutifully at the trickle of blood from his lip. The situation looked bad but no longer disastrous.

"I didn't enjoy that, Tory."

He couldn't contain a small shocked laugh, though it made the left side of his face ache sharply. "I wasn't too crazy about it either."

Mr. B. shook his head and laughed too. "Always with a wisecrack," he chided quietly after a pause. "Sometimes you get too big for your britches. You're as bad as my five-year-old grandson. He keeps pushing, just wondering how much he can get away with, and he's not satisfied until he gets his ass paddled." He frowned paternally over the upraised cup. "Just remember who's boss."

"Yes, sir," Tory replied, daring a small tinge of sarcasm in his voice.

"You're lucky I like you. Nobody gets away with what I put up with from you. Except my smart-ass daughter, and only because she's the mother of my grandsons." His expression recalled the business at hand. "The numbers are coming here, Tory. My mind is made up. You were a smart boy with this building, smarter than you realize. I was humoring you at first, giving you a new toy to play with. The accountants said it was a good idea, so I thought, 'Go ahead! Have fun!' " He chuckled. "When I got some of the bills for what you were filling this playhouse with, I was amazed. It seemed impossible that anyone could spend that much money, even you. But the accountants said not to worry. So when it came time to put in the security system and they're still saying 'Spend! Spend!' I decided to go all out." He paused dramatically. "We've got Fort Knox here. It's perfect for the numbers."

Tory doubted that there was any point in arguing but still needed to voice his feelings. With an intimidating awareness of Nick in the corner, he prefaced his words with a humble sigh. "I don't feel right about the numbers, Mr. B. The club and the girls and the casino are one thing. My rich people come and have a good time—it's like a party every night. I've never felt that I'm actually breaking the law, at least not the laws that count. But the numbers . . . it's different."

"What's wrong with the numbers?" Mr. B. asked perturbedly. "Nobody forces anybody to play."

"But if they don't pay up," Tory replied quietly, "they disappear in Tinicum Marsh."

A pained expression spread across Mr. B.'s face. "I'm not going to lie to you, Tory, and say it's never happened. Once in a great while we come across a jerk who gives me no choice. But I'm not Al Capone. Times are different now. If it ever has to happen, it will have nothing to do with you."

"I won't be able to help feeling partially responsible if they're operating from under my roof," Tory replied, pleased with his moral fortitude.

A sly expression crept over Mr. B.'s face as he sipped coffee. "All right," he began slowly, "I'll make you an offer." He gave Tory a long, appraising stare. "I'll give you your salary for showing your face in the club four or five nights a week. You can give up the telephone operation, move out of this apartment, just become another salaried employee, and wash your hands of anything that goes on in the building. There would be no hard feelings, Tory."

Tory reached quickly for his champagne, wishing he could be knocked out of his chair again instead of replying to the proposition. At least physical violence didn't require any reaction from him except pain. It seemed cruel to force him to make a moral decision that had no pleasing alternatives. Could he live with his conscience if he harbored possible murderers in his home? On the other hand, could he give up the apartment with uncounted thousands in antiques, a staff of over a hundred to cater to every whim, a position at the center of a personal ten-story universe with thousands of applauding guests, to step down to a position as "another salaried employee"? Mr. B.'s business had always seemed like a game of cops and robbers before. It wasn't pleasant to be forced so abruptly to face the facts.

"I have three spare rooms at the far end of the hall we can set up."

Mr. B.'s face broke into an infuriatingly smug smile as he rose from the table. He patted Tory's shoulder on his way to the door. "I'll see what I can do to soothe your troubled conscience."

Tory finished the champagne in his glass. He reached for the wine bucket to pour more, then changed his mind and went to the sideboard for a brandy snifter and a bottle of Courvoisier. He poured at the sideboard and took a deep swallow, the painful-pleasant burning in his throat feeling so much more satisfying than the champagne. From the corner of his eye he caught a movement at the door and turned to discover Mae's glowering face.

"Did you miss anything, J. Edgar?" he asked without humor. He knew that Mae eavesdropped on his meetings with Mr. B. and it didn't usually concern him, but he was in no mood to listen to the inevitable lecture.

"I heard enough." She continued to glower in the doorway, showing no trace of the underlying fondness that usually accompanied her reprimands. "And I couldn't believe my ears, that those words dropped out of your mouth."

Tory refused to let her upset him. "This is almost like reliving my childhood," he laughed flatly. "I have a father figure to smack me around and a big mama to make me feel guilty about it."

"Maybe what you *need* is a good beating, knock some sense into your thick head. It's high time you grew up, Buster." Her tone was unsettlingly harsh. "You're supposed to be an adult, and you got some big decisions to make, bigger ones than most of us ever have to face. You know, ever since that day two years ago you told me you was selling your tail, I told myself, 'Calm down, Mae. He's a sensible boy underneath all that foolishness and he knows right from wrong. And he won't do nothing that's out-and-out evil.' Ever since that day I've been wondering now and then, thinking maybe I'm wrong. I stuck around to keep an eye on you, give you a helping hand to make the right decisions, and till tonight you never disappointed me too bad." She shook her head sadly. "You been flirting with the devil for years and it looks like this time he's finally got you."

"Looks that way, doesn't it?"

She stared at him for an eternal moment, weighing her words with the utmost care. The look on her face had to be identical to the one a president would wear before pushing the button for a nuclear holocaust. With a startling flash of intuition, Tory saw into her mind: she was going to invoke David's memory, the ultimate weapon of guilt she'd always possessed but never resorted to in the years since his death. She was deliberately and self-righteously going to strike him to the marrow with it, the use of it's power finally justified. She shook her head sorrowfully and discharged an abysmal, foreshadowing sigh.

"I only thank the Good Lord that poor David isn't here to see what you finally come to."

Tory floundered for an excuse to avoid the guilt. "If he hadn't gone and died, this wouldn't be what I've finally come to."

"How long are you going to go on blaming him?" she shot back angrily. "You been using him as an excuse for everything that needs excusing ever since he died."

Tory's senses reeled at her words. He knew she spoke a truth that he'd never allowed himself to recognize. David had been his most cherished memory, buried with the innocence they'd shared, the ambitions and ideals and burning passions of rose-tinted youth and perfect first love. Thoughts of him had become a sanctified dream, the only full romance of his life. Suddenly he saw that it had gone before it had a chance to go sour and that he remembered it all through gauze and soft lighting. In a painfully blinding flash, he recognized that he'd turned David's death into the perfect alibi for anything that had gone wrong ever since, the ultimate rationalization to justify embezzled funds, peddled flesh, and everything else that "You owe it to yourself" had ever covered for. Suddenly he knew that it was all so wrong. He'd stretched the excuse past its final limit and it had burst, exploding in his face with six years of self-indulgence. It left no one to blame but himself, and he was furious at Mae for pointing it out to him, furious at himself for giving her the reason, and furious at David for dying.

"David is dead!" He didn't recognize the harsh, guttural voice that issued from his throat. His eyes cut into his tormentor with a cold-blooded viciousness. "I'm alive. And I'll answer to no one."

Mae shrank back at his words but managed to recover for a bitter reply. "You was mighty meek answering to Mr. B. though, wasn't you?"

Anger with himself drove him on to sustain the frightening wickedness that gripped each nerve of his body. "I'll make you the same offer he made to me," he rasped satanically. "If you don't like it, get the hell out!"

He'd never seen Mae less than indomitable before. It frightened him to see her flinch as if from a slap, to deflate suddenly with a painful gasp and tremble in silent misery. He was shocked to discover such a black power in himself and horrified to find that he could use it on someone he loved. A strong hope that the evening held no more surprises of self-discovery suddenly gripped him, and he reached instinctively for the cognac.

"I'm sorry, Mae. I didn't mean it." He wanted to embrace her but he was no longer sure if he was entitled to her affection. "Please don't go away."

"I ain't going nowhere," she finally replied, a trace of her old manner returning. "I don't know what more I can say to make you see what's right, but I'm staying."

"I can see what's right," he replied with a quiet sadness.

"That makes it ten times worse, if you can see it and don't do nothing about it."

He watched a tear come to her eye and a new wave of self-hatred swept over him. He poured more Courvoisier to avoid it.

"Baby, I don't know what's to become of you. After David died and you was so deep in the blues, it was good to see you perk up one day and go out and buy a new shirt. I said to myself, 'Mae, it looked like an uncommon bad case but he's going to pull through. New clothes is a good sign.' But you just kept buying like there was no tomorrow, reckless-like, and none of it was giving you no real pleasure. It got you into a heap of trouble at the supermarket and you jumped right out of the pan and into the fire." She paused to give him a wistful smile. "But you seemed to be leading a charmed life. Always landed on your feet like a cat with nine lives, like David was in heaven pulling some strings for you. I hoped he'd see you through till you got this recklessness worked out of your system. Then along comes George and I said, 'Thank you, Lord. You finally come up with a suitable replacement—' "

"And the good Lord screws me again," Tory interrupted with a grating laugh. "He took a second look and said, 'What the hell am I giving this evil bitch a man for? I'll send him out to Bucks County for a needy lush.' "

"That ain't no way to talk," she said with her reassuringly familiar sternness as a hint of a smile crossed her lips. "Besides, the game ain't over till the last card's been played."

Chapter Thirty-two

THE numbers moved in the following week, three or four quiet, nondescript men that Tory would see occasionally getting on or off the elevator. They always smiled and nodded politely, like barely known neighbors on one's floor in an apartment building. Then they disappeared into the small corner suite to answer their silent telephones. The suite had been an afterthought, unnecessary space on the eighth floor that Tory had decided would be a gracious touch for houseguests he didn't want constantly underfoot. It had been used only once. With his sprawling apartment, it hadn't been necessary. Giving it up was no physical hardship, but it was a constant mental irritation to be reminded of his new tenants' presence. No one had been murdered yet, as far as he could ascertain. It gave him some comfort, but it was the comfort of an appliance on its last legs, a relief to avoid the problem soured by the knowledge that eventually it would have to be dealt with.

The cocaine operation followed the numbers a few months later. There was no decision for Tory to make, and it was easier to accept. Victor and his people needed only one room of the numbers suite, and they spent little time there. It was no more than a warehouse and wholesale showroom. It irked Mona to have Victor make impromptu appearances instead of waiting for an arranged meeting. More than once he'd unexpectedly interrupted her in the middle of a flirtation in the Mahogany Room. But compromise seemed to be the password of the day.

It had its rewards. Mr. B. doubled his salary with the onset of the numbers. Tory imagined that it was most likely small change to him, but he sent it to Freeport without question. The cocaine trade provided him with extra money on an irregular schedule plus unlimited free samples which in some weeks exceeded the cash. The white powder was more precious than gold dust, and Tory sometimes took pleasure in distributing it with princely extravagance.

Tory gazed up at the Rialto Room's lighting booth from his ringside table, hoping that everyone was duly appreciative of his unusual patience. He'd been calmly putting the technician through his paces for fifteen minutes, mixing and remixing various lights directed at the black-dressed waitress on the stage. The rest of the windowless room was a twilight world unto itself, oblivious to the early-afternoon December sun outside.

"You're doing a dazzling job, darling," he shouted to the man in the dim distance, vaguely gauging his drunkenness by the affectation in his speech. He started to sprinkle it with "dazzling" and "darling" and other new standards of his vocabulary after three cognacs. It was so much easier than remembering names or searching for the best adjective. After five drinks he noticed a change in his pronunciation of certain words. He assumed the trace of a nasal Main Line tone and enunciated carefully to compensate for the slur that became markedly noticeable after the sixth drink. He turned to Ginny and Jimmy playing backgammon at the next table. "What was his name?" he whispered loudly. Jimmy cued him patiently. "Donald, darling, I think I liked the set best that you did before we wandered off on the pinks. The one with all the blues and just enough pink to make this poor girl look less than deathly pale. Why don't you set that one up again?" He gazed beyond Eugene's prone form on the edge of the stage to give the piano player a dazzling smile. "Don't fall asleep on us, Mr. Music. We'll be with you directly. Just try to look interested and concentrate on the triple time you're earning. And darling," he remembered the waitress stage center, "I think we won't need you anymore. Just bring Mr. Music and me another Courvoisier, then you can go back to whatever it is you people do when I'm not here to brighten up your drab little lives. Get a drink for yourself, too. You've been an absolute lamb."

"Thank you, Tory," she smiled as she climbed off the stage. It was the same smile he used to see some people give to the lady who talked to herself and made animal noises on the corner of Broad and Walnut, kind but uneasy.

"Is this part of tonight's big secret?" the reporter at Tory's table asked.

"DeeDee, my plump little peach," he continued in his stilted voice, "I'm dreadfully sorry but this isn't a scoop. You know I love you dearly but you'll simply have to join the rest of the media and wait with bated breath until the stroke of midnight to find out." He gestured negligently to the stage. "This is just a little family fun. Mona's been working her stylish little toes off with tap-dancing lessons, and I promised her that when she's good enough she could be an opening act. The routine's coming along nicely," he cheerily informed her before dropping his voice to a stage whisper, "but frankly it still needs some work."

"What happened to *your* lessons, Tory? After I printed that you were going to be the next Fred Astaire, I hope you're not going to make me look like a fool."

"How could he possibly do a thing like that?" Ginny asked with an innocent ambiguity, sending Jimmy into a fit of constrained hysterics.

Tory sighed dramatically, the signal of a coming anecdote. "Poor Mr. Keenan. He's our instructor, you know. We were doing so well. Mona and I had the most darling little matching costumes with top hats and we were tapping our little hearts out almost every afternoon in what was once known in the vernacular as Joan Crawford come-fuck-me pumps. We were working on a routine to 'A Little Girl from Little Rock', with myself in the Lorelei Lee role, of course, and had gotten as far as the canes. The finale was to be a dazzling series of high kicks, but in my unbridled enthusiasm, one of my kicks somehow connected with the cane and it landed on poor old Mr. Keenan's graying skull." He paused for another dramatic sigh. "But he's mending quite nicely. It only needed twelve stitches. The old darling's almost persuaded to come back if we promise to give up the props for a few months."

DeeDee wrote voluminously. "That's a good filler for a slow day."

He lowered his voice to an urgent murmur. "When Mona finishes her number, I expect you all to applaud wildly. The poor angel's been working so hard at it, and she needs the encouragement." He knew DeeDee would stand on her head if he asked. He provided her with many of her slow-day fillers and frequent headlines for her about-town column. She'd have had to put in twice as many hours without Steven Sachs to write material for her.

"Jimmy," DeeDee pleaded with a galling flirtatiousness, "give me a tiny little hint about tonight."

Ginny looked up from the backgammon board to give her a stare of unabashed distaste, but Jimmy maintained his usual poised smile. "I know as much as you do, DeeDee. It's been top secret since October."

"We'll discuss it no further," Tory closed the subject imperiously. "I'll only say that at midnight, I shall descend from the heavens as Baby New Year in a production that will dazzle my two thousand guests on the rooftop garden and turn every red-blooded American queen absolutely chartreuse with envy."

They'd begun hyping his New Year's Eve Gala in October with mysterious references to his plans. Curiosity had reached fever pitch in the last week of December with the activity on the roof of construction men building a fifty-foot square gold-painted platform and workers assembling a heated gold-and-white tent big enough for most three-ring circuses. Months before that, one of DeeDee's competitors led a column with an interview with Tory's florist, claiming a sixty-thousand-dollar holiday order featuring thousands of gold and white orchids. DeeDee countered with a scoop on the entertainment, which would include a new sound system in the Mahogany Room, three impressive acts in the Rialto Room, a sixty-piece Dorsey-style band in the roof-top tent, and a few surprises. Other professionally timed leaks promised a midnight supper with roast suckling pigs and a Roman-orgy theme followed by a breakfast buffet that would feature Beluga caviar served in an exact replica of Empress Josephine's bathtub. Tory started dropping hints about a spellbinding entrance two weeks before Christmas, though the publicity was no longer necessary. The five-hundred-dollar-a-couple tickets had been sold out by Thanksgiving, and he spent December trying to cope graciously with desperate requests, tears, and an occasional suicide threat.

DeeDee didn't give up easily. "At least give me a hint on what you'll wear. You can't possibly outdo your peek-a-boo caftan at the Halloween Ball."

Tory gazed ethereally toward heaven. "My lips are sealed. Except to say that tonight . . . tonight . . . I shall transcend Fashion."

The costumes had become a tasteless joke to him. The crowd applauded each new excess, and their laughter had begun to sound more malicious than kind to his ears. He decided to turn the joke on them after some rude catcalls at his Labor Day party, and he exaggerated his image until it had become a cartoon. He gave himself a white Rolls-Royce for his birthday in October and complemented it with an ermine lap robe and ermine-trimmed uniforms for Eugene and the new footman. He bought a lynx cape in November, wore it once before deciding that the shade was wrong for his coloring, gave it to Goodwill, and ordered a new one in chinchilla. He sometimes appeared upstairs in sequined jumpsuits or, claiming an early-morning appointment, in silk pajamas. Caftans always seemed to get a hoot from the crowd, and he wore them often. They were frequently mentioned in the columns, and he smiled his secret fuck-you smile as he watched the money roll in.

Being outrageous helped to fill the hours. At some point his personal universe had ceased to be a perpetual party. Some nights, he'd look at the crowd and want to say sweetly, "It's been such fun, but you're beginning to bore me. Why don't you all go home?" Being outrageous sometimes made it more bearable. It was a little game he could play with Mona when she wasn't stalking a man and Jimmy when he wasn't with Hal and Mae on the rare occassions when she was in a light mood. By letting his friends know that he knew the crowds were laughing at him, he could play along.

Eugene began to snore lightly on the edge of the stage,

and Tory turned to DeeDee in disbelief. "How can he possibly sleep in my scintillating presence?" He took two steps to the stage and grasped Eugene's crotch. Eugene quickly awoke and pushed the hand away in annoyance. "Let's go to my boudoir and take a nap together."

"No thanks."

"You dare refuse me?"

"You're not my type."

Tory turned again to DeeDee. "How's that for a head-line? 'Tory's Chauffeur Refuses Him a Miscegenous Affair.' Will it sell?"

It was a running joke that didn't amuse him anymore. It had never been funny, it was too close to the truth. As far as life had taken him into contact with black people, he'd often overcompensate to appear liberal. Hypocrisy wasn't necessary with Mae and Eugene, but at other times he'd find himself unconsciously trying to please because of color. He imagined that they could sense it and that it must be insulting, the coaxed cordiality that covered an ingrained aloofness based on fear. His own rural childhood far from a black face hadn't been notably prejudiced, but the fear had always been there. A vestige of it remained under his veneer of enlightened sophistication, the subconscious thought that black people were dangerous, filthy animals. Any contact with them was sullying and sex with them the ultimate self-abuse.

He knew it would never occur with Eugene—his frighteningly powerful black body on top of him, forcing him to do debasing things, reveling in his humiliation. But he wanted it. And it was readily available elsewhere. He gave in to the urge every month or so and quietly disappeared to a cheap hotel in Greenwich Village for a few days. Then he could go to the trucks and the leather bars and cruise for hustlers and come home with a fresh supply of self-disgust.

Eugene seemed to sense it. Tory couldn't read how he felt about it, but he was taking it well. And he was always looming in the background, looking serious about his power. He seemed to be expecting trouble at some point in the near future when the outrageousness went too far, and he was ready to deal with it. Tory often wondered why so many people seemed to worry about him lately.

"That headline won't do for a family newspaper. Tell me about your Christmas instead."

"Dreary, dreary, dreary," he moaned dramatically. "I hate Christmas."

"Because there's nothing left for you to find under the tree?"

"Perhaps." He waved the subject off. "This is my holiday. New Year's Eve."

He hadn't wanted any gifts. They would have been superfluous. But the people who weren't pleased with the gifts he gave depressed him. Mae had appreciated the thoughtfulness of the mink he'd picked for her but gave her envelope to the church. His mother had seemed more troubled than pleased with the new car. Going home for Christmas Eve dinner had been like visiting a polite family of strangers. There had been nothing to say beyond the civilities, and even those were fraught with uncomfortable silences. His father joked uneasily about the publicity items he read in the Philadelphia newspapers. Tory tried to imply that his success was due to hard work, luck, and ability, but he sensed that his parents weren't buying the story. It would have been unbearable without the cognac.

"Ain't you going to eat lunch again today?" Mae shouted as she threaded her way through the tables. "Those fellows can't rustle something up when the mood hits you today. They can hardly walk in that kitchen with all the party food."

"Milly can make me a sandwich later."

She shook her head at the brandy snifter. "You better make time for a nap this afternoon, it's going to be a long day. You know how you get with all that brandy on an empty stomach."

"I'm pacing myself," he smiled affably. "I should pass out around cocktail hour and be fresh as a daisy for midnight."

He knew the cognac was turning into a problem, but it worked so well at dulling the hollow chill that seemed always to be with him lately. He'd drunk wine for years, ever since David had died. After a few years it didn't make him silly, it just imparted a pleasant outlook. Most people couldn't even tell he'd been drinking. The cognac gave him an incandescent glow that was so much more pleasant to him. It had taken him a while to adjust to the scorching of his insides, but the effects were immediate. He often slurred his words and took numerous catnaps. He even fell down occasionally. But it had its compensations.

"I just got off the phone with my man," she smiled.

"Who's that?"

"George!" she scowled at his feigned ignorance.

"George who?"

"Stop acting stupid. He's got to close up the restaurant and he won't be in time for your big entrance, but he's dropping by around three."

Tory had mixed feelings about the whole idea. He knew that Mae talked to George on the telephone once or twice a week lately, that she even went out to New Hope for dinner occasionally. Tory asked polite questions about him that would usually be enough to prompt Mae into a comprehensive summary of every detail of their conversation, but she was strangely taciturn lately.

It made Tory nervous. He hoped she wasn't repeating some of the more tawdry details of his life. He was so much more comfortable thinking that the only news about him should be from press releases and approved interviews. Mae had sent George the invitation for New Year's and told Tory about it later. He'd been at a loss for words, not knowing how he felt about it or how he would act, after not seeing him since the previous New Year's Eve.

"Janice should be incoherent by three." He laughed suddenly. "But by then we might start to make sense to each other."

"Janice ain't coming. She's drying out at Chitchat, hasn't touched a drop in two weeks."

"Poor darling."

"He's coming alone." She gazed at him in a familiar reprimand. "I hope you don't do anything tonight to embarrass yourself."

"How can I?" he giggled. "I'm shameless."

"You just make sure you take a long nap," she ordered.

The supper-club manager approached as she ambled away. "Tory," he smiled with a condescending deference, "I hate to bother you, but we really have to get this room set up for the party. Do you think you'll be done soon?"

Tory attempted to throw back his head in haughty disdain. "We shall be done when we are done," he decreed. "And in the future, when you have something to say that's going to displease me, my name is Mr. Bacher."

The manager hastily retreated as Ginny looked up from the backgammon board. "Have I told you lately that you're getting obnoxious?"

"Yes, madam, you have," he answered with a serene smile. "Repeatedly. And it seems to be the general consensus of opinion."

"Tory," Mona's excited voice echoed from offstage, "I'm ready."

"We're waiting with bated breath, my darling. Eugene, sit up and prepare to be dazzled by true talent. Music please, Mr. Maestro."

To the opening notes of "The Lady Is a Tramp," Mona appeared in tuxedo jacket, top hat, and fishnet stockings, with a black cane in her hand. She launched into the song with vigor, carrying the tune without great power but almost on key. The spotlight gamely attempted to follow her as she burst into dance after the first chorus, tapping inimitably across the stage in a blare of metallic clicks and a blur of unsteady black props. She finished the dance segment only a few steps from her intended mark, and the spotlight quickly rediscovered her. Shortness of breath failed to dampen her enthusiasm as she finished the song and high-kicked her way offstage in a one-woman chorus line. Tory and DeeDee led the applause and coaxed her back for three ecstatic curtain calls.

Tory's applause was almost sincere. He was so fond of Mona, she seemed to be the only one who understood him anymore. She'd always understood. She knew the same feelings of emptiness and dealt with them in the same way. They brushed off their problems with a smile, a smart remark, a pretty purchase, or a handsome man. It used to seem such a valiant attitude.

Chapter Thirty-three

TORY was starting to feel claustrophobic after four hours in the tiny airport office with Germaine and his two assistants, but the end was finally in sight, and it was beginning to seem worth the effort. His growing certainty that the coming scene was going to be totally outrageous caused excitement to replace his usual cynicism, something that hadn't occurred in months.

The hairdressers were using artist's brushes to touch up the final finish on the metallic gold paint that covered him from head to toe. They tickled his eyelids and ears and the spaces between his fingers, but he persevered. He tried to dwell on being thankful that he was done bending over the tiny sink while Germaine gave his hair rinse after rinse of gold until it matched his skin. Pasting the sequins onto his body from eyelash to ankle in artistic swirls had been painless but tedious, and now they all sparkled so brightly, like a thousand tiny diamonds. They'd had to sew the gold lamé loincloth onto his body to get just the right drape to keep him on the borderline between vulgar and indecent. He couldn't watch the darting needle so close to his crotch, but everything seemed securely in place now. Germaine was doing the finishing touches on his hair, attaching rhinestones to the tip of each small clump of hair in such a way that the glue would come out with a trim the next day. An assistant decorated him with twenty fake diamond rings, one for each finger and toe.

"Now take a deep breath and hold it for ten minutes," the other assistant requested.

Tory bravely attempted the feat while the assistant knelt to glue the thirty-carat Wellington into his navel.

"Hurry up, Ronnie," Johnny commanded as he finished with the rings. "We can't stop for one red light or he's going to land on the roof before we get there."

"One more minute. Get my coat."

"Only three more rhinestones, darling," Germaine promised. "And I must say that your patience has been heroic."

Tory smiled through his closed lips.

"Tory, can I have some more coke before we leave?" Johnny asked.

He nodded and motioned to his bag on the desk.

"Thanks."

"OK. Breathe out slowly."

He did so and the stone seemed well anchored.

"Marvelous. Hurry up, Johnny. If I miss this I'll never forgive myself."

Tory recovered his breath and gave Ronnie and Johnny a threatening look. "One word of this to the crowd and I'll have both your tongues cut out."

They seemed to consider his words seriously for a split second. People were no longer sure that there were whims left that Tory couldn't have fulfilled. "Our lips are sealed," they answered in unison before scurrying out the door.

Germaine finished with a sigh of accomplishment and looked at his watch. "Perfect timing. It was touch and go for a few hours, but we pulled through."

"You're a trouper, Germaine."

"And you, darling, are a bona fide star. Pity all the fools who are watching the ball fall in Times Square." He gave a final adjustment to the Happy New Year streamer across Tory's bare chest. "We better throw on your sable, it's raw out there."

"Two good snorts and I'm about ready. Can you hold the spoon for me, please?"

"Certainly."

Germaine measured a grossly oversized coke spoon and held it to Tory's nostril, gently pressing the other with a tissue to preserve the paint, then repeated the process.

"Ready now?"

Tory took two deep breaths of air. "For anything."

They crossed the runway to the small crowd assembled around the gold-painted helicopter. The crowd broke into disbelieving laughter as they approached, and Tory smiled and waved gaily. The pilot only shook his head as they climbed in, then started the engine for a vertical ascent.

As the airport faded from view, Tory felt the beginnings of the Novocained feeling in his mouth and nose with relief. As they whirred toward the center of town he tasted the first medicinal post-nasal drip. He knew it would be only another minute before the cocaine swept over him in surging waves, the joyous total confidence that all things were possible and that nothing could go wrong. Two thousand waiting party-goers in an expectant froth gave him nothing to worry about. He was certain that everything would be perfect and that he was going to be ecstatic through every minute of it. The first jubilant smile crossed his lips as he thought fondly of the nameless person who had cleverly dubbed cocaine "the Cadillac of highs." Feelings of admiration for him and even of love swept over Tory's body. It was almost a substitute for the vibrations that never came anymore.

Germaine shrieked as the gold-and-white-striped tent came into view, but Tory forced himself not to peer out of the open door, fearing what havoc the gusting wind might play with his coiffure. As the helicopter turned ninety degrees and began its descent, Tory found he could see the tent by standing on his seat and looking downward, much to the displeasure of the pilot. He felt a chill of anticipation as a helicopter-sized flap unfolded on the top of the tent to reveal the golden platform shimmering in the spotlights. It loomed closer and closer until they passed through the roof and landed with a soft thud.

The helicopter abruptly ceased its ear-splitting racket, only to be replaced by the din of expectant shouts and laughter from the pressing mob. They were obviously impressed. Tory slumped in his seat to avoid their gaze and peered out the bottom of the window while Germaine used the coat to tent his head. He searched for Mona or Jimmy or another favorite face, but it was difficult to distinguish anyone through the glare of the spotlights.

A hidden mechanic took the helicopter's silence as

his cue, and the front of the platform slowly unfolded into a glittering golden staircase, prodding the crowd into more laughter and Tory into a fresh rush of coked exhilaration. The staircase's hydraulic motor shut off and the side flaps of the platform slid back to unleash a horde of marching Mummers in white sequins and feathers who proceeded to strut frenetically before the crowd. Their tinny banjos somehow managed to quiet the growing hysteria as they strummed "Stairway to the Stars" and assembled themselves in precise formation three abreast on each side of the staircase. They finished their number to howling applause, then silenced the crowd as they launched into "Pennies from Heaven."

The platform panels slid back once again to disgorge the most statuesque girls of the crew clad in white-satin-and-sequin angel robes tailored in Frederick's of Hollywood tradition to reveal torsos to the navel and legs to the hip. After hours of rehearsal, they were able to balance their six-foot spans of white ostrich-feather wings and traverse the distance to the staircase with Ziegfeldesque grace. The wings made it necessary for them to ascend the steps in stately single file and pivot with poised caution as they positioned themselves in a glittering white inner border to the Mummers.

All but the tip of the golden helicopter was obscured from the crowd by a sea of luminous white feathers. Germaine prodded Tory at the final notes of "Pennies from Heaven" and he slipped out of the helicopter to take his place behind the wings of Doreen and Gloria at the top of the staircase. Doreen almost lost her footing as she glanced over her shoulder to see him but managed to recover as the song ended and smile angelically for the frenzied crowd.

When silence was restored, the girls raised their best soprano voices and stunned the mob with three quick hallelujahs from Handel's *Messiah*. The Mummers immediately burst into an upbeat rendition of "Love for Sale," and Doreen and Gloria gracefully pivoted their wings to reveal Tory spotlighted in his best showgirl stance, a golden apparition against the sea of white.

The effect produced the expected devastated response, and the crowd drowned out the music. Tory remained at the top of the staircase in immobile ecstasy, allowing the riotous applause to sweep over him in wave after euphoric wave. He wanted to remain in his stately pose for eternity, simply stand there forever and have the applause never end.

He didn't know how much time had passed when Gloria finally prodded him. It seemed a lifetime, but not long enough. She prodded him more roughly the second time and in order to avoid losing his balance he had to begin a regretful descent. The clouds of golden confetti and the hysterical shouts and the flashing cameras were all very pleasant, but he knew it was the beginning of the end. He'd been safe at the pinnacle of the staircase, an idol to be worshiped from a distance. The crowd seemed so much friendlier to him while it remained faceless. Descending back into reality was an unpleasant prospect, but he maintained his smile.

The din continued for several minutes. Tory was grateful to it for saving him from making clever remarks to the gathered reporters. He needed only to beam and shout 'Happy New Year!' and accept the awed compliments graciously. The first rush of the cocaine began to wear off, and he nervously searched the crowd for Germaine. He appeared behind him like an efficient field medic, leather clutch in hand, and administered the powder behind a mob that obscured him from the photographers. Being outrageous was one thing, but Tory knew that even *he* might have to face the consequences of such a picture in the local papers.

The cocaine made everything so much easier. He floated through the crowd, greeting guests with unfeigned delight, fascinated with whatever trivialities they had to utter, being genuinely amused by the most mundane remarks. The periodic snorts made time fly and constantly renewed his energy. By three o'clock, he was certain that he'd spoken to each of his two thousand guests, working his way through the rooftop tent, the casino and private lounges on the tenth floor, the dining rooms, the Rialto Room, and the Mahogany Room.

He finally perched himself atop the mahogany bar with a snifter of Courvoisier, a royal presence for his subjects to approach and pay homage. The photographers had departed, much to his relief. Three hours of cocaine had rendered his eyes and running nose less than photogenic, and their absence allowed Germaine to revive him without first searching the room for incriminating camera angles. They were in the process of another resuscitation when George was suddenly by his side. Tory smiled weakly over the gold spoon embedded in his golden nostril.

George's expression was so familiar, the one of equal parts of adoration and irritation that he'd so often directed at Tory. His sameness extended beyond the expression. The lean face and tousled hair hadn't changed, except perhaps for a subtle deepening of the crow's-feet that only enhanced his handsomeness. The hard masculine body looked the same under the black tuxedo, and Tory felt the same familiar emotions stirring in his heart and other regions of his anatomy.

Tory couldn't pinpoint the change, but something about George was different. He thought perhaps it was his mouth. It no longer seemed quite so set in a tight-lipped frown. His lips had always reminded Tory that things were less than perfect. They used to tell him volumes without ever moving, about how unhappy George was being a hustler, how impatient he was to become independent and respectable, how frustrated he was not to be capable of a relationship. The tight-lipped frown was now almost a complacent shadow of a smile. It said nothing to Tory, but he found it very appealing.

Germaine dislodged the spoon and began to refill it for the other nostril. Tory struggled with the feelings of guilt that George's sudden appearance provoked in him and decided to brazen it out. "Would you care for some?" he cordially asked, motioning to the spoon.

"No thanks," George answered. "And I'd rather you didn't either." The tone was more polite than critical, stopping Tory from an angrily defensive reply.

"Why?"

"I want to talk to you," he answered simply.

The cocaine or the excitement of the evening or the confusion at George's presence had left Tory's brain in a less than alert state. "About what?" was all he could manage in childlike curiosity.

"Us.'"

The familiar old emotion of injured pride fought its way through the jumble in his mind, and he carefully tilted his head to its angle of greatest arrogance. "I didn't realize that there was anything left to be said."

"There's plenty. Let's find someplace quiet." Another familiar expression crossed George's face, the unabashedly predatory, frankly sexual look that Tory remembered so well from their first day in Freeport. He cursed himself for allowing it to bring on the same nerve-tingling sensation of flustered desire. "How about your apartment?"

Tory wanted to be offended, to indignantly refuse this man who had the audacity to think he could suddenly appear after over two years of uninterest and calmly lead him off to bed. He knew he should be incensed at such impudence, especially on the night he'd reached a new pinnacle of success and his company for the evening would be a singular honor. But suddenly the hollow chill inside him ached more than his offended pride.

George seemed to sense the battle being fought in his mind, and a different smile crossed his face, a wistful meditation on treasured memories. "Do you remember a spring afternoon three years ago?" he reminisced quietly. "The day you finally tracked me down in a bookstore after I hadn't called you for two weeks after that night with Andrew Arledge?"

"Vaguely," Tory managed to lie. It seemed like a memory from another lifetime, but it was crystal-clear.

"We went back to my apartment at the Locust Towers." He laughed suddenly at a remembered detail. "Because you were ten seconds from humiliating me to death in the middle of the bookstore. You were bound and determined that day to lead me off in chains to connubial bliss."

Another familiar feeling came back to Tory, a feeling of annoyance that George always managed to provoke by not ignoring unpleasant thoughts. Tory missed that feeling, too. "Does this story have a point, or do you always spend New Year's Eve cheerily reopening old wounds?"

"It's coming," he laughed. "After we talked it over and I stubbornly refused to cooperate with your plans to straighten out my whole future and you were looking for a way to make one of your grand exits, you marched to the door and turned to me dramatically and tried to look like Doris Day—"

"It was Lauren Bacall!" Tory laughed in outrage.

"Really?" George asked, trying to look seriously perplexed. "I thought it was Doris Day in *Pillow Talk*. Anyway, you struck a dramatic pose at the door and said, 'If you want me . . .' Remember?" Tory nodded dumbly as George puckered his lips into a soft whistle. "There's a point of honor at stake here," he continued gently. "You wouldn't go back on your word, would you?"

"Do you expect me to fall for such a ridiculously flimsy, mawkishly sentimental excuse?" Tory asked without conviction. He answered his own question as he slid down from the bar, too intent on George to notice Germaine's gaping stare. He had to laugh at the absurdity of his pounding heart and weak knees, sensations that he thought his cynicism had dimmed forever. He felt idiotically sophomoric as he had to grasp George's arm for support and follow entranced as they negotiated their way through the mob. There were a few drunken catcalls and some scattered applause, but none of it mattered. The crowd didn't exist, and his image was suddenly unimportant. He followed George through the mahogany doors without a backward glance.

Chapter Thirty-four

TORY awoke to sounds from the bathroom. He'd expected to have his usual hangover, but the sharp jabbing pains that began in the back of his head and continued down to his calves were a new sensation. He wondered if perhaps the Courvoisier and cocaine had finally gotten out of hand. With tremendous effort he rolled on his side and the tiny stabs miraculously ceased. He groped behind him and came back with a handful of rhinestones and sequins, relieved to find an external source for his discomfort. Forcing himself slowly into a sitting position to sweep them from the bed, he groaned as he noticed the gold paint smeared on the Porthault sheets and pillowcases. He collapsed helplessly back into the mess, too exhausted to ring for clean linen.

He wondered why it hadn't bothered them during the night. It all seemed like a dream, everything had been so perfect. The cocaine haze, the discomforts of the costume, the two years of separation, it had all been unimportant. They'd been together with total rapport, a night that almost equaled the enchanted afternoon in Freeport. But Tory couldn't remember vibrations. If they'd been there, he assumed with a vague uneasiness that they'd been emanating from George.

He was in no mood to analyze the components of the situation, only delighted to have things finally straightened out. He was even willing to forgive George the ridiculous amount of time it had taken him to come to his senses. It had been two wasted years, but he planned to be nobly magnanimous. He wouldn't let even the trace of a smug smile cross his lips, nor would he utter one word about how he'd been right all along.

There were other emotions he didn't plan to show either. He felt like a silent movie heroine being untied from the railroad tracks in the nick of time, but he didn't think it was necessary for George to know that. He hoped George would take him away from the club immediately, and Tory was ready to leave. He didn't need a psychic to tell him that danger was making a rapid approach. It would be a relief to leave behind the sinister men in the corner suite and the vicious smile on Victor's lips and the demeaning self-caricature he had become and the snickering crowd that goaded him on. It would be a relief to stop the cocaine and cognac he needed to cope with it all. He tried to remember how it felt to be sober without a hangover.

George emerged from the bathroom, a slight golden hue covering the front of his body and a smile that bordered on arrogance splitting his face. He ignored the painted sheets and climbed back into bed for a demanding kiss.

Tory responded as best he could through his postparty stupor, hoping his mouth didn't taste as bad to George as it did to him. "Doesn't the paint taste funny?" he asked, trying to camouflage his discomfort.

"Yeah," George grinned lecherously. "But fortunately, the most delicious parts weren't covered."

Tory laughed, despite the throbbing it caused in his forehead. It felt so right to have George back in bed beside him. But memories suddenly struck him of past moments of contentment and how quickly they'd disappeared. "We never did get much talking done last night," he stated tentatively.

"I'm a man of action," George replied lightly as he ran his hand down Tory's sequinned side. Noticing Tory's expression, he changed his own to match it and met his eyes through a serious pause. "Tory, I want you back."

The hangover made clear thinking impossible. He knew he should be thrilled, embrace him meaningfully, perhaps even shed a few tears. All he could manage was a frail smile.

"On my terms," George continued.

"OK."

"I want you out of this place," he ordered. "It's destroying you."

"Today?" he asked meekly, trying not to look as sick as he felt.

"Today?" George repeated with a laugh. "I've been psyching myself up for an argument and you're not even going to give me the least bit of resistance?"

Tory tried to sound indifferent. "I'm ready to get out. If there's one thing I've learned from entertaining the public it's a sense of timing. And I can't think of a better time to draw the curtain than after last night's show-stopper. What can I possibly do to top it?" He managed a theatrical sigh as he lit a cigarette from the sterling box on the night table and sank back unsteadily into the pillows. "If I go now, I can take my rightful place in local history as a living legend. Sort of like Christ ascending to heaven after the Crucifixion."

"I don't think Billy Graham would approve of you taking your stage cues from the Bible," George laughed.

"You've got to hand it to the guy," Tory shrugged pragmatically. "He sure knew which end was up when it came to making a flashy exit."

"Someday when you get me mad I'm going to repeat that to Mae and you'll get the lecture of your life."

"I've had it already," Tory stated flatly. "Besides, I'm never going to get you mad again."

George looked dubious.

"Really," Tory smiled wanly.

"What will we do for entertainment?"

Tory gave him a suggestive stare, then changed the subject. "So what are our plans? When do I get out of here and where are we going? To New Hope?"

"No," he answered with finality. "As soon as I'm sure Janice is on her feet I'm selling out."

"Good," Tory sighed, relieved not to be subjected to the tourists in New Hope. "Let's go someplace warm. I'm so tired of being cold all the time."

"I'm afraid I can't do anything about that for the rest of the winter. Janice won't be back until February, and I'll need, at the very least, a month after that to square things away. Why don't you take a vacation?"

"I could go to Ginny's place in Florida until I wore out my welcome," Tory answered quietly. "With her old man up here, she might let me stay a month or two. I'd do it if you promise to come visit me on weekends."

"Sure," George hastily agreed with a puzzled smile. "But what will you tell Mr. B.?"

Tory concentrated his energy on tugging the bell pull for coffee. "I don't know," he wondered vaguely. "What can he say? If I want out, I want out. He's usually a reasonable man."

George gave him a perplexed smile through a long pause. "This is too easy. I was prepared to browbeat you for days until you gave in. Such cooperation is unlike you. Can you actually walk away from all this decadent splendor just like that?"

Tory nonchalantly picked sequins from his thigh and tossed them on the carpet, avoiding George's eyes so he wouldn't see how pathetically eager he was to give it all up. "It's been fun," he answered with a shrug. "But the novelty has worn off. Having spent most of my life hovering forlornly about the poverty line, I'm grateful to have had the chance to live in such absurd opulence. But now I've had a satisfying taste of it and it isn't necessary anymore. Besides, it's not like I'll have to exchange it all for a tenement slum. I paid attention when Ginny was giving me lessons. There's no reason why we can't live comfortably on my interest."

"You've stashed that much away?" George asked with surprised respect.

"Mr. B. has been a generous employer," he answered in an offhand tone. "And there are no withholding taxes on the wages of sin."

"I was expecting to have to rescue you from a life of dissipation," George chuckled in an irritating way. "Mae didn't tell me that you'd taken up saving."

"Mae doesn't know everything" he almost snapped. "I'm no dummy. It's all been put away very discreetly. Only one other person knows where it is."

George was impressed. "It's good to know you've been smart about *something* for the past two years."

"I hope you didn't lose too much sleep over it," Tory answered, a trace of pique creeping into his voice. "I may appear less than sensible at times, but all things taken into consideration, I think I've done a half-decent job with my life." He hoped he sounded as if he believed it. "I'll admit that I get a bit carried away on occasion, but I know when to stop."

"Tory," George began in an annoyingly omniscient tone, "I know exactly what's been going on for the past six months, and if we could leave today it wouldn't be a minute too soon. I wish it could be that way but I have other obligations. I'm tied up until March with Janice. If I took off now I'm afraid all her progress would go down the drain. I can't be with you every day, but I'll be there as often as I can. And this will be a big first step in itself, just getting you out of this environment."

"What do you mean?"

"You know what I mean," he continued kindly. "I can imagine what it must be like to live with everything that's on your mind. Hell," he asked sympathetically, "who can blame you for the abuse you've put your body through? But it's all over now, Tory. A couple of months in Florida will do wonders for you. And by March, I'll be there to help you." He flashed Tory another irritating smile. "Trust me. You're going to enjoy seeing the world sober again."

Tory valiantly overcame his pounding head to prop himself against the pillows in ramrod indignation. "Please!" He stretched the word into several syllables of haughty disdain. "I can give up the liquor at any time I choose."

George ignored his words with a patronizingly charitable smile. "Tory, I've been a fool. It's all my fault that you've become what you are, and I apologize. We can't change the past but we can work on the future. I'll help you. I've done wonders for Janice," he enticed, as if offering candy to a four-year-old. "After two years, she's almost ready to face things on her own."

Only the hangover stopped him from interrupting. A patronizing attitude was one thing, but being classified with Janice quite another.

"It's been tearing me apart ever since you opened this place," George continued sadly. "The stories kept getting worse. Finally, you're running a numbers operation and dealing coke. But I had to stick it out with Janice after I used her so shamelessly for the restaurant. She needed me, too. I had a moral obligation."

With a hangover or without, enough was enough. He

tossed a handful of sequins across George to the floor and somehow managed to sit up without support. "So now it's my turn to be saved?" he shouted incredulously. "All this time I thought you were out there in the boondocks in your rustic little restaurant being tormented with unrequited love while you were actually chomping at the bit to reclaim a lost soul. This is a good joke on me."

"Don't be flippant, Tory," George replied with an infuriating patience. "You know that's not how it is. I love you! But until recently, I wasn't ready to deal with it. You can't have forgotten how I was. I wasn't ready for you. I had my own problems to work out first, and two years back in reality with me finally coming out on top has solved them. I needed the time to straighten myself out. But it was worth it, I can deal with you now and the way you make me feel. It was too one-sided before." He laughed with a condescending tolerance at the memory, as if he'd been a silly schoolboy. "It can work between us now, Tory. You need me more than I need you." George seemed to regret his last sentence immediately, and he looked warily at Tory, who looked back with eyes widened in rage.

His throbbing head and shaking hands were suddenly forgotten, and he jumped out of bed with a surprising energy. Spotting a pile of the previous evening's diamond rings on the night table, he grabbed a handful and hurled them at George. "You self-righteous prick!" he screamed, bringing a stunned look to George's face. "I'm ready to give all of this up for you! In a minute!" He gestured wildly, at nothing in particular. "All the money! All the service. All the publicity. I don't need it if I can have you. But not the way it apparently has to be for you to accept me. Do I look like some heathen waiting to be saved by a born-again Christian? Some wino on Skid Row waiting desperately for St. George of the Barflies to come along? If that's the only way we can have a relationship, it's not worth having. If you still need to play your little macho games about dominance and masculine ego and who has the upper hand, you'll have to find someone else to play with. When you grow up enough to accept me as an equal partner, if that ever happens, perhaps we'll have something to talk about."

He snatched a silk robe from the bedside chaise and

stormed through his dressing room and into the hall. He stalked past Mae, approaching with a breakfast tray for two, and her beaming smile dimmed.

"Oh, baby!" she moaned after him. "Don't tell me you went and done it again."

"It's all his fault," Tory screamed over his shoulder. "And I want him out of my apartment, out of my building, immediately!" He then disappeared through the main foyer in search of a bottle of Courvoisier.

Chapter Thirty-five

TORY made his expected grand entrance into the Mahogany Room at midnight with a pink follow spot and the sounds of "My Funny Valentine." His caftan was a riot of alternating red and white hearts, accessorized with tiny hearts dangling from his curls and pasted to his cheeks. The crowd's reaction was gratifying, though no match for New Year's Eve.

He wondered how long he'd be able to coast on that evening's performance. The crowd still packed the club every night and the waiting list for new memberships continued to grow, but he was sure that the public must find anything he'd done since that night to be anticlimactic. He depended on the cocaine to help him through until a more extravagant idea occurred. It gave him the strength to be effervescently flamboyant night after night and made the most outlandish behavior to please the crowd seem like sensible fun. They all applauded wildly when he tapdanced the length of the mahogany bar, and at least one crystal brandy snifter tossed nonchalantly into a fireplace had come to be an expected part of the evening. A surprising number of guests were good sports about a bottle of champagne poured over their heads, and most of the waiters cooperated when he flipped them dramatically across a table for a passionate kiss. He usually had to wait until the next day to get a full report on his latest antics, so many of them slipped his mind. Mae seemed to take grim satisfaction in catching him with a hangover and informing him of his misdeeds while he was too ill to fend off the guilt and humiliation. Only a few quick belts would calm his hands and make her recitation bearable.

He was relieved to have the rationalization that it was all good for the club, something he could convince himself of after the fifth or sixth cognac. Each excess since New Year's Eve had been covered with heightened interest by the press, and Steven Sachs had even gotten feelers from New York about opening a second club. But most important of all, Tory was sure that his behavior irritated the hell out of George.

George would appear at the club two or three nights a week since New Year's. He'd telephoned the apartment almost hourly for the first few days of January, but Tory wouldn't accept his calls. It would have been a simple matter to have had him barred from the club. Tory considered it, but decided a total lack of interest would be more insulting. It was another rationalization to satisfy the part of him that still wanted George to be there, one he could believe by lunch-hour cocktails. He made it a point to treat George as just another guest. If George happened to be in earshot, he'd blithely continue in his party image, telling outrageous anecdotes against himself and making frivolous remarks. It was usually easy to do with the assistance of cocaine. If he concentrated on it, George was just another nondescript face in the audience.

Sometimes he couldn't maintain the fantasy. He'd be in the middle of a story and catch George's smug smile, the one that said he knew exactly what was going on in Tory's head and that he knew it was little more than an adolescent phase that Tory would someday outgrow. It was too infuriating for words, especially when Tory was sober enough to realize that George was probably right and only his own stubborn pride stood in their way. When Tory would catch one of these expressions, he'd chug-a-lug his Courvoisier to addle his brain into more rationalizations, then try to do something exceptionally vulgar. It gave him a bitter satisfaction to turn George's smug smile into a pained frown. He despised himself for it, but he despised himself for many things. There was even a rationalization for the pain he caused. When the cognac and cocaine weren't enough to overcome his guilt he could tell himself that he was doing George a favor by trying to alienate him. When he was in one of his ever-more-frequent martyred states of mind, he was sure that George would be better off without him.

He spotted his three self-appointed consciences huddled at a table directly in his path. Mae and Brad were no more than irritating when taken alone. He could make a joke of their remonstrances and laugh almost anything off. It was easier to avoid them when they teamed up with George, as they were prone to do since New Year's. He often thought that the three of them together was like having his own personal Greek chorus to chant predictions of doom.

There was no way to gracefully avoid them. He always stopped at the tables in his path for a few boisterous remarks, and to bypass theirs would betray the discomfort he didn't want to show. He armed himself with a few superficial lines and hoped they wouldn't try to steer the conversation into a serious area.

They looked up suddenly as he approached, three somber faces interrupted in the middle of an undoubtedly earnest conversation. Tory was sure they were plotting to abduct him to Bucks County, hold him prisoner with well-balanced meals and mineral water until he saw the error of his ways. He prayed to get through with no more than a few casual words.

"Happy Valentine's Day!" he shouted merrily, bending to kiss Mae's cheek. "Wasn't it clever of Ginny to have them set aside a day to honor the noble employees of the escort service?"

The remark met with polite smiles and a few giggles from an adjoining table.

"It's our equivalent to Labor Day, you know. Mona gave the crew a day off and all their drinks are on the house tonight."

"Damn generous, that Mona," Brad smirked.

"Baby," Mae coaxed in her nursery school teacher's voice, "don't you want to thank George for the pretty flowers he sent you?"

"But of course!" he enthused. "Thank you, George. They were divine." He turned to Mae blankly. "What flowers?"

Her only answer was a disgusted frown, but he preferred it to the fleeting look of hurt that passed over George's face.

"Don't be too upset with him, Mae," Brad advised sarcastically. "Loss of memory is one of the typical intermediate symptoms."

"Symptoms?" Tory asked valiantly, raising a hand to his forehead. "What have you been keeping from me? Is it a brain tumor, like Bette Davis in . . . in . . . what was the name of that movie?" He looked up in sudden horror. "Oh, Bradley! You're right! I can't remember the name of that movie. It's a brain tumor, isn't it?" He grasped Brad by the shoulders. "Give it to me straight. I have a right to know. I'm going to be out in the garden one day, puttering with the petunias, and suddenly it will start getting dark. That's what's going to happen, it's a brain tumor, isn't it?"

"Something along those lines," Brad answered humorlessly.

"How much longer do I have?"

"It may be a matter of minutes," he smirked.

"Then I better get moving," Tory exclaimed with a sudden sense of purpose, delighted to find an exit line so quickly. "I've got a lot of living to squeeze in."

He rushed off to the next few tables and extricated himself quickly from each, intent on putting as much distance between himself and the three sober faces as possible. Spotting Mona and Jimmy at the far side of the bar with a handsome young man wedged between them, he decided they'd be a pleasant change of pace.

Even they had taken to mild criticism, though they still enjoyed a good time. Mona was always ready to join him on the dance floor for a steamy tango or an energetic polka. She'd even maintained her sense of humor when he'd lost his grip on her hand in the middle of a spin and crashed her into three barstools. And she never told him to stop being a fool and make amends with George before it was too late. He didn't doubt that she'd thought it, but she never put it into words.

Mona and Jimmy watched his progress toward them with wary eyes, like two dogs fighting over a bone and unhappy with the prospect of more competition. The young man between them looked painfully uncomfortable, a sure sign that Mona had coaxed Jimmy into playing one of her favorite parlor games. They'd find a man who appealed to both of them, preferably someone young and unsophisticated, then swoop down on either side of him and make outrageous advances. The winner of the game was naturally the one who exited with the prey, but most of the pleasure was in goading each other on to be shockingly forward and watching the young man's reactions.

Tory decided to join the game just to harass them. He searched his mind for a totally shocking course of action that would give them something to laugh about when the young man was gone. He opted for an approach on top of the bar that would put his caftan to attention-getting use. It would allow him to hoist the garment high, let everyone know that he was wearing nothing under it. The routine was always good for a few laughs. Caught without his tap shoes, he hoped that a nonchalant stroll up the sixty-foot length of the mahogany would be sufficient cause for attention. He planned to chat to everyone on the way to Jimmy and Mona and swing the caftan a bit, just underplay the whole thing as if it were his normal way of traversing the room. The red-headed bartender whose name Tory could never remember helped him up with an exasperated grin. People began to laugh, but it wasn't spontaneous. It was the laughter for a slightly amusing anecdote heard the second time. Losing his audience's attention was one of his most nightmarish fantasies, but he persevered, shouting out greetings and shaking hands as he threaded his way through the field of cocktail glasses and ashtrays.

Disappointment and the beginnings of panic finally began to set in as he approached the halfway point. He needed another snort of cocaine to make it amusing to him, to make him not feel like a summer rerun. Fortunately, the caftan had a pocket, and he knew he looked chicly decadent holding the heart-shaped enamel snuffbox to his nostril. The gesture was usually good for scattered applause. After several previous snorts, the exhilaration was almost immediate. It brought to mind his latest attention-getting idea: invisible wires from the ceiling that would let him cross the room in Peter Pan style. He made a mental note to have them rigged up for St. Patrick's Day and pictured himself making an entrance as a debauched leprechaun in green tights and a funny little hat. He was sure that his audience would love it. And as his foggy brain collected childhood memories of Mary Martin flying across the television screen, he knew that he'd enjoy it too. He pictured himself bursting in through the ceiling and when a conversation began to bore him, floating off through the air. He spotted the chandelier a few feet above his head and decided that it would be good practice, besides perking up the sluggish crowd.

The brass loops between the prisms looked sturdy enough for a hand grip. With a running start, he imagined he could make it swing and give everyone a laugh, besides giving Jimmy and Mona's young man good cause for apprehension. And George was sure to give him one of his censorious, pained stares. With four quick steps and a jump, he was floating. The gasps and hoots were satisfying. He was glad to have discovered the missing ingredient to get the party rolling, the needed spur to break the ice. And he was exhilarated to be alone above them all. They made him giggle, the field of upturned, open-mouthed faces that swung in and out of view, getting a good gaze up his caftan. As another cocaine rush hit him, he felt nothing but love for his audience. They were such a burden at times but at the moment such a pleasure. He generously decided that they deserved a gay wave and a smile.

The crowd gave a gratifying, in-unison gasp at the one-handed feat. He felt like a circus acrobat, and the exhilaration was becoming almost unbearable, coursing through his limbs like an electric current. With a two-legged kick at the end of each arc, he was certain that he could go on and on, happily swinging for hours. He didn't doubt that a truly energetic kick would sail him to the ceiling, letting the caftan float above his waist and giving the crowd an even better show.

It was a beautiful kick, perfectly timed. He wondered happily if he might not float right through the ceiling and make an early dramatic exit for the evening. He couldn't decide if he was more curious or alarmed as he felt his hand beginning to lose its grip. It all seemed to be happening in fascinating slow motion. He could see the inevitable doom looming ahead of him and wondered how much it was going to hurt, how many bones he would break, how it would feel to be impaled on the broken glass.

Flying through the air without benefit of wires was a new sensation for him, more exciting than the roller coaster. He could only feel slightly annoyed that it would be such a short trip and quickly decided to enjoy it and worry about the consequences when it became absolutely necessary. Even as he landed behind the bar with a thud and the pain began to register, he could only feel a sense of accomplishment at having cleverly avoided the glasses.

Chapter Thirty-six

SPRAWLED across one of the sofas in his tiny office, Tory studied the seashore real estate ads as Yvonne De Carlo croaked through "I'm Still Here" in the background. The room no longer had any practical purpose, but its modern lines and cozy dimensions were sometimes a welcome change from the museumlike tone of the rest of the apartment. The walls and floor were covered in bright-red suede, the matching sofas were the same color in velvet. A large mirrored cube between them served as a table, complementing the mirrored fireplace mantel and the matching wall unit which housed the desk and shelves. The only decorations were pieces of Steuben and Baccarat crystal on the table and mantel in sparkling animal figures and geometric forms.

Mae ventured into the room after a perfunctory rap on the door, carrying a tray with champagne and one stemmed glass. "Cocktail hour, baby."

Tory sighed with exaggerated relief. "I thought it would never come."

"You just hang in there, you're doing fine. I'm right proud of you the past couple weeks."

Tory had quit the Courvoisier after his fall. While he recuperated in the hospital, he'd decided that he could live without alcohol in such quantity, but he still needed a little something to help him through the day. He returned to Dom Pérignon, as to an old friend. Even after two bottles, he could still function without major lapses of judgment. He moved back his starting time in April,

333

waiting for cocktail hour instead of ringing for the first bottle after breakfast coffee at noon. It cut his consumption almost in half. He still needed two spoons of cocaine before his nightly appearance in the Mahogany Room, but it always stopped with two.

He was proud of himself, though he hated to be complimented on it. Mae and Brad continually gave him patronizing encouragement. He'd often catch George watching him across the bar with a smugly hopeful grin. It was sometimes almost annoying enough to tempt him back to the Courvoisier.

"See anything interesting?" Mae asked, glancing at the classified section in his lap.

He shrugged. "There are a few decent places still available in Stone Harbor. But I don't know. The whole city seems to transplant itself to the Jersey shore in the summer. Maybe we should go someplace farther away. How do you feel about Cape Cod or Fire Island?"

"Baby," she answered with a touch of impatience, "I'll go to the moon to get out of this city. I just wish you'd make up your mind. Here it is almost the first of June and you're still hemming and hawing. We ain't never going to get anything on the beach this close to the season."

"We'll work something out," Tory sighed in exhaustion.

He wished he could make up his mind. He'd almost convinced himself that he wanted out of the club. It was too much for him to handle relatively sober. The rationalizations didn't work without the catalytic effects of ample depressants and stimulants. But the alternatives looked less than exciting. He toyed with the idea of moving to New York or Los Angeles, using his connections to get an undemanding position in something glamorous. A job wouldn't be a financial necessity, but it seemed the best way to establish himself in a new city. The problem with such a move was that he couldn't quite accept the step down to a secondary position in entertainment or public relations. He also considered retiring to a remote resort. Going into seclusion on a tropic island would preserve his legend as taking a mere job never would, but he wasn't sure that he was ready to become a recluse. His latest thought was to spend the slack summer season at the seashore to give himself time to think things over.

George was another annoying quandary. It was a

constant temptation to swallow his pride and make up, giving George reason for his smug smile. Whenever the temptation started to get out of hand, Tory would tell himself what a foolish move it would be. Even though George was right in so much of his criticism and Tory was prepared to admit it, it seemed a lopsided way to resume a relationship. Tory still loved him, but he didn't know if he could deal with the superior attitude that such a capitulation would reinforce. He finally began to understand George's old misgivings about an unequal relationship, but understanding didn't help him come to a solution. He sighed and decided that it was one more thing to think over at the beach, if only he could get himself motivated to find a beach house.

"Did you change your mind about Jimmy's birthday party?" Mae gently coaxed in her increasingly familiar nursery school tone. "There's still plenty of time to get ready. You really ought to show your face. If not for dinner, at least for the cake. That's no way to treat a friend like Jimmy."

"Jimmy understands," he snapped. "And stop talking to me like a four-year-old."

The command had no effect on her tone. "I don't know why you won't go. You're most likely to run into George in the club afterward anyway."

"That's different. I'm the host and he's a member. It's business. I don't have to socialize with him outside the club, even if you have half the world conspiring with you to arrange it."

"I wish you'd stop being so mule-headed," she shouted, lapsing into her usual voice. "Any fool can see that it was meant to be, and the sooner you stop fighting it and trying that poor man's patience to death, the sooner you two can work out your little differences and settle down."

"Little differences?" Tory shouted back. "Why won't anyone listen to my side of the story? You make it sound like we had a fight over which sterling pattern to register at Caldwells."

"It ain't nothing that couldn't be ironed out if you'd just show some sense for once."

"It's two entirely different ways of looking at a relationship. He wants to do me a big favor and take me under his wing, like I'm a helpless orphan sitting on the curb."

"He just wants you to get out of this racket and straighten out some of your personal habits. And we're all proud of the progress you've made so far."

"Sometimes I wish the three of you would pack up and move to a convent or Boys' Town or somewhere." He paused dramatically and located his persecuted tone before delivering his current favorite point-winner in arguments with Mae. "Sometimes you're enough to drive me back to hard liquor."

"Now just calm down, baby. I was only trying to help. That's all George is trying to do, too. He only wants for the two of you to be happy."

"Tell him to take in a foster child," he muttered. "I don't need another father, I need a man."

"Maybe you need a little of both, baby."

Tory began an angry reply when the private line rang. Less than a dozen people had the number, and all other calls were screened through the switchboard. Mae opened a mirrored cabinet and answered, then nodded to him.

"It's Mona calling in from San Francisco."

"I should've gone with her. At least she doesn't nag me and treat me like an adolescent."

"Takes one to know one."

Mona had flown out the previous morning, a last fling with Victor before dumping him. She hadn't looked forward to it, but he'd begged her piteously until he'd uncovered a soft spot in her heart.

Tory picked up the telephone. "A postcard would have been sufficient."

She didn't stop to acknowledge his humor. "Tory, have you seen Victor?"

"Not since he drove you to the airport yesterday. What's wrong?"

"Something, apparently. He was supposed to have been here two hours ago."

"Maybe there was no one around to read his watch and he missed the flight."

"I think something peculiar is afoot."

"What problems are you manufacturing now?"

"This is serious, Tory. Listen to me." It wasn't Mona's usual light tone.

"So tell me already."

"It started three days ago when he gave me a lame excuse about business holding him up until today. I didn't argue, I was relieved to avoid his conversation for a transcontinental flight. Then when he dropped me off at the airport yesterday, he insisted that I take his suitcase with me so he could travel today with only a flight bag and avoid the luggage claim. Believe me, I was not pleased. It was one of those red plaid numbers that people get for trading stamps. It absolutely destroyed the picture of me with the Cartier bags and the white de la Renta."

"You did it for him?" Tory asked in amazement, understanding her horror perfectly.

"He wouldn't take no for an answer, carried on like his life depended on it. I'm going to concentrate on northern European men next, Italians are too spoiled. Anyway, the story gets more bizarre when I landed in San Francisco."

"It figures."

"He had his two friends pick me up at the airport. I told him not to bother, knowing what sort of 'friends' I could most likely expect, but he insisted. My worst fears were fulfilled. Two thugs who looked like they just walked off the set of a *Godfather* sequel loaded the bags in the back seat of a less than attractive car, squeezed me into the front seat between them, and drove off to the Huntington. I tried to make polite conversation—"

"But of course."

"But all they'd do was grunt or answer in monosyllables."

"Perhaps they didn't speak the language."

"Listen to me, this is the most bizarre part. We arrived at the Huntington, I got out and turned to talk to the doorman as a bellhop unloaded the bags, and before I could thank them they'd driven off. With Victor's bag!"

Tory's stomach began to tighten. "You're right. That's very strange."

"And Victor was supposed to be in at eleven-thirty and here it is well past the luncheon hour and not word one from him. I can't reach him anywhere. His wife doesn't even know where he is."

"You didn't happen to open the bag, did you?"

"Of course not."

"Did you get a good look at the two guys and the car?"

"They were foreign and the car wasn't. What are you driving at?"

"I'm not sure. Just stay put while I make a few phone calls to see what's going on and I'll get back to you."

"This is beginning to sound less than pleasant."

"I don't want to upset you, but it may be serious. Just to be cautious, why don't you check into the St. Francis or the Hyatt? Use an assumed name."

"An assumed name!"

"And call me when you're settled. In fact, maybe you should rent a car and get out of San Francisco. Go someplace quiet and relax for a while."

"Tory, you're frightening me."

"You always said that the danger was a kick. Just do as I say. Now."

He hung up the telephone with a chill. He'd often entertained dark fantasies of what might go wrong since the club had become a base for Mr. B.'s numbers and cocaine operations. Mona's call was eerily close to one of his imaginary scenes.

"Now why'd you go and tell her to call here?" Mae asked perturbedly. "If there's trouble and Mr. B. wants her, this is the first place he's going to look."

Tory was annoyed to see her point. "Why didn't you think of that before I hung up?"

"Good question, baby. What's the problem? I couldn't hear it all over your shoulder."

"If it's as bad as it looks, Victor used her as a dupe to deliver a suitcase, probably full of stolen coke, and he's nowhere to be found. I don't even know if they've discovered it's missing yet, if it is."

"I knew all this gangster business would come to no good someday," she observed with a hint of satisfaction at being proved right.

"I needed that, Mae."

"So what are you going to do?"

"First, I'm going to make some calls and try to find out the whole story. If it's all the way I think it is, I'll try to explain things to Mr. B. I hope I'm overreacting, but I have a feeling he's not going to laugh the whole thing off."

"Maybe we should pack up and get out of Dodge before the shooting starts."

"Mr. B. will be unhappy, but I think I can talk to him," Tory replied uncertainly. "I hope I can."

"Looks to me like you got yourself in over your head this time."

"This isn't the time for discouraging words. Go check your gossip rounds to see if you can find anything out."

Mae left the room without another word, and Tory went to work with the telephone. No one knew where Victor was, and if they knew anything about a cocaine deal, they weren't talking. Mr. B.'s whereabouts were ominously unknown until Mildred ushered him into the office, his hulking bodyguard behind him.

"Hello, Tory." His face and his voice indicated a raging anger just below the usual serene surface. He reminded Tory of a lion considering whether or not to pounce.

"Mr. B." His feet remained planted in front of the mirrored cabinet.

Mr. B. nodded to the sofas. "Sit down." The words were a command. Tory sat, searching his mind vainly for the right words. "Where's your friend, Tory?"

"California," he answered weakly after a long pause.

"No games tonight." There wasn't a touch of the usual humor in his tone.

"She had nothing to do with it, Mr. B. Victor set her up. He put her on the plane with a piece of his luggage. She thought they were going on a vacation."

"I didn't ask for an explanation. Just answer my question."

The harshness of his tone prevented Tory from replying.

"Now tell me where she is and don't give me any more cute answers."

"She was at the Huntington until an hour ago. I honestly don't know where she is at this moment."

"You told her to clear out?"

Tory nodded timidly. Mr. B. took two steps forward and swung an open palm at his face. The pain passed quickly, but Tory was more frightened than he'd been when Nick had knocked him across his dining room.

"Where is she headed?"

Tory hoped that Mr. B. could read his expression to be truthful. "I honestly don't know."

"Remember the night I had to have Nick hit you? That was a love tap."

"I'm not lying!" He fought to keep his voice from trembling. "I told her to get out of San Francisco. We didn't discuss where. She could be on her way to Hawaii by now, for all I know."

Tory forced his eyes to hold Mr. B.'s burning stare.

"You know what happens to people who work against me?"

"I'm not working against you."

"You're helping someone who is. You're an accomplice. Are you getting a cut?"

"You know that's ridiculous." His indignation gave him his first touch of boldness.

"I always knew that it was a matter of time before Victor turned on me. I knew he was trouble from the start. But you, Tory. I thought I could trust you. All this wild living must have gone to your head."

"I'm trying to protect an innocent friend. Is that wrong?"

"Why didn't you listen to me all the times I told you to keep her away from Victor?"

Tory considered his words and wondered why, indeed, he hadn't. "It would have saved us all a lot of bother," he sighed.

"No changing it now," Mr. B. shrugged. "When is your friend going to call in?"

"Any day now."

"Don't get cute. Tonight?"

"I told her to call when she got settled somewhere. We didn't set a time and date."

"You're pushing, you little bastard," he said calmly. "And you're on thin ice. Here's what you're going to do. You and Nick are going to sit here by the telephone and wait for her call. You're going to find out where she is. Then you're going to tell her that everything is all straightened out back here but she should come back immediately anyway, just to clear up a few details."

"Do you think she doesn't have enough common sense to see through that?"

Mr. B. paused only briefly to consider. "I'd say the

chances are about fifty-fifty. If not, be sure you find out where she is first."

"What makes you think I'm going to do this to my best friend?"

"Nick standing behind you with orders not to be gentle." He smiled smugly. "You think it over until she calls. She's not worth being a hero for."

"Isn't there another alternative? Perhaps you can recover the cash if you find Victor and we can just pretend the whole thing never happened."

Mr. B.'s expression said that the idea didn't appeal to him.

"Or maybe we can cover the loss for you."

"You got six hundred thousand dollars?"

Tory's stomach felt queasy as he thought of the steadily growing figure in the Freeport bank, the figure he'd so lovingly nurtured like a growing plant. "Almost. I could give you two-thirds down and Mona could cover the rest of it with her jewelry."

Mr. B. smiled. "I'm happy to hear you've been sensible enough to put something aside. It's a touching gesture, too. And dumb, Tory. She isn't worth it."

Tory shrugged with an indifference he was far from feeling. "It's only money."

"You're right," Mr. B. agreed unhappily. "It's only money. There's something more important at stake here. I've got to set an example."

"Why don't you stop picking on innocent women and concentrate on finding Victor and using him for an example?"

"When mercilessness is called for, I've got to show it. Even to you." He examined Tory's masklike expression through a long pause. "You think maybe I'm bluffing, don't you? You're playing with expensive chips if you'd care to satisfy your curiosity."

Tory felt no vibrations.

"Nick, you get in touch with me at home if the call comes through. I'll send someone to relieve you at midnight. Get used to company, Tory. You'll have it around the clock until she's back here."

"I'm expected in the club."

"I'll send your regrets. Anyone else in the apartment besides the maid that let us in?"

He wondered where Mae had disappeared to. "Eugene and Mae are in and out. And somebody from the kitchen will probably be sending dinner down if I don't come up. I never know who's floating around in here."

Mr. B. gave him another of his smug smiles. "I guess it doesn't much matter. Even if you were foolish enough to try to get around Nick, you'd never make it out of Fort Knox."

Chapter Thirty-seven

EVEN the most routine waiting had always tried Tory's patience, but the evening's vigil by the telephone was sheer torture. He paged through magazines, chain-smoked until nauseated, sent Mildred for a Valium, then changed his mind. He paced nervously from time to time, but Nick always complained that he was blocking the television.

Nick seemed totally and annoyingly oblivious to the suspense of the situation. He sprawled on the sofa and watched television with Heineken in hand, as if he'd dropped by a neighbor's house for a casual visit. He wasn't even good company. Tory went into spurts of nervous chatter and they fell on either uncomprehending or ill-mannered ears.

He tried to pass the time hatching plots, but only a miracle seemed effective. With Nick's total absorption in *Hawaii Five-O*, he considered some Errol Flynn tactics to take him by surprise. Periodically eyeing a heavy crystal obelisk on the table, he thought he had a sporting chance to sweep it into his hand and make a lunge in one quick gesture before Nick had time to defend himself. The thought of physical violence made him queasy, but he gave it serious thought. A second solution would be for the beer and the television's drone to lull Nick off, allowing Tory to tiptoe nonviolently out of the room. It was an appealing alternative to shattered crystal and bloodstains.

But his mind kept repeating Mr. B's words about

Fort Knox. He'd had every reason for a maddening smug smile. It would be impossible to get through the guards and electronic equipment at any of the three exits. Even a fire ladder of two or three dozen Porthault sheets would be discovered by an outdoor watchman. The same extreme precautions that kept unwanted guests out would serve just as effectively to keep Tory in.

Escape plans seemed futile so he turned his mind to the inevitable telephone call. Inspiration hit him almost immediately. He was startled by the simplicity of his plan and wondered why Mr. B. hadn't thought of it. He'd simply pick up the telephone and say, "Hello . . . oh, Lisa! What a surprise! It's my cousin, Nick." Nick didn't seem bright enough to catch on, even if he overheard Mona's voice. Mona would pick it up quickly, he hoped. He could chat for a few minutes, say, "Give my regards to Alex and I'll call you soon." Alex was a mutual acquaintance in Los Angeles, and she'd be sure to figure it out. Tory had no idea of what he'd do afterward when the expected call never came through, but at least it would give him a few days to think. Mr. B. might even cool off in a few days. The future could sometimes be delightfully unpredictable.

He rehearsed the telephone conversation in his head, overjoyed to have found a temporary salvation and confident that his acting ability would be sufficient to fool Nick. Deep in his mental dress rehearsal, he barely noticed the door behind Nick slowly begin to open. It moved so slowly that at first he thought it was just his agitated imagination. He forced himself not to stare. He paged through his magazine, letting his eyes dart occasionally to Nick or the creeping door. His mind catalogued possibilities, and he nervously hoped that it was only Mae on a routine snooping expedition. The only other possibility that came to his mind was the start of some foolishly heroic rescue attempt, doomed to failure at all exits. He wanted to get up and slam the door shut and pretend that the whole thing wasn't happening. His plan seemed much more sensible.

The door slowly inched open to a noticeable crack, and Tory tried to make out the facial features in the dark hall. The broken brown void where a face would logically be cheered him briefly, convincing him that it was indeed Mae. But as he stared he realized that there were no features to be made out and that the brown patch didn't have the texture of flesh. The door moved another inch and he swallowed a shriek as he realized it was a stockinged head.

He wondered briefly if it could be a burglar. It seemed an absurd possibility but not totally out of character with the rest of the evening. Whoever it was, he seemed intent on taking Nick by surprise, an event that Tory didn't look forward to explaining to Mr. B. After the interrogation he'd been through, he could only stifle a nervous laugh at his chances of explaining that Nick had been jumped by a burglar.

Four fingers appeared on the doorjamb, and Tory's stomach sank as he recognized them instantly. He would have preferred an armed burglar with murderous intentions, but the man under the stocking was unquestionably George. He felt the familiar resentment at George's meddling in his affairs, nobly trying to rescue him from his latest foolishness. The idea was irritating in itself, maddening since it was doomed to failure.

The door opened another inch to reveal George clutching a Courvoisier bottle by its neck. Tory's stomach jumped violently as his worst fears were realized. But there was no turning back. Anything but cooperation could prove fatal to George. He decided that some nervous patter might distract Nick from any creaks of the floorboards.

"Nick, what's it worth to you to let me go?"

"Come off it." Nick seemed infinitely more interested in the television.

"I've got six thousand in cash in my bedroom. I've got keys to the cash drawers in the club, and you know what kind of money is up there. I've got a safe-deposit box crammed with Mr. B.'s envelopes."

Nick concentrated even more intently on the television as George edged himself into the room.

"I've got gold jewelry by the pound and diamond rings I haven't even worn yet. I've got cufflinks and shirt studs and stickpins worth thousands. I've got the key to Mona's apartment, you can have all the emeralds that Victor gave her."

George slid down the wall until he was directly behind Nick.

"Nick, I've got negotiable securities. I've got unregistered municipal bonds. I've got oriental jade you can take out in a shoebox and fence for twenty thousand."

George took two steps forward and raised the bottle. Tory's words spewed out in an agitated torrent.

"Nick, I've got a fortune in a Swiss account. Millions, Nick. Just name your price and I'll mail it to you from Gstaad. Whatever you want, Nick. It's all yours."

The bottle came down in an arc and cracked on contact with Nick's skull in a sickening thud. Nick slumped sideways across the cushions, and a trickle of blood began to ooze down the front of his balding forehead. Mae suddenly appeared with an Irish-linen tablecloth. She threw it over his head and handed George the velvet bell pull from Tory's bedroom.

"Come on, baby," she shouted. "Make tracks."

Tory remained motionless as George secured the unconscious form. A patch of blood began to grow on the tablecloth.

"Come on! Move!" She pulled Tory unceremoniously to his feet.

"Where?" he shouted back. "How do you plan to get out the front door?" The futility of their next move had him close to panic.

Mae shoved him toward the door. "The kitchen entrance. Out on the fire stairs."

Tory balked. "You're crazy! What do we do when we get downstairs? That entrance is just as well guarded as the front."

She shoved him viciously. "Just do as you're told!"

Tory shook his head and prepared to meet his fate stoically. He wondered if perhaps he might not be safer in the guards' hands then at the mercy of a screaming madwoman. She grabbed him roughly by the wrist and led him through the dim kitchen.

He balked again. "Where's George?"

A rough push from behind answered him. "Right behind you. Keep moving."

Tory was considering an angry complaint at the rough handling and harsh words to which he was being subjected when they reached the heavy door to the fire stairs. It swung open under the force of Mae's shoulder, and she dragged him through. He was about to start down the stairs when his arm suffered a jolt that he thought had dislocated his shoulder.

"Up, baby, up."

He thought he was past becoming more confused until he noticed George disappearing in the opposite direction. But there was no possibility of questioning the obviously raving psychopath who clutched his arm with the strength of a vise. They ran up three flights of stairs, and Mae kicked the door. It seemed incongruous to suddenly be on the rooftop garden, in the process of being prepared for a gala Memorial Day reopening. Empty flower pots lined the railings, and plastic tarpaulins covered the white wrought-iron furniture. The metal frame of the New Year's tent looked ghostly without its canvas, and the gold paint was chipping sadly off of the helicopter pad. The workmen had even neglected to raise the hydraulic staircase.

His worst fears for Mae's sanity were confirmed as she began to run back and forth across the roof, waving her hands frantically over her head. Tory barely noticed his three best pieces of Vuitton luggage at her feet when she stopped and turned to him with an ear-to-ear grin.

"Here she comes, baby!"

He suddenly became aware of the overhead hum, steadily growing louder. The speck to the south grew larger by the second. He looked at Mae in disbelief.

The helicopter hovered downward and landed on the platform. Even from fifty feet the gusts of wind it created were gale-strength, and Tory was sure that the deafening racket would have every guard on the roof within seconds.

"Grab the bags, baby!"

Mae picked up one bag and he followed her up the staircase with the others. They handed them up to a confused-looking pilot and climbed in.

"Hit that gas pedal, sweetheart!"

They began a vertical ascent. As they swung out over the building, Tory noticed several uniformed figures staring skyward from the fire stairs. He waved a gay farewell.

The building grew smaller and smaller until Tory could only distinguish his name in glaring neon above the main entrance. As they moved farther into the horizon, even the twelve-foot letters became a minor component of the network of jewel-like twinkling lights. It was all so beautiful from their vantage point in the sky.

"James Bond's got nothing on you, lady," he laughed. It was difficult to sound nonchalant.

Mae looked skyward from the helicopter. "Thank you, Lord! Thank you, David!" She turned back to Tory. "I can't take all the credit. Your guardian angel's still looking out for you, though I thought you had even *him* stumped this time. And it was you-know-who's quick thinking that come up with the plan." She leaned close to whisper. "No need to mention any names in front of our friend here."

Tory felt an uncomfortable feeling creep over him as he glanced at the pilot. "That poor man could be in big trouble," he whispered back.

"Not unless your boss wants to be unreasonable. As far as this guy knows, we're just another fare. Except we happened to have our own landing pad. And he don't know where we're going after he drops us off in Jersey."

"Where *are* we going?"

"You-know-who is picking us up—not the you-know-who we was talking about a minute ago, the other you-know-who who usually does the picking up."

Tory winced. "What about the first you-know-who? He could have gotten himself you-know-what."

"He's OK. He went back to you-know-where, to you-know-who's you-know-what party, like he'd never left. Mr. You-know-who will never figure it out. It's just going to be me and you with you-know-whats on our heads." She turned to the pilot with a bright smile. "You driving careful there, sweetheart?"

"And Mona. What about Mona?"

"She ought to have sense enough to hang up when you don't answer. And the way you two got minds that work in the same fool way, you're sure to track each other down sooner or later. We didn't have time to work out all the details."

"How did you work out this many?"

Mae gave him a perturbed look. "You know I always

eavesdrop, baby. And I wasn't going to miss a word to-night. He sounded mean."

"Sure did," he laughed nervously.

"I didn't know what to do, how we could get you out of this mess with all the goons at the doors. I called you-know-who at the party and he thought this up right off the top of his handsome head. What a man. You owe him a great big thank you."

The thought annoyed him. "I guess I do."

"You might even owe him your life."

"Oh hell."

Mae pursued her advantage. "The least you can do now is mend some of your ways."

"If you two hadn't been meddling again I could have straightened it out. I was going to pretend that Mona was my cousin when she called."

"Then what?"

"I don't know. But it would have kept Mona out of it and given me time to think. And Mr. B. time to cool off."

Mae made a lame attempt at hiding her satisfaction under a sigh of philosophical acceptance. "This way, you're out of that racket once and for all."

Tory laughed after a thoughtful pause. "I guess I am, aren't I?"

"Praise the Lord!"

"At least I got to do a dazzling exit," he giggled. "So what do we do now?"

Mae lowered her voice even more. "We're heading for JFK in New York."

"Yes."

"Catch the red-eye to Miami."

"Miami," Tory repeated distastefully. "Mona will never think to look for me there."

"Then we go to the Bahamas so we can be close to your money."

Tory wasn't terribly surprised that she knew where his money was. "Did you bring passports?"

"Of course. It's a good thing you talked me into that trip to Paris last year or I'd be sitting on the dock waving goodbye to you. Eugene says he can get a passport in Miami. I don't think he means one from the State Department, but I suppose this ain't the time to ask questions."

"Then what do we do?"

"Oh, we can lay on the beach and get suntans. Play cards. Collect seashells. All sorts of things to do. We could all do with a vacation."

"Did you pack my swim trunks?"

"Now don't go asking me fool questions, boy. I packed everything I could on short notice. Somebody might've got suspicious if I ordered a U-haul."

"Good point."

"I brought enough clothes to see us all through for a while—ain't like we're going to be doing much socializing. And all your jewelry. And the cash you keep stashed behind your books in the den. And the emeralds that Mona didn't have room for in her pocketbook. She might be needing them someday."

"Did you pack David's goblet?" It had been Tory's twentieth-birthday present from him, worth ten dollars at a flea market and millions in memories.

"Yes, baby," she smiled gently.

He thought of the apartment of antiques, the piles of Georgian silver, the crammed dressing-room closets, the fur coats, the white Rolls-Royce. "I guess you got everything that was important."

"Well," she drawled, "we had to leave a man behind, but he's got two legs."

Tory felt an unpleasant jolt every time he thought of George. "Mae, you could have gotten him killed."

She turned to him with angrily narrowed eyes. "Don't let's start shifting the blame, buster. We all know who got us into this fix in the first place. Ain't nobody for you to blame but yourself. I ain't going to dwell on it, but you know damn well you been putting everyone's life on the line with that racket. I just hope you finally had some sense knocked into your thick skull."

"It's given me something to think about."

"I hope some good comes out of it."

"Me too," he laughed. "I keep wondering lately when I'm going to grow up."

"That makes at least three or four of us, baby." She paused before continuing in a meaningful voice, "Maybe you'll start seeing some sense in a lot of things."

Tory was uncomfortably aware of her meaning. But

too confused to give serious thought to a future with George, he decided to try to divert her attention. "Doesn't much matter," he sighed. "I'm being exiled to a tropic island to spend the rest of my life looking over my shoulder for a hit man."

"Everything will work out in time, baby."

Chapter Thirty-eight

TORY kicked off his Dr. Scholl's outside the kitchen door and carefully brushed the sand from his feet, not wanting to provoke one of Mae's reprimands. He didn't understand her concern. It wasn't as if he'd be soiling Tabrizes and Bokharas. The rambling furnished house they'd found far from the crowds of Freeport had beige wall-to-wall carpeting that showed years of wear and furniture that complemented it perfectly. Sometimes Tory would look at a sagging chair or a wobbly table and break into a cheerful chorus or two of "If They Could See Me Now."

He didn't have to pretend to take it lightly. It actually didn't bother him much. He missed the steamroom in his bath and the gargantuan bed with its piles of goosedown pillows and Germaine coming in every day or two, but otherwise he was physically content. The house's view made up for its lack of elegance. Two sides looked out on the beach, and the other two offered acres of tropical greenery. There were two patios and a screened in porch and twelve rooms for solitude away from Mae and Eugene, and the forest insulated them from the sounds of civilization. The only noise came from squawking seagulls and crashing waves. There was even a gazebo on a little hill that offered a panoramic view of sand and sky and trees and ocean. Tory spent hours there with his morning coffee or evening Campari, reading anything that crossed his path, watching the boats and the birds or just letting his mind wander aimlessly.

With his feet dutifully sand-free he opened the screen

door and entered the kitchen, heading directly for the watering bucket next to the sink. He filled it and moved to the hanging baskets of scrawny spider plants, checking for signs of improvement. He laughed at himself for worrying over houseplants when the lawn was filled with lush greenery, but it was part of his daily routine. After morning coffee in the gazebo and a few hours of reading, he'd have an early lunch. Then he'd go for a swim and a long walk on the beach, or send Eugene to rent a motorboat. Tory didn't like all the noise it made but he wasn't ready to tackle the intricacies of sailboating. The motorboat was as easy as driving a car without the annoyances of red lights and rush-hour traffic, and it could take him even farther into a world of total tranquillity. A few hours of sun and salt air prepared him for his nap, usually in a shaded hammock or the sunporch glider. After a crossword puzzle and the evening news it was time for dinner, then a few hours of television or backgammon or three-handed pinochle before bed around eleven. Some nights he'd go to bed as Johnny Carson started his monologue and remember how he'd often still be preparing for an evening in the club at the hour. It made him laugh as much as the fading wallpaper.

Finishing with the spider plants, he went to the refrigerator for a tall glass of Perrier. Drinking water made him laugh too. His nerves had been bad the first month on the island, and Mae had watched the wine disappear with a frown. With Mona and George and hit men to worry about, he'd felt justified in ignoring her dark looks. But the news that trickled in over the summer was encouraging, and he gradually relaxed enough to be content with two glasses of wine with dinner and an occasional Campari on the gazebo with the sunset.

Victor's mysterious disappearance made headlines in the Philadelphia newspapers. The case remained unsolved, and the police seemed to have lost interest in it. Tory had located Mona in Los Angeles with their mutual friend, Alex, three weeks after he left Philadelphia. She told him harrowing tales of fear and deprivation living the life of a marked woman in Big Sur, Tahoe, and Zuma Beach. With Tory's call, she decided the time was ripe to visit some out-of-the-way resorts in Europe. She shrugged off the loss of most of her worldly possessions, relieved to have her passport and the security of her emeralds. Tory got news of her over the summer by having Mae telephone Alex on her weekly trip to Freeport. Alex reported sporadic but cheery postcards from Yugoslavia and Greece. Mae also made regular calls to George, who reported that things were relatively calm back in Philadelphia. Tory's dramatic exit had been the talk of the town for weeks, and Mr. B. was said to have been more amazed than angry. The club was still packed nightly without benefit of a host, and Tory's name continued to blaze outside in twelve-foot neon letters. He was relieved not to be there but it gave him a secret satisfaction to still have his name a part of the evening skyline.

He was also relieved to have the excuse of anonymity to get out of the weekly telephone trips with Mae. He always sent George polite greetings, but he didn't want to talk to him. Most of his resentment had passed. He couldn't rouse much ill will about a person meddling in his life when that person had felt strongly enough about it to risk his own. And since he'd started to lead such a harmless, if unproductive, life, there was little left for George to criticize. Sometimes it seemed useless to worry about it. The nagging feeling that Mr. B. would find him someday gave him an adequate excuse to ignore any thoughts of a reconciliation. He could ignore his own muddled feelings by nobly sighing to Mae that it wouldn't be fair to George.

Thoughts of Mr. B. were always with him, but he refused to dwell on them, as he'd always refused to dwell on unpleasant thoughts. Passing from the kitchen to the hall, he gave his attention to the reflection in the mirror instead. His old vanity had returned as the hollows in his cheeks disappeared. He hated to admit that moderate living made such a difference, but the proof was irrefutable. Liquor and cocaine had been replaced with a healthy appetite, and his former fashionably emaciated frame was once again padded with a layer of healthy-looking flesh. Hours of sun made the highlights in his hair glimmer and his skin glow. He brushed off vague worries over wrinkles with plans for a facelift when it became necessary. The deep tan that made his eyes sparkle and his teeth flash made a facelift seem a fair price to pay. It made him laugh, too, to be better-looking than he'd been in two years and have no one to see it.

He was four steps into the living room before he saw them. Nick was sprawled on the sofa. Mr. B. sat kinglike in the high-backed chair. Tory froze in his tracks. The silence was sepulchral. Mr. B.'s face was inscrutable.

"Hello, Tory."

He was too far into the room to run out, and too stunned to move his legs in any case. A flash of heat suffused his face and neck. A cold trickle of perspiration ran down his spine.

"Mr. B.," he murmured.

Mr B. didn't speak. He only stared with a strange wisp of a smile. Tory's heart pounded. He wondered how much longer his legs would support him. The perspiration was beginning to soak through his shirt.

"You left without saying good-bye."

"We were in a rush." He had no idea how the flippant remark found its way to his lips. Mr. B.'s smile didn't change.

"It wasn't a very polite thing to do."

Tory wondered how long he could hold out, how long it would be until his frozen nerves thawed into pathetic hysteria. He wasn't surprised that the inevitable had happened. But he couldn't understand why he was being tortured. It was so unlike Mr. B.

"I have to give you credit." Mr. B.'s smile didn't change. "You outsmarted me."

Tory couldn't believe that Mr. B. could be so cruel. Ruthless, surely. Cold-blooded, yes. But he'd never seen him be cruel.

"Maybe it's time for me to retire, when a young punk like you can outsmart me."

The numb terror was beginning to fade. He was afraid he'd be groveling despicably any moment, begging for mercy, pleading to be spared.

"Don't you have anything to say for yourself?"

Please don't kill me! flashed through Tory's mind. He had plenty to say, but he refused to say it, begrudging the unexpected barbarian sitting in judgment before him the pleasure of revenge.

"No, sir."

"You're trembling, Tory," he smirked. "What's wrong?"

Tory had never suspected such a sadistic streak in Mr.
B., the man who'd so often reminded him of his Uncle
Joe. He'd always been a gentleman, relatively speaking.

"Nothing to say?"

Please don't do it, Tory thought. Or get it over with before I start to scream.

"I've got something for you, Tory." Mr. B. reached
slowly inside his jacket.

Tory watched his motions with disbelief. He couldn't
believe that Mr. B. would actually perform the act himself, and from the smile on his face, probably relish every
moment of the terror. Mr. B. fumbled inside his jacket
interminably. His eyes and the small smile never left
Tory's face.

Tory stubbornly refused to give him the satisfaction of
tears. It was a new test of the limits of his self-control, but
a bitter sense of disgust drove him on. He'd often wondered how he'd react, if he'd be able to face death like a
movie hero. He'd always doubted it but noted with some
satisfaction that he was merely on the verge of panic and
gratefully not groveling on the floor. He hoped his nerves
would hold out and that he'd be able to die with the same
nonchalant style with which he'd always tried to live. A
feeling of regret somehow managed to break through the
wall of panic, a regret that there wasn't a larger audience
to watch him perform so admirably. Then he wondered if
the workings of his mind would make more sense to him
from the perspective of an afterlife.

Mr. B.'s hand finally emerged, with an envelope. Tory
wondered if it was a death warrant, if Mr. B. planned to
take him back to Philadelphia and stretch out the ordeal
for days. He tossed the envelope at Tory's feet.

"Open it," he commanded roughly.

Tory bent to pick it up. He dropped it. He bent again.
His hands shook as he ripped the envelope unevenly. He
dropped it again. He bent again and his eyes tried to register the exposed papers.

"Tickets?" he whispered under his breath. He examined
them carefully, wondering if the panic had affected his
eyes. But even on third examination they remained three
one-way, first-class tickets, Freeport to Philadelphia. Tory
gave Mr. B. a bewildered look. Mr. B.'s smile broadened
almost imperceptibly.

"Get back to work," he ordered gruffly. "The joint isn't the same without you."

Tory's mind went blank and his mouth fell open. A few seconds later he felt tears in his eyes. Mr. B. laughed.

"You little bastard, you *ought* to be shot." He shook his head with an introspective sigh. "Maybe it really *is* time for me to throw in the towel."

Tory collapsed into the closest chair, still speechless.

"I hope you've learned your lesson." Mr. B. tossed him his handkerchief.

Tory searched a long moment to regain his power of speech. Only the panic lingering in his mind gave him the rashness to go on. "Mr. B., I don't want to come back."

A hurt frown crossed Mr. B.'s face, and Tory remembered his fear.

"If the club's in bad shape," he continued hurriedly, "I'll come back and do what I can for as long as it takes. But Steven can come up with a new gimmick, fabricate some new character to replace me. I want out, Mr. B."

There was a long silence.

"Do you really mean it?"

"I can't handle it anymore, Mr. B. It was tearing me apart. I'd either end up in a nuthouse or killing myself if I kept it up. This summer down here with peace and quiet has changed me. It's what I want. The fast pace and neon lights were almost a necessity to me at one time, but it's out of my system now, thank God. I just want peace and quiet and no decisions to consider and no compromises to make. I'll come back if you need me, Mr. B., but I want it to be temporary."

There was another long silence and a hurt stare.

"I'll miss you, Tory."

The tears started anew. Mr. B. rose.

"Come here," he commanded.

Tory struggled from his seat and kissed the proffered cheek with a torrent of gratitude. For a brief moment he almost wanted to go back with him.

"You stay here and be a beach bum," Mr. B. smirked. "I'm not going to argue with you. You wouldn't be worth a damn at the club in this frame of mind anyway. But it will change. And you'll be back. You can't stay away from those neon lights for long. They're in your blood."

"Not anymore," Tory quietly replied, wondering if it was true.

"Don't argue with me, I'm seldom wrong. And I say you can't stay away. When you're over your back-to-nature kick, you give me a call. You'll have to beg a little, but I'll take you back."

He disappeared through the door with Nick. Tory collapsed back into the chair and indulged himself in maudlin sobs.

Chapter Thirty-nine

"I don't know *where* Ginny could be," Tory muttered in exasperation as he spread Bain de Soleil over his midriff. He tossed the bottle back on the table, which Eugene had carried out to the dock along with three deck chairs, an umbrella, an ice chest, and a tape deck from which Barbra Streisand asked, "How Lucky Can You Get?," before collapsing for a nap in the motorboat moored below. "She said she'd be here at three and here it is almost cocktail time."

Jimmy looked unconcerned as he glanced up from filing his toenails. "Maybe she got confused with the time zones. They always throw *me* for a loop."

"Not Ginny," Tory replied. "I called her last night as soon as I got off the phone with you and she said she'd have the yacht docked in Porto Banus before sunrise, hire a car and get to Málaga in time for the morning flight, land in New York, change planes for Miami, borrow a friend's boat there, and arrive here promptly at three this afternoon."

"Maybe one of her flights was delayed."

Tory gave him a totally unconvinced look. "If you were an airplane and Ginny was on you, would you have the nerve to be delayed?"

"Never. She'd hit me with one of her evil looks and melt my propeller."

Tory peered into the horizon. "Is that a sail?"

"It looks more like a seagull to me," Jimmy answered patiently. "What's Brad doing in the house?"

"Shuffling papers in his briefcase, no doubt. And trying to think of ways to make me feel guilty about dragging him away from work. It's so good to see my old friends again."

"Home just isn't the same without you," Jimmy mused. "Maybe you'll come back someday, now that everything is straightened out with Mr. B."

"Maybe."

"How long can you sit down here and be a hermit?"

"I don't know." He shrugged. "Until it doesn't feel good anymore. Or until something better comes along."

Jimmy spent a long moment concentrating on his left big toe before speaking again. "When is George coming?"

"I don't know."

"You don't know? He is coming, isn't he?"

"I think so," Tory answered flatly.

"You're not sure?"

"Not positive."

"Did you have another fight?"

"We haven't even spoken. Mae called him."

Jimmy tossed away his emery board in disgust. "What the hell is it going to take to get the two of you to stop acting like a pair of dumbbells?" he shouted in a startlingly angry voice. "I've had about all I can take."

Tory looked at him in amazement. "I didn't realize that you felt so strongly about it."

"Of course I do. You and George are two of my best friends, and I'd like to see you happy together. It just seemed like I'd be wasting my breath to mention it before. You're both such hammerheads. But after all you've been through since New Year's, I thought you might finally have found some common sense."

"I must be in awful shape for *you* to lecture me about common sense." Tory laughed.

"It's not all your fault," Jimmy continued charitably. "George is just as stubborn. You left the club, you got out of the Mafia, you don't do coke, and you hardly drink anymore. What more does he want from you?"

"That's one of our problems," Tory sighed enigmatically. "He wants to come down here and see me living an exemplary life and give me one of his smug redeemer smiles like he's so happy I've finally seen the error of my ways. And forever after I'll be on parole, in need of his advice and guidance to keep me on the right path. What kind of relationship is that?"

Jimmy flashed him a familiar look of confusion. "It sounds sort of like Lucy and Ricky."

Tory glanced over his shoulder at Brad approaching the length of the dock. "No, darling. It's only Brad."

"What about Lucy and Ricky?" Brad asked.

"They can't make it this weekend, but Fred and Ethel are going to try to pop down for Sunday brunch. I just hope Ginny makes it by then. It's not at all like her to be late."

"Give her a break," Brad said, looking at his watch. "You can't expect precision timing from the middle of the Mediterranean."

"Of course I can," he answered indignantly. "Ginny wouldn't let a few thousand miles throw her off schedule. Now if it were Mona expected from across town and she showed up within a week one way or the other, I wouldn't bat an eye. But Ginny's never been late in her life. I'm sure she's met with a natural disaster or political unrest."

Brad refused to acknowledge his dark musings. "What's the latest on Mona?"

"Do you miss her?" Tory asked brightly.

"No. I just want to be forewarned when she approaches the territorial limits."

"How ungallant. But you need not fear. The last news is a three-week-old postcard from Crete that has her approaching Ibiza by a no doubt circuitous route." He sighed. "I must have spoken to every decent hotel in southern Europe trying to find her last night."

"Don't worry," Jimmy assured him. "She'll turn up one of these days."

"Like a bad penny," Brad agreed. "Where's George?"

"Your guess is as good as mine," Tory answered with a stab at indifference.

"When are you going to stop acting like a child about him?"

"I haven't the vaguest idea. When he stops treating me like one, perhaps." Tory turned as he heard Mae's tread on the planks. "I'll give you a more detailed explanation later. If you mention one word about him in front of Mae and get her started again, I personally guarantee that you'll find your briefcase floating face down in this exact spot before the day is over."

Mae reached the edge of the dock with an accusing finger. "I don't want no more gangster talk around here!"

"We were discussing the Summer Olympics." Tory nodded toward the house. "Do you have your new help under control?"

" 'Course I do," she answered indignantly. "What's three part-timers to me after I used to run a staff of a hundred?"

"Maybe we'll keep them after our houseguests leave."

"What are we going to do with three in help in this little place? Be bumping into each other every time they turn a corner."

"We need more than a twice-a-week cleaning lady." He turned to Jimmy. "Do you know that sometimes I even have to unload the dishwasher?"

"All by yourself?" Jimmy asked in admiration.

"Awful, isn't it? We're in dire need of domestic help down here."

"I wouldn't go making any long-range plans," Mae advised cryptically. "You might up and leave this place in a week or two. Who knows?"

"It sounds like *you* know something. What are you driving at?"

"Nothing," she answered quickly. "Just that now you're out of hot water with the mob, you might go through some changes. George might want to take you away someplace."

Tory laughed without amusement. "And you'll be waiting at the door with my leash and flea collar, no doubt."

"Now you just cut that out!" she scolded. "With you giving attitude like that, no wonder it's taking half of my golden years to get you two together."

"Well, what the hell do you mean, he might want to take me away someplace? Do I look like a Panasonic portable?"

"I just meant that you two might talk things over and decide to go someplace different. Or he might surprise you and offer to take you someplace you'd like to go. That's all I meant, baby."

"Look!" Jimmy shouted. "It's a yacht!"

"It's about time." Tory jumped down into the motor-boat. "Wake up, Eugene. Your favorite former employer is on the horizon." He looked back up to the dock. "Are you coming with us, Jimmy?"

"Not me," Jimmy answered with a look at Mae. "I smell gossip."

"You won't get word one from her," Tory shouted as they pulled away from the dock. "She knows I'd get it out of you."

Eugene avoided his eyes as they moved across the water. Tory fixed him with an expectant look.

"What do you know that I don't?" he asked in the escort-service voice that expected an answer.

"What makes you think that I know anything?" Eugene laughed, pretending to concentrate on maneuvering the motorboat. "I mind my own business."

"What was going on this morning when you drove Mae into town?" he accused. "It didn't take two of you to pick up a case of champagne."

"I'm not saying," Eugene shot back. "You'd just repeat it if I did and then I'd have Mae on my back for the rest of the month."

"Is he here on the island?"

"Who?"

Tory's only answer was a glare.

"Might be," Eugene finally answered.

"What's he doing?"

"Getting a tan."

Tory continued to glare.

"Look," Eugene finally said uncomfortably, "I've never been one of the insiders in this conspiracy. After watching you two fight since the day you met, I'm to the point where I don't care if you both decide to go straight and marry women. I don't get all the inside information. All I know is that he's been looking at a lot of real estate."

"You're holding out on me, Eugene. I know that look."

"Well, that's all you're getting from me. You'll find out the rest soon enough, I expect. Don't ask me for any more. That's all I'm saying."

Tory spent the rest of the ride frowning viciously at Eugene, but to no avail. He lost interest in the pursuit when he spotted Ginny on deck and shouted futilely at her over the roar of the motor. Eugene finally maneuvered the boat into position and they climbed the ladder. Ginny embraced him warmly, a change from her usual curt nod or occasional polite peck on the cheek.

"I was sure I'd seen the last of you," she laughed. "It's not like Mr. B. to forgive and forget."

"We've always had a special understanding," Tory replied nonchalantly. "More importantly, what could possibly have gone wrong to make you two hours late?"

"It's a long story," she laughed. "Wait until you see the present I brought you." She walked to the stairs and shouted belowdeck. "Playtime's over. We're here."

She was answered with a familiar shriek.

"It couldn't be!" Tory shouted.

As his words faded into the air, Mona emerged from below in a white satin negligee and a matching marabou-collared wrapper. *"Mon cher!"* she shrieked.

They rushed into each other's arms and exchanged their customary greeting, kissing the air beside each other's cheeks with a loud smack of the lips.

"I suppose I shouldn't be surprised," Tory laughed.

"It was all a very peculiar chain of events," she began to explain breathlessly, obviously about to launch into an imaginatively embellished account. "We were strolling the docks at Porto Banus after a late espresso when I heard a familiar voice shouting orders at some sailors. Imagine my surprise to look up and find our own Virginia parking her little yacht right at my chicly sandaled feet. Without the least hint of a polite greeting, she started shouting orders at us also, and the next thing I knew we were back at the Marbella Club packing our bags and on the way to Málaga. Unfortunately, the regular flight was booked solid. Not even a barefaced bribe was effective. As a final act of desperation, Ginny had to commandeer three seats on a charter. Would you believe that they only have a tourist section on those charter flights?" she asked, appalled. "We crossed an entire ocean packed in the back of the airplane like common sardines. With a group of English teachers from Passaic, New Jersey, and several members of the Glassboro Township Kiwanis Club."

"Why did you need three seats?"

"I was just getting to that part." She indicated her negligee. "Notice the bridal white?"

"You didn't!" Tory gasped.

"Last Tuesday," she said, seeming vaguely surprised
herself. "It was a whirlwind romance." She held up her
left hand to display an emerald that made Tory squint as
it reflected the sunlight.

"You were supposed to be over there fearing for your
life and you got married instead?" He shook his head in
disbelief. "I always thought it was a toss-up between
us for who was missing the most marbles, but you've
definitely outdone me this time, my dear."

"It's the brightest move I ever made," she gushed. "I'm
in love! My cynical days are over. It happened just like
in a Cole Porter song."

"You always promised me I could be your brides-
maid."

"We couldn't wait. You'll understand as soon as he
wakes up and you meet him. Jet lag has simply done the
poor lamb in."

"Jet lag, my ass." Ginny laughed. "You haven't given
him a moment's rest since we left Porto Banus."

"Who is he?"

"Martin Hoffmann," Mona said dreamily. "He's German from a very old family, blond, gorgeous, and need-
less to say—"

"Hung like a stallion?"

She gasped in ecstasy.

"Is he rich?"

"He talks about marks and pesetas and things. It's
all beyond me." She shrugged. "It's not important anyway."

"Good God!" Tory gasped as he clutched his heart.
"Wheel in my respirator!"

"Don't be such a cynic. I'm in love."

Tory turned to Ginny. "I'm living like a Spartan, Brad
took time off from work, Mr. B.'s getting soft, Jimmy
yelled at me, you're late, and Mona's in love. What's this
world coming to?"

"I don't know about the rest of the world, but what
the hell are you doing with yourself? What's all this nonsense between you and George?"

"Yes, Tory," Mona replied self-righteously. "Far be

it from me to criticize, but don't you think it's time you stopped being so perversely pertinacious and settled your little differences with that man?"

Tory considered throwing himself overboard for dramatic emphasis but gave them an exasperated glare instead.

Chapter Forty

TORY climbed the stairs to the gazebo and sank into his chair, hoping not to be missed for thirty minutes so he could enjoy his Campari and his sunset in solitude. Everyone had been occupied when he'd eased his way off the patio. Eugene and Jimmy had been intently watching Ginny hustle Brad at quarter-a-point backgammon, and Mae had been immersed in directing the excavation of a crater-sized clambake pit on the beach. Mona was off somewhere with her husband, as she'd been for the better part of three days.

He wondered vaguely why he was fighting off the early symptoms of a depression. There was little reason for one, he told himself as he reviewed his advantages. After months of expecting to be murdered, he appreciated the simple fact of being alive. After years of abusing his body, he was amazed to have emerged unscathed. He had money and he was surrounded by friends. He might not have George, but he'd coped competently with that for years. Searching his mind for an explanation, he decided to blame Mona. For the first time in their friendship, he felt an undeniable jealousy toward one of her men. Tory had never seen her look at a man with anything more than affectionate lust before. Her former conspiratorial glances at Tory had been replaced with an almost nauseatingly sweet smile, and he couldn't deny he felt bereft. He was happy to see her so obviously in love, but a part of him wished that her husband would disappear back to Germany and not be heard from again.

The first star of the evening emerged, a small pinpoint

of light barely noticeable in the rays of the setting sun. It reminded Tory of the city skyline at dusk, when the first neon signs would flash on and skyscraper windows would light up one by one until the horizon was ablaze in artificial glory. The thought of city lights still gave him a chill of excitement, and he wondered if they might not be part of his depression. He'd always be grateful to the lights. They'd offered an escape from an unsophisticated, far-from-glamorous rural life, and he'd accepted the offer gladly. They'd offered conspicuous consumption hand in hand with embezzlement and a brush with bankruptcy, livelihoods as hustler, pimp, and town character, absurd splendor accompanied by flirtations with alcoholism and drug abuse, and a run-in with the underworld. The lights had offered, and he'd accepted it all with an ingenuous smile.

They'd also offered him love. City lights had been a common bond that had lured him to escape the hinterlands with David. After they'd taken him away, David had become a deified shrine and then the perfect alibi and finally a bittersweet memory. Tory couldn't regret it. It still seemed worth the price.

Finally, they'd offered him George. They'd taken their toll and he was no longer sure it would be right to accept, but he was glad that they'd made him the offer. It had always been so convenient to blame them for the things in his life that needed an excuse, but they'd never done more than offer. He'd always made the final decision to accept, and he wondered if perhaps now was the time to refuse, for George's sake.

As he thought of the changes the lights had put him through, all the drawbacks of a relationship between himself and George came to mind. The changes had taken the form of one temptation after another, a continuing series of tests of his morals. As he looked back on them, he could only stifle an embarrassed laugh at his cumulative score. There was little to be proud of, and it was his weaknesses that seemed to have given George the strength to finally accept him, the assurance that he'd have the upper hand. It seemed a poor foundation for a relationship, with or without love. Tory tried to analyze it as he stared out blankly at the ocean, and he could find no rational reason for them to be together. They had few common interests. Their temperaments clashed regularly. They shared a cynicism and a stubbornness, but that was about all. Common sense said they'd be better off apart. But the unexplainable vibrations that had been present since their first meeting magnetically pulled Tory to him.

He heard a rustle on the wooded path to the gazebo and wasn't the least bit surprised when George appeared from behind the trees. George stared for a moment, then took the seat beside him.

"Hello, George."

"Hi," he replied with a tentative smile.

"Have you come to take me away?"

"Something like that." He propped his legs against the rail. "But first we've got to straighten a few things out."

Tory shot him a nervous glance but quickly covered it behind the motions of lighting a cigarette. "If you're here for an unconditional surrender there's not much point in a discussion."

George suddenly swung his feet to the floor and clamped his fingers under Tory's chin. "Drop it, Tory!" His burning eyes bored into Tory's, which were widened in surprise. "For once I'd like to have a conversation without you answering me in flip rejoinders. This is you and me we're talking about. And if our relationship means anything at all to you, I think you can try to be serious for a few minutes."

"I'm sorry," Tory meekly replied.

"That's better." George arose from the chair to slowly pace the floor while Tory's still-surprised eyes followed him. "Now, tell me what's been going on in your head since you came down here. Why wouldn't you talk to me? Are you just being stubborn?"

"Partly, I suppose." So many thoughts were racing through his head, and he barely knew where to begin. "But I think through all that's happened since spring, we've lost sight of the original problem. I'm still not sure I'm over last New Year's Eve and what was said between us."

George stopped pacing to lean against the rail in front of Tory's chair. "All right. I'll admit that maybe I went too far, that I didn't give you credit for any sense at all. But that was back then, when there was no reason to believe there was still anything left between your ears that was capable of rational thought." He shrugged. "In the last three months you've proved me wrong. And it's in the past anyway. Can't we forget it and go on from there?"

"Can we?" Tory asked. "Circumstances may have changed, but the basic attitudes are still the same. You're still convinced that I'll fall apart if you're not around to keep an eye on me."

"Some things aren't going to change, Tory. I worry about you. And I'm going to go on worrying about you, thinking that you'll be better off if you listen to me more often. And you're not going to change either. You'll always act first and worry about consequences later. But I think we can reach a compromise. As long as I can keep you from stumbling into the really bad situations, like gangsters and heavy drugs, I don't see that there will be a problem between us."

"I can buy that," Tory agreed. "I'm hoping that the whole thing I've just been through has knocked some sense into me and it won't happen again. But is this what you want to do with your life, George? Live with the constant realization that I may do something insane again at any moment and be forever watching me to make sure that I don't?"

"It's not quite that bad," George smiled.

Tory looked up at the smile and thought he felt something snap in his chest. He saw such feeling in that smile, such a warmth and affection he knew he didn't deserve. A melancholy chill ran through him, and a tear began to form in the corner of his eye. "But it *is*, George. Let's face it. I'm a mess. A walking disaster area. I've been doing a lot of thinking down here. About us. But especially about myself. How did I get to this point in my life? After the way I've lived, is there any logic to it, that I should be sitting down here alive and healthy, capable of retiring at twenty-seven with a small fortune stashed in the bank? When I look back on it all, I can hardly believe the luck I've had. They say that you make your own luck, but it isn't true. If Mona hadn't been dizzy enough to get involved with a double crossing dope dealer, and if you and Mae hadn't rescued me by whisking me off with such absurdly theatrical tactics, I'd probably still be in Philadelphia mulling over seashore rental ads and wondering what I was going to do with my life.

"And I still don't know what's going to happen to my life. I think I still subconsciously believe that I just mind my own business and for some unexplainable reason these strange things simply happen to me. It's not in my control. I've blamed Fate for taking a touchingly noble young man and turning him into an impulsive, immature, frivolous, superficial ornament. And I've believed that given the right circumstances, that noble creature would reemerge. But it isn't so. Underneath this superficial veneer, there's very little in the way of redeeming social value to stand up and applaud.

"I don't know about the future, George. Perhaps I've learned a lesson. Perhaps I haven't. I hope it's all taught me something and keeps me from repeating some of the more serious mistakes I've made. But who knows? Not me. Something dubious may cross my path anyday now and I may jump into it just as heedlessly. And screw up all over again. It's a distinct possibility.

"But it's the way I am, and I've come to accept it. I have a total lack of self-discipline, and I'm a constant threat to myself. And to you, too. You could have been killed because of me. People probably think I'm incapable of letting something like that bother me, but it does. More than you can imagine. I'll never forgive myself for it and I never want it to happen again. You deserve someone better than me, George."

"You're right," George cordially agreed. "I deserve somebody sensible and stable with a rational mind. But I got you. And I'm glad. You bring something into my life that's been missing. You have more than your share of faults, but you're never dull. Your next move is always a surprise to me, and I'm constantly fascinated by the workings of your mind. Maybe that's why I love you."

"I don't know why I love *you*. I've never stopped to figure it out, and I guess I'm not too interested in the reasons. I only know that there was something special there from the day I met you, and it's kept growing and growing until now I don't want to imagine my life without you. I do love you, George. I know it's been hard to tell at times, but I do."

George pulled him from the chair and wrapped him in

his arms for a long kiss. Tory melted at the tenderness he felt in the embrace but couldn't deny the erotic undertones threatening to erupt.

George finally pulled himself away. "It's not going to be easy, you know. Love is going to see us through some rough spots, but we'll probably still find reason for a knock-down drag-out fight at least once a week."

Tory reentwined himself and began nibbling George's earlobe. "No we won't. I'm never going to make you angry again."

"Yes you will. I hate to be the one to break it to you, little boy, but real people don't get to live happily ever after."

"We'll be the exception to the rule."

"We can try. I've got the future all mapped out for us."

Tory moved down to George's neck. "Whatever you say, George."

"I say that you haven't looked so good in years."

"Thank you."

"The climate agrees with you."

"It's good vacation weather. Though I have suspicions that too much salt air tends to corrode one's lungs. You've seen what it can do to housepaint." Tory ran his fingertips down the front of George's shirt. "Why don't we take a little walk? I know a beautiful secluded spot near the beach not five minutes from here."

George smiled but shook his head. "Let's talk some more first."

Tory looked up at him in vague puzzlement. "OK. If that's what you'd rather do."

"Why don't we borrow Ginny's boat tomorrow and sail over to Paradise Island?"

"If you'd like."

"There's a hotel I want you to look at."

Tory pulled his head back to give George a confused frown. "I'd rather look at you sprawled across my bed, but if you want me to look at hotels, I guess we'll look at hotels."

"This one's special," George smiled. "We're buying it."

Tory took a step backward to stare in disbelief.

"I closed the deal this morning. Settlement's in sixty days."

"Hold it!" Tory lit another Gauloise, and his chin jutted

forward threateningly. "I'm willing to play along and let some things slide so you can coddle your fragile macho ego, but there are definite lines to be drawn. Do you actually have the audacity to sit there and tell me that you went out and bought a hotel and expect dizzy old Tory to just pack up and follow you, trusting in your infinitely superior powers of judgment? I'm willing to humor you, George, but don't get too carried away with yourself."

"Relax," George smiled sheepishly. "It was just a security deposit. We'll sail over tomorrow and you can look at it. If it doesn't suit you, we'll look for something else."

"That's more like it."

"Would I do something like that?"

"It wouldn't surprise me," he snorted.

"We'll need some of your money for a down payment, anyway."

"You son of a bitch!"

"Calm down," George laughed. "You'll love it."

"I hate it already! I want a co-op on Park Avenue."

"It's right on the beach. Eight suites, twenty-two doubles, six bungalows in the garden behind it. There's even a little restaurant. You can be the maître d'."

Tory looked to the sky for sympathy. "Not only does he want to pack me up and drag me off like a piece of American Tourister, he expects me to earn my keep, too."

"So don't work if you don't want to. Just sit in the house on the hill and watch the sunset. I'll even buy you a gazebo."

"There's a house on a hill?" Tory asked tentatively.

"Yeah."

"With an ocean view?"

"Yeah."

"How big is it?"

"Eight or ten rooms," George shrugged.

"Forget it. How can I possibly entertain houseguests in eight or ten rooms?"

"You'll have a hotel and six bungalows for houseguests, dummy."

"Oh," he said thoughtfully. "What color is it?"

"Tan, I think."

"That won't do at all."

"So we'll paint it."

"White."

"Why not?"

"And I want a white picket fence. With roses."

"I'll buy you one."

"Would you?"

"If you're ready for it. I've been waiting almost a year for you to come to your senses."

"And how long did I wait for you, you bastard?"

"Maybe we both needed the time," he shrugged.

"Perhaps you're right," Tory sighed. "Three and a half years doesn't seem so long now. It gave us both the chance to become semi-affluent. And I shudder to think of some of the fascinating anecdotes it's added to my cocktail-party repertoire."

George extended his hand. "Is it a deal?"

"I hope you know what you're doing, George. I'm not exactly a blue-chip risk. I may flit off to the nearest opium den without notice."

"I'm willing to take a chance."

"And I'm not signing anything until I've seen the property."

"Just wait, you're going to love it. Maybe we *will* get to live happily ever after."

Tory clasped the extended hand in both of his as he looked out on the sun slowly sinking into the sea. "What the hell," he sighed. "I guess it's worth a shot."

GAY PAPERBOUND